❧ ❧

Kinau began to chant and sway on the edge. She was calling on the goddess Pele. "We need advice," she was saying. "We need your approval and wisdom, oh, Pele," she was singing. "Give us counsel, and bless us in our adventures. Bless the child Victor, who is of your own people and kin."

......The rumble increased. Rosalind threw in the *leis,* and they were consumed into burning ashes before they had gone a dozen feet. Kinau tossed in the wine, and the bottles exploded as they touched the hot lava. Kinau kept on singing, even as the sulfur odor increased.

Hoke shouted, and they turned to listen. He was pointing frantically to the cindery road they had taken.

In the path had sprung up little tongues of flame!

The volcano was going to erupt!

Also by Janet Louise Roberts
Published by Ballantine Books:

*ISLAND OF DESIRE*

# BLACK PEARLS

Janet Louise Roberts

BALLANTINE BOOKS • NEW YORK

Library of Congress Catalog Card Number: 78-61825

ISBN 0-345-26012-0

Manufactured in the United States of America

First Edition: March 1979

To: Barbara,
   Mary and Marion,
   Mildred and Virginia,
      with many happy memories of
      beautiful Hawaii

# 1

❦ ❦ ❦ ❦

THE HOWLING MARCH winds made Rosalind Murray stir restlessly on her narrow bed. There had been so many storms this year. Only yesterday, the waves had risen so high that she had feared they would strike against their small house, located near the beach. She got up, finally, and padded to the living room, to peer beyond the bamboo lattice.

As she watched the crashing seas, Rosalind listened for the sound of her father awakening. He hated storms. They disturbed and upset him. It was during a hurricane in 1865 that her mother had died giving birth to Rosalind, nineteen years ago.

Her softly shaped mouth drooped a little, thinking about it. The gentle woman, Rose, dying here in this wilderness of sand and stark cliffs, with the Pacific savagely beating near the front door. Her quiet musical mother, with her smile, of which all that remained was a faded photograph in a simple frame placed on the living room table.

The roar of the waves was so strong tonight. Again, Rosalind stared into the darkness, lit with flashes of lightning. The rain was beating down steadily, noisily on the woven-mat roof. It was a wonder her father had not risen, nor dear Kinau. Kinau slept heavily, she worked so hard. Yet her ear was always attuned to her little charge, her Lokelina, for Kinau had taken care of Rosalind from the moment of her first breath.

There—it came again. Tonight the wind sounded like a baby crying. Rosalind frowned and swept back her dark hair, in its neat long braids. She was getting nervous, and that would not do. She must keep her sanity, and be decisive for herself and her father. He lived in the dream-world of his legends and stories. He must be kept free of worries, for he was not strong. He must not be told how low the money was, how few checks had come in for his stories, how they had lived for the past year on their vegetables, the fruit of the trees, and the fish brought to them by Kinau's sons.

They lived on the edge of the ocean, on the leeward side of Hawaii. Many years ago, Rose and Alfred Murray had come to the big island, their ship blown off course on their way to the South Seas, where he had hoped to regain his health and to have his honeymoon. A kindly plantation owner had taken them in, given them the shack of one of his sugar workers, and there they had stayed. Forever more, said Alfred, contentedly, in the days when his wife lived, and the sun shone brightly, and he learned Hawaiian, and loved the great-hearted natives.

Rosalind rubbed her slender arms. It was chilly tonight, and the full muumuu she wore as a nightdress provided little protection. Her feet were cold. She must return to bed and get warm. . . .

Abruptly, it came again; the wailing of a child, a hungry baby. She shivered. Was she going mad? To hear such wails in a normal end-of-winter tempest?

She lit the lamp on the table, holding the match with a steady hand. She would read for a time, she would correct the typescript of her father's latest effort, one of the Hawaiian legends of which he was so fond. That would make her calm and sleepy enough to rest.

Rosalind sat down in the wicker chair and picked up the manuscript. The squall blew about the house, but fortunately the building had been erected against the cliff at its back, to shelter it from fierce gales. She would forget the fury outside, and lose herself in the legend of Pele, the queen of fire and goddess of volcanoes.

Pele was a favorite of Rosalind's nurse, Kinau. Rosalind had helped to record this story by gathering the many versions from her Hawaiian friends, and by talking to Kinau. Kinau was full of tales, and she told them with a chuckle, or a shaking of her ample body, or with big round eyes of awe.

Pele now preferred to reside in the seething crater of Kilauea, on the slope of Mauna Loa, and Kinau sometimes went there to fling an offering of fruit and drink into the volcano, to request some blessing of the goddess. It was a number of miles, but Kinau would walk, or borrow a donkey from a friend or relative. It was not too much trouble to go to the goddess. And fortune would smile on them, she vowed.

Rosalind lost herself in the account. She picked up a sharp pencil to change a word here and there, curling up in the chair with her bare feet under her. The cushions she had made softened the hard lines of the chair.

When the door burst open, she started up with a great leap of her heart, fear and shock making her gasp with alarm. The great figure that staggered in was like some god out of the past. Black wet hair, a bronzed face, a thick blanket wrapped about him, blood on the long arms and shoulders—a bundle in his arm.

He stared at her, then thrust the package towards her. Rosalind took it automatically. "Take . . . it . . . Help . . ." he gasped, and fell at her feet.

Her arms had curled about the cloth, and she heard a feeble cry before she was able to take in the message her arms were sending her. An infant! A baby who couldn't be more than six-months-old—emaciated, but bronzed like the man, with thick dark hair, and an opened mouth squealing as though it were a sad little bird. . . .

The man was unconscious on the floor. From his shoulder blood gushed thickly, shocking Rosalind from her stupor.

She dashed to the door of her room, and whispered, "Kinau, come quick! Kinau!"

The heavy-set woman got up yawning, then stared wide eyed when she heard the unexpected though unmistakable cries. "What you got there, huh?"

"Come."

Rosalind hurried back to the living room. The man had not moved. The baby wailed again, lustily, angrily, hungrily.

Kinau padded into the room, rubbing her eyes. Her great body in the flowered muumuu shivered in the cold wind from the open front door. She shut it firmly, then turned to look at the prone body.

"That Peter Darien."

Rosalind nodded. "Take the baby, get it some milk. I'll get cloths and medicine. Mr. Darien is badly injured."

Kinau took the child, unwrapped it from the blanket, and began to croon. "Oh, little baby, you so hungry, you so cold, huh? Kinau fix, Kinau take care of you," and she carried him off to the kitchen. Food first, that was Kinau's motto, on any occasion.

Rosalind had brought cloths, and while the kettle heated she examined the wound. She was puzzled. It looked like a great gash, such as a huge fish would receive from a cruel hook. Had someone struck him with a spear?

After a few minutes, Kinau brought the kettle of water, still rocking the baby—a boy, she had discovered—in her great gentle arms. She had had many children and grandchildren. She knew how to hold a baby, how to soothe it, how to croon and take away fear and hunger. She watched Rosalind as the girl knelt beside the unconscious man.

"Is father awake?"

"No. I look in, him sleep like little one should," said Kinau cheerfully.

"That's good. I don't want him to see Mr. Darien like this. It always upsets him," murmured Rosalind absently. "Wounds—blood—it makes him remember."

Deftly she staunched the blood, and it stopped at last. She folded a pad, and bound it to the shoulder, after smearing the injury generously with salve. She was accustomed to nursing. There was no doctor for many miles, and the Hawaiians took care of themselves, or came to Miss Rosalind or Kinau for help.

4

When a foot was punctured on the coral reefs, or a shoulder scraped open on the rocks, or a fishhook caught in some sturdy young body, they came cheerfully to Miss Rosalind, and laughingly told of their misadventures, and she bound them up, and teased them for their clumsiness.

"I put baby in my bed, get him good and warm," said Kinau, and carried him off once again. The weak wailing had stopped and long lashes curled on his dark cheeks. He was a handsome child, though too thin for her liking. She looked at him thoughtfully as she took him away. This baby was not all Hawaiian, she thought. He was part *Haole*. It was there in the shape of his eyes, the set of his chin, the lighter tone of his hair.

Rosalind found the mat on which she slept on exceptionally hot nights. She laid it on the floor, covering it with a blanket. A pillow at the head, more blankets, and it was ready. But how to move him? She stood looking down at the long young man. His was a muscular body, naked to the waist, his trousers torn. How did wealthy young Peter Darien come to such a state? His shoulders were wide and bronzed, like his face. His black curly hair was long and shaggy, unlike its usual neat appearance. He looked as though he had lived in wilderness for a time. She had seen him twice before, in Kailua, at the church there. He had been well-dressed in his white drill uniform, with a large white sombrero in his hand, and a red scarf at his throat. What could have happened to him?

Kinau returned. "Him ready for bed, like baby?" she whispered, with a gusty chuckle. She stooped, picked him up in her great arms, and let him down gently onto the mat, before Rosalind could protest. Her strength had always amazed Rosalind. They covered him with a second blanket, and he lay quietly.

"I had best stay up with him," whispered Rosalind, worriedly.

Kinau shook her head. "No. Him sleep good. You go to bed. We hear if he not sleep. He be good, I think."

Rosalind finally nodded. Kinau had a wealth of experience in her life. She noted that Kinau went over to the door, and dropped the bar across it, fitting it sturdily into its posts. They rarely barred the door.

So Kinau thought the wound was strange also.

Rosalind blew out the lamp, and thoughtfully went to bed. She had thought she would not rest, but the wind had died some, and the waves had calmed before morning, and she slept.

They wakened to a fresh new world, rain-swept and cleared of dust, with the sky a brilliant blue. Small clouds drifted across the mountains behind them, and in the distance Mauna Loa wore a stately cap of white, the steam circling her beautiful head. The sky was echoed by the sea, coyly blue and peaceful after its wild actions of the night before. Hawaiian boys were already fishing, yelling to each other with delight at their catch, and the shells they found strewn on the beach.

Rosalind washed at the basin, and slipped into a fresh muumuu of green leaves and hibiscus flowers of scarlet. She had few dresses of Western wear. It was simply easier to sew native garb out of cloth from the trading store.

When Rosalind wanted a bath, Kinau went down to the sand, sternly shooed away the Hawaiian boys, and she and Rosalind shed their muumuus and immersed themselves in the turquoise waters of the lagoon, inside the coral reefs. They washed their hair there, clothes, and themselves. It was their giant bathtub. Rosalind had known no other.

Rosalind re-entered the house, moving softly in her sandaled feet. The man lay motionless, but had moved in the night, and his bandages were stained with red. She brought salves, and gently removed the bandages, to examine the wound. Her mouth tightened in concern. If he got worse, they would have to send for a doctor. She cleansed the injury thoroughly, and Peter moved and moaned, without opening his eyes. The lashes lay long on his cheeks.

His hair had dried, and lay in soft curls on his forehead and along his bronzed head to the back of his shoulders. His chest was covered with curling dark hair, down to his trouser belt. She put on a fresh dressing, and looked at him, and was suddenly aware of him as a man. He was not like a Hawaiian boy, young and grinning and amiable. He was a tall man, and she remembered that once he had glanced at her after church, his dark brown eyes going up and down her in the slim muumuu which was her best dress. She had felt—awful. She and Kinau had left early, without stopping to talk to friends. The other ladies had been so dressed up in tight silk and lace gowns from the Mainland, with funny bustles on their hips, smart shoes on their feet, and flowered bonnets on their heads. She had not gone back to that church for a long time.

Peter's family owned the whole island of Darien. It was theirs—all the cattle they raised, a huge house, jewels and everything. She wondered how it felt to be so wealthy, to have so much. It must be strange.

She got up from her knees, and stood gazing down at him. His cheeks were flushed with fever, the dark eyes opened abruptly and stared up at her. He muttered something, then his lids closed again, and he was still.

She took the blood-stained cloths out to the kitchen, and put them in a woven basket. Kinau would wash them and they would use them again. Cloth was so precious.

Kinau, cleaning vegetables, glanced at her. "I tell my eldest son to bring a chicken," she said briskly. "The man, he needs meat and some broth. He all bones. Big man."

Rosalind frowned. "I—I cannot pay him, Kinau," she said finally. "I must save what money we have left for paper and stamps for father's stories. Do not ask him."

"Huh," said Kinau. "My boy bring me chicken. Should I tell him I cannot pay for chicken for his old mother? He scold me and tell me I crazy in the head." She chuckled and gave Rosalind a shrewd kindly look.

"Besides, your father need chicken sometimes. We get."

Rosalind swallowed her pride, and nodded reluctantly. "All right. Once. No more."

"Huh," said Kinau, and turned back to scraping the vegetables. Rosalind wandered back to the living room, still worried about the chicken. It was all right to accept fish, and fruit. They came from the sea and the land, no one owned them, one took from the ocean and trees what one needed; it was free to all. Chickens were different. One had to raise them, one could sell the eggs and the fowl.

She found her father standing in the living room, staring down at the man on the mat.

"Good heavens," said Alfred Murray mildly. "Where did he come from? What's wrong with him? Got a fever, huh?"

"Yes, Father. Kinau is taking care of him."

Her father bent down and peered more closely with his near-sighted eyes. "Oh, it's young Peter Darien. What is he doing here? And no shirt on."

"I expect he lost it, Father."

"Lost it? Young men are strange. One doesn't lose one's clothes," he said, and wandered over to his desk, sat down, and picked up the pages there. He began going over them, having completely forgotten Peter Darien.

Rosalind smiled quietly to herself. Her father was different, absent-minded, a scholar, and a brilliant man. She had taken care of him since she was old enough to realize he was different from other people's fathers. Now his dark hair was greying, his thin shoulders were stooped. But he did not cough so much, and the doctor on one of his infrequent visits had told Rosalind he thought he did not have tuberculosis any more. Something about the fresh air and the sea, and good plain food.

The day passed slowly and serenely, as most of their days did. Kinau's big son brought a chicken, dressed and ready to cook, a big grin on his bronzed face when Rosalind thanked him. They had chicken for dinner that evening, and Mr. Murray ate it with pleasure.

"Hum, I don't think we have had this a week or two, have we, Rose?"

They had not had it since Christmas, but she did not remind him. It was sufficient that there was some for him, broth with mashed chicken for their guest, and a bit for the baby.

The wind murmured over the house that night. Kinau's son slept outside. Rosalind had noticed him in his hammock, with his spear nearby, stuck in the earth. She would have asked Kinau why, but Kinau would have had some cheerful answer that meant nothing.

The next day, Rosalind asked, "Do you think we ought to send to Mr. Darien's relatives? They should know he is here, and ill. And perhaps the doctor—"

"No," said Kinau, shaking her head decisively. "No, no."

"Why not?"

"Wait till Mr. Peter, he wake up and say what he wants. Now, let him sleep."

Rosalind thought about that. And she thought about Mr. Darien's shoulder, and the condition of the baby. And she kept quiet. Kinau always knew what she was doing.

Toward nightfall, Peter's fever rose. He tossed and muttered unintelligibly. Mr. Murray had gone to bed early, Rosalind was thankful for that.

Peter opened his eyes and looked straight at Rosalind. She was sitting on a mat near him, her legs crossed beneath her.

"You can't have the baby," he said, distinctly.

She started. She was cuddling the child. It seemed to crave handling even when it was not being fed. She held him in her strong young arms, against her rounded breasts, and the baby put his head against her and cooed contentedly.

Peter's face was flushed, he half-rose from his mat. "You can't have the baby," he said again. "He's a

Darien, and a Darien he will be raised! I'll fight you to the death for that!"

Rosalind realized he was delirious. "Of course, Mr. Darien," she said soothingly. "Lie down again, and rest. You are at peace here."

He stared at her, his dark brown eyes glittering. He shook his head impatiently, winced at the pain in his shoulder. "Doesn't matter what you say," he said, less distinctly. "I'll take the baby—raise him myself. He's a Darien!"

"Of course he is," she said quietly. She began to hum a tune, to the infant and to him. Finally Peter lay back, and the dark eyes closed. He seemed to listen, smile faintly at the Hawaiian words of the lullaby, and slid into sleep. She sat in thought, still holding the baby to her.

Peter was more restless that night. Rosalind rose several times in the night, to give him chicken broth, hot tea, herbs, whatever she could think of to help him regain his strength. His body must fight the fever. She talked to him, and in a quiet voice sang songs to him, which seemed to calm him. She would even get out her flute, and would play it quietly, and finally he would rest again.

By morning he slept deeply. She rose, yawning, to face the bright day.

"We get baths today," announced Kinau. "Baby better, we take him in water and give him bath."

"So soon? Is he strong enough?" Rosalind put the back of her hand against the baby's cheeks. He gurgled at her, held out his thin arms to her. He knew her already, it seemed. She smiled, and took him.

"He stronger, and very dirty," said Kinau. "Sea good for him, it be warm today in lagoon."

She went out and dismissed the boys, and the women had the lagoon to themselves. Kinau bathed briskly, then with her big body moving in the shallows, she scrubbed the bloody cloths. Rosalind enjoyed holding the baby in the water, he cooed and splashed delightedly. He had been in water like this before, she thought. He laughed when a wave came up and splashed over them. He caught at her long loose brown hair and grabbed fistfuls of it and pulled, beaming up at her.

Later, the sun dried them on the creamy white sand. Rosalind stepped into a clean dress and placed a brief cloth on the baby—he needed no more. She played with him on the shore until the sun rose close to its mid-day position. Sensing the heat might be too much for the boy, she took him inside.

He seemed to be a happy baby, who clapped his small hands and laughed when she sang. His dark brown eyes danced with mirth when he was fed, delighting in the milk bubbles he created. He spanked at the liquid and gurgled with pleasure at the bright day and the joy of living. A typical Hawaiian boy, she thought.

Only he was a Haole, and he was a Darien.

In fact, he rather looked like Peter Darien. Rosalind had studied him carefully as she held the baby in her arms. The same formation of the face, the same winged eyebrows, the dark curly hair grew the same way on the forehead. Peter's son? By a Hawaiian girl? She was not surprised, only she had not thought he would be that kind. Still, the white men here had few choices for mates. Many thought little of taking a Hawaiian girl for a few weeks or months or even years. Until they married, sometimes a girl from the Mainland, a prim proper girl who would look down on the native woman who had been the mistress of her husband. It made Rosalind feel sad that handsome Peter Darien had done this. Somehow she had thought he would not have succumbed to such behavior.

She was not sure why she felt so disappointed in Peter. Had she formed pictures in her mind about him? She sat nearby with the baby against her full breasts, watching Peter as he moved restlessly on his mat.

She had seen him standing tall and proud. She knew his story, how his grandfather and father had bought the island and named it Darien. How they had brought in steers from Texas and bred fine cattle

11

which stood the heat. How they had built ships, and sailed them to the Mainland with their beef, and prospered.

They had trained Hawaiians as cowhands. The business had grown. Mr. Barton Darien was widely-respected, for all his quick temper and fierceness. His son Peter was like him, dark and strong and quick, and respected, and sometimes feared. She had heard that Barton Darien had been ill, and Peter was now the guiding force. She knew little else about them—except that they were wealthy, and the Darien women wore silks, laces, pearls and diamonds.

The baby fussed a bit, frowning, stuffing his fingers to his gums. She picked up a rounded stick, a dowel that Kinau's son had smoothed, and put it in his mouth. He sucked on it, cuddling down contentedly, and she sang to him softly. She thought Peter Darien stirred, but the dark eyes did not open. The lashes only fluttered on the bronzed cheeks as she continued with the song.

Her father came in, paused and smiled at the maternal scene. "One of Kinau's?" he asked, amiably. "My, how he has grown!"

Rosalind only smiled, and nodded. Her father was not to be bothered with such mundane matters.

He brought over a handful of pages. "When you have time, look through this, will you, Rose? See if I said everything right. I want to mail it off next week. I think it is one of the finest of stories," and he went outdoors into the sunshine, putting his shabby Panama hat on at a jaunty angle.

She set the papers beside her, and gently joggled the infant while she read. It helped to say the words aloud and the baby seemed to enjoy the melodious sound of her voice. It was a good story, and her father told it well. The legends and myths of Hawaii were so fascinating, and there were so many of them. The American magazines often paid good sums for them. Maybe this would sell well. She might even be able to buy a few chickens and try to raise them in a small area behind the house.

12

As she finished one page and looked up, she saw Peter staring straight at her. She looked back, in surprise.

"The baby . . ." she said weakly. "The . . . baby. . . ."

"He is fine, just fine, look!" she said, and held him out to Peter. Peter reached up his left arm, and touched the baby's leg, sighed a little, and his eyes closed again. His arm fell limply to his side.

Then Rosalind touched his forehead, smoothing back stray hair. His head was still hot to the touch. He must still be delirious.

She wondered again if she had been foolish not to send for the doctor. Kinau had been so positive that they should not notify anyone.

Kinau entered just then to relieve her of the child.

"Kinau, do you not think we should send word to the doctor—to someone?" Rosalind asked anxiously.

"No, no. Not till Mr. Darien, he say so." She seemed calmly final about that, and took the baby away to sleep.

Rosalind got up, and went to the desk. She carried the pages with her, and marked them carefully in a few places where they did not seem clear. As she bent over the manuscript, she had a feeling someone was looking at her. She glanced towards the mat, Peter was gazing at her. He said nothing and soon closed his eyes again.

The shack was very peaceful with the afternoon light streaming through the open windows. The lattices had been pegged back, the little living room was bright with sun, clean with the salty ocean air. She could smell the flowers from their little garden; the plumeria, the hibiscus, the herbs. Sunshine sparkled on the blue waves beyond their sandy beach. Perhaps the storms were over for a season.

This week she would retype father's latest efforts on the battered machine which the plantation owner had given them when he sold out. The buyer was someone in the United States, though no one had yet come to claim the land and to begin planting sugar once more. One day, someone would arrive. But perhaps the gods would be kind to them, and the new owner would be good, and let them remain in this peaceful house.

All the time she was correcting the story, her thoughts ran to what they could do with the much needed money. Besides the chickens, they could get more material to make clothes. Her father needed some new shirts, and that meant buying more thread and needles.

Peter sighed, and turned over, laying with his face toward her. The dark lashes were shadowed on his cheeks, the blanket was pushed down to his waist. She glanced at his strong bare shoulders and chest, then away again, uneasily. She did not know why the sight of the bare shoulders of a man should make her feel so odd. . . .

# 2

🌷 🌷 🌷 🌷

PETER DARIEN WAS NOT SURE when he had become aware of the house. It was the silence and the peace he had vaguely noticed first through the mists that seemed to envelope his mind.

He had nightmares of stumbling through the rain, across rocks, falling over a small cliff, trying to protect the baby in his arms. Nightmares of the pain stabbing his shoulder, the warm trickle of blood, the feel, like cotton, in his mouth as he ran—ran—ran—. No water, no food, no rifle. He could not go on, but he must, there was the baby—and his own life at stake. . . .

Sunshine shimmered across his body and made him warm. He pushed down the blanket that covered his shoulders, stretched out his arms and yawned. The pain in one shoulder made him wince in surprise and he opened his eyes. He seemed to be on the floor. He looked about, frowning in surprise. Where was he, what was he doing here?

He lay on a blanket, with a mat of rushes beneath that. A few pieces of shabby furniture half-filled the airy room. The lattices had been drawn against the night air and mosquitoes, and now the sunlight was beginning to poke inquisitive fingers between the blinds.

He heard a low musical voice, a woman's voice, then a soft laugh. He had heard the voice before, his memory faintly recalled. And a delicate, cool hand had soothed him when he tossed in fever. Someone had coaxed him to eat a mash of chicken and *poi*.

He closed his eyes, trying to visualize what had happened. Something terrible. He was sure of it, and

15

the horror of it filled his spirit. The memories began to rush back, his fists clenched the blanket.

Soft sandaled feet—the sound of them entered the room. He kept his eyes shut. Someone knelt beside him, the gentle hand touched his forehead again.

"It is cooler, Kinau," said a soft woman's voice.

"Him be much better now, better by-m-by," said a husky older voice. "You come eat now, huh?"

"I'll feed the baby first, he is so hungry," and a whispery laugh filled the pretty voice. Peter slowly opened his eyes, to see the girl next to him, with the baby in the crook of her arm.

She held a bowl and a crude spoon in the other hand. The baby seemed quite content. She smiled down at the child, pursed her lips, and made encouraging sounds.

"See? He knows now how to eat from a bowl, Kinau."

"Hunger is a good teacher," said the older woman with a fat chuckle, and she left the room.

Peter studied the girl's face as she fed the baby. She had a lovely oval face, serene and intelligent, somehow older for her years. He remembered her now, she was the daughter of Alfred Murray. He had seen her at church a few times, noticed her shyness, and the huge Hawaiian woman who hovered protectively beside her. They had worn native garb, and some women had laughed at them.

Her name? He should remember it. He fought against the mists that hazed over his mind. It was something in a play by Shakespeare.

Ah, he half smiled as he repeated the lines to himself:

> From the east to western Ind,
> No jewel is like Rosalind.

Yes, that was it, her name was Rosalind. His clouded mind wandered about, aimlessly thinking of how, in the Shakespeare play *As You Like It,* the love-struck Orlando had wandered through the Forest of Arden pinning up his verses to Rosalind on the trees. He had seen the play once, been amused at the quick wit of the heroine, her grace in masculine attire, the garish background of green-painted trees and shrubs.

The girl beside him was humming, she had laid down the bowl of *poi* and was rocking the baby in her sturdy brown arms. He liked her voice; it was low and soothing. She sang a Hawaiian song, pronouncing the words like a true islander. What a strange person she must be, knowing English, speaking Hawaiian fluently, living in a hut like this, wearing muumuus—apparently happy with her lot.

Time must have passed, for the sunlight flowed full across his body, and the lattices had been pegged back. Through the windows he could see the vivid blue sky, shimmering reflections of the sea far beyond the reefs.

A tall lean man came into the room, glanced down absently at him, and nodded. "Well, young man, feeling better?"

"Yes . . . thank . . . you. . . ." Peter found he had to force his voice. The man smiled kindly, he looked like a nice absent-minded teacher.

"You should have something to eat, get your strength back," he said, and called softly, "Rosalind! The fellow is awake!"

The girl came quickly, her bare feet nearly soundless on the mats. When she bent over him, Peter noticed her golden brown eyes, and the dark lashes that fringed them beautifully. Her hair was glossy brown and straight, hanging in two braids well below her shoulders.

"Hello, *aloha,* how do you feel?" she smiled.

"Fine. I wonder . . . where I am. . . ."

On the leeward side of Hawaii," she said briskly. "Kailua is north of us about twenty miles. Do you remember my father, Alfred Murray, Mr. Darien?"

He nodded weakly. It was surprising how weak he felt, as though he could scarcely lift his head or his hand. "And you are . . . Rosalind. I . . . remember you . . . now. . . ."

His eyes traveled down the length of her shiny braids to her slim figure, accented by the revealing flow of the faded muumuu, to her slender tan legs and trim ankles. She drew back a little, her smile becoming set.

"Yes, Mr. Darien. I was wondering . . . do you wish us to inform your relatives that you are here?" The golden brown eyes were anxious.

"Good heavens," said Mr. Murray. "Do you mean to tell me you haven't sent word to his father. . . ."

"No," interrupted Peter firmly. His mind was not clear yet, but this he knew. He did not want anyone notified of where he was, not until he was able to get up and walk. "Who knows I am here?"

"Why, no one," replied Alfred Murray. "But we should send word. Surely Kinau could send one of her sons. . . ."

"No," said Peter again, weakly. "Not until . . . I can . . . get up . . . don't let anyone . . . know. . . ." He turned his head and sighed. It was important that nobody should know where he was. But he could not recall just yet, not very clearly, why it was so.

Mr. Murray muttered to Rosalind. He brushed his hand through his greying dark hair, ruffling it worriedly. She was shaking her head firmly.

"No, Father, not until he wishes it. Kinau said so also."

"Well, well, I don't understand," he commented irritably. "Not that he isn't welcome. . . ."

"Don't fret about it, Father," said Rosalind. "Have you gone over the Pele story? I thought we should change a few words. Let me show you."

Her father was distracted, and soon sat down at his desk to go over the corrections. Peter heard the rustle and muttering of his host and Rosalind tiptoe out of the room. He fell asleep again, feeling comforted and secure. They would not tell anyone he was here. The villagers must know, but they seldom went far afield.

Kinau fed him supper some hours later. He was able

to half-sit up for it, but his arm ached, and he was glad to lie back again. Presently, Rosalind brought in a lamp, and carefully set it at a distance from Peter so the glare would not shine in his eyes.

"You are better tonight," she murmured. Her voice was like the summer wind through the trees.

"Yes. The baby . . . he is. . . ."

"Fine. Kinau and I are taking care of him," she said firmly.

Thankfully, she asked no questions, for he did not feel able to answer any. Her father wandered in to join the women in drinking a fragrant herb tea, the scent of which permeated the room like incense. Peter gave in to the intoxicating smell, letting his mind wander.

He was beginning to remember. The cliff high in the wind, the frightened crying girl, the wailing child. The ominous approach of the husky Hawaiians. And Lydia Pauahi, poor young Lydia . . . He flinched, recalling her gaunt form, the unnatural shallowness of her once-lovely face. She had wept and begged him to take her baby and flee.

"My father will hate you forever, but the baby must be safe. Father would kill the child. You will promise this, Peter? Make safe my child! I can die happy. . . ."

"You are not dying," he had said firmly. Her pallid lips had curled in a little smile.

"Yes, I am. I began to die . . . when Terry left me . . . he left me. . . . " She groaned, and her eyelids began to droop. He had stayed with her, until the death rattle came in her throat and the lovely body had gone limp.

The Hawaiians had caught up with him, three stalwart men sent by the haughty Chief Kaahumanu Pauahi, Lydia's father. They had orders to kill his daughter and the *Haole* baby she had brought into the world. Peter had stood them off, shot one with his pistol, fought the other two with spears. One had been shoved from the cliff, the other had wounded him, but had been seriously hurt in turn.

He had escaped, the baby in his arms, wrapped in

the thin coverlet Lydia had given him. She had sheltered her child from the storm and the rains, but she had not cared about herself. Peter had walked, run, staggered over the miles, from the cliffs near Mauna Loa, toward the coast. Other Hawaiians had taken up the chase; her father was furious, obstinate, and menacing. Chief Pauahi was a proud, difficult, arrogant man. He was Peter's enemy now, and he knew the Chief would not hesitate to have him killed.

Yet Peter felt a softness in his heart for the old man, strange as it was. For Lydia was the apple of her father's eye. He had named her Hoakanui, for an early queen of Hawaii, one of the wives of the legendary Laa-Mai-Kahiki. Lovely young Hoakanui had come to Darien to stay with the family for a time, winning all with her beauty, charm, and shy grace. They had given her the Christian name Lydia, against Kaahumanu's wishes. She had accepted it though, laughing, pleased that she was now one of them, with an English name.

Hoakanui Pauahi had attracted the attention of all the single men. Too much attention, thought Peter, with a painful grimace as he moved on the mat. Such attention would have turned the head of any girl. And Lydia had been so sheltered and protected until then. The freedom had gone to her head, and it had destroyed her.

Peter felt weak and languid with relief. He had won, nevertheless. The baby was safe. As he lay there, ate what was brought him, slept, and wakened, he thought about what to do. One clear shining strand of meaning came through. The boy was a Darien. He would be raised a Darien and be proud of his heritage.

He observed the set-up of the little house where the Murrays and Kinau lived. It was a small, four room building, one of many such dwellings of the sugar plantation workers. He had spoken before to Alfred Murray; the man was intelligent, even brilliant, coming to know and live among the Hawaiians. It was said he was writing down the myths and legends of the people, and they liked him.

The home was small, ocean breezes sweeping through it. Rosalind wore the same shabby muumuus day after day, and either went barefoot or wore rush sandals. She was always clean and neat, however. When she knelt beside him he could smell the perfume of her body, the fragrance of a frangipani flower she would set in her glossy hair. But this was no life for a young *wahine,* he thought. Not a white *wahine;* intelligent, educated by her capable father, and gently bred. So Peter lay and thought, and put the pieces of a puzzle together.

The day came when he was able to sit up without help, feed himself, and wash himself. He stretched his hard body, and rejoiced that his strength was returning. Kinau grinned down at him.

"You much better, huh? No need doctor, Kinau fix."

"You're a fine doctor, Kinau," he teased her. "And even better as a cook."

She laughed until her plump body shook, and brought him another dish of baked chicken and plantain.

The day came soon after that he was able to stand up, and while holding onto a chair, take a few cautious steps.

"I feel weak as Victor," he told Rosalind, who stood to watch his first steps gravely.

"Victor?"

"That's the child's name. Victor Darien," he informed her. "His mother named him."

There was a question on her open face, but she only nodded, and helped him to a wicker chair. He sank into it with relief. From here he could look out over the veranda to the ivory colored beach, and beyond to the blue sparkling water. Hawaiian boys were bobbing up and down in the waves, yelling to each other, splashing, diving under the next wave in exuberant youthful spirits.

"Tomorrow I'll go swimming," he said presently. Rosalind was sitting in a nearby chair, sewing with neat stitches on a bright piece of Hawaiian cloth. It appeared to be a new shirt for her father.

"It may be too soon," she noted dubiously.

"I think he be good for swim, the water good," Kinau said firmly.

So the next morning, Peter went out to the sea, first holding to the veranda post, then to the sturdy shoulder of one of Kinau's sons. Hoke remained with him, not obviously holding him up, but watchful that Peter should not fall.

Once in the water, he was buoyed up by the waves. The salt stung his wound, but the gash was healing. Hoke paddled near him, and another of Kinau's sons was sitting on the beach, facing the cliffs behind the Murrays' little house.

"Do any men come here, strangers?" asked Peter quietly.

Hoke nodded. "They come, they look, they go away again. Carry spears."

"You sleep at night outside the house with a spear in the ground."

"I do what Mama tell me," grinned Hoke, his black eyes flashing with mirth. "I am not so old that I disobey!" And he laughed and flung water on Peter.

"I am grateful."

Hoke shrugged, embarrassed. "You are our guest."

When Peter came out, he found that Kinau had laid a piece of cloth on the sand and taken away his blood-stained trousers. He wrapped the material about his waist, tucked it in with a practiced motion, slicked back his dark hair, and lay down in the sunshine. The warmth was gratifying on his weakened body. He slept for a time, before going indoors.

Rosalind was setting the table. Peter noticed she'd neatly rolled up the mat and was smiling at him.

"You are much better now, Mr. Darien. There is a shirt for you, if you wish to wear it after I have bandaged your shoulder again."

He stared at the shirt in her hand. She had been making it for him! She brought the ointment and fresh bandages, and her gentle fingers eased the ache in his shoulder as much as the salve did. She helped him put on the garment, sliding it carefully across his broad shoulders.

"Perfect fit," he grinned appreciatively. A soft rose color tinted her tanned cheeks.

"I am glad," she said, and turned away. She went to wash her hands in the kitchen, and he heard her speaking to Kinau. Peter sat in his favorite chair near the window, and thought some more.

When he left this family, the men of Chief Kaahumanu Pauahi might choose to attack the Murrays. After all, they had taken in Peter and cared for him. The Murrays were no longer safe here. Chief Pauahi's men hated all whites since the loss of Lydia, the lovely young princess.

Another piece of the puzzle had fit into place, he decided. He ate with Rosalind and her father that noon, then Rosalind laid out his mat again.

"I don't need to rest anymore," he protested.

"I think it is better if you do," she responded firmly, and laid out a fresh, sweet-smelling blanket on the mat. He lay down and, within minutes, was asleep again. He wakened toward evening, to the sound of humming.

Rosalind's face was bent over the child. She tickled his chin and he gave a little chuckle, reaching up to grab one of her braids. She rocked him, singing a lullaby with her melodious voice.

Peter lay watching them, lazily, not wanting to rise. He was so comfortable. She was lovely, he thought, so slim and yet curvacious. Her sun-darkened throat rose above the edge of the muumuu, and he longed to touch it. Her breasts were softly outlined against the cloth. As he gazed at her, lying on his side, he saw the long slim brown legs where the skirt had ridden up from her ankles.

She stood up gracefully and carried the baby back to her bedroom. He watched her go, the ease of her movements, the beauty of her walk.

That evening, Rosalind set the table with a single lantern. The battered silverplate looked lovely in the dim light. And Rosalind, wearing rose-colored cotton, would have graced any table. They were celebrating Peter's first meal with them.

The group discussed island politics, and Darien found the others unusually knowledgeable about the controversies of king against king, Hawaiians against the white intruders. The landgrabbers were taking sugar cane fields which had long been the property of the chiefs, and many were furious and ready to rise against them. How could a payment of a few lengths of silk cloth and some mirrors and trinkets pay for land which had belonged to their fathers and their fathers' fathers for many long years?

"Do you think your Hawaiians here will rise up?" asked Peter. "The ones on Darien are loyal and faithful, however; they have been working a long time for us, and have received their own homes and payment. On Hawaii it is different, and in Honolulu the talk is fierce."

Alfred Murray looked troubled. "I fear the old days are gone forever," he said with a sigh. "I long to lose myself in the oral traditions of this great people. But the realities press in on us. Why must there always be some to despoil and wrench the land from those who have owned and worked it for centuries? Why must there be wars?"

"When men take what belongs to others, when they have hot and bitter feelings, they will make war," said Rosalind, unexpectedly. She usually spoke little at the table, but tonight her eyes flashed in the lamplight. "If someone tried to take what belonged to me, I would fight!"

"Now, Rosalind, that is not Christian," her father rebuked her gently.

"It is not Christian either to allow greedy foreigners to come in and ruin the land and fish from the waters until there is little left! It is not Christian to kill and murder those who try to protect their families and their homes! The land is sacred to the Hawaiian gods, and the spirits will be angry!"

Peter stared at her speculatively, at the flushed

cheeks and sparkling eyes. Obviously, she felt strongly about this, or she would not have spoken so adamantly.

"Do you think the Dariens have no right to their land?" he asked, tautly.

"The Dariens?" She stared at him, perplexed. "What does that have to do with it? You use the land wisely, men work for you because they wish to do so. There is no whip over their heads, no poverty in your village. I have heard wise ones speak in this manner."

"Thank you," he said, oddly relieved at her approval. "We try to treat all fairly. The island, when we came . . . my grandfather, I mean . . . was barren and empty of people. We brought in cattle to graze, we built reservoirs to catch the fresh rain water. We asked Hawaiians to come and learn how to be cowboys from the Mexican vaqueros whom we imported. Now all live and work together . . . happily, I hope."

He went on to speak of his beloved island, his home. He found a fascinated audience as he spoke of the work of his grandfather and father, how they had cultivated the land, built vegetable patches, encouraged fruit trees to grow, until the island was completely self-sufficient. The cattle ranged through half the island freely until round-up, when some beef were slaughtered, salted, and sent to Honolulu.

"And we have flowers also," he smiled at Rosalind's wide eyes and soft cheeks. "Aunt Norma and Aunt Honora have made it their concern to see to that. We have the native plumeria, frangipani, bougainvillea, ginger, allamanda, as well as some attempts at roses and carnations. Some days, when the wind is from the east, the whole house is filled with a wonderful fragrance."

"It sounds beautiful," said Rosalind softly. "Kinau and I try to raise what we can, but we are busy with vegetables and herbs."

"When you see my home and gardens, I think you will enjoy them," Peter said deliberately.

Her face looked startled; she glanced at her father,

then down at her plate. "I am sure of it," she commented, with cool politeness. He smiled, and complimented her on the taro pudding.

After a few more days, Peter regained most of his strength. He sent word to Darien, a note to his second cousin Terence and one to Aunt Honora, and waited. They would be puzzled by several items he'd mentioned!

A week later, Terence Darien came to the thatched home beside the sea. He strolled up from his carriage, gave a startled look around, and walked up to the veranda where Peter sat with his feet braced on the railing. His arm was in a sling, otherwise there was no sign of injury.

"Well, Peter, what have you been up to?" asked Terence, standing with his hands on his hips. His white tropical suit and white sombrero set off his blond good looks. Peter studied him dispassionately, noted again the too handsome face, the weak chin, the petulent blue eyes.

"You brought my suitcases?"

"In the carriage. Oh, boy!" Terence called to Hoke who had appeared around the corner of the house. "Get the cases," and he jerked his head casually toward the carriage.

Peter's eyes narrowed slightly, the only indication of annoyance. Hoke looked at him, nodded, and did as ordered.

"Lazy bastards," said Terry, and looked disdainfully at the battered wicker chairs. He chose to stand. "Well, I'm here. Come on, how long do we have to stand around?"

"As long as I wish. Have a seat."

Terence's mouth tightened, he looked ready to utter a curse. But he restrained himself and carefully sat down as though worried for fear he would dirty his white suit.

"Well?" demanded Terry, after a pause.

"Well, what?"

"What did you find?"

26

"I wasn't sure you were interested," Peter responded drily.

Terry flung out his hand. "Of course I'm interested! What did the crazy girl do?"

"She died."

Jolted, Terry swallowed, his blue eyes reflecting shock. "Suicide?" he whispered, "Jumped off a cliff?"

"Nothing so easy," said Peter. "She took her baby to the caves, so her father would not kill them both. She slowly starved to death . . . Slowly."

Terry jumped to his feet. "God damn you for a devil!" he burst out. "What do you want from me? Regret? She asked for it, she hung around me until I was sick of her. . . ."

"She was the daughter of a chief, and you chased her like hell. You broke up her engagement to a fine young man chosen by her father. Because she was unavailable, you had to pursue her, didn't you? When she got pregnant, you flung her away like a worn-out shoe."

"Her father would have taken her back." Terry stood with his back to Peter, staring out at the azure sea, the white-capped waves sliding gently up against the shore. "If she wanted to run away and kill herself and the baby, that was her problem."

"The baby is not dead. I was in time to save him. I will bring up the boy, since you have denied your responsibility."

Just then, the child's cry echoed through the house. Terry spun around, staring inside.

"A baby . . . you brought him here? You crazy. . . ."

The soft pad of bare feet, the mellow sound of Rosalind's soothing voice, and the screaming stopped.

"Give him to Lydia's father!" urged Terry, lines white at the corners of his mouth. "Give him up! Who wants a half-white child? Not me! I won't be saddled with him! Give him to his grandfather! Let them raise him!"

"Lydia broke the taboo," Peter pointed out, his eyes flashing with rage. "She had to pay for that. Her father sent warriors to kill her and the child. That's where I got this . . ." he motioned to his right shoulder.

"Why did you bother? She was nothing, nothing, I tell you! Oh, cute and funny, and kinda sweet . . . but she was not a white girl!"

Peter gazed across the sands to the ocean, not trusting himself to speak. He had stood beside the girl, held her in his arms as the death wind shook her, had witnessed her emaciated body, the light in her eyes as she gazed for one last time on her child.

"The boy is a Darien. Victor Darien. I shall raise him as my son."

Terry laughed, chokingly. "Oh, fine, fine! I can hear the gossip now! The gay bachelor Peter Darien comes home with a half-*haole* boy, adopts him, and makes him his heir! You don't care who talks about you, do you? Well, I do! You won't bring that bastard to my ranch!"

"Your ranch?" asked Peter, gazing up at him, tauntingly. "Think again, cousin. It is Darien, and I run it! What happens is my responsibility and my duty. Victor shall grow up on our island, and live there, and be proud of his heritage . . . both of them!"

"You are mad," yelled Terry with conviction, his cheeks red with anger. "You are insane! You can't bring that boy to Darien and say he is your son! Everyone will laugh at us! Think of our guests! Think of the people from the Mainland. . . ."

"The guests who come will accept him, as I do. The only people I invite are those who think as we do."

Terry laughed hysterically. "Oh, do you think so? You're the only one who can invite guests! You're the big boss of Darien now that your father is laid up! Well, think again, cousin! I invited a guest, and he may be there by the time we get back!"

Peter stiffened. "Whom did you invite?" he snapped.

"A man named Glendon Corey. He is interested in ranching around here. . . ."

"Damn you! You know I won't have people come to

28

Darien, unless I look them over first! Who is the man? Where did you meet him?"

"I met him in Honolulu. He's a fine chap, you'll like him."

"And what were you doing in Honolulu? I told you to stay home and take charge until I got back! What do you mean by running off to play around the minute my back is turned?"

Terry shrugged sulkily. "A man has to have some fun," he muttered.

"Fun! You have no sense of responsibility! You can't be trusted with a calf, to say nothing of a whole cattle ranch! You think of nothing but fun; gambling, women, and horse races! By God . . . I ought to. . . ." He stopped at the look on Terry's face.

His cousin had changed expression. He suddenly looked charming, eager. "Well, well! Introduce me to the little Hawaiian peach!" he breathed.

Peter knew before he turned awkwardly around that Rosalind stood behind them in the doorway. He wrenched his arm and smothered a curse. Rosalind's large eyes were gazing at Terry intently. Her feet were bare, her plaits hung down beside her tanned cheeks. The muumuu she wore was faded, but attractive, the pink color flaring against her breasts and rounded hips.

Peter bit his lips savagely, forcing himself to be calm. He wondered how much she had overheard.

"I came to make you welcome."

"*Aloha,* darling, and who are you?" grinned Terry, looking her up and down, until she shrank back into the doorway. "Peter living here, huh? Soft cushiony place. No wonder he didn't want to leave!"

She stared at him. Peter could have pitched him down the steps.

"Miss Rosalind Murray," he said formally. "Permit me to introduce you to my second cousin, Terence Darien."

"You a white girl, or part *Haole?*" grinned Terry. "Happy to meet you, honey! Do I get a bed in the house also?"

"No, you don't," said Peter, brusquely. "If you're lucky the Hawaiians might make up a hut for you. Otherwise, you sleep on the beach . . . with the mosquitoes."

Rosalind looked at him in surprise. Peter took a deep breath, and leaned back. It never did any good to lose his temper with Terence. The man just took advantage of him. He was clever, shrewd. A man had to be, to live all his life without working.

If it were not for Terry's mother, who had raised Peter following his own mother's death, Peter would have pitched out Terry long ago. It might yet come to that, he thought somberly.

Rosalind retreated into the house, saying she would see to luncheon. Terry sat down again on the steps, wagging his head roguishly.

"No wonder . . . no wonder you didn't want to leave! Gone almost three months, Peter, my dear cousin! Won't this make some story, on Darien and in Honolulu? I can't wait to get back home!"

"You'll wait until I'm ready to go," growled his cousin, leaning back in his chair with grim patience.

# 3

🌷 🌷 🌷 🌷

ROSALIND WONDERED how these two cousins could be as different as night and day.

Peter was tough, arrogant, domineering. What he said must be done. The Hawaiians obeyed him cheerfully, Kinau almost ran to do his bidding. Now that he was over the fever, he seemed to have taken over the small house, yes, even the nearby village.

There was a tone in his voice that said, "Do this at once," no matter how quiet his voice. He was a leader of men. She enjoyed hearing him talk; he was decisive, intelligent, far-sighted. Her father sometimes argued mildly with him, usually ending it with a laugh, for he disliked disagreeing with anyone.

Terence had brought a subtle difference to them. Terry slept in a grass hut erected by Kinau's sons, and grumbled at how uncomfortable he was, in spite of the blankets and mosquito nets. During the day he hung around the house, swam, or stared at Rosalind. She felt uncomfortable around him. The blond man seemed too charming, too easy and much too friendly and forward.

Rosalind had overheard several arguments between Peter and Terence. It seemed that Terence wanted to return at once and complained bitterly at remaining here. Peter had cut him off, abruptly, sent him out on errands, ordered him about.

Terence did what Peter told him. Rosalind noted that, thoughtfully. No matter how he protested, the younger cousin did as ordered.

Peter was much better now, his strength had returned. The wound had healed, Rosalind noted when she bandaged his shoulder after he had been swimming. He would soon leave, she thought, and take darling Victor with him.

She would miss the little boy. He had been such a sweet, unexpected addition to her life. How would she endure it, not having the sweet plump arms about her neck, the chuckle echoing when she tickled him, the gentle demands of his crying for food. His soft body seemed to belong to her now as he murmured and cuddled against her breasts, his eyes closing in sleep. Who would take care of him on Darien? Did Peter have someone patient enough?

Rosalind had heard them speak of their relatives. There was Aunt Norma, who had raised both Peter and Terence, her own son. There was eccentric Aunt Honora, who spent much time with her roses. And there was someone named Eileen, Terry's sister, about whom Terry teased Peter, saying she would be anxious to have him back at Darien.

Then came a bright sunny day when Peter sent Terence into Kailua to see about hiring some carriages to take them all back to the port. Rosalind wondered why Peter would need several vehicles. He and Terry could easily fit into the one Terry had driven to the Murrays. Terry wondered also, and protested about going to Kailua. Peter sent him off anyway.

After Terry had left, Peter turned to Rosalind. "I want to talk to you, Rosalind," he said abruptly. "Shall we walk along the beach?"

He was serious, even grim. She wondered what was on his mind. Although Hoke slept in his hammock beside the veranda every night, his spear in the ground, there surely was no real danger about.

"Yes, of course," she said, and came down the steps with him. She wore her new green rush sandals, and a dress of green cotton. She had washed her hair in the sea that morning, brushed it dry, and set a white tiare flower beside her ear. She saw him looking thoughtfully at it. Was it too brazen? To the Hawaiian girls, the flower meant "I am looking for a lover." Rosalind hoped that he would think she just wore it for the gardenia fragrance. He would be going soon, and she might never see him again, except from a distance. It would leave a vacant place in her life, as much as the leaving of Victor.

They strolled across the sand. Peter was gazing out over the water, his eyes crinkling against the brilliant sunshine sparkling on the blue waves. She walked with her eyes cast demurely downward. She longed to look up to him, so well-muscled and wide-shouldered. Standing, he was much taller than she had thought when he had lain helplessly on the mat. He was no longer an invalid to be coaxed into taking *poi* and chicken, to be soothed from his nightmares, to be bathed and cooled from the fever.

"You have lived here all your life," he began abruptly.

"Yes. I was born here."

"Have you never longed to see the rest of the world?"

She hesitated. "Yes, but it is not possible."

He must know they were poor, that their only income was from her father's writing.

"It is possible," he said, with calm conviction. "Rosalind, you must leave this place. And your father also. You have shut yourselves away from your own people. I realize your father's health was poor, but now it's better."

"The islands have helped to cure him," she said, with reserve.

"He still needs care. How often does the doctor come to see him here?"

"He came before Christmas, and said father was improving. Indeed, he is well again."

Peter was silent. She realized he did not think so.

Peter finally said, "My father suffered a stroke about a year ago. He is not recovered at all. He sits in a wheelchair, and grumbles at his idleness. I have the doctor come from Honolulu once a month to check on him." He paused, and looked down at her.

"That is good," she said.

"I am doing this badly," said Peter, with an exasperated sigh. "You know that I mean to adopt Victor. But I am a bachelor, and people would talk, as my dear cousin pointed out to me rather nastily. I need a wife, someone who would love the child and care for him well. I also need a wife . . . for myself. I am the boss of Darien, and I should have sons . . . and daughters. I am twenty-eight. How old are you, Rosalind?"

Her throat felt choked, but she managed to stammer, "Nineteen."

"You seem . . . older, more mature," he said quietly. "You have cared for your father, you take care of the Hawaiian people here who need medical help and encouragement. Rosalind, I need you more than they do. Will you come back to Darien with me?"

She was silent, gazing up at him with wide incredulous eyes. Her? What did he want with her? A nursemaid for Victor? But he had said *he* needed her, he, Peter. Peter Darien, who did not seem to need anyone.

When she was without words, he added, impatiently, "I am asking you to marry me, Rosalind! Will you?"

"Me?" she squeaked, her voice almost closed off completely.

"Yes, you."

"But I . . . I am not. . . ."

"Not what?"

"A . . . a fine lady . . . like the ones in church . . . with lace and velvet," she finally stammered.

He shrugged his shoulders, and winced. The right one was not completely healed inside. "What does that matter? I shall buy you dresses as fine as theirs. You shall wear silks and velvets, lace and jewels, whatever you chose! And you will be as beautiful as any of them, even more so."

"I mean," she said, carefully, "I am not educated in their fine finishing schools. I have heard them talk about New England, and their years in the United States. I do not know about such matters. I would . . . disgrace you."

"You would never be an embarrassment to me, Rosalind," he said gently. "I would be proud of you."

She shook her head, and gazed out to sea. It shimmered more than ever because of the tears in her eyes. It was impossible. How the ladies would laugh at her, and titter behind their fans! The men would joke and look her up and down as Terence did, and ask if she was a *Haole* because of her tanned skin and dark hair. They might even wonder if Peter had had to marry her, that the child Victor might be hers. Though she did not care so much about that, she loved the child already, as though he did belong to her.

They continued to walk in silence. The native children ran past them with fish strung on their lines, their wide grins triumphant. One called out to Rosalind, "Lokelina, I take fish to your house for you!"

She managed to smile and answer him, "Thank you, son of Hoke. You are very good to us."

The boys ran on. "Lokelina, is that what they call you?" asked Peter. "Yes, of course, it is the name for Rosalind."

He put his hand under her arm as they came to some rocks. They sat down on the sun-warmed black lava that stuck out of the sand like so many ancient monsters.

"I thought," said Peter, not letting her arm go, "we could be married at the church in Kailua."

She thought of that large church, and the grand people, and flinched. "No . . . no . . . " she muttered.

He went on quickly, "Or the small mission church you like. Would you prefer that? I have written to the pastor at Kailua to wait for word from me, and to obtain a wedding license for us. Then we will go to Kailua, and order some clothes for you . . . and for your father. It is the last chance before we go on to Darien, we don't have women's shops on our island," he went on quickly, before she could protest. He must have felt her stiffness as they sat close together.

She was shocked and rather repelled by his audacity. He had dared to go ahead with the arrangements before he had even spoken to her about the matter! How dare he!

Well, she was not bound to him. She could say no, and he could do nothing about it. He could not force her to marry him.

She knew what freedom she had would be lost if she gave in to him. She could picture him now, all arrogance and dictation as to what she should do and what she should think and feel. She was silent, biting her lips, feeling his body heat against hers. She gazed at the velvety silk of the waves as they rippled inland, grazing her dangling legs.

Yet—yet how safe he would be! She would be able to rest against his strength. Arrogant, yes, but hard and sure of himself. Caring for those who belonged to him. She was torn, undecided.

She flinched at the quick memory of the mockery in the eyes of the women at church when she and Kinau had come. No, Peter should marry someone grand—like himself.

"I . . . I cannot marry you," she muttered, torn between desire and a quiet understanding of reality. He was the powerful and wealthy owner and boss of Darien. He was grateful to her, that was all. And he felt sorry for her, cut off from her own people here on this fragment of Hawaii's coast.

"Why not? Don't you like me?"

She gazed steadily out to sea. "Yes, I like you," she admitted, reluctantly.

"Don't you think I would be a patient lover, and a kind one?"

She flushed violently, and put her free hand to her face shyly. He laughed a little, close to her neck, and pressed a quick kiss to her bare shoulder. "I would, you know," he murmured.

Rosalind shivered. She felt tingly all over at his kiss. "We . . . we are of different worlds," she began, drawing back from him.

"Nonsense. You are of my race, you are of my interests. You speak English and Hawaiian, the people here love you. You would take an interest in those on

Darien and help me to rule wisely. It is a large job, Rosalind," he said seriously. "Sometimes I wonder how I can continue alone. There is so much to do. And the women will not confide in me. They would talk to you, and you could tell me what is wrong, what needs doing."

It was tempting, she thought briefly. To be his wife, his partner, his helper. To have his strong arms about her, to know his embraces at night, to bear his children.

To be allowed to love him! That idea came to her, and made her feel breathless and enchanted. Could this be Rosalind Murray, sitting on this boulder, where she had sat so often to watch the sunset spread its rose and crimson and scarlet banners across the sky, listening to a man tell her he wished to marry her? She felt as though she were dreaming and did not want to waken.

But she must be practical. Whites would not accept her. They would be scornful and sneer at her if she dared to marry Peter Darien. And that would hurt Peter.

Twisting her hands, she said presently, "I cannot leave my father."

"Of course not," he said promptly. "We will take him with us. I think he will enjoy Darien. My father knows many stories, and the Hawaiians there would talk to him of the old legends."

"And Kinau?" murmured Rosalind, rather frantically.

Peter laughed. "You may bring Kinau, and all her children and grandchildren! As many as you like, so long as you come also."

"You are teasing me," she said finally with a sigh. "You do not mean this. I am not the wife for you. There are beautiful and educated ladies in Kailua and Honolulu, look for your wife there."

"I have looked at them," said Peter Darien grimly. "Don't you think I have? For years, I have endured their simpers, and their empty conversations; they flirt and wave their fans. And not one of them has the sympathy and compassion and inner loveliness that you have. Why do you draw back? Don't you think I know what I want?"

She remained quiet, letting her eyes roam over the lush vegetation. Her mind was spinning frantically. Did he truly mean it? Or did he feel grateful to her and her father; perhaps he was sorry for her that she was cut off from all white people here? She did not want anyone to pity her, it was humiliating. When he had left, he would forget her again.

Peter squeezed her arm. "I think you are bewildered. Talk to Kinau. You trust her, don't you?"

Rosalind nodded, not looking at him.

"Talk to her. She will advise you. Think it over. We should leave here in a few days. I won't rush you. Just let me know soon what you wish. I want your decision as soon as you can give it to me. . . . "

"Don't rush! But hurry up and tell you I will do whatever you say!" she interjected spiritedly, with a toss of her dark head. "Really, Mr. Darien, you are . . . you are. . . ."

He flung back his black curly head and laughed aloud, and a tingling warmth ran through Rosalind's whole body. They sat together so closely on the rock, that she felt his joy race through him, and it seemed to enter her also.

He bent his head, caught her even closer to him, and boldly pressed his lips against hers. It was the first masculine kiss she had ever felt. Only her father had ever kissed her, and his dry papery lips had just touched her cheeks. The urgency of this man's lips caught her breath. She pulled away and stared at him. She saw the dark brown eyes so close to hers, laughing, with something flickering in the darkness. A blaze that made her a little afraid.

"You must not do that," she protested primly.

"Why not? We are practically engaged," he said, and caressed her mouth again, running his sensuous lips over her rounded cheeks, and down to her throat.

Several Hawaiian boys ran past them, and laughingly called out to them, "Look out, Lokelina, he means business, that one!"

"I should say I do," said Peter, softly in her ear, nibbling at it, until shivers raced up and down her spine. Rosalind pushed his hands from her. Somehow she felt colder without them on her body.

"I . . . I have to talk to Kinau," she said, and tore away from him.

Rosalind found Kinau in the vegetable patch, weeding and hoeing busily. The older woman looked at her questioningly, with keen eyes that had watched the girl grow from baby to child to young woman.

"Oh, Kinau, I am disturbed."

"What is it, my dear child?"

Rosalind automatically began to help, bending to pull out a weed. "Mr. Darien . . . he. . . ."

"Which one?"

"It is Peter Darien," she said, rather surprised. She never thought of the other cousin, except in distaste.

"The blond one, he thinks too much mischief," said Kinau bluntly.

Rosalind nodded. "Mr. Peter Darien . . . he asked me to marry him . . . to go to his island, to be his wife!"

"Hummmm," muttered Kinau, not seeming surprised. "What you say to him?"

"I . . . I must think about it. He is grateful to me . . . to us. We took him in, sheltered him. And he is . . . sorry for me, I think."

"Hummmmm." Kinau straightened and put her hand to the small of her back. "And your father? What he do?"

Rosalind had not even thought to ask her father. "Mr. Darien . . . Peter . . . wishes for us all to go with him. Father . . . and you . . . and all your children—"

"My children not leave here," said Kinau thoughtfully. "They have their homes, their land. But I go wherever you go. You need me still."

Rosalind sighed. "I don't know what to do."

"You like him much, huh?"

Rosalind nodded, blushing. "But he . . . he will for-

get me, when he goes away," she said in a low tone.
"Maybe so, maybe not."

They carried a basket of vegetables and some taro
roots into the kitchen, working together as they always
did. Kinau was silent for a time, then finally she
nodded, having made up her mind.

"We talk to Pele," she said. "We go to the home of
Pele, and ask her what she wishes you to do."

Rosalind thought of protesting, but at least this trip
would give her time to think over his extraordinary offer. "Yes. How shall we go?"

"Too far to walk. You not used to donkey. We borrow Mr. Peter's carriage."

"Oh. But do we have to tell him where we are going?" She thought somehow that Peter would be displeased, or tease her. To consult a Hawaiian goddess
about her future! She felt confused. She wished someone would take her hand and tell her quite simply what
she must do.

"No. We tell later if we must." And Kinau proceeded to change the subject as they prepared the evening meal.


Terence returned toward evening, tired and cross from
the heat. He grumbled about being sent hither and
yon on his cousin's errands. Refreshed by the simple
evening meal, he began to tease Rosalind.

"Next time I go to Kailua, I'll take you with me.
Buy you a pretty gown," he said, grinning at Rosalind.
"You'll be the belle of the place. What color do you
like best? We could go to a party at the hotel there.
Have you been to a dance? Can you dance American
style?"

She finally shook her head. "Only Hawaiian," Rosalind admitted, quietly.

Terence laughed at her. Peter watched the byplay,
then finally cut off Terry sharply, and sent him outside.

In the kitchen, Rosalind whispered to Kinau, "What
about the carriage?"

"It is set for tomorrow. We take lunch and blankets.
Be gone overnight, maybe. Hoke drive us."

It was all set. Early the next morning, Rosalind and Kinau set out in the carriage, with a shade over the top, and Hoke grandly in the driver's seat. They watched the dawn break over the peaks of Mauna Loa. White steam wreathed the head of the volcano, and blended with the reds and pinks of the sunrise. They drove all the day, into the evening, and finally reached the crater road before sundown.

On the way, they had stopped to pick plumeria and fragrant ginger blossoms, and in the carriage they had woven the flowers into leis. Kinau had a wealth of tales to while away the time, all about Pele and her family, and the events of the centuries which made up the legends of Pele. They drove around Mauna Loa, to the other side, to the slopes of Kilauea, where Pele now lived and sent up her volcanic steam and sulphurous fumes, and sometimes threw out chunks of red-hot lava down the slopes.

Rosalind could smell the sulphur now. It was growing more pungent as they approached the volcano, which rumbled and grumbled under their feet.

Hoke had grown silent, his eyes filled with awe. They drove close to the rim of the great crater and got out of the carriage. Hoke tied the carriage securely to a tree. Kinau brought with her two bottles of strong coconut wine and the flower leis.

She padded over the volcanic rocks, walking easily on the sharp cinder path. Rosalind followed her timidly, suddenly afraid when she traveled on the verge of the boiling red mass that lay beneath them. At the cracked brim they stopped, and looked down into the mass of lava that seethed and bubbled below.

Kinau began an eerie wailing and crying to Pele. Hoke crouched on the rim, staring in fascination at the steaming cauldron. Rosalind stood silently, her hands clasped together. Could Pele hear them? Was the goddess favorable? Was it all just crazy superstition?

Kinau turned to Rosalind. "Tell Pele what is in your heart," she urged. Her plump face was bathed in perspiration from the ascending heat.

"What shall I do, Pele?" asked Rosalind obediently. "Tell me what is right. Shall I continue to take care of the child Victor? What is your will?"

Kinau poked her impatiently. "Tell her what you wish!" she urged, and then took herself and Hoke away to another part of the rim. Once alone, Rosalind felt more free to speak.

"Pele," she said, in a low tone, "I admire Peter Darien, and I should like more than anything in the world to be his wife. Yet, I feel unworthy. I am not good enough for him. All will ridicule me, and I will be ashamed and hide my face. He will grow weary of me. Oh, Pele, what shall I do?"

Kinau returned then, and handed some coconut wine to her. "Fling it into the lava," she said. "Pele, she likes wine very much!"

Rosalind threw it carefully into the molten mass. Then they flung the flower leis down after it, to see them caught in the fires and consumed in moments.

From the fire rose steam and smoke, then a great tongue of flame, almost to their feet. Hoke cried out, and shrank back. Rosalind was frozen in fear, but Kinau only nodded and beamed in satisfaction.

"It is good." She cried out a weird chant, singing it over and over, and Hoke joined her earnestly. They praised Pele for her beauty, her wisdom, her goodness to her people. They promised to bring more liquor and blossoms.

Finally, Kinau paused and wiped her wet brow. "It is good; we are finished. We go now."

Rosalind was glad to get away from the crumbling edge. The flames seemed to leap up toward her very feet. They moved back from the crater, and finally Hoke untied the horse.

It was dusk, and they could still see the red flames leaping against the purpling sky. The very earth shook beneath them, rattling the carriage.

They went down the slopes and found a grassy mound on which to rest for the night. Kinau took food from the baskets. They ate, and drank of cool spring water from bottles. Hoke curled up afterwards and went to sleep peacefully. Kinau lay awake on her blanket, gazing up at the brilliant sparkling stars in the indigo sky. Rosalind could not sleep either, she tossed and turned. Had Pele answered her? What was the answer?

She finally slept, but her dreams were troubled. Terence Darien was running after her with mocking laughter. Then Peter came, took her hand tenderly, and shook his head. "No, I don't really want to marry you," he said. His voice echoed in her ears as she wakened.

She gazed about the grassy mound. Kinau was up, and shaking out her blankets and her dress. Hoke was feeding the horse, and giving it water.

Kinau found a hot sulphurous crack in the earth, from which steam rose, and boiled a kettle of water over it. They had hot tea, cold fish, and *poi*. Then they were ready to depart.

In the carriage, Rosalind finally asked her timidly, "What is the answer of Pele, Kinau?"

Kinau turned to her, and gave her a great beaming smile. "Pele, the goddess of volcanoes and fire, who gives us life and heat, she say, you take care of her child for her."

Rosalind stared at her. "Her child?" she echoed.

"Yes, Victor. He is now dedicated to Pele. He will grow up strong and big. He will be leader, he will be chief. You will raise him and teach him the legends of his people. Also he will know English and all that he must know. You take care of him until he is grown."

"You mean . . . I should offer to be a nursemaid for him?" asked Rosalind.

Kinau shook her head. "No. You marry with Peter Darien. You be his wife, have his children. Pele say you will have fine sons and daughters. But you must care tenderly for her child Victor, bring him up to be strong and fine. One day he will be fine chief of his people."

She lapsed into silence, and would not be drawn out, her face serene and happy in the morning light.

Rosalind leaned back in the carriage, her heart strangely light. She would do what Kinau said. She did not know if Pele had said it, or Kinau. She thought Kinau was probably the wisest woman she knew, and she had said to marry Peter.

She glanced back over her shoulder at the brooding black volcano behind them. Did it flare up in red flames, or was it the rays of the sun that burned so brightly against the sky?

The idea of marriage troubled her. She was not sure if she was equal to the task. To be Peter's hostess, the mother of his children, to carry on the Darien traditions, to help him in his work. But she would try very hard—if he wanted her to do so.

It was evening when they reached home. Peter came out to meet them, his face troubled. Hoke jumped down, gave him a broad grin, and led the horse away.

"Where have you been? I never dreamed you would be gone so long," Peter asked Rosalind, sternly.

Kinau interposed. "Tomorrow you talk. Not tonight. She very tired. She sleep good tonight," she said cheerfully.

Rosalind managed a faint smile, and a weary nod of her head. "Tomorrow," she echoed. "We'll talk tomorrow."

"Very well. Tomorrow," he said. But by the grim set of his mouth, the young tyrant was not pleased.

# 4

❧ ❧ ❧ ❧

ROSALIND ROSE early the next morning. She bathed from a blue china bowl, and put on her favorite green print dress. Kinau had been up before her, and was preparing breakfast when Rosalind went to the kitchen.

The older woman's seamed face was serene as she hummed over her cooking. She was satisfied. "Today you tell him okay to marry."

Rosalind nodded. "I think . . . I will."

Kinau patted her shoulder. "You will be fine."

Peter was sitting on the veranda. By his wet hair and shining face it was apparent he had been in swimming already. He turned as Rosalind came out shyly with his plate of food and cup of tea.

He stood up and said, "Good morning." The keen eyes searched her face.

"Good morning," she said gravely.

"Bring your plate and eat with me," he ordered. She nodded, and went back for her food. She was glad Terence was not present, somehow he spoiled things.

They ate in silence, looking out over the lagoon to the western sky, skimmed in pink with the reflection of the sunrise. She sighed to think she might leave this place soon, the place of her birth, and never return to it again. She knew the rocks, the sand, the shape of every palm tree, the looming black cliffs behind their small white house, the face and voice of every Hawaiian here.

Peter was shifting restlessly in his chair. She was awkward, not knowing how to bring up the subject.

"Have you decided, Rosalind? You will marry me?"

She nodded. "I talked with Kinau," she said slowly. "I think . . . I am needed to take care of Victor."

"That also," said Peter abruptly. "But first of all, you are to be my wife. That comes first."

"Oh. She looked at him directly, caught by surprise. Her mind had been full of the words that Kinau had spoken about Pele, about Victor and how he would be a great chief. Peter's dark brown eyes were direct and piercing, as though he could see into her heart and soul. "Yes," she said softly. "I will be . . . your wife . . . first."

It was a promise and a pledge, and he was satisfied. His handsome face relaxed, he finally smiled and held out his hand to her. She put her slim hand in his great tanned one, and he squeezed her fingers reassuringly. He put his other hand in the pocket of his trousers and took out a ring. He slid it gently onto the finger of her left hand. Instinctively, she caught her breath.

It was a gold band with a great black pearl on it, a black pearl that shone and glimmered with secret silvery light. She had seen small ones in the stores, but never anything like this one.

How had he obtained this, and in the right size? She knew he had sent his cousin here and there with errands. Was this one of the chores, to obtain a ring for her before she had even given her consent? It troubled her, that in his confidence he had taken for granted that she would agree, and had ordered the ring be made.

She twisted it about on her finger. The beauty of it, the deep shining shimmer, held her heart captive.

"Oh . . . how beautiful," she gasped. "Where . . . did you find this?"

A little secret smile curling his large generous mouth. "One day I will tell you," he said, as though amused by something in his mind.

She continued to turn it about gravely, admiring it. He looked down at her bent head, satisfied.

"Now we can make plans," he said briskly. "I have requested some dresses for you at a store in Kailua. The seamstress will send out your wedding dress today. I will ask for the pastor to come to the mission church two days from now. The license is here already. Terence has brought several trunks with him, lined with tin. I think your father will want to take his books and papers with him."

She caught her breath. He swept all before him like a great typhoon! He saw the expression on her face.

"There is no need to wait, is there?" he asked, more gently, taking her hand in his again.

"I . . . suppose . . . not. . . ."

She was troubled. She wanted some time to think about her new status, to consider whether she was doing the right thing.

"What is it?"

"Father," she said, grasping the idea. "I have not even told him."

"I will tell him today," said Peter, and raised her delicate hand to his lips and kissed it. "Don't worry. You're in my charge from now on."

In his charge. And he had ordered dresses made for her, without waiting to see if she would consent! He could have waited for her to say yes, but no—he must go ahead and plan without speaking to her first!

She tried to whip up her anger against him. But he was like one of those powerful ocean currents which took control of one's body—useless to struggle.

In his charge. It was comforting, yet irritating as well. He had requested to have this made and that made, bonnets and shoes, all without her knowledge, even before he had asked her to marry him.

Was this a warning about their marriage? Would he always go arrogantly on his way without asking her consent? She felt as though she had agreed now to let him take over her life and mind and thoughts, completely.

He had Hoke bring in the great trunks and had some Hawaiian boys begin to pack her father's papers and books. Another Hawaiian was sent to Kailua to bring back the carriages, horses, and dresses. Messages flew here and there. Terence wakened and was put right to work, to his grumbling amazement.

"You never said you were going to marry the girl!" Rosalind heard him say to his cousin.

"Since when do I tell you my plans first? Was I supposed to propose to you before I did to Rosalind?" Peter asked cuttingly. "Will you get down to work, and do what I say?"

"Well, all right, all right, but why the rush? Why not take the girl back to Darien and see if she fits in? Maybe they won't like her. Maybe she won't like the island. It's damn lonely there."

"It's more lonely here," said Peter curtly. "And she is marrying me, not anyone else." With that he strode away, to talk to Hoke, leaving Terence to scratch his head and mumble to himself.

The talk wakened more misgivings in Rosalind. It became worse when her father wandered in from his walk and found boys busily packing his belongings.

"My word, whatever is going on? Boys, stop this at once! Rosalind, stop the boys, they are putting everything in boxes!"

Rosalind hurried in to take her father's thin arm in hers and lead him away. "Didn't Peter tell you, dearest? We are going to be married, and go to live with the Dariens on his island."

Her father looked at her blankly. "He said something about a wedding. But I didn't know he meant right away. And why are my books being packed?"

"You are going with us," she said firmly. "He wants you to come with us."

Peter came up on the veranda as she was attempting to explain matters. His dark eyes alert, he took in their troubled expressions.

"What's the matter, Mr. Murray?"

"Why . . . why I never realized . . . you meant immediately. And why am I leaving here? I have not yet finished my work!"

"You can work on Darien. There are many people there to tell you what you want to know," said Peter, patiently. "I don't think Rosalind would agree to leaving you behind."

"Oh, no, I could not, " she said quickly. Her father was brilliant, but he had no sense at all. He must be looked after, his clothes mended, his work encouraged.

"Well, well," said Alfred Murray fretfully, brushing back his greying hair. "It seems like everything is taking place in such a hurry! Why don't you wait until Christmas? Christmas is a nice time for ceremonies."

Rosalind sighed, and began again. "Peter is anxious to return to Darien, and take up his work there, Father. You will have a room in which to work, a desk . . ." She looked anxiously at Peter.

"Two rooms," said Peter seriously. "A bedroom and a sitting room where you can write in privacy. However, you may want to spend much time in the library. My father and grandfather have collected a vast number of books and papers on Hawaii, and I have tried to add to them as time permitted."

"A library?" Arthur Murray's eyes lit up with incredulous pleasure. "Truly? It is the one thing I have missed!"

"Over two thousand volumes, plus documents and magazines," said Peter, and smiled at Rosalind with a little wink, as though to share her concern.

"Well . . . well . . . I may come for a time, then," said her father, and wandered back to see that his things were being packed properly.

"Father does not realize," Rosalind said anxiously, "that we are not going to return here."

"I know." He took her hand, and held it in his strong one. "Leave it to me. He will adjust to Darien and enjoy it, believe me. And so will you. I promise."

Hoke returned with the carriages, several other drivers, enormous boxes and a big grin. Rosalind wondered why he was so pleased—unless he was planning to come with them. Then Peter explained that Hoke and his growing family were to have the Murray house after she and her father moved out.

Kinau said, "Hoke and my sons have to learn to do without me. They get good sense and know what to do. I come back and see them sometimes. I tell them they must be good boys, and work hard, and watch for any enemy." Seeing the worry in Rosalind's face, she added quickly, "That is only sense, my baby," and patted Rosalind's face as though she were but a child.

Boxes were carried through to Rosalind's bedroom where she and Kinau opened them. Dresses of cotton, silk, and lace—pink gowns, green and blue ones like the sea and the sky. Rosalind handled them in wonder, gasping over their beauty. She had never seen anything like them before, except on the ladies at church.

There were dresses of fashion, with ruffles on the bosoms and lace on the sleeves, and a funny bundle at the back that Peter said was called a bustle. But there were also smartly-made muumuus and slim holomus. They fit Rosalind like the comfortable ones she already owned. It seemed Peter had managed to get to the dressmaker a sample from her wardrobe that was used as a pattern for the others.

And the wedding gown! It was of white satin, simply styled, with a scooped neck, and a skirt to her ankles. Lace trimmed the sleeves from elbow to cuff and additional lace filled the side slits of the skirt, which resembled sea foam.

"This is too much," Rosalind cried awkwardly. "I can never wear them all . . ."

Peter only smiled, brushing back his hair where the curls had fallen on his forehead. He was helping pack up the boxes, nailing them shut. "Yes, you will, and more. You will be the hostess of Darien now, and entertain guests. Do not worry about it," he added quickly. "You will soon become accustomed to it. But I want you to be the most beautiful lady of them all, and you will."

She shook her head, her eyes shadowing. "I cannot be like that, Peter," she whispered.

"Yes, you will," he said firmly.

She wondered if anyone dared to say "No," to him and get away with it. When he closed his lips like that, and nodded his head so firmly, did anyone defy him?

But even this might be beyond his capacity, to take a shy brown bird and turn her into a bird of paradise. She began to turn away in embarrassment.

"I asked the dressmaker to keep the wedding gown simple. Ask Kinau to have the girls make leis of plumeria—the white kind—for you to wear. And I should like you to wear tiare in your hair."

This was something she could do, and would take pleasure in. "Yes, I will," she said, and went out with one of Kinau's daughters to gather the plumeria and to find the tiare blossoms to weave into a net over her hair.

So they were married by the pastor in the little white Congregational Church of the mission. Peter wore a pale tropical suit, with a royal blue tie. Terence was the best man, in a sleek white suit and a discontented expression.

Rosalind allowed her chestnut hair to hang loose over her shoulders. The fragile tiare gave the allure of mist about her head and two leis of plumeria blossoms circled her slim throat, creamy against the white silk of her gown. She carried a small Bible that had been her mother's, and Peter placed a gold band on her finger that matched that of the black pearl. He gave her another wider gold band, and she put that on his left hand, her fingers cold and chilled with awe at what she was doing.

The church was filled with their friends, Kinau's family, a few from Kailua. The pastor's wife kissed her cheek and wished her well, some other ladies stared at her as though to ask how she had managed to pull this off. She tried not to think of them, but only of Peter, whom she wished to make happy, and of Victor, whom she wanted so much to protect.

The carriages were ready by afternoon and they drove to Kailua, leaving behind them the small house with peeling paint. She glanced back once, to see it looking lost and fragile against the looming black cliffs, the waves beating up on the shore—the waves where she had swam and played, the house where she had slept, where they had worked and been content all those years—and her mother's grave, up on the cliff.

Peter drove her himself in one carriage. Kinau rode with Hoke, and someone else drove her father, hugging his latest manuscript which he had refused to allow to be packed. Terence had driven impatiently ahead with some smart lady from Kailua, and they were laughing and talking, the echo coming back along the trail.

Until now, Rosalind had not thought about exactly where they were going. She thought they would go to the docks and get onto a ship, what kind of vessel she did not know.

They entered the town on the dusty road, and Peter reined up to a grand, huge building.

"This is the hotel where we shall be staying for several days."

Hotel? She had heard of staying in places like this, but she had been in the dining room here only twice. She looked at it shyly, then followed her husband as he entered. Men ran to do his bidding, a man in a frock-coat kept bowing to him and saying, "Yes, sir, at once, sir." He bowed to Rosalind also, and she was not sure whether she should bow back to him, but her dress was so stiff and tight she did not think she could manage it.

They were shown to a large suite with a veranda facing south. Peter looked about him critically, and nodded. "This will do very well." Rosalind thought the sitting room was bigger than the whole of her small home in the cove, left far behind now.

Then the thought came back to her—Victor! How could she have forgotten the child? She started for the door.

## Black Pearls

"Where are you going?" asked Peter sharply. He was taking off his jacket.

"To get Victor. I must give him his supper, he must be hungry," said Rosalind, tugging at the door handle.

"Nonsense. Kinau will look after him." His voice gentled, he came after her, and took her hand from the lock. "Don't you want to change your dress and put on something comfortable?"

"Oh . . . yes . . . but I should look after Victor. I promised to look after him. . . ."

"Of course you will. You will see to his education and his training. But Kinau will look after his feeding and his sleeping," he said patiently. "Don't forget, you have a husband to look after now."

She smiled, that seemed ridiculous. "Oh, you don't need to be looked after," she said. "You're an adult!"

"Oh, but I require a great deal of attention," he teased, and caught her to him, pressing a kiss gently on her lips. "There now, go and change. Wear something pink, I have not seen you in that color yet."

That seemed easy enough, she smiled and went to the bedroom, where a Hawaiian girl was unpacking the boxes. She smiled and bowed to Rosalind, and seemed amazed when Rosalind spoke to her in Hawaiian. They were soon chatting away, and the girl told Rosalind she was her maid for the time she was in the hotel.

The maid, Akela, helped Rosalind take off the wedding gown with its numerous covered buttons running down the back, and slip on a simple pink muslin dress with ruffles about the throat. It was loose like her muumuus, and felt so much better. The tight satin slippers were removed, and she put on sandals.

Akela continued to remove garments from the boxes, and hold them up, exclaiming delightedly over each. One set of garments was very scanty, with only straps for the shoulders. Rosalind puzzled over them. Akela said, "For the night wear, Mrs. Darien!"

"Oh," said Rosalind, and began to blush. She knew that on marriage a husband and wife slept together

53

on one mat, or in one bed. However, did one really wear such brief garments to do this?

Akela looked over the assortment, then laid out a beautiful ivory muslin gown with cornflower colored ribbons threaded through the bodice of lace. "This is for tonight," she said decidedly, with a beaming smile.

Rosalind escaped from the room, leaving the maid to hum happily over the lovely boxes. She found Peter in the living room, in white shirt sleeves, reading a newspaper. He lowered it, and smiled.

"Feeling better, darling?"

She felt a little thrill of pleasure race along her spine. "Darling," he said, and it sounded natural on his lips. But to say darling to her. . . . She had read the word in books, but had never heard anyone speak it like this.

"Darling," he had said. His voice had lingered over the word, and he looked at her as though he liked what he saw, his gaze going from her smooth brown throat to her thin sandals. She shivered a little from some odd feeling of the change in her life.

She was married, she was wife to this strange man. Could she ever call him "darling" in that natural way? She could not imagine doing so.

"Rosalind . . . you do feel comfortable, don't you?" he persisted when she did not answer.

She nodded. She felt odd, not having chores to do, such as peeling the vegetables for dinner. Not even Victor was there and she missed his soft little body against hers. She walked about the room, looking at the objects: the pretty sandalwood tables with glossy magazines spilling over them, a lamp with shades of green ruffles, a green flowered china dish, flowers everywhere in vases and bowls. Peter was watching her.

"You are as restless as a cat in a strange house," he teased gently.

"I feel . . . strange," she admitted. "Everything has happened so very . . . rapidly."

"Come over here." He was sitting on the plump sofa, and she went to sit down beside him. He reached out his uninjured arm, and scooped her closer to him. He pressed his cheek against her glossy hair. "You are beginning a quite new life, my dear," he said presently. "I want you to be happy, that is what I want most. Remember that, will you?"

She nodded, but she did not understand. He had married her to have a wife and children, and to have someone undertake the care of Victor. Happiness came in doing one's duty, pride was a part of it, that one did one's duty well.

Someone tapped at the door. Peter muttered a curse and got up. He opened the door. A man stood there.

"Mr. Darien? I know you must be busy, but I must speak to you tonight. . . . " He was turning his sombrero over and over in his hands, his tanned face a flushed red.

"Did you know I was just married today?" asked Peter Darien, a dangerous ring to his voice.

Another man stood behind them. "I know, but it is important . . . I have waited . . . you have been gone for more than three months. . . ."

Rosalind stood up. She recognized the urgent appeal in their voices. "I will rest in my room, please, excuse me."

Peter invited the men in, and they talked for more than an hour. Rosalind sat in a comfortable chair near the veranda watching the sunset over the waters of the bay. There were ships in the harbor, and she enjoyed the swelling sails, the masts looming over the tops of the houses by the wharves, the bustle of activity on the street below her windows.

Peter was an important man, she must remember that. Many decisions waited for him, they needed him. If she was to help, she must remember how important he was, and how much his decisions meant to them. He was like a great Hawaiian chief, big and strong and intelligent and wise, and they listened to him, and followed his advice.

The rumble of the voices finally ceased. She heard the hall door close, then Peter came to her. His hair was ruffled; he looked grim.

"I am sorry, Rosalind. I did not mean for this to happen," he said, coming to stand behind her chair.

She turned her head and smiled. "I have been watching the ships and the people. There are so many people here. Is that big ship the one on which we will sail to Darien?"

He bent his head to peer out the window. "No, that is a sailing vessel. We shall go by steamship," he said, his voice lighter. "It is very luxurious. We go next Thursday."

That was another five days off. She wondered why the wait, but he would tell her if he wanted to.

"I ordered our meal to be brought here," he said, sounding a little impatient again. "If we go to the dining room, we will be interrupted constantly."

"People want to speak to you," she said gently.

"And see how beautiful my bride is," he smiled, and kissed her forehead. "No, I shall keep you to myself. Come in, and have some champagne. I told them to send it right up."

He poured wine for her into sparkling crystal glasses. The drink bubbled up in fizzy bursts that tickled her nose. He lifted his glass to her.

"To my wife," he said. He kept saying that. My bride, my wife. He sounded proud, possessive. Yes, he was a very possessive man. What was his was his, and no one should touch or take.

Three Hawaiian men brought their dinner shortly thereafter. They had appetizers of raw fish with assorted sauces to dip it in, shrimp, and *poi*. Then hot dishes of beef in another sauce, and delicious fresh-cooked green beans and pork. For dessert there was chilled mango in champagne. She felt quite dizzy from all the alcohol.

Rosalind was not accustomed to wine; so she stayed away from the fermented coconut milk and rice wines. But Peter insisted she must try everything tonight.

Finally they were left alone. The mosquito nets had been drawn across the windows, and the shutters partially closed. Lamps were lit, creating an intimate atmosphere.

She wondered briefly about her father, where he was, and how he managed. Did someone see that he ate regularly and went to bed at a reasonable hour instead of staying up all night reading? And Victor, did he cry for her?

Peter read the disturbed expression that flitted across her face. "What now?" he asked, filling her glass again.

"Father," she admitted. "And Victor."

"Kinau is taking care of them both. You do not need to worry about anything."

Didn't she? There was the whole new world she was entering, a worrisome world, with new people, new habits and customs. Would they like her, or would they turn up their noses and talk behind her back? She shrank from all the challenges that were coming.

"Let me tell you about Darien," said Peter, as though realizing what she felt.

Like the other Hawaiian islands, it had been formed by volcanoes many thousands of years ago, as the lava spewed forth from the ocean depths. The volcanoes erupted again and again, and molten lava boiled forth, sizzled as it hit the ocean waves, and formed new soil. And finally the volcanoes stopped erupting, green grasses grew, and birds dropped seeds for new growth.

Darien was a small island compared to some, about nine miles by twelve. The center was an extinct volcano, and at the far northwest and far southwest were two other smaller extinct volcanoes. On the northeast were high sheer cliffs, and all around the eastern end of Darien were more high cliffs, against which the first Darien had built his home.

Peter sketched a map of the island, and she looked at it with interest. The three-story house was long, with two wings extending from the ends. It stood not far from the shipping dock, where they would land. Behind the mansion were stables and rooms for the carriages. To the west were gardens for vegetables, fruit trees, and the smaller dwellings of his cowboys, the *paniolos*. On the slopes of the central volcano the soil was fertile and the grass soft and fragrant. There the cattle roamed, until time for the round-up, when beef was shipped off to Honolulu. A dirt road wound most of the way around the island, but horses gave everyone easy mobility over the plains.

"How many people live on Darien?" she asked as she studied the map.

"About two hundred. Maybe two more," he grinned. "The wives of two *paniolos* were expecting when I left."

So Peter was responsible for more than two hundred people! No wonder he looked so grave and even cross sometimes. She must remember that, and help him all she could.

She yawned, unexpectedly. The champagne made her feel light headed and sleepy. He set down the map, and kissed her forehead. "Go and get ready for bed, darling. It has been a long day."

"Yes." She got up with relief, and said shyly, "Goodnight, Peter."

He looked a little surprised. "I'll be along presently." His eyebrows were raised at her, and she began to blush.

She hurried into the bedroom, forgetting to take a lamp with her. She undressed in the half-darkness, groped for the nightdress. It slid silkily over her body. She washed at the basin and brushed out her hair, then braided it neatly. She got into bed, marveling at how wide and long it was. She would be lost in it! The bed creaked as she turned over, and laid her warm cheek against the cool pillow.

Peter came in, and set a lamp on the dresser. Then he blew it out, and began to undress. She heard the sounds of his shoes dropping, the rustle of his clothes. She was trembling. If only she had talked to Kinau! She had meant to, but things had happened so rapidly the past few days. . . .

Peter slid into bed, and reached out his long arm for her. She tensed, and he felt the stiffening. He scooped her against him.

"Tired, my dear?"

"Yes . . . rather . . ."

"Kiss me."

He was bending over her, and she turned her face obediently to his. His lips brushed against hers and she felt the strength of them, and the warmth. He kissed her deliberately, she lay motionless, savoring the feel of the mouth, the generous width of his lips. His fingers caressed her cheek, then traced the length of her shoulder and arm. It was so odd, to have him holding her like this, touching her.

He lay back on the pillow, and drew her more tightly against him. She put her head on his bare chest, wondering at the rough texture of the hair, the smoothness yet hardness of his flesh, the differentness that was him. She wondered if he liked touching her. His fingers were stroking lightly over her back.

"You are tense," he said presently. "Go to sleep, darling. Too much has happened too fast for you."

She agreed, but wondered how he knew that. She snuggled her face more closely against him, and closed her eyes. She began to relax, drifting away into sleep. And even in sleep, she felt his arms about her, holding her to him, and under her cheek she heard the steady beating of his heart, as firm as the waves of the sea.

When she wakened in the morning the sun's rays were already coming through the shutters. She heard deep masculine voices in the living room, her husband's, and those of other men. She frowned a little. Today also?

She sat up, and presently got up to bathe and dress. She put on a pretty lavender gown that was loose and fresh. It was going to be a hot day, she knew by the glaze of the sky.

Peter tapped on the door. "Awake, Rosalind?" He put his head inside, and smiled to see her up. "I have to talk a while longer. I'll send for your breakfast. Would you like it on the veranda?"

"*Aloha.* Yes, please."

She ate the crisp melon, the bacon, and the biscuits on the terrace, and still the deep voices went on and on. She wondered all the more. They could not even leave him alone for a single day! She had glimpsed one man, an important Hawaiian politician in Honolulu. How did he come to be here, and what did he want with Peter?

Finally they went away, and Peter joined her. He stretched himself out beside her with a sigh, and put his feet up on another chair.

"We have a great many errands to do today, darling," he said, looking at her as she drank her tea. His gaze seemed to go all over her, as it had that day in the churchyard at Kailua.

"Errands? What errands?"

"More dresses. Shoes. Bonnets."

"Oh, Peter! I have so many. Don't say that."

He only smiled. "And then you must buy more paper for your father. We sometimes don't get back to this island for a time. How much would he need for six months or so?"

She calculated, frowning a little. "Six reams, maybe more."

"And a typewriter. I left the old one there. We should be able to find a new model here, or I'll send to Honolulu for one. What else? Pens, ink . . . you make a list, and we'll start out soon," and he got up briskly to get a pencil and paper for her.

He was rarely still for long, she thought.

She made the list, finished her tea, and found him waiting to leave, shrugging into his crisp white jacket. He looked so handsome, she thought proudly. He carried himself with an air of authority that made everyone look at him with respect!

She had thought they would go first to the stationery shops. But instead, he directed their driver to stop at a row of shops in town. The first place they visited, she discovered, was a jeweler's.

Several discreet rows of locked glass cases lined the sides of the store. Clocks chimed in unison on the walls, large grandfather clocks and short mantel clocks, little darling watches, and turnip-shaped golden ones for a man.

A short dark Asian came forward, bowing almost double. "Mr. Darien, sir, you honor my place!" he exclaimed. The man was part Chinese, thought Rosalind. He lisped the English in a cute way. And his bright eyes were in a network of deep lines, slanted unlike the large Hawaiian eyes.

"How do you do, Mr. Chan? This is my wife, Mrs. Darien."

The man bowed double again. "How honored my humble place is today!" he chanted.

He showed them back into another room, waving the other clerks to take his place in the showroom. He shut the door after them, and bowed Peter and Rosalind to chairs. Then, on a glass table, he laid out a black velvet cloth. Like a magician, he flicked his fingers, smoothed the velvet reverently, then brought out a Chinese lacquer box, in brilliant red with design of peacocks and dragons. He opened the box before Rosalind, gently lifting out the golden necklace inside.

She caught her breath. The gems sparkled like green fire. She looked at Peter appealingly. He had given her so much, surely he did not expect. . . .

"These are emeralds, Rosalind." Peter took the necklace and set it about her throat. Mr. Chan brought a silvered mirror, and showed her the reflection of herself. It showed a wide-eyed girl with amber eyes, a long slender neck—and a necklace of glittering gold and green. "Do you like emeralds?"

She faltered, "I've never . . . seen . . . any . . . before. I have only heard of them in stories."

Mr. Chan smiled with pleasure, his old face crinkled up into a vast network of wrinkles. "Stories, yes, yes, many good stories about emeralds. And the little drops for the ears, yes?"

He placed them in Peter's hand, he helped her adjust them since Rosalind had never worn earrings before. They twinkled back at her from the mirror.

"And the ring, in the lady's size," said Mr. Chan, magically producing an enormous square-cut emerald on a gold band.

It was then Chan noticed her engagement ring.

"Ahhhhh," he sucked in his breath. "The lady permits?" Gently he reached for her left hand, and reverently lifted it to examine the pearl. Mr. Chan glanced at Peter. "Black pearl, of fine quality. You permit I examine?"

"You have not seen such pearls before?" asked Peter blandly, his eyes narrowed.

"Rarely have I seen black pearls, and never of such quality," responded the jeweler. He hesitated, his finger on his lower lip. "There was a man who came in and asked if I had black pearls. I told him, none in Hawaii. I must have been mistaken, yes? I should like so very much to examine this rare pearl. You permit?"

"No one else would be permitted. But since Mr. Chan is my friend of long standing, and he has a reputation of keeping silence about matters, he may be permitted to examine this pearl." And Peter took the ring from Rosalind's hand and held it out to Mr. Chan.

Mr. Chan bowed even more deeply than ever before. He lifted a magnifying glass from his desk, and held the ring near the light. He turned it this way and that, looking at it intently. Peter watched him keenly. The Oriental finally laid down the glass, and returned the ring to Peter, who slipped it again onto Rosalind's finger.

"I ask no questions," said Mr. Chan very softly, as though there was a secret between them. "But if ever you should find such pearls again . . . if a poor merchant such as myself might be permitted to handle such exquisite pearls for someone . . . it would be the greatest of honors. It is of such quality I have rarely seen. Truly beautiful."

Peter bowed to him, Mr. Chan bowed back, and all seemed understood between them. Rosalind was bewildered again. When and where had Peter purchased such a ring, if not from one such as Mr. Chan? And why the secrecy? So much was puzzling to her.

"Do you like the emeralds?" Peter turned to her, changing the subject quite abruptly. He lifted her right hand, and let the lamplight play on the precious stone.

"I have never seen such an exquisite set," she said honestly. "Even the flowers are not so beautiful . . .

except when they are fresh, and the tiare gives off a scent . . ."

Both men smiled, and Mr. Chan said sweetly, "Truly your new flower is of a radiance, Mr. Darien. My congratulations to you, and my very best wishes for your great joy and happiness."

"I thank you, Mr. Chan. You have my wishes about the diamonds? I wish a necklace made up, and a tiara, with matching rings and two bracelets. You have the lady's size, and know what I wish."

"You may trust me in this, and in all matters." The jeweler set the emeralds back into the red lacquer box, then handed the box to Rosalind with a smile and a deep bow. "May you wear these in happiness, Mrs. Darien. It will always be my pleasure to serve you."

She clutched the box to her, bewildered. Had Peter just bought these? They must be horribly expensive. But yes, they were bowing again, and Mr. Chan was showing them out of the shop, and all the clerks were bowing and echoing good wishes all the way to the door.

"And now the dressmaker," said Peter. "Just up the street, we'll leave the carriage here." He took over the box, tucked it carelessly under his arm, and put his hand under her elbow to guide her.

Rosalind whispered frantically, "Peter, pray do not purchase anything else for me! Just father's paper, and that is all. . . ."

"Nonsense," said Peter, in his arrogant young fashion. "I enjoy dressing you, much better than a doll," and he grinned down at her, his eyes sparkling. "You are very lovely, you know. You shall be the belle of every ball at Darien's. Come along, love. I want you to choose a dozen more gowns. Do you like blue better than green? Truly, you seem more beautiful in every color. I thought green was your color, but in pink you are delicious. And in white, like your nightdress this morning, you were so charming, I could scarcely leave you."

"Peter!" she whispered, aghast and blushing furiously. Everyone could hear them, she imagined.

Peter nodded to someone on the street, she noticed it was the newspaper editor, and then a fine lady in a red and white striped silk gown. He knew everyone, and everyone knew him. She had known he was important on Darien—but in Kailua also? And in Honolulu? And all over Hawaii? Oh, what had she done to marry such a grand important man? She felt turned inside out and upside down.

She wished she could sit down on the beach for a day, and think. Just think. Everything was so confused and upsetting. If she could only get things straight in her mind.

There was so much to puzzle her. The men last night, urgently needing to see Peter and talk to him, so urgently that they had interrupted him when he was angry. And the men this morning, that man from Honolulu, an important politician. And everyone on the street, knowing him, pausing to greet him.

"I say, Mr. Darien, do you have time to come to lunch?"

"There you are, Mr. Darien, it has been a long time. Couldn't you stop by the office . . . or I can come to the hotel. . . ."

"Why, my dear Mr. Darien," and this was a coy simpering older woman. "How you have neglected us! Is this your dear bride? How pretty, won't you introduce us? I could give a tea tomorrow. . . ."

To all of them, he smiled and shook his head. "So sorry, terribly busy, see my agent," or "No time this week, I fear. Perhaps next time, so kind of you to ask," and he whipped Rosalind along with his hand under her arm.

They went into the dressmaker's, a grand one where Rosalind had only dared to peep in the windows before. Now Madame Rosario came to the door herself, bowing until her stays creaked under her black satin dress. Everyone else was forgotten, only Mr. Darien and Madame Darien were there, her dark eyes snapped.

Had Madame Darien liked her wedding gown? She had! Perfecto! Did Madame Darien prefer rose or green? Blue or yellow? Would she care to suggest a favorite flower? The new silk prints were exquisite, would Madame Darien care to make a choice? Would Madame Darien please remove her little bonnet, and allow one to be tried on her head? Would Madame Darien permit her to send for a hairdresser, to show her how to fasten her hair in a coronet for special occasions?

Peter sent for the hairdresser, and seemed to be amused and pleased to be an onlooker as hair styles were tried, bonnets set on Madame's head, pieces of silk and lace and satin examined. He knew more what he wanted than Rosalind, her head was soon turned completely around.

He ended the session by promising to return the next day with Madame, and swept Rosalind off to a fine restaurant, "To show you off," he said with a grin. And all during luncheon, people kept coming up to their table to be introduced, to shake her hand, to congratulate Peter and wish her well. She knew a few of them, but most she did not.

It was amazing, and something to be pondered. Peter knew everybody.

# 5

❦　❦　❦　❦

AFTER LUNCH, Rosalind and Peter walked
back to the hotel. "I have an appointment," he said,
frowning slightly.

"And I should like to see Victor," she replied
quickly. "I have not seen him since yesterday! And
not much then."

Peter hesitated, then nodded. "Kinau is with him
on the second floor, on the other side. I'll take you up
to them. Do not wander around town on your own,
will you?"

She felt surprised, and rebellious. "Why not? I have
before, when I came into town."

His mouth tightened. "I do not want you to," he
said definitely. "There are always rough sailors and
town louts. They might accost you. Promise me, Rosalind, you will not go out alone."

She sighed. "I don't see what difference. . . ."

"You belong to me now. And nothing is going to
happen to you."

"Oh, Peter. But. . . ."

He shook his head, and led her into the hotel, his
arm in hers. He could have picked her up with just
one arm. He was very strong, and very sure of himself, she thought.

Peter took her upstairs on the other side of the hotel. There she found Victor playing on the floor,
watched over by Kinau, sitting in a rocking chair.
They both beamed to see her. Victor held up his arms
to her. Rosalind knelt down to pick him up and hug
him.

She pressed her face against his small neck, and he

67

gurgled with pleasure. Peter watched them, a slight smile on his bronzed face.

"Oh, baby, darling, have you missed me?"

Kinau got up with some difficulty. "I take him to the beach this morning, but it no good," she said, with some scorn. "All dirty with bottles about. I bring him home, to hotel. Darien much better, huh?" She looked hopefully at Peter.

"Much better. Victor will like that, and so will you both. I must go, Kinau. See that Rosalind does not go out alone. This isn't her own little cove. Okay?"

"Okay," said Kinau, and patted him on the back, as she would have her own stalwart sons. "I look after her. Hoke still here, he watch."

Rosalind crinkled her face at them both, they puzzled her, as though they spoke some other language. Why were they so disturbed about watching and looking after her?

"Where is Mr. Murray?" Peter asked, looking about.

"Him go out, Hoke watch."

Just then, Mr. Murray returned, walking in the door, and smiled absently at Rosalind. "There you are, dear, I was looking for you. I want you to have a look at my story."

Hoke followed, standing just inside the door. He was unusually dressed up, with white trousers and a flowered shirt. His alert dark eyes glanced at Peter. Peter nodded.

"Well, I must leave. Be sure to get some rest this afternoon, Rosalind. I'll be back later," and he disappeared.

Rosalind gave a little moue of disgust. "What is this? Why am I to rest, not to go out walking?" Hoke had closed the door.

"He look after you now, he your husband. He always the boss, yes?"

"He certainly is," said Rosalind.

Her father picked up the story from the table, and this week before we return home."

flipped over the pages. "Do you think you could look

over this now?" he asked patiently. "We might mail it
this week before we return home."

Kinau gave Rosalind a significant look. She felt a
sinking in her stomach. Her father had grown even
more absent-minded in recent months. Was something
wrong with him? Or did he just live in such a dream
world that nothing else mattered to him?

She sat in the rocking chair, with Victor clinging to
her, bobbing up and down in her arms. He was trying
his best to talk, gurgling earnestly and making sounds.
She read at the same time that she rocked him, and
made several suggestions to her father for the story.

Kinau and Hoke sat on the veranda and talked in
low tones. Presently Kinau returned. "Victor sleep
now, and you sleep too, Lokelina," she said. "Hoke
take you back to your rooms."

Rosalind was about to protest, but Kinau looked
stern, and shooed her away. Hoke escorted her
through the maze of hallways and stairs, back to her
room on the other side of the hotel. There, Akela
waited for her and helped her remove the gown, wrapping her in white cambric.

She lay down for a time, thinking how much hotter
it was in town than in the countryside. She must have
fallen asleep, because she wakened as the door
opened. Peter came in quietly. She blinked at him.

"I did not think I would sleep," she said drowsily.

"I'm glad you did. It's a very hot day, muggy. We
may have a storm soon." He stripped off his tie impatiently, shrugged out of his jacket, then his shirt,
and went to wash at the basin. She could not keep
from watching him, noticed how the bronzed skin
shone in the lamplight, how wide his shoulders were,
narrowing to the slim waist.

When he had dried his shoulders, toweling them
roughly, he came over to the bed, and bent over her.
He kissed the tip of her nose teasingly, then his mouth
came down over hers and pressed more urgently.

His large hand stroked over the fabric of her wrap-
per, to her bare throat, and his fingers gently moved
over the soft flesh.

"Want to get up now?" he asked finally. She nodded. She felt breathless and disturbed for him to be so close to her.

He went to the wardrobe, taking out a loose rose-flowered muumuu. "I think this would be comfortable," he said, and laid it over a chair.

To her relief, he went to the other room, leaving her to dress alone.

He called back to her. "I'll order dinner in the room, too hot to dress up for the dining room. Okay?"

"All right. Fine." After a few minutes she padded barefoot into the other room and curled up in a chair, her legs under her.

He was sitting at a table, going over some papers, already absorbed in them. He looked different there, stern and distant, frowning over the pages, ticking off points with a black pencil.

There were so many Peter Dariens, she mused, as she watched him from the shelter of her thick lashes. The helpless man, lying on the mat in her living room, depending on her for food and water. The giant of a man staggering in with the baby in his arms, a fanatical light in his eyes, as though he had driven himself to the shelter through sheer willpower. The man in white tropical suit receiving the politicians and businessmen. The frowning man who worked over pages and studied ledgers. The autocratic man who ordered her about. The man with the half-smile on his wide mouth as he bent over her, studied her face, and pressed a kiss on her lips.

He was a complex person. Could she ever hope to know him? Why had he married her, when he could have married anyone? He had given her reasons, but she did not think he told the entire truth. There was something else, something to do with the fact that Hoke remained in Kailua, guarding her and her father.

She gazed out the window at the growing dusk, as the storm approached. Rosalind could see it coming across the waters. Sailors scrambled over the ships, tying up the sails, and securing the boats to the docks.

The streets were almost empty, a gusty wind blew the flags on the warehouses. Now the clouds scudded across the purpling sky, darkening it to black streaked with an angry crimson.

A gust of wind blew sharply against their windows and a shutter banged shut. Peter got up, closed the shutters, and locked them into place.

"The storm is coming now," he said. He lifted his long arms in a stretch and yawned. "About time for dinner. I'm hungry. Aren't you, honey?"

She nodded, and he stroked his hand slowly over the long shining braids of her hair. "I like storms sometimes," she said.

"You do? Not afraid of them?" He watched her, half-smiling, his attention wholly on her.

"Well, yes, a person would be foolish not to be afraid and to take precautions," she said seriously. "But when the wind blows and the rains fall, the earth renews. It is splendid. One feels that the gods are aware of us and our needs, and that we are not alone in the world."

His dark eyes narrowed. "The gods . . . you mean, the Hawaiian gods?"

"All gods, the ones of the rains and the volcanoes, and the trees, the rocks . . . all nature."

"I thought you had a Christian training," he said thoughtfully, as he sat down on the arm of a chair near hers.

"Well . . . yes, I did, some. I read the Bible. In the Old Testament, that is the way of it. The Lord speaks in the voice of the storm, and in a still small voice as well."

"Oh, yes, I remember that." Still he frowned slightly. "Well, I'll tell the waiters we are ready for dinner." And he went to the door, to ring a buzzer.

They had dinner in their suite and it was peaceful although the storm raged outside. She felt cozy and sheltered, sitting at the beautiful mahogany table opposite Peter. There was a tablecloth on the table, silver serving dishes, blue and white china plates, and the same pretty glasses as last night for the champagne.

The Hawaiian waiters served them, then departed, closing the door. Peter got up to pour more champagne into their glasses. The wind and rain rattled the shutters, a great gust shaking the wooden building.

"I hope this is finished before we sail on Thursday."

"Oh, yes, I should not like to be on the open seas in this storm," Rosalind shuddered. "Once, I was out in a fishing boat when a storm hit. We crouched in the bottom of the boat for protection. We were out all night."

"Who was with you?"

"Kinau, Hoke, and one of her other sons."

He frowned. "Why did you go out?"

"We needed the fish and several of the men were ill. The storm came up suddenly." She mused about it, remembering. She had been about twelve, but the memory was as clear as yesterday. The terrible fright, the long pounding of the wind and rain, then finally the calming, and coming into port. Kinau had made several sacrifices to her favorite Pele after that incident.

"Did your father ever think of taking you home . . . to the States?" asked Peter as he sipped at his champagne and watched her over the rim of the glass.

"Home? No, our home is here," she said, surprised.

"No relatives there?"

"We correspond with no one. I think his brother was angry because father left home and his brother had to do all the farm work. But father was not a farmer, and he was not strong even then."

"And your mother?"

"I do not know of anyone belonging to her."

She finished her chilled papaya with a sigh of satisfaction. They lingered over the wine, talking idly. He told her more of Darien, asked her about what she remembered of her childhood. She talked of the life in the little cove; of fishing, swimming, and learning to sew, learning to read and write. Most of her education was from her father and his books, a little library of about fifty volumes. She had practiced writing in the sand.

Peter set the trays of empty dishes outside on the hall table, came back in and locked the doors. "The storm will go on all night. Sounds like it has settled down to be a good one. Well, that should fill the reservoirs on Darien."

He told her more about that, how they had built earthen dams on his island, so they would always have fresh water to drink.

She sat down on the soft cushioned couch, and he sat down beside her, still speaking casually of Darien. His good arm slid around her and she curled up and leaned against him. His hand lay on her waist, where he tenderly rubbed it back and forth.

"I have not put salve on your shoulder," she remembered presently. "Is it all right?"

"It is just about healed. I put some on this morning. It just needs exercising. I'll have a workout with some fresh horses back on the island," he said with a grin. "That should work out the kinks!"

He told her, in a lazy way, about the ranch life, and how they raised their part-Arabian horses to be sturdy work animals. About the long-horned cattle and their meanness, and how they had to keep the small boys away from them. "Some of the cattle are from those turned loose on the island long ago, and they grew wild for years. Now they are mostly culled, but we sometimes have a vicious old bull, cunning as hell, hiding out in the hills. Some of the *paniolos* enjoy trying their hand at the mean ones, but mostly it's a waste of time. They're too nasty to breed, and too old to eat."

She could have listened to him for a long time. When he got started talking, and spoke in his low drawling voice about the men and the cattle, about his beloved island and his people, he was fascinating, even more than usual. She lay with her head on his chest, and heard the deep pounding of his heartbeat, and did not want to move.

"You're getting sleepy," he said presently, bending

over to see her face. "Yes, your eyes are closed." He kissed her eyelids, moved his lips down to her mouth. She felt the firm pressure, and a thrill went through her body from her head to her heels. "You go off to bed, I'll come in soon. Nobody is going to bother us tonight. They'd have to be mad to come out in this weather."

There was an intimate murmur in his voice, a deep husky tone that seemed to warn her. She straightened up, groped with her feet for her sandals, and slid into them. "Yes, I must go to bed, goodnight, Peter," she said shyly.

He smiled up at her, his hands lingering over her hips as he let her go. "I'll come in soon," he repeated.

She lit a lamp that night, the room was so dark with the shutters closed. She took off the muumuu, and washed, then put on the crisp fresh white night-dress Akela had laid out, this one with rose ribbons threaded through the lace about the neck. She crept into bed, yawned, and put her head down. She could sleep in spite of the storm.

Peter came in and shut the door after him. He had blown out the lamps in the living room, the room was in darkness. He undressed, washed at the basin, and came to bed. He slid into the big bed beside her.

She felt very shy with him. His hands were so big and sure, he was so certain of himself. What did he want with her? Why had he married her? The questions still plagued her. She was not smart, fashionable, with a fund of talk like the ladies in the churchyard. She had never gone to a dance, never gone to boarding school, not even attended school or had a governess. It was so strange that Peter had married her—and so fast.

He drew her over to him, against his naked body. He had not put on a nightshirt tonight. She trembled at the feel of his warmth against her slim body. His hand stroked over her shoulders and arms, down her back.

"Are you cold?" he asked, as she shivered again.

"No . . . no . . . it may turn colder tonight."

"Yes, after the storm."

He pressed her back against the pillows, and leaned over her. He had blown out the bedroom lamp. She could not see his face tonight, for the room was in darkness. His lips found her cheek, slid down to her mouth, pressed gently.

As he kissed her, his hand came from her back, around to her front, and moved to rest over her breasts. She squirmed, no one had ever touched her there before—not like this. His fingers closed over one breast, through the thin material of her gown. His thumb moved over the nipple, until it rose up tautly.

His other arm went beneath her, and held her closely to him. She felt a little frightened. This was not like last night. He seemed to have some determined purpose in him tonight. He was not tired and lazy and quiet. He was like—like a stranger—like a panther—a dark god bending over her.

His hands roamed over her, his lips moved against hers, urging her. He finally whispered, "Kiss me, Rosalind. Kiss my mouth. Open your lips."

She obeyed, drawing a frightened little breath. His tongue pressed inside her lips, causing strange sensations inside her. He was so close, too close, too intimately close.

"Has no man kissed you like this?" he whispered.

"No, of course not!" she said indignantly.

He chuckled against her throat. "I would have been angry if you had said yes. I am glad you have not known other men, that you have lived all your life at the cove . . . though it is selfish of me. You are so sweet, so unspoiled, so fresh. . . ."

She wondered at his words. But she forgot them for the time, for he was moving against her more insistently. His whole body was rubbing against hers, his legs pressing on her legs, his hands moving over her soft breasts, around to her back, and down to her hips. His lips were everywhere—on her cheeks, chin, throat, shoulders. He gently drew aside the neckline of her nightdress, and pressed his mouth to her breasts. A wild thrill went through her, like nothing she had felt in her life.

She was absorbed in the new sensations. She was frightened a little, but he was gentle with her, and slow. When he finally lay on her, and thrust to join their bodies, it hurt—the pain sharp and quickly gone. He had played with her so long, and his hands had prepared her so, that she did not feel too badly. Still, it was a shock. She had not known how a man was with a woman.

"That is enough for tonight," he groaned. He seemed to have difficulty breathing, and gave great gasps until he had calmed down. His arm lay across her, he straightened her nightdress and soothed her with his hands and voice. She fell asleep against his shoulder.

In the morning he had not left her. He was watching her face as she wakened. He had opened the shutters, and the fresh rain-washed breeze came in to cool the room. The blanket shielded them both from the wind. His hand moved under the blanket, gently exploring her.

"*Aloha,* my darling," he said in her ear.

"*Aloha* . . . Peter."

"You are very beautiful today."

She blushed. His eyes were telling her more, and his hands. She shut her eyes and he bent and kissed the eyelids, then her cheeks and forehead, and her lips. His hand moved possessively over her breasts, down to her waist and thighs.

Presently he got up. "I have to go, darling. Meeting this morning. You sleep as long as you want to."

"Yes . . . all right, Peter." She did feel weary. And she wanted to be alone to explore the sensations she had felt, to think about what had happened to her.

He washed and dressed in his smart white drill suit, with the blue tie she liked. He left the room quietly, and presently the outer room was silent also. She thought for a long time before she got up.

Rosalind felt stiff. She wanted to ask Kinau about it, yet she felt shy. She dressed in a blue print muumuu, and presently, feeling hungry, she rang the service buzzer. A beaming Hawaiian boy came, and she told him what she wanted for breakfast.

She ate on the veranda. The sunshine today beamed as though no storm had ever swept over the town. Yet she saw trees knocked down, some roofs had been blown away, and a ship in the harbor was tilting into the water.

She still felt some pain. She bit her lips. It was little enough for Peter, if he felt pleasure in it. She owed him so much. She had been worried about her father, and about Kinau, and herself. And Victor— the small boy was such a joy. She could live with him and watch him develop and grow. And she would take care of him as Pele had instructed.

Peter dashed back about noon, looking harassed. He had a file of papers under his arm, his curly hair was ruffled. "How are you, darling? Have you been lonesome?"

"Oh, no," she assured him eagerly. "You do not need to entertain me."

The answer did not seem to please him. She felt perplexed. "Well, I have to go out again, have luncheon with some men. However I will be back about five, we'll go out to dinner, shall we? The seamstress is sending over some dresses. Get the maid to help you try them on. Everything all right?" He gave her a keen look.

"Yes, yes, I am . . . fine. I mean to express my gratitude to you, Peter," she added shyly.

He did frown then. "Gratitude?" he asked sharply.

"Yes, for all that you are doing for me, and for father and Kinau. You understand how it is with me, and I want to do everything possible to show my gratitude for your concern for us. . . ."

She had been composing this pretty little speech for quite two hours. It was a pity it did not have a good reception. Peter gave her a fiery look.

"Gratitude!" he exclaimed loudly. "Of all the . . . what the devil are you talking about?"

She flushed, disturbed, twisting a strand of long hair in her fingers. "I mean . . . father," she stammered. "He is . . . difficult . . . and I did not want to leave Kinau . . . it is good of you . . . to understand everything. . . ."

"*You* don't understand anything at all!" he shouted, and stormed out, slamming the door after him so violently that the room shook.

"Well, my word, I don't know why he is angry," she said aloud to the door. She remained perplexed until she finally got angry. He left her alone for hours, ordered her not to go outside, and then when she tried to be nice to him he shouted at her!

"Well, I'll go see Victor, he won't shout at me." She left the room, and wandered about the hallways, until she found a boy who showed her where Kinau's room was.

Kinau looked quite startled when Rosalind appeared. "Well, you come, eh? Where is the good husband?"

Rosalind shrugged. "Meetings," she answered, and held out her arms for Victor. He beamed in his ecstasy upon seeing her.

Rosalind stayed to have lunch with them, after which Victor curled up for his nap, settling down with his dark head on a mat. His long limbs were golden-tan now, plump and sturdy, not looking much like the mite who had come half-starved to them.

She talked to Kinau for a time, and finally went back to her own apartments. She found Peter there, sprawled on the couch, going over papers.

"Where have you been?" he inquired ominously, his dark eyes flashing.

She drew a deep breath to control her temper. "Really, Peter, you fuss like . . . like Kinau! I went over to see Victor, and give him his lunch."

"And didn't I tell you to go nowhere alone?"

She said, in satisfaction, "You said not to go out on the streets alone! I went through the hotel."

He flung a sheaf of papers across the room, toward the windows. She stared at him, then with dignity

78

retreated to the bedroom. She had never seen his face so livid.

Once there, her anger simmered down. After all, he worked hard, and was probably tired. Kinau had told her sometimes that she advised her daughters and daughters-in-law always to talk soft and be nice when her men were weary and cross. "Feed them and pet them," she advised, with a knowing chuckle. Maybe that was the answer.

Several fresh boxes of dresses were set on the floor of the bedroom. Oh, she had forgotten the dressmaker was sending more dresses. Guiltily, she opened a box, held up one dress after another. Peter was so good to her, and she was being ungrateful! Perhaps he would be pleased if she wore something especially pretty tonight.

She found a white muslin dress printed with bright yellow flowers, and tried it on. It was lovely, simple, and dainty, with a wide lace collar, and lace from the elbows to the wrists. She managed to fasten the frogs that ran down the length of the bodice to below the waist, and brushed her hair into a coronet, the way the hairdresser had shown her. Someone had put fresh plumeria on the table, she took several of them, wove them into a bouquet, and set them low on the folds of the coronet.

Peter tapped at the door as she was finishing. He came in, stared at her, and his face lightened. "Why . . . you look quite wonderful, Rosalind."

"Do you like it?" she asked, holding out the full skirt anxiously.

"Yes, very nice."

"Shall I wear the satin shoes?" She asked because tight shoes were still very painful for her.

"No, wear sandals, be comfortable. We'll dine downstairs tonight."

"Thank you," she said with relief.

"You look . . . quite grown up," he said, as he stripped off his mussed shirt.

"I am grown up!" she protested, turning to look at him in surprise. "I am nineteen . . . and married."

"Growing up is a state of mind, my dear, not of age or appearance," he said drily, scowling at the fresh white shirt he had taken out.

She wandered into the living room while he got ready. She had more to ponder. Would all the mysteries of life ever be solved? Perhaps not, for then one would be bored and weary. She smiled over her own thoughts, and picked up a book she had left on the table. Reading books she had never seen before was such a luxury! Father would be so happy to see the library on Darien.

People turned to look at Peter as they walked into the dining room together. He was a tall man and important looking, she thought proudly. How they stared at him! The head waiter in a frock coat rushed to take him to just the right table near the windows. Other waiters came at the snap of the fingers, bringing menus, wine glasses, and a bucket for chilling the wine.

She was not used to ordering from a menu. When Peter said, "Shall I?" and gestured, she nodded, and he ordered for them.

She looked about the room curiously. People were still staring at Peter. One man was staring at her also. He was a thin man, with greying brown straight hair, and grey flinty eyes. His heavy mustache covered his mouth, and he had to part it to eat hs soup. She wondered how it tasted, flavored with mustache. She felt a little giggle rising in her, and suppressed it. She must sit up straight and act like a lady.

The first course was brought, with the wine. Peter seemed abstracted, and spoke little. Rosalind was content to sit and eat, enjoy the view from the window as the sunset crimsoned the sky and made the sail boats look as though they were on fire. Out on the dock, lamps were flaring in the early dusk and people were hurrying to get home to their families. She saw a big burly man with a small boy on his shoulders. They were laughing and talking, and in a rush. Maybe they were anxious to get home to supper, she thought, and he was the father who had been working all day, and his son had come down to the boat docks to meet him.

The second course arrived, delicious thin slices of beef marinated and cooked quickly. Peter seemed to relax.

"Well . . . did you have a good day?" he asked.

"Yes, I played with Victor quite a long time."

"Tomorrow we must get your father's supplies and make sure they are sent to the ship."

"Oh, is it in harbor?"

"It came in this afternoon. We can see it from our windows, I'll show you later. Not as much fun as a sailing vessel, but considerably faster and smoother. Those steamships will take the place of sails before many more years."

They were finishing dessert when the man came up to them. Peter glanced up, a frown crossed his forehead. The man bowed first to Rosalind, then stuck out his hand to Peter. Peter rose, and shook it briefly.

"Glendon Corey," said the man with a smile. "Thought I had better introduce myself! I've been looking all over for Terence Darien, but he seems to have disappeared!"

Peter's mouth tightened. "I sent him back to Darien . . . on business."

"Mind if I join you?" The man did not wait for approval, he snapped his fingers for the boy to bring a chair. Rosalind thought her husband would burst out at him, but he did not, though his dark eyes blazed dangerously.

The chair was brought, Mr. Corey sat down with them, and accepted some coffee. "Thought I'd wait till you finished eating, Mr. Darien," he said jovially. "Since I'm going out to Darien with you, I wanted to get acquainted."

Peter kept stirring his coffee, letting his lids shadow his eyes. Rosalind felt a twinge of uneasiness. She hoped he would not make a scene in public.

"What is your purpose in wishing to visit Darien?" Peter asked finally, looking at the man levelly.

"Purpose? I thought Terence had told you!" Another jovial laugh. "I'm a cattleman. I want to see how your ranch is run, on an island, with no fresh water, and everything brought in. Thought if it looked like a success, I might buy an island and try it myself."

"There are no other Hawaiian islands available," said Peter, evenly, drinking his coffee. "You would be wasting your time."

"Oh, I may not do it here! Lots of other islands in the world, you know." The bright grey flinty eyes caught sight of Rosalind's hand, and before she knew it he had taken her hand in his. "I say, what a beautiful ring, mind if I look. . . ."

"Don't touch my wife!" The words rang out like a bell. The man jerked and dropped Rosalind's hand as though it burned.

A dull flush came into his cheeks. "I say, I am sorry. Just wanted to look at her ring, you know. . . ."

He seemed so shocked and abashed that Rosalind felt momentarily sorry for him. "It's all right. Don't worry," she said. Peter gave her a fiery look.

There was a long awkward silence. Glendon Corey finally said, "I'm terribly sorry. Guess I've been away from civilization too long. I just wanted to make sure it was all right for me to come on the steamship with you on Thursday. I've booked my passage."

"Terence invited you," said Peter curtly. "I still don't see why you are interested in coming."

The man seemed to gain more confidence. "Well, I am interested, very keen," he said with a smile. He looked down at Rosalind's hand, as she stirred her coffee. The black pearl glimmered in the lamplight. "Very interested," he said softly. "I hear you have quite a fine operation on Darien. I want to see how you work and manage everything. You have a high reputation, Mr. Darien."

Rosalind thought that Peter's mouth was curled, ever so slightly.

"I think you will be bored, Mr. Corey. However,

if you wish to come . . . you are our guest, of course."

The man rose, bowed to Rosalind, and made his departure. Peter gazed after him thoughtfully, his mouth hard, his bronzed face set as though in a mask. What his thoughts were, Rosalind could not even begin to guess.

# 6

❧ ❧ ❧ ❧

"Do you like Akela?" asked Peter, on Thursday morning when Akela was in the bedroom, busily packing up Rosalind's dresses, setting the bonnets in their boxes, wrapping shoes in tissue paper.

"Oh . . . yes . . . . she is very pleasant. But I do think I should help her pack."

Peter frowned. "Not at all. I have thought if you like her, I would hire her to come to Darien to be your maid. She seems quick and intelligent."

Rosalind stared at him. "But . . . Peter, I do not need a maid! I mean . . . on Darien . . . surely I can take care of myself . . . "

"It will be simpler to have someone take care of your clothes for you," he said flatly, and strolled into the bedroom. Rosalind heard him speaking pleasantly in Hawaiian to Akela.

Presently Rosalind went in also. Peter had left by another door. Akela beamed at her, and broke into breathless speech.

"You wish me to go with you? I shall be so happy! My mama hoped I would have a position with you, Mrs. Darien. Do I make you pleased? You will be pleased with me, very much! I learn hairdressing, the ironing of laces, all to please you very much!"

The girl was so delighted that Rosalind had not the heart to express her doubts. Akela was about eighteen. Did she really want to leave her home, her family? It seemed so.

What in the world would Rosalind do on Darien, if all her work was done for her? She could not understand it. She had thought Peter had married her

85

to help with Victor—but he left Victor with Kinau and seemed displeased if Rosalind spent much time with them. Then she had thought she would help with the housework. However, Peter hired more servants with such casualness.

He had rushed her so, she had not had time to think about it. Now she brooded, gazing out the windows to the silky blue of the sea and the busy wharves. Everyone worked, what was she to do? What would her function be? She could not picture her role on Darien. It made her feel very uneasy.

Akela dashed home to inform her family. Later she met them at the dock, surrounded by father, mother, numerous brothers, sisters, small nieces and nephews, all laughing and crying and hanging leis on her small capable shoulders. Akela was weeping herself when she came on board.

Rosalind introduced herself to Akela's parents, and assured them she would take good care of their daughter and make sure she came back sometimes to pay visits to them. They shook her hand enthusiastically, assured her they were all most happy, with tears streaming down their broad cheeks.

"I am not sure she wishes to come," Rosalind said dubiously to Peter, in their grand cabin.

"Of course she does. I am paying her a good salary and she is sending half of it home every month. They need the money, her father was injured and cannot go out on his boat as frequently."

"Oh," said Rosalind. He smiled at her, and tilted up her chin with one big finger.

"Happier now?" he asked. She nodded. He laughed, and bent to kiss her mouth, lingering over her lips.

She took time to look around the large cabin. It was lavish with red plush, huge beds, and large mirrored dressers. Akela had unpacked three dresses for her, with matching shoes.

Peter said, watching her face, "We shall dress up. Dinner is served in the dining room."

"A dining room—on a ship?" she gasped. Of course, this huge steamship was nothing like the small fishing boats she had been on. It was more like a small hotel.

"Yes, with musicians. You will enjoy that."

And she did. Peter escorted her into dinner. Rosalind wore one of her grand rose lace gowns, with the bustle at her hips which stuck out so strangely. But the other ladies in the dining room wore much the same outfits, and even more jewels in their ears and on their necks. She walked cautiously in her pretty matching silk shoes, the heels were too high for her. Peter held onto her, and she knew he would not let her fall. In fact he held onto her so possessively, she thought he would not let her go even to sit down.

The were seated at the captain's table, Rosalind on the right of the captain and Peter next to her. On the other side was an older grey-haired lady who kept lifting an eyeglass to stare at Rosalind. Rosalind was as fascinated with her as she was with Rosalind. She spoke so crisply that Rosalind could scarcely understand her. Peter whispered that the lady was British, and going on to Honolulu.

The dinner was pleasant, very elaborate, with many wines. Rosalind decided to avoid them, and only sipped cautiously when she had to. The ship was going up and down on the waves, and she did not want to get sick. Hawaiians with flutes, guitars, and small drums came around from time to time and played lively music for them. She recognized many of the tunes.

Glendon Corey was at another table at the side of the room. He was with two pretty ladies, but he kept looking at Rosalind and Peter as though he longed to be at their table. Rosalind wondered why Peter had not invited him, and decided that her husband did not like the man. Being frank with herself, she admitted she didn't either. He smiled too much, which gave her a vague reason to distrust him.

After dinner, Peter sent for Rosalind's cloak, and they strolled on deck, mostly alone, for the others were gambling in the brightly lit salon. They heard the laughter and click of a wheel, and saw people bent intently over cards. Mr. Corey was in there, his face bright and his eyes glittering.

"Would you rather gamble, Peter?" Rosalind asked, as they circled the deck once again. She enjoyed the fresh sea air on her face, the look of the purpling sky, the outlines of the islands off to the right, as they proceeded toward Darien. They would reach his land tomorrow noon, and she was very excited and apprehensive about that.

"Not at all. Life is enough of a challenge for me," he said, with a short laugh. His hand was tucked in her arm, his fingers closed over hers warmly, and he held her close to his side.

She pondered his words. She was learning he said nothing by chance, he meant every word he said, and often there were hidden meanings behind the obvious ones.

They paused at the rail, and looked down at the water. Silvery phosphorescent fish glimmered below them, shooting through the deep. It was a beautiful night, and she wanted it never to end.

"How lovely it is here, how peaceful," she murmured. Suddenly, a burst of laughter came from the salon.

"Some of the time," said Peter. "I shall be glad to be home on Darien. I think you will like it there, Rosalind. I want you to be very happy and contented with me."

"I am sure I will be." She wanted to express her gratitude again to him for taking care of her. But he had been so angry with her she did not dare. Maybe he did not like to be thanked.

"If there is ever anything you want, or wish to talk about, you must come at once to me," he said. "Aunt Honora and Aunt Norma are difficult women, but you are the head of the house now, with me. It is your home, first of all, and they must bow to you."

"Bow to me?" she gasped. "Oh, I would not like

that! They are older and respected, I would not wish . . ."

"I don't mean literally bow down, like the Hawaiians to their chiefs," he said impatiently. "I mean, you are their hostess, the house is your domain. Whatever you wish to be done shall be done. They must listen to you."

She was inwardly horrified. She was but nineteen. The two women had run the house at Darien for many years. How insulting to them to install a younger woman and tell them they must "bow down" to Rosalind! She was silent, troubled.

Finally, as they continued circling the deck, Rosalind demanded, "What about your father? Is he not really the boss, he is the eldest. . . ."

"Father can scarcely speak and it's almost impossible to understand him. He had a stroke that has crippled him. He lives in a wheelchair. He has turned it all over to me, to run the ranch. He made that clear, to Terry and Nick and all of them."

"Who is Nick?"

"Another cousin of mine. You'll like him. He is quiet and capable, a good cowboy, none better with cattle. His parents died many years ago and he came to live with us."

She wondered how many other relatives he had, but decided she would discover that soon enough. She sighed a little.

"Tired?" he asked, gently, his voice softening.

"It has been a long day. I think I should like to rest. But first, I'll look in on Victor."

"Oh, he went to sleep long ago. Kinau sent word to me," said Peter casually. "Come along, let's retire." And he turned her around, and led her through the maze of passageways, to their luxurious cabin.

Akela had laid out a nightdress, then disappeared to her own cabin. Rosalind undressed, washed, and went to bed in the carved wood bunk which was fastened cleverly to the wall so that it would not move about with the rocking of the ship.

Peter soon joined her, naked and virile in the glowing light. He blew out the lamp, and got into the narrow bed with her. She settled down to sleep, her head on his chest, but he had other ideas.

His big hands moved slowly over her skin, deliberately teasing and caressing her. He kissed her delicately shaped mouth, then brushed her cheeks with his lips, her throat, and her bared breasts. He moved his fingers over her nipples until they rose tautly, and then he kissed them also. Her breathing became more rapid, he was somehow alarming.

This time she knew a little more what to expect. He took her arms and put them around his neck, and moved on top of her. When he brought their bodies together, to her surprise she felt very little pain. He moved deliberately, then more quickly, their hips matched rhythms, and the excitement built up and up in her. She was half-sobbing as he finished, and lay back.

"Lovely," he whispered. "You are my lovely, my bride."

He held her closely, kissing her fiercely on the lips, then more gently as she stiffened. His hand stroked over her back, down to her hips, and up again. He kept whispering to her, possessive words, sometimes using Hawaiian words to show how he wanted and desired her, how she was his woman.

She wakened to find him up and dressing. His hard body gleamed as the sunlight glanced off the water he splashed on himself. He was humming and smiling to himself.

Peter pulled on his trousers and fastened them. Then he saw that she was awake, but still blinking drowsily. He came over to the bed, his chest gleamed bronze and gold as he sat down on the edge of the cot. He kissed her mouth and her chin teasingly.

"You slept late, darling."

"Um, am I late, Peter?" Rosalind was looking at the cruel scar on his right shoulder, and she traced it lightly with her long fingers. "Does this hurt still?" she asked anxiously.

"No, it is about well." He seemed to enjoy her touch. She moved them slowly over the scar, then down over his chest timidly, over the thick black curly hairs to his waist. Then her hand dropped away. He was watching her with that odd fierce gleam at the back of his brown eyes.

"What shall I wear today?" she asked.

"Your wedding dress. I want them to see you in that beautiful white gown. Akela is making leis for you, and sewing tiare on your veil. The Hawaiians will meet the boat, and make music for us. There will be ceremonies, but not lengthy ones because we won't want to stand in the hot sunlight for long."

He got up, and went to put on his shirt. When he had finished he went out, and sent Akela to her. Rosalind ate some breakfast hurriedly, it was quite late in the morning, and they would dock at noon.

When she went out on deck, she felt very shy. People were staring openly at Rosalind in her wedding garb. Akela accompanied her proudly, in her best muumuu of blue and white. In the distance, she saw the pier at Darien, and the outline of the island, the tall cone of the central extinct volcano, the dimness of the huge white house which stood out beyond the docks.

Hawaiians were coming out toward the boat in long canoes, calling and singing. Peter leaned over the railing, laughing, and waving at them, his face open and boyish. He was excited about coming home. He put his arm about Rosalind. They waved to her and circled the steamboat dangerously close to get a better look.

The steamship puffed into the landing, and the long plank was laid down. Mr. Corey started down, someone grabbed him and pulled him back.

"No, Mr. Darien gets off first," said the sailor fiercely. Mr. Corey was momentarily taken aback, but quickly acquiesced.

Peter Darien swept Rosalind into his arms, and

carried her off the boat, setting her down gently on the pier. She straightened her veil, rather dazed, as people began to crowd around. Some Hawaiians were playing and singing, and she listened to the music. They were welcoming the bride of Peter Darien. Someone had made up a song, and they sang it again and again. "Welcome to the lovely bride of Peter Darien, who will have fine sons and daughters for him, and make our island happy."

Kinau carried Victor off the ship and Rosalind noticed the Hawaiians staring at them, whispering among themselves. But the white people had come up to her, two older women in the front.

One woman was blond, with severe blue eyes, wearing stiff black clothes and a white widow's cap over her hair. She held out her hand and smiled at Rosalind.

"This is Aunt Norma Darien," said Peter. "She raised me from a baby. Aunt Norma, this is Rosalind, my wife."

"Welcome to Darien, my dear. May you be happy always, may the sun shine often on you," said the woman, with a touch of Hawaiian poetry in her words.

Rosalind smiled in relief. She had feared they would resent her so much. "Thank you. I hope . . . may I call you Aunt Norma?"

"I shall be happy if you will. This is my sister-in-law, your Aunt Honora," said Norma formally. She drew forward the other older woman.

Honora was smaller, with greying, black curly hair. Rosalind recognized something of Peter in the snapping brown eyes, the quick summing-up way of looking. Her old-fashioned frizz fell over her forehead. She was tanned as leather from the sun. Honora shook Rosalind's hand briskly in a pumping motion.

"Welcome, welcome. It's about time Peter married. You're very pretty. Do you speak Hawaiian? Terry said you were practically a native, but he never gets things right."

"Rosalind speaks Hawaiian better than I do," said

Peter. There was a slight frown on his face. "Where is Terry?"

"Arranging a *luau*," said Norma quickly. "Eileen is helping him." She seemed oddly nervous. Peter gave her a look, as though he didn't quite believe her.

A tall thin man, with a cowboy hat in his hand, come forward. Leathery, with a stillness to his face, his black hair and dark eyes showed his resemblance to Peter.

"Nick Darien," he was introduced, and he took Rosalind's hand in his timidly, as though afraid of crushing her.

"How d'ya do?" he muttered, and stepped back.

"We'll go on up to the house," said Peter.

The Hawaiians crowded around them, still singing and laughing, waving their leis. Some managed to get close enough to fling several leis around Rosalind's neck.

She smiled, and called to them in Hawaiian, "Thank you for your welcome! You make me feel at home at once, gracious friends!" They laughed as though she had pleased them very much, and loudly called flattering remarks about her to each other so she could hear.

"Look how she smiles, like the sunshine! Look how her hair shines under the tiare! She is a blessed one. She brings us much luck! Good fortune will shine on Darien! She speaks our tongue as one born to it! Our Peter has done well for himself! She has the kind face of a good wife and mother!"

She was soon blushing rosily, and Peter laughed down at her.

One husky Hawaiian caught up with them, waiting for Peter's attention anxiously, with a beaming grin on his broad face. Peter caught sight of him, and the procession stopped while they shook hands vigorously.

"Rosalind, may I introduce my foreman, Hilohilo. He taught me much about cattle. He is a very good man. Hilohilo, this is my wife, Lokelina," he said in Hawaiian.

Hilohilo bowed and beamed at her, and shook the

hand she held out to him. They exchanged greetings, then they walked on.

"You will meet many of my people at the *luau* tonight," said Peter. "Soon you will have them all sorted out."

They came up to the wide-winged house made of stone and wood. In the courtyard, a man sat in a wheelchair, leaning forward, as though he longed to leap out of it to greet them. His dark eyes were fierce, his hair streaked with iron grey. His shoulders were stooped, his left arm hung limply. Yet there was enough of him left to show how he must have been once, as big and husky and tough as Peter himself.

"My father," said Peter softly. They came up to the man, who struggled to say a few words.

Rosalind shook the still firm right hand of Peter's father. Then at the look in his eyes, she bent and pressed her lips to the leathery cheek. "I am happy to meet you," she said.

Mr. Darien seemed to relax. "Meet . . . you," he struggled to say, licking his lips. "Happy . . ."

Kinau came up with Victor in her arms. The man stared at them, scowling.

"This is Kinau, and her charge, Victor Darien," Peter said, his voice deliberately carrying.

Kinau smiled at them happily, and went past into the house led by Aunt Honora, who seemed to have her in charge. Behind Norma came Alfred Murray, looking about in bewilderment. Farther back came Glendon Corey, rather uncomfortably out of it.

Peter introduced her father to them all, then a Hawaiian girl came to show him to his rooms.

Norma said, "I have prepared the two rooms next to the library, Peter, as you suggested."

At the mention of the library, Alfred Murray brightened. "Oh, yes, I came to see the books," he said, and hurried inside after the girl.

Peter took Rosalind up to their rooms. They had a suite on the second floor in the East Wing, the opposite one from where Norma and her two children, Terry and Eileen, lived. Kinau and Victor had rooms at the back of the third floor, where he might play and cry and laugh to his heart's content.

Rosalind's impressions were a blur at first. Later she came to enjoy the massive home. That first day, though, it seemed impossibly huge, terribly large, frightening in its grandeur and elegance.

Norma had arranged the rooms in Peter's suite, putting in a huge bed for them and adding more feminine touches: a vanity and bench, a tall mirror, and two more wardrobes for Rosalind's dresses.

The rooms were simply decorated, suitable for the tropical weather. However, even the hotel rooms in Kailua were not so elegant in their furnishings as their suite here. Rosalind wandered from one item to another, touching the ivory figurines, the Chinese blue porcelain vases, the smooth sandalwood tables holding books and magazines. The living room contained two long sofas covered with blue silk, several matching armchairs, lamps of rose porcelain, candlesticks of silver.

A glass cabinet held treasures which Peter told her he had collected on his travels. She promised herself some leisurely time studying them, for they might serve as keys to his nature. She noted the jade figures, a huge baroque black pearl set in marble, a tray of uncut jewel stones of all colors and shapes, a small marble Venus statuette, the wooden figure of a large horned bull, and several grotesque Hawaiian figures in lava rock like those of gods.

Akela came to help her change to a more comfortable dress. Peter had suggested the rose muumuu and a necklace of one of the leis. Behind the large house, the fires were burning in open pits, cooking several roast pigs for the *luau*. The odor filled the house, making her feel hungry for the first time in days.

Peter also changed to a more comfortable outfit; dark trousers, a flowered shirt, and a red scarf. He went out to see how the preparations were going and Rosalind felt sure that the men would be asking him questions, telling him what had happened while he was gone.

Norma Darien came in softly, to glance around anxiously.

"I do hope you will like this, Rosalind," she said. "It is difficult to plan when one does not know the other person's likes. If you want anything changed . . . the colors. . . ."

"Oh, I think it is perfect. Please, do not worry. Nothing could be more charming than the blues and roses of these rooms."

Norma's stern face relaxed, her widow's cap bobbed as she nodded. "I tried to follow Peter's instructions. We all want to please him. He is a dear boy, but difficult at times," she said simply. "I must apologize that Terry and Eileen were not at the boat to meet you. They are . . . disobedient and willful. I hope you will not be insulted by their behavior. I have spoken to them severely and they will be at the *luau*."

So she had been right, as had Peter, thought Rosalind. Terry and Eileen had not come to the dock deliberately. But she could not disappoint the anxious woman before her. She smiled.

"Please do not worry. I shall not," she said, with more confidence than she felt. "They probably feel resentful, that a stranger has come here."

"Oh, not a stranger, not a stranger," said Norma quickly. She patted Rosalind's arm kindly. "Never a stranger. You are Peter's choice and we shall love you. Only, Eileen can be so outspoken. You must not pay attention to her."

She said a few more kind remarks, cast another anxious look about the rooms and departed, leaving Rosalind in a thoughtful state. Akela was unpacking the rest of the trunks, humming happily in the bedroom. Rosalind sat down cautiously on the sofa, running her hand slowly over the silk cushion at her side. Had Peter designed all this for her? She had thought he had lived here all his life, and this was the way he liked it. He could not have pleased her more, she loved these colors. But how quickly they must have worked, to have all this done.

Peter came up presently, looking harassed. "Prob-

lems, problems. Now I know I have been gone more
than three months," he groaned, then smiled at her.
"How charming you look, my dear. Everyone will love
you."

"Thank you," she said shyly, wishing she could believe him.

"I thought you should wear jewelry, but you look
perfect this way," he said. "Wait for me while I wash
up, I have dust all over me," and he disappeared into
the bathroom.

They went down together, as dusk gathered over
the island of Darien. On the huge patio in the back,
Hawaiians and all the Dariens had gathered, even
Barton Darien in his wheelchair. Alfred Murray was
seated at a little distance from the others, watching
them benignly, probably a little bewildered about it
all.

Norma came up to Rosalind, drawing with her a
slim, blonde girl with large blue eyes, wearing a costly
blue silk dress with lace from her shoulders to her
wrists, and at her throat. Diamonds gleamed from
her neck and ears. She was overdressed for the *luau*,
quite out of place, but she seemed pleased with her
own appearance, by the peacocky way she walked,
thought Rosalind.

"Dear Rosalind, this is your cousin, Eileen, my
daughter," said Norma.

"How do you do, Eileen?" said Rosalind, pleasantly, very aware of Peter silently by her side, glaring
at Eileen.

"How do you do?" The voice was pleasant, but not
the gaze, that slowly, insolently analyzed Rosalind,
taking in the rose muumuu, the leis, the slippers of
grass. Her lip curled. "I thought you would be formally dressed. This was such an . . . important occasion! Forgive me if I am out of place!"

"It is quite all right, please feel free to dress as
you choose," said Rosalind, taking a perverse delight
in playing the grand lady. She gave Eileen a gracious
nod, and put her hand on Peter's arm. They went on,
leaving Eileen staring after them.

Terry came up to them, turning on the charm and the smile. "Dear Rosalind," he said, and bent toward her as though to kiss her. Rosalind drew back sharply, and Peter put out his hand. "What's this? I'm going to kiss my cousin and make her welcome!"

"You will not kiss my wife," said Peter, his voice knife-sharp. "And you could have welcomed her at the boat dock this afternoon!"

"Oh, am I out of favor? After all the errands I have run for you!" chuckled Terry. But Rosalind felt the sneering behind the laughter, and was uneasy with him. She was glad to go on, to be introduced to the Hawaiians who waited eagerly for her, their faces beaming in the firelight.

Kinau was there, big in her favorite muumuu. She had made friends rapidly and now sat with some of the women. Rosalind met them all, and also some of the cowboys. Most were Hawaiian, but Hilohilo introduced her to Joe Smith, a lean dark laconic American, with somber eyes.

The feasting started, and went on until midnight. The pigs were carved, and eaten with fingers. They ate corn roasted in the fire, bowls of pineapple and papaya and passion fruit, more bowls of greens and nuts. Then there were the desserts, puddings and pastries, and coffee, dark as Peter's eyes, thought Rosalind.

The fires gleamed on laughing faces. The flutes were brought out, and the guitars, and concertinas, and much music was sung. Then some of the women danced, the graceful swaying dances of the islands. Rosalind longed to jump up and join them, but Peter might be shocked. He did not know she knew these dances.

Barton Darien motioned to Norma, and she bent over him. She stood, and said, "Barton wishes us to toast the newly married couple. I will say the words for him," she said formally.

Eileen muttered from behind them, "Hasn't enough been said?"

Rosalind hoped Peter had not heard. She was

much aware of the undercurrents of jealousy from Eileen and Terry.

They disliked and resented Peter, as well as herself. She did not understand it all, but the reasons would come out eventually. She must be patient, and try to help Peter all she could.

Norma was saying the words slowly, so all would understand. "To Peter and Rosalind, who will rule over Darien and make it a happy island of peace and prosperity. May they be blessed with many children and good lives full of honor and justice and charity. Our love to them, our blessings on them."

The Hawaiians cheered. Mr. Murray smiled and murmured in pleasure. Barton thumped on the arm of his wheelchair, in the approval his tongue could not say.

Peter said to Rosalind, "Will you answer my aunt, darling? I think all would like to hear what you say."

She had not expected this. She gasped, then stood in the firelight, groping for something to say. What would he have her say? Then it came to her.

"I would . . . like to sing a song for you. It expresses how I feel . . . how we both feel . . . at your welcome."

She clasped her hands before her, and looked at Peter. He nodded encouragingly, a little surprised.

She took a deep breath. She had never sung for such a group before. But her heart felt warm, she felt hopeful for the future.

She sang a Hawaiian song that they all knew, about a man who had left his islands and finally returned home.

"When I came in sight of the islands, how my heart gave a great jump. I am home again, I am home again," she sang. "I know the trees that will welcome me, I know the scent of the plumeria. They will set leis about my neck, and kiss my cheeks, and I shall set my feet on my own soil once more. I am home again, I am home again."

She finished, and they were silent for a moment. Then they cheered and sang the final lines for her, all the Hawaiians clustered about the fires. Peter put his arm about her, hugged her before them, and put his lips to her cheek.

"That was perfect, my darling," he whispered, for her ears alone.

The singing went on, and the dancing, and it was very late when the first ones moved to go home to their huts, to their homes beyond the great house. Several of the men went about putting out the flames, so the grasses beyond would not catch fire.

Peter went over to speak to Hilohilo. They spoke intently, their faces gleaming in the firelight.

From behind Rosalind came a whispery voice, full of malice. "Oh, that was very charming!" murmured Eileen. Rosalind turned around, startled. "Oh, so pretty! And such a deep sexy voice, sensuous as hell!"

Rosalind drew a startled breath. She had never heard such words, not from any woman. She saw the flame in Eileen's blue eyes. "What do you mean?" she asked.

"The child," said Eileen. "It is your child, isn't it?"

"It is now," said Rosalind, more calmly, over the thumping of her heart. "Peter and I shall adopt him."

"Peter! One might know he would come home with a child! Nothing else would have persuaded him to marry . . . and such a . . . woman!" Her contemptuous look went over Rosalind again, as though scorning her slyly. "Like a native woman! Peter is very fond of native women! No wonder he settled for you! A respectable woman, but like a native woman! Don't expect him to be loyal to you, though, that would be too much to expect from somebody like him! His needs are too big to be satisfied by any one woman!"

"You do not need to be insulting," said Rosalind, her mouth firm, her stomach a little sick. Such malice was both cruel and unexpected. "Keep your tongue to yourself!"

Eileen must have seen Peter returning. Her whisper was lower, like the hiss of a snake.

"He says the child is Terry's. Well, I don't think so. Terry would have had a blonder child! It is more likely Peter's, and I don't care if you tell him I said so!" She smiled snidely. "Peter is . . . very virile. I'm not surprised he had a Hawaiian child! But it is too much to drag the boy back here saying he is a Darien and that we must accept him! I shall never accept such a bastard!"

Eileen moved away from Rosalind and tossed her head. She put her hand in Terry's arm and said something to him in a low tone.

Peter came to Rosalind, and glared at Eileen. "What was she saying? You look strange."

"She is full of strange ideas," she managed to say off-handedly.

"Don't listen to her," he said curtly. "Let us go upstairs. It has been a long day."

She went with him, but her heart, which had been light when singing for the welcome of the Hawaiians, had fallen down into a darker mood. Was there truth in what Eileen had said? If only she knew Peter better, and could judge for herself! She had taken his word for it, that the child was Terry's. But what if Eileen was right, and the child was Peter's?

She thought about it, argued one way and another. But she was too tired for straight thinking. Peter fell asleep almost at once. Rosalind lay awake, brooding.

The dark hours of the night are not good for serious pondering. One sees matters only in a distorted fashion, twisted out of context. Problems seem larger, solutions farther away, some matters overwhelming. And the middle of the night seems to bring out demons of doubt which could be driven away if viewed in the daylight and sunshine. She tossed and turned, and could not sleep.

If the child were Peter's, and he had lied about it— then he was not the man she had thought he was. She knew he was a complex man. But a liar and a cheat? A man who would rape a girl, and leave her to have the baby alone? Oh, he had rescued the infant later, and meant to bring him up. But why, why, why would he lie about it?

Peter stirred, muttered, flung out his arm and

searched for her in the darkness. He found her, put his arm around her, and drew her closer.

"Not asleep?" he murmured, against her hair.

"Not yet."

He nuzzled his face against her, and stroked her shoulder comfortingly.

"Tomorrow will be better," he said vaguely, out of the mists of sleep, as though someone had said that to him sometimes, perhaps when he was a boy, plagued with nightmares.

He slept against her, and she went to sleep comforted that yes, tomorrow would be better, she would make it better. She had vowed to do her duty, and make him happy, and take care of Victor, and she would do it.

# 7

### ❦ ❦ ❦ ❦

TERRY SPLASHED in the blue waters of the lagoon, keeping a lazy lookout toward the beach and the trees. He was supposed to be herding cattle, but it was too hot for that today.

He had told Hilohilo that he would round-up the cattle from the far leeward side, then had snuck off by himself to swim. Nobody would know the difference. He would reappear about sunset and tell them the cattle were hidden in the brush, and that he hadn't found any.

He resented it that a Hawaiian gave him orders. Peter had made Hilohilo chief foreman over Terry, and that was a gross insult. A native—foreman over him! It had been bad enough when Peter was the foreman, and Barton Darien had told Terry he had to follow his cousin's orders.

He scowled to himself, swimming around in the cool waters. Damn it, it had all gone bad, much worse since Barton had had his stroke. Before it had been difficult, but Norma had protected him saying he was not strong enough to stay out in that hot sun all day. Barton had growled, but he had been too busy bossing Peter around to pay much attention to Terry.

Peter was far stricter than his father. His tone bit sharply, he did not care if he bawled out Terry in front of his mother or anyone else. He had no manners, in spite of his fine appearance and everyone bowing down to him.

Eileen was jealous as hell. No wonder. She had expected confidently to marry Peter herself. They were second cousins, she made a beautiful appearance. They

103

had all been shocked as could be when Peter told them he was going to marry Alfred Murray's daughter. That native-looking girl, that brown-skinned quiet thing—how had she captured Peter Darien, the wealthy boss of Darien?

Unless he had been caught out with her by the father. Terry's blond eyebrows knitted in puzzlement. Murray seemed a bit dim, always going around in a daze, his nose in a book. Would he have seen Peter sneaking up to Rosalind even if they had done it right in front of him? Funny. But why else would Peter have married the girl? She was twelve years younger, and seemed very naive.

Of course, the girl looked nice in the fine silks Peter had bought her. Any woman would. But he could have had Eileen like a shot, she was ready to fall into his arms. Or he could have married any of the well-educated women of Honolulu or the mainland. He had been chased by some of the best. And their mamas! Lord, how they would be raging now! All sorts of lures had been cast at Peter, and he had not been caught. Until now.

He wondered if Rosalind had gotten pregnant right away, and Peter had felt he had to do his duty by her. Still, she was quite slim. Time would tell.

He dismissed them from his mind. He turned lazily into the surf and rode a wave to the beach, exulting in the lift of the water under his tanned body. This was living! Much better than riding a half-tamed horse around the hot plateau.

Near the beach, he saw the Hawaiian girl standing there, bare feet digging into the clean sand. He waved at her, grinning, "Come on in, Dorisa!"

He had been right, she must have been watching where he went. She had been coy before. Maybe today his luck would turn. He watched her through half-closed lids as the girl ran down to the water and plunged in, her sarong wrapped about her, getting soaked in an instant. He could see the lines of her rounded figure.

She was about fifteen, the daughter of one of the

*paniolos*. She was full-grown and the glances she had given him meant she was ready to give out. He grinned to himself as he followed her into the waves. She was ripe, beautiful. Later she would be fat and lazy, but now—now she was just the way he wanted her.

She swam in long strokes out beyond where the waves were forming and foaming in the Pacific. Then she stood up and balanced herself, laughing with her beautiful red mouth as she rode a wave in on her bare feet. Terry rode beside her, ecstatic as the waves tried to tumble them over. He felt exhilarated, alive, happy. This was the life!

They rode in again and again, swimming out to the reef, and back in again on the cresting waves. It was a perfect day for it, the waves formed and rolled, and they rode them in, until they finally dropped exhausted down onto the beach. It was quiet there, hot and still under the waving green palms.

Terry clamped a lazy, strong arm about Dorisa's waist. She felt warm under the wet cloth. He stroked her brown arm, bent over, and kissed her as she panted from the swimming.

She let him kiss her, and her tongue stroked into his mouth. Then she pulled at his arm and tried to get away. Not today, he thought. He was hot for it, he wanted her badly.

He held her harder and laughed at her. "Afraid?" he teased. "Afraid of me?"

"You are a bad man. Papa says so," she said, her lashes fluttering.

"You always listen to your papa?"

"He is a smart man!"

"Sure, sure. And he knows where you go everyday?"

The lashes fluttered again, she closed her eyes, and color came into her cheeks like dark roses. He bent over and kissed her cheeks, travelling down to her wet brown throat. She writhed under him, trying desperately to throw him off. But he had her pinned firmly beneath him.

"You let me up, Mr. Terry!"

"Huh. You want this," he said thickly, against her

wet arm. "You want this . . . as much as I do. . . ."

"You would . . . be my man alone?" she asked anxiously, her body growing quieter under his. His tanned leg wrapped around hers.

"Sure . . . sure, you bet . . . I'll be your man. . . ." he muttered, and drew away the sarong from her breasts. He had it ripped from her body before she could protest. It was fastened only with a loose loop in the cloth, and he spread it out and looked greedily down at the rounded plump body.

He ran his hand over her and she shivered. He pressed his mouth to the brown breast and licked at the red nipple. She trembled, and he knew he would have her today.

He wore nothing, and now she was nude as well. It was silent under the palms, only the dim murmuring of the waves and the distant lowing of some cattle. Those damn cattle, he was sick of them. He was sick of trying to work for Peter. One day soon he would demand his share of the money and leave here. He didn't have to stay, he was no slave.

He pressed himself to her urgently. She cried out, "Do not do that, Mr. Terry . . . do not. . . ."

He was in no mood for just kissing, but she wanted petting. He drew off a little, and stroked her breasts and her round thighs, telling her how beautiful she was. He put his hands on her, and fondled her until his experience told him she was ready. Then he lay on her again, and this time her voice was cooing and soft, not objecting and wild. He pressed home into her, laying luxuriously on her. Oh, God, he needed this, he thought. He had wanted a girl, any girl, for so long— Peter was a slave-driver, he was sick of Peter—

As he lay in her, he lifted his head, and caught the wild exuberant expression of her face, the glitter of tears in the dark eyes. He smiled down at her triumphantly. He was a good lover, girls had told him so.

"You like this, Dorisa?" he asked softly, and moved himself on her.

"Yes, yes, good . . . oh, good," she muttered, her hips moving under his. Her arms clutched at him.

"You are my man now, eh, Mr. Terry? You are only my man?"

"Are you my girl, only my girl?"

"Yes, yes, only yours. You will speak soon to my father?"

He had no intention of speaking to her father. Fathers made trouble, big trouble. If she was smart, she would keep her mouth shut.

"You best not tell him," said Terry. "He might be angry and whip you."

Trouble gleamed in her eyes, she moved, and then lay still. "Not . . . tell?" she faltered dubiously.

"You want to get whipped? We aren't married."

"But you are my man," she whispered.

"Um," said Terry, and bent to kiss her mouth shut. Women talked too much. He wanted her again, and he rolled her over and played with her until he was so hot, he had to have her quickly.

He slept afterwards, and wakened to find her bending over him, tickling his nose with a ginger blossom. He caught her to him, rolled her over and kissed her again. She finally pulled back, and he kissed her throat passionately.

"I must go home," she said uneasily. "It is the noon time, my mother will say where am I? I must go home."

"You come tomorrow, same time," he commanded. "We will swim . . . and play again, huh?"

"Maybe," she said coyly, with a smile. She jumped up and wrapped the dry cotton cloth about herself, turning her smooth young back to him. He ran his hand down her leg, and laughed as she kicked at him. She ran off, and he lay chuckling to himself.

It had been a good morning. He got up and ran into the surf, splashing about happily. It had been just the kind of morning he had liked best. He had met Lydia here—a shadow crossed his face at the thought of her. She had been the most beautiful Hawaiian girl he had ever had. So young, so sweet and tender. He hated to think of her dying, starving. . . . He grimaced to himself. She had been foolish and stupid. She should have

107

gone to Honolulu and lived in that house the way he told her. He would have paid for her—for a time anyway. Instead, she had tried to return to her father and his land, and her father had been deadly angry.

He deliberately wiped out the thought of her. It did not do any good to worry about the dead. What was past, was past.

Peter was waiting at the stables when Terry returned that evening. He stared at him. Terry hated that look, that haughty "I am the lord of all I survey" look.

He laughed, tipped his hat to Peter, and bowed low. "Hello, boss," he mocked, in the high voice of a Hawaiian tenor, drawling out the words. "You wait for me, I guess, huh?"

"Where have you been all day?" asked Peter sharply.

"Didn't your mighty foreman tell you? I was rounding up strays on the leeward."

Peter ran his hand deliberately over the neck of the horse. "Not even sweating, not worked at all. You had him in the shade. I'm asking you again, where were you all day?"

"We worked all day," repeated Terry, sliding down lazily. "Then we went for a ride in the surf, didn't we, boy?" And he patted the neck of his horse, and took him off to the stalls. He left him with the Hawaiian stable boy, and strolled back to the patio. Peter had left, and Terry grinned. Peter had no idea if Terry had told the truth or not. He could not prove anything.

"Mr. Peter see you in his study," said a Hawaiian servant when Terry went into the great house. Terry grimaced.

"I'll have a shower first," he said.

The Hawaiian did not move from before him. His great height towered over Terry. "Mr. Peter say now."

"Oh, hell," said Terry, and went to the study. He hated a fuss. He went in without knocking, and tossed his hat onto the mahogany desk where Peter sat.

"I'm asking you again, where were you all day?"

"What difference does it make? I'm not your slave."

"No, your work doesn't qualify you for any such status. You don't work enough to earn your food."

Terry scowled. Peter could get under his skin sometimes. "What are you going to do? Send me to bed without my supper?"

"I'd like to, only Eileen would slip you food, the way she did when you were kids," said Peter without expression, only a hard glint in his eyes. "Did you think you fooled us all the time, Terry? Tomorrow, you'll go out with Joe Smith. He has orders to keep you with him the whole time."

"Damn it to hell, you won't treat me like a child!" exploded Terry, grabbing his hat and turning to leave the room.

"Not after you grow up. When you learn to work and earn your keep, you'll be treated like an adult."

Terry slammed the door after him, and raced up the stairs to his own room. He was cursing under his breath. He knew Smith. Quiet, deadly, thorough, owing everything to Peter, who had rescued him from something back in Texas. They never said what, but Terry would give a lot to find out. It would be something to hold over Joe.

Eileen came out of her room next to his, wearing a lace peignoir over her petticoats, her hair loose. She was brushing the long blonde curls.

"What has you all steamed up, Terry?"

He pushed her back into her room, and shut the door. "It's that damn cousin of ours," he said angrily. "Treats me like a child."

"Why? What have you done now?"

"Oh, I didn't go round up his precious cattle," grumbled Terry. "Now he's going to sic Joe Smith on me all day."

"Joe Smith?" Eileen's little red tongue curled around her lips thoughtfully. She looked like a satisfied little cat, searching for more cream. "That man intrigues me."

"All men intrigue you, sis," he said with a grin, his ill humor fast evaporating. He was never angry for long, it was too wearing. He sat down on the end of her bed and watched her seat herself gracefully on her dressing stool and continue brushing her long hair lovingly.

"I could help," she said, after a pause. "If you want to get away from Joe . . . I could help."

"Oh? How would you do that?" he asked alertly, watching her narrowed blue eyes in the mirror.

"Oh . . . he might be too busy . . . to watch you. What about it, Terry?"

"What favor do you want in return?" he asked wryly. He knew his sister. She was fond of him, more fond than of anyone else in the world. But she never did anything for free.

"I want Peter," she said, carefully, "under my thumb—humiliated and begging."

"If you think I can get him for you . . ." he began, exasperated.

"I almost had him, until he saw that . . . that female," Eileen said, angrily. "When he came back with that . . . that brown-faced native girl, I could have spit! But I'll get him back, I know I can. Only . . . get that girl off his neck!"

"Rosalind?" asked Terry, and began to laugh. He rolled on the bed and chuckled to himself. The idea interested him very much. "Peter would be jealous as fire!"

"Of her? No, he'll be angry and get rid of her. I know him. He is very possessive. If he thinks you have her . . . and you can do it, Terry! . . . you're very attractive to women . . . he won't want your leavings," she said, daintily brushing a powder brush across her face, and eyeing herself critically.

He sobered and sat up, thinking about it. "What if she won't play? She's rather a stick-in-the-mud."

"You can get her alone somewhere, can't you? That shouldn't be hard."

He eyed her, and gave a little shudder. Sometimes Eileen surprised him, she was so cold-blooded about what she wanted. His blood was hot, and he liked women quite a lot. His sister experimented with emotions, she knew all the time what she was going after and why. If their mother ever found out what Eileen did, she would faint dead away. But Eileen was quiet as a cat, and her mother never found out.

"Just pay her little flattering attentions, where Peter can see you. Then, when you get her really, he'll believe you and send her back where she belongs," said Eileen, with cool satisfaction. She finished fastening up her hair into a smooth coronet, and examined her reflection again. She added diamond ear studs and stood up gracefully.

She shed her peignoir and stood to put on the blue lace gown lying ready for her. Terry looked at his sister appreciatively. She was very lovely, slim and rounded in the right places. No wonder the men fell for her like ninepins. But she wanted only Peter, his wealth and power. That was all she had ever really wanted that she had not obtained—yet.

"Fasten me up," she commanded.

He stood up and helped.

"A bargain?" she asked softly, with a gentle smile, and patting his cheek.

He nodded. "A bargain."

At dinner that night, Terry was very gay. He flattered Rosalind about the dinner table—she had arranged the anthuriums in red and ivory clusters in three low vases. The candle sticks of silver were filled with burning red candles. The lace tablecloth and the beautiful rose and white china were set beautifully.

She thanked him soberly, her attention more on the maids. She was helping to train a new maid, and she kept an anxious eye on the young girl, who was inclined to giggle and drop things.

After dinner, they retired to the formal drawing room where Barton Darien joined them. He ate in his room, because someone had to feed him and that infuriated him. He was growling now and trying to talk to Norma about some complaint.

Eileen sat next to Peter on the sofa, and talked to him in a low tone, reaching over to light his cigar or pat his knee with her slim white hand, murmuring things that no one else could hear. Rosalind sat quietly at the coffee trolley and served the cups until all had enough. Then she moved to a wing chair near the windows.

The French windows were open to the night air. She could look up and see the stars, the same ones which had shone over her little home near the cliffs. But they did not look the same here. They looked faded.

She repressed a sigh. "Have a drink, pretty Rosalind," Terry said, and handed her a snifter of brandy before she knew what he was doing.

"Oh . . . no, thank you," she said hastily, and tried to hand it back. He would not take it.

"It will do you good, you look pale." Peter was glancing toward them, frowning slightly.

"I don't care for it, it's too strong," she commented firmly, and set the bulbous glass on a table next to her chair.

Aunt Honora got up from her couch and came over, taking the next chair. "About the roses, my dear," she said firmly. "Have you thought where we might put the new stalks?"

Terry hung around for a few moments, but Rosalind started talking desperately to Aunt Honora, and he soon got tired and went back to his chair, flinging himself down with his own brandy snifter and hers. Eileen remained next to Peter, talking in a low tone, and laughing.

". . . near the back of the house," said Aunt Honora. "Don't you think that is a good idea? They will have more shelter there, the sun does not burn so brightly. We might have the boys put up an arbor. . . ."

"That sounds lovely," said Rosalind, fixing her attention firmly on the subject of roses. She was startled by a roar from Barton Darien.

He was pounding the chair, his face was red. He managed to articulate, "Want the damn cattle moved . . . now . . . right now . . . be too late. . . ."

Peter said quietly, "It's being done, Father. We

have to move them slowly, it is so hot. When it gets cooler. . . ."

"Too late . . . too late . . . got to attend. . . ."

"We're taking care of it, Father." There were white lines about his mouth.

"I told you we should have moved them last month, Peter. You preferred to stick around at the Murrays'," Terry said brightly, with a wink at Eileen.

Peter did not attempt to answer that. Rosalind thought indignantly that Peter had been recovering from his wound, and Terry could have seen to the moving of the cattle. Instead Terry was egging his uncle to further anger.

Peter stood up abruptly. "I'm doing the best I can, Father," he said, with weary patience. "The cattle will be ready when the ships come at the end of the month. We were butchering today and will go on all this week. They are being salted down. . . ."

"Should . . . should have been done . . . done . . ." Barton tried to say.

Alfred Murray wandered in, a book in his hand. "Any coffee, Rosalind?" he asked, innocent of interrupting the conversation. "I say, I've found the finest book of stories! All twisted about, of course, but someone tried to write up the stories of the Menehune. Got it all wrong. I must figure out what is the right story . . . do you think Kinau will know? I must talk to her . . . where is she?"

"Let me get you some coffee," said Rosalind, rising. She moved over to the trolley to pour some coffee from the large silver urn. She brought the cup to him as he sat down with a sigh of satisfaction. His greying hair was ruffled, she smoothed down a standing tuft gently. "Kinau is taking care of Victor just now. She will talk to you tomorrow, Father."

"You should talk to Hilohilo's woman, his wife," said Aunt Honora unexpectedly, a light of interest in her eyes. "She has a fund of stories, I'll ask her to come over and talk to you."

"Who is that? Who is that?"

"A fine woman, she knows many stories," said Rosalind. "You will have a chance to learn many more stories."

"I hope so. Oh, you must look over my latest manuscript, I asked you about that, didn't I?"

His rambling conversation had helped smooth over the argument. Barton Darien was mumbling to himself, but no longer red of face.

Presently a sturdy Hawaiian came in, and wheeled Barton away to his rooms. His head was sagging to one side, he was visibly exhausted. Rosalind wondered why he argued so with his son. He had given up the reins to him, he must know he could not cope with the huge ranch. Peter looked so tired and grim.

In their bedroom later, she ventured to ask about it.

"Why does your father persist in trying to manage the ranch, Peter? He must know he cannot cope with it, and you have everything in hand."

He did not take offense. He came over to her, and rubbed her shoulders with the palms of his large hands. "Oh, it's habit, Rosalind. I must not get angry with him. It is bad for him to lose his temper. Brought on a stroke before, it could again. I try to remember that. But he ran everything with an iron hand for so many years, it is hard for him to believe anyone else can handle it."

"I don't think anyone else could but you, Peter."

He murmured in her ear, "Trying to flatter me, my dear?"

Her heart lifted at his teasing tone. "No, it is just the truth, Peter. Terry is too weak; he lacks responsibility. Joe Smith is good, I believe, but he is a loner. He cannot handle people. Hilohilo would not look far enough ahead. And you handle it all and keep everything in your hands. No wonder they missed you when you were gone so many months."

He kissed her neck, sending a shiver of delight through her. "You've been keeping close to the house, trying to handle it all. I wonder . . . would you like a horse to ride? I can teach you, I think you would learn quickly."

"A horse? Oh, Peter, I should love to try!" she said, glowing.

"Aunt Norma rides sidesaddle, but Aunt Honora puts on pants and rides like the hands. You can ask them which would be best for you. Do what you wish, this is your home."

"You are . . . very good to me," she said, and turned into his arms.

"And you are beginning to feel at home?" he asked, his arms closing hungrily about her.

She evaded that. "It is a beautiful house, Peter, you must be very proud of it."

"I am, and I want you to love it as I do."

Peter kept his word, and chose a horse for her the very next day. The mare was older, brown and with soft brown eyes, gentle and docile. Rosalind decided to ride astride, as the *paniolos* did, and once she lost her fear of being so high off the ground she delighted in going off in the morning for a long ride.

She learned to love the wide plains, to ride under the palms on the creamy beaches, to amble along the edge of the surf where her mare stepped daintily in the foam. She would go off for an hour or two in the afternoons when she had time, and return glowing and tanned, happy to have been alone and quiet, with time to think.

She could sing on the back of her horse, with none to hear and mock, as Eileen did when she sang in the drawing room. She could sing and chant to herself all the old Hawaiian songs she loved, and jog along on the brown mare, feeling free, with the wind in her hair, her cowboy hat hanging by its cord around her throat.

And she found a quiet lagoon where she could swim. She had missed swimming in the surf. No one was about, and she brought with her a sarong, undressed behind a palm tree, hung up her clothes on the branches of the tree or a nearby shrub, and let her horse browse on the scant grass nearby while she swam.

She would brush out her wet hair, and it would dry on the ride home, with no one the wiser.

Peter was very busy, he never came home during the afternoon, he rarely came home for lunch. She thought nothing of it until one morning she was later than usual.

She was riding past the houses of the *paniolos* when she saw Peter come out. A Hawaiian girl came out with him, a pretty young girl with long brown curly hair flowing down her back. She wore a blue and white sarong, and as Rosalind saw them, the girl unwrapped the sarong and in an easy gesture wrapped it again, and fastened it at her breast. The gesture was so intimate, so easy, that Rosalind stared, her breath caught in her throat. She rode on, full of shock. She did not wait for Peter, she hoped he had not seen her.

Peter did not come home for lunch. He arrived back about five o'clock, tired and dusty. He had been herding cattle all day, he said. He said nothing about the girl, and Rosalind could not ask. The words stuck in her throat.

But she did not forget. Eileen's taunts had come back to haunt her. Peter was a virile man, and no one woman could satisfy him. And Rosalind had seen him coming from that hut.

She did not know what to think, she felt numb and sick. A burning heat filled her, an anger. She was knowing a terrible jealousy for the first time in her life.

Peter was so possessive of her, he wanted to know even what she thought. But secretly he went off to see his Hawaiian mistress! Could it be true? Did he go to that girl regularly? If he had only said—if he had spoken naturally of her, if he had told her, "I had to go to see one of the Hawaiian women, her husband was injured," or something like that. But no, he had told her nothing.

She was ashamed of her own jealousy. She hated it when Eileen touched his knee, lit his cigar, or leaned over him when he read a book, speaking in whispers to him. She hated it more when she thought of Peter coming out of that house, the girl wrapping her sarong more closely about her—as though she had just put it on!

That night in bed, she could not relax. Peter was impatient, and put his arm about her, and tried to draw her close. But she was stiff, and slow tears burned behind her eyes.

"What is it? What is wrong?" he demanded.

"Oh . . . I must be tired. I rode far today," she said in a faltering voice.

"You should not ride so far. Take Aunt Honora with you when you ride after this, she has common sense." And his hand stroked her shoulders soothingly. But she could not unwind and relax against him. She kept thinking of that girl. . . .

Long after his easy breathing told her he was asleep, she lay awake, staring into the darkness. On her quiet beach, she had not thought such harsh emotions existed in this world. Now she felt torn with anger, hate, jealousy—

And love. Yes, she had come to love Peter, to think of him as her own husband, a dear good man who loved her. But he did not say that he loved her. He had merely married her, taken possession of her. And he had not asked her to love him. She was his wife, the mistress of his house. She had wanted to take care of Victor, Peter had needed a wife so he could adopt Victor. It was supposed to be a bargain.

She had not counted on falling in love with him. She had thought it would be good to respect him, to honor him, to assist him in his work.

But she loved, and it hurt her. Something like a knife twisting around inside her. Perhaps Eileen was right, perhaps Victor was really Peter's son and he had deceived her all along. But it was too late to do anything about it; she was caught in a trap, with no way out.

# 8

🌷 🌷 🌷 🌷

PETER RODE out early in the mornings of these
hot days. He liked to get as much done as possible
while the day was cooler. Toward noon, the burning
sun boiled down over the plains and the cowboys
sought relief among the palms and on the beaches,
where they ate their lunches, and lazed until three
in the afternoon.

Sometimes a brief rain storm came up around four,
and they rode around laughing, enjoying the brief coolness of the downpour, not bothering to shelter. The
cattle enjoyed it also, lowing mournfully and moving
more quickly, heads up, searching for little puddles to
drink from.

Peter kept thinking about Glendon Corey. He had
tried to be courteous to the man. He had taken him
out on round-ups, sent him around with Joe or
Hilohilo, and explained the problems of ranching on an
island. The man showed great interest, asked searching questions about the island and rainfall, water sup-
ply and the difficulties of shipping.

Yet Peter had an uneasy feeling that the man knew
little about cattle and how to handle them. So why
was he here?

Perhaps he really did know something about beef,
but planned only to finance a project. That could be.
He was more the well-dressed financier than any cattleman. Glendon Corey was not comfortable on a
horse, he wearied early and went back to the ranch-
house or wandered around on his own. Yet—still he
lingered on this island that offered little in the way of
amusements.

Peter pondered about that, hooking his leg over the saddle horn, lighting up a cigar. It was late in the afternoon, he would go home soon. These very hot days took it out of him.

And Terry was a problem. Joe had tried to take him in hand, but he reported Terry kept slipping off.

He saw Hilohilo in a distance, waved his hat. The foreman started toward him, pausing to chase in a stray bull with lowering horns. Peter ambled toward him, they met in the shade of some *koa* trees on a gentle slope of the old extinct volcano in the center of Darien. Beneath their feet was the black lava dust and rock from the volcano which had formed Darien many thousands of years ago. Over it grew the lush green grass which the cattle enjoyed.

"They go well," said Hilohilo, pausing beside Peter. He accepted a light from Peter's cigar, and puffed away vigorously on his own thick cigar.

"We have almost two ship loads of meat salted down. Should be enough in a week," said Peter.

Hilohilo nodded, and waited. The big boss had something on his mind.

"Where is Glendon Corey?"

Hilohilo shrugged. "He go out with me, then disappear. I look around, poof, he is gone, like smoke. Over in the slopes of the small volcano."

The smallest volcano was the one in the southwest. Peter nodded, frowning. "Why is he still here?" he mused out loud. "I cannot understand it. I have told him all he needs to know. I wish he would leave. The ship called last week. I wanted to put him on it."

"He stays, and rides alone," said Hilohilo. The steady gaze met Peter's.

"What does he want?"

The bronzed shoulders in the open shirt shrugged. "Maybe in time we find out. I think he does not like cows."

"I think so also. If he stays longer, I will put him on a ship and bundle him away."

Hilohilo grinned around the cigar, a brief fierce grin. They understood each other. Neither liked strangers on their island. They were both suspicious of the townman with his neat suits and sharp eyes.

"Is it going to rain today?" Peter asked after a pause, gazing up at the hot blue sky.

"Not today I think."

"We'll go in, then. Set the night guards, and we'll head for home."

Hilohilo hesitated. Peter looked at him. The man was pondering, his broad face grave.

"Boss, I think you better know something."

"What?"

"Men have come from other islands."

"What men?"

"Some Hawaiian men. They came in canoe. Yesterday, I see them, I ask what they want. They say they will fish. I watch them, they have spears."

Peter stiffened. "Where do they come from?"

"They do not say. But I think I know two of them. I think they are of the people of Lydia Pauahi."

Peter gave a little groan of fury. "What? Do they still pursue the matter?"

"I have heard stories," said Hilohilo slowly. "The sailors on ships tell me. The chief, Kaahumanu Pauahi smoulders like volcano. He hears of his daughter's death. He hears that his warriors die by your doing. He hears that his grandson lives here under your protection." He paused, as though gathering up his thoughts.

"So he still pursues it?" asked Peter bitterly. "He turned away his daughter and his grandson from his village and his island. He sent them away to die. Is he not satisfied that his daughter *is* dead?"

"He mourns her," said Hilohilo, looking toward the peak of the central volcano as though drawing inspiration from it. "She was his best-loved child, everyone said so. His heart mourns her, though he is very angry. And he hates the man who brought her down."

"Terry."

Hilohilo nodded. "He hates the man Terry Darien. He hates all the Dariens, and especially you, who took his grandson from his vengeful warriors. He says

121

that the white men must be wiped from the islands, all the islands, before he will be appeased, and the gods satisfied."

"Ah." Peter mused, over his cigar, his face grim. This was worse. Not just a blood feud between the Dariens and Chief Pauahi, but a vendetta against all white men. That was serious and could be deadly. When the gentle Hawaiians were aroused, and their pride wakened, they would fight on to the death— their blood demanded it. He knew them: laughing and serious, loving and hating, amiable and proud. They would stop at nothing if once they began to kill.

"These men," said Peter. "Those who came to Darien. Who are they?"

"They are led by one young warrior, a great man, named Maleko. He is cunning and laughing with his mouth, but his eyes are keen and smart. He tells me they fish, and they do. But he moves among the people, he tells things and makes them listen to him because of his skill. None suspect that he comes from Chief Pauahi, as I believe he does."

"I would meet this man Maleko."

They were still speaking in Hawaiian, as Joe Smith rode up. The somber Texan had his sombrero low over his eyes, his rifle lay loosely in his left arm.

"Howdy."

They greeted him, and lounged in the saddles as they talked in the shade of the tree. They switched to English, for Joe knew only a bit of Hawaiian so far.

"Hilohilo tells me of the strange Hawaiians who came by fishing canoe."

Smith nodded, and spat accurately at a lizard sunning itself on a rock. "Saw them."

"What do you make of them?"

He shrugged. "Trouble, maybe."

"My idea. We'll have to post guard around the great house, and around the *paniolos'* houses. Not conspicuous; say that the cattle are restless and may break loose."

They discussed the arrangements briefly. Joe Smith would be in charge of the guards at the great house.

Hilohilo would manage the guards at the houses of the cowboys. They would also post guards at far ends of the islands to watch for any further "fishermen" coming.

Especially in the long canoes, the long boats of the warriors. They would not come at night, probably, the seas were too dangerous. But they might come at dawn, or evening.

Behind Darien mansion rose the huge cliffs. They could not come that way, the cliffs rose starkly a thousand feet into the air, and no man could climb them. But a guard could be posted at the top, and he could see the oceans for miles around the island on a fairly clear day.

Peter finally said, "Let's go back to the house and work all this out. It's damn hot out here."

Joe nodded. "Terry got away from me again," he said briefly, his brow wrinkling under his low hat.

"When?"

"About middle of the morning. Never saw him again."

"Damn. He's as slippery as an eel." Peter frowned. "Not your fault, Joe. Keep trying, though. Damn it, that man has to grow up sometime. There is some good in him, I know it, he had good parents. But to dig it out is going to take every bit of patience I have."

Hilohilo grinned mischievously. "How much you got, boss?" he laughed, and ducked as Peter swung at him. They were all laughing, even Joe, as they rode out of the shade and toward the great house.

Peter talked to the men, dismissed them, and strode up to his room to bathe off the dust. He luxuriated in the tub of hot water, then dried off, put on fresh clothes and his cool white tropical suit with the blue flowered shirt. He was just brushing back his wet hair as Rosalind came in.

"Oh, Peter, you finished early. I'm so glad," she smiled. "It's so very hot today, and it must be boiling out on the plains."

"Boiling," he agreed, and bent to snatch a quick kiss

from her lips. She still blushed when he kissed her, and he laughed down at her. "You look pretty and cool," he said, with satisfaction, putting his arm about her waist.

She wore a blue and green patterned muumuu with ruffles about the low neck, short sleeves, and hem. "I was just going to change for dinner," she said. "I thought the rose dress with the lace?"

"No, too hot," he said. "I appreciate that you want to dress beautifully as my hostess," and he ducked to press a kiss on an entrancing bit of shoulder. "But it's too damn hot to put on those tight clothes."

She drew a quick breath of relief, and he teased her cheek with the tip of his finger. "I want to do whatever you wish," she said with sober anxiety. "Your cousin and aunt always dress so properly. . . ."

"And don't move a muscle in this heat," he said grimly. "You and Aunt Honora do all the work, don't think I haven't realized. No, you be comfortable. And leave the running around to the servants, that's their job."

He frowned slightly, thinking of how Eileen rested the whole day, then wanted to stay up the entire night, drinking and playing cards and gossiping. Even Aunt Norma was prone to do that on the hot days. Rosalind would be wilted by all the work she did, while Eileen was fresh and cool and contemptuous of her hostess. There was no way to get Eileen to contribute, she had deftly slid out of it all her life. Terry was different, he had to learn and earn his salt. If Eileen married, some poor sap would have to gain control of her, or put up with her.

Perhaps it would be best to send Eileen with her mother to the mainland one day. Eileen would meet no one here suitable for her to marry. Yet he needed to keep his eye on her, she got away with too much. If only he could find someone to marry her—

Rosalind was watching him, and he smoothed out the worry lines on his face, and smiled down at her. "Ready to go down?" he asked.

"I must just see Victor a little while. He is teething and has been fussy."

"I'll come with you. Haven't played with the rascal for a time." He slid his arm about her waist again, he liked the feel of her slimness in his hold. His fingers stroked over the smoothness of her bare arm.

They could hear Victor's crying as they approached the room on the third floor. Rosalind opened the door and went in to bend over the baby on the floor.

"Poor love," she murmured. "Are you so uncomfortable?" She picked him up, he stopped wailing and beamed at her, the tears still running down his chubby cheeks. He put a plump finger into his mouth fretfully.

Kinau got up from her chair. "I'll get some salve for his gums," she said. She padded over to a medicine chest and brought out a small jar.

Rosalind sat down, the baby on her lap, and applied the salve carefully, rubbing with her finger over the hot gums. "I can feel a couple of little teeth trying to come through," she said, pleased.

Peter watched the pink color rising in her cheeks, the sparkle in her golden brown eyes. She laughed down at the baby as he cooed and bounced in her lap, and tried to grab at her braid. What a picture they made, his lovely wife and the brown child. One day she would have a son, his son, and it would be even better. To see her with his child in her arms—or a little daughter, round and beautiful, with her mother's eyes. She would be beautiful with children, she had such a warmth and gentleness in her.

When the baby had calmed down, Peter lifted him. "Hey, he's getting heavy, a real chunk," he said, bouncing him and making him laugh. He carried him to the window. "Look, Victor, this is our land. Look at the stables, see the horses? One day soon you will ride a horse."

Victor cooed approvingly, snuggling up to the big man.

The baby caught sight of some horses in the corral,

and leaned toward the window so suddenly that Peter had to hold tight.

"Hey, wait a minute, Victor! You can't ride today!"

"Victor like to look at horses," said Kinau, beaming. "He pats dogs, pats horses, he gonna be real boy real soon."

"Yes, he will grow up so fast," sighed Rosalind.

"He will be chief," said Kinau proudly. "Big Hawaiian chief of his people. Pele says so."

Peter turned to give her a stern look. "What are you saying? Victor is a Darien."

Rosalind caught her breath, she looked anxiously toward Kinau.

The older woman said firmly, "Victor is Hawaiian, he will be chief of his people. He need to learn much about Hawaiian ways. He will be great chief. It is promised."

Peter felt as though he had been struck. He knew the Hawaiian people, and how subtly they felt things. He looked down at the baby, sucking his finger now, gazing out at the animals moving below them in the corral. An Hawaiian chief? It could be. The boy was husky, he might grow tall and big. If he was intelligent, as his mother and father had been—if he learned—if he was a leader—he might one day lead the Hawaiian people of whom his grandfather was now chief. What did Kinau know of it? Had she talked to people of the Pauahi?

Victor put his brown curly head down on Peter's shoulder, and heaved a big sigh. His eyelids were drooping. Peter carried him over to the crib, laid him down gently, and gazed at him for a long moment before drawing the mosquito netting over the crib. Victor flung out his fist, sighed again with contentment, and was asleep in a minute.

Peter went down thoughtfully to dinner with Rosalind. He sat at one end of the long teak table, she at the other end. She was a gracious hostess, a little anxious yet that all was going well, but poised and calm.

Her father was conversing with Aunt Honora, talking of the Hawaiian legends. It seemed that Hilohilo's wife had come over that day and told him many stories. He was very happy and excited over the tales. He could scarcely wait to write them down.

"She knows a great many, and the chronology makes sense now," said Mr. Murray, his cheeks pink with pleasure. "I must write them down quickly, quickly. Dear me, Rosalind must help me. My dear, we must spend the next few weeks writing them down."

Rosalind smiled gently at her father. "We can work on them tomorrow morning for an hour or two, Father."

"I'll help you later," said Aunt Honora quickly. "I have heard the stories so many times."

"Good of you, good of you, but Rose is my helper," said Alfred Murray. He seemed to have forgotten that Rosalind was married. Peter frowned at Rosalind, she shook her head at him slightly, her mouth rueful.

Eileen was bored and sulky. Terry had not appeared for dinner. Eileen had dressed in her most beautiful lace and silk gown, but it was so hot. Peter suppressed a smile as his cousin wriggled and squirmed in her chair. The dining room had a ceiling fan which revolved slowly over their heads. But it was still too hot for all her layers of clothing.

Glendon Corey was ill at ease also, in his silk suit and wide tight white collar. He kept putting his finger under the collar and running it around, and sweat rolled down his cheeks. Peter wondered again why he remained.

Well, patience would tell. The man would open up and give his reasons one of these days.

After dinner, they moved to the coolest of the drawing rooms, at the northeast of the house, where the grand piano had been set. French windows were open to the slight night wind which had risen. Eileen took a chair next to the window, and fanned herself vigorously. Mr. Corey sat near to her, waving another palm leaf fan.

Peter went to the piano. He had not played for weeks. He sat down, feeling like music tonight. He put his hands on the keys, his mind drifting from problems to contentment. He was married, things were going rather well, he was happy.

He began to play. Something dreamy, soft, something to bring a smile to Rosalind's red mouth as she poured refreshing drinks into the shell-like cups. She was listening, he knew by the tilt of her head. He looked across at her, how lovely she was, how sweet. Sweet like honey, not cloying, but infinitely satisfying. She was still very modest with him, but she was learning to respond. In time, he would teach her to loosen up, and let loose with all the passion that he sensed was in her.

And to love him. He did not think that she loved him yet, but in time she would. He hated it when she was "grateful." He didn't want gratitude, to think that she had married him to help her father be secure. He wanted her love and passion, all of it, from her head to her heels, everything inside her. Heart and mind and soul.

Nothing less would do. He must have her all.

And one day she would give it.

He played more passionately, absorbed in the music and his thoughts. Eileen was murmuring to Mr. Corey, never so pleased as when a man paid attention to her, admired her with his eyes. Aunt Norma was nodding her white-capped head, Aunt Honora was tapping her slender feet briskly on the mat floor.

Presently Rosalind got up and went over to the shelf where her flutes were. Demurely she returned with one of them. "May I . . . play along with you?"

Peter smiled up at her, delighted, and moved over on the bench to make room for her. She seated herself beside him, looked at the music intently as he played. He indicated the place, she nodded, and raised the instrument to her lips.

He had set out an album of Beethoven *Sonatas*. She picked up the melody and played along with him, and they became completely absorbed in the composition. It was delightful, and soothing to him. He forgot the others in the room, none of them mattered to him, just Rosalind and her flute, her body close to his on the piano bench, and the music weaving magically around them.

She read music well, she must have taught herself, he thought. Unless she had learned from one of the mission ladies. One of them played the piano in the Congregational church, she might have taught Rosalind. Yes, that might be it. The lady had played for their wedding, he remembered now, and seemed happy for Rosalind.

They completed one sonata, and he smiled across at her. "Beautiful," he said, for her alone.

"That was very lovely," said Alfred Murray. "You play better than ever, Rosalind! You must get out your violin."

A shadow crossed over her face. She murmured to Peter, "He forgets . . . it fell apart years ago."

"I'll get you another, I did not know you played."

"Oh, I should like that so much," she said. Her voice lilted, there was no pretense in her. When she was happy, she showed it.

Barton Darien's voice boomed behind them, "Good . . . good . . . play . . . more!" His fist banged down on his chair for approval.

"Right, Father," said Peter, cheerfully. He turned over the pages, they began again, the *Moonlight Sonata*. They seemed to play as though they had always played together, knowing instinctively when to pause, when to lengthen a phrase, when to rush through.

When they had finished, Aunt Honora sighed, "So lovely, so lovely. It reminds me of years ago. . . ."

Eileen interrupted. "Play a waltz, Peter," she demanded imperiously. "Mr. Corey and I want to dance!"

Peter grimaced at the piano. He felt Rosalind stiffening. "I don't feel like waltz music tonight, sorry. And isn't it too hot to go cavorting around?" He began again, without waiting for her answer, turning to some Chopin sheets on the rack.

After a pause, Rosalind picked up the melody and played along. Peter's keen ear picked up a rustle of lace and silk, a disgruntled mutter from Eileen. Evidently, she and Mr. Corey had gone onto the patio. Good riddance, he thought. She was always spoiling a mood.

Those who remained enjoyed the classical music that followed. They went through more Chopin, to Brahms, a Mozart, and then to Bach. He was delighted to find that Rosalind could follow even the difficult Bach tempos. She was innately musical. The big Hawaiian butler came in with cool drinks, moved out again silently; a maid came in, hovered to listen for a time, her dark eyes shining. They all loved music, their own and the music of the Americans. It was a long time, they whispered, since Mr. Peter had played for an evening. The music filled the big gracious Darien home, echoed along the hallways of mahogany and sandalwood, through the rooms of Persian and Turkish rugs, the rosewood furniture, the elegant portraits on the walls, the treasures of two civilizations.

It was past eleven when they finally stopped. Barton had grown weary, sagging in his wheelchair, but he utterly refused to leave. His old face glowed with pleasure as he listened to the music and thought his own thoughts.

Peter helped Rosalind up, pressing a kiss lightly on her cheek. "That was glorious, we must do it often."

Her cheeks were rosy with pleasure, her amber eyes glowed. "Oh, I did enjoy it," she breathed. "I did not know you played so well, Peter."

"I have not had time for it . . . but I must make the time. There are many more important things in life than just working."

"Don't let Terry hear you say that," advised Aunt Honora drily, folding up her crocheting. Her hook had gone ahead busily as she listened all the evening, a quiet smile about her mouth. She was very pleased with this marriage, and all evening she had been thinking some line about "The marriage of true minds. . . ." Yes, it was a good marriage, Peter and Rosalind. When she had first met the quiet tanned-faced girl, had seen the shy fearful look, she had been very worried. But no more. Rosalind could manage. Peter had seen the depths in her.

They went to bed. Eileen had gone up before them, her mother said. Peter hoped she was right. He didn't want to go chasing Glendon Corey with a shotgun.

He went upstairs with his wife, his arm across her shoulders. He was tired, satisfied, and exhilarated all at once. They had something else in common, something good.

After disrobing in his dressing room, Peter yawned and stretched. He would sleep well tonight. He returned to their bedroom to find Rosalind donning a sheer nightgown. It seemed it would be awhile yet before she could show him her body without shame. He climbed into bed where he waited for his timid wife. His pulses pounded. She was lovely, curvaceous, beautiful, and so sweet.

Finally, Rosalind joined Peter and he drew the mosquito netting over them both, so that the folds hung down from the high posts of the rosewood bed. It was like another misty world inside there.

He turned to her, and put his arm across her. She curled up against him confidingly. She was not afraid of him as she had been for a time. He pressed his lips to her smooth shoulder.

"I discover new talents in you all the time," he murmured. "Where did you learn to read music?"

"At church. One of the ladies, the one who plays the piano. . . ."

He smiled to himself. He liked to find that his theories were correct. "She taught you well. But you have natural ability. What kind of violin would you like? I'll send to San Francisco for one."

"Oh, whatever you can get."

He would have one of the best sent out, something with a fine tone, and a package of extra strings as well, since they would have to wait so long for replacements.

"Some evening, we must have a real concert with

131

all our Hawaiians, playing and singing and dancing," he mused. "Wouldn't that be fun?"

"I should like it immensely!" she responded sincerely.

Peter traced a fine line along her shoulder and bare arm, and was pleased when she shivered and drew even closer to him. She was easier to arouse now. He bent over her, and pressed a kiss to the hollow of her tawny throat, and down to her taut breasts through the thin muslin. He could just make out the outline of her face in the moonlight and he cupped it in his hands. His thumbs lightly caressed her cheekbones as he kissed her mouth, her cheeks, down again to her throat. One hand slid down over her breasts, to her waist, then urgently to her inner thighs.

As he caressed her Rosalind thrilled to his tenderness and wrapped her arms about his back. The music had stirred her also. The music, and discovering a special harmony to share with Peter. She made no attempt at reproof when he lifted the hem of her short gown in order to stroke over her warm silky flesh.

Peter found he could not get enough of her. Thoughts of her filled his mind at the oddest times of the day, making him long to be with her. Often he looked at her at the other end of the dining table, wishing to throw everybody out so he could make love to her. Sometimes he wanted them to return to the shack in which Rosalind had been raised, that remained huddled under the black cliffs. There they could be completely alone, night and day, making love in both the moonlight and the sunlight. He wanted her on a beach, under the hot sun, moaning deliciously under him.

The round-up would soon be over, then there would be more time to spend together. They would take a carriage or their horses, and spend the day at an isolated beach, where they could love lazily under the swaying palms. Or he might take her back to her old home, and stay with her there. Surely it was safe by now. The old cunning chief Pauahi knew they were on Darien, he would not bother them elsewhere. His brow knitted slightly at the knowledge of the strange Hawaiians on his island, coming from Pauahi.

Rosalind stirred under him, and her hands clenched on his strong shoulders. "Peter . . . Peter," she muttered.

He forgot everything else and began to move with her, learning again the raptures of her young body. He kissed her ardently as her hips repeatedly met his. She cried out softly, clenching him with her fingers. His lips devoured the honey sweetness of her mouth, his tongue probing inside for more.

She sighed when it was over, and lay breathing quickly, and he rested too but would not release his hold. Oh, she made him crazy with desire. He had never felt this way with any woman in the world. He wanted her again, though did not have the energy to act.

It was as though they were two halves of a whole, parted when the world began. Now they had found each other, and the hunger to be reunited was overwhelming. It seemed as though they could not get enough of each other.

He longed to say all these things, but did not know how she would react. Would she think him mad? He contented himself with brushing little kisses over her bare shoulder, nibbling at her flesh, teasing at the nipples which stood up proudly after their embrace. She went to sleep in his arms, and he lay awake only a short while longer, holding her, loving her, not yet sure of her.

She had responded to him, he was awakening her passions. But he wanted all her love and devotion, forever. He never wanted her to look at another man, to smile at anyone else. It was selfish, but he was greedy for her. Unaware of it, he had looked all his life, searching to find someone to be totally his. Rosalind was that woman, and he'd swept her away with him. But would she understand? Would she be contented? She must be. She had to be.

# 9

❦ ❦ ❦ ❦

IN THE COOL of the late afternoon Rosalind hummed to Victor on the patio behind the big house. Peter would be home soon, and the house would come to life again, to ring with laughter and music in the evening.

She smiled at Victor sitting in her lap, patted his legs, and watched his alert face as he gazed toward the stables. Already he was struggling to talk.

Bougainvillea twined in rose and purple splendor over the arbor which surrounded the patio. Beds of roses, allamanda, hibiscus bushes, even pansies glowed with color and perfume in the shadows.

She loved the house now, huge though it was. During the day she always found time to dust one of the rooms, opening the cabinets to study the precious treasures inside.

The music room was her favorite, with the large rosewood piano, her flutes, the racks of scores, the books on music and art. In a glass cupboard were set precious ivories, porcelains from England and France, green and white jade from China.

The front drawing room was more formal. It too had glass cabinets of treasures. It was there Peter kept the formal china set of his family, a beautiful design in blue and gold, with the center a hibiscus flower in rose. In another cabinet were set miniatures of his grandfather, grandmother, mother and father, aunts, uncles, and cousins. Peter would tell her about them one day. Aunt Honora had started to explain them all one day, but had been called away.

The wide hallway had its own strange charm. On

the walls were hung Hawaiian spears, still bright and sharpened with deadly tips. In cases were beautifully carved wood calabashes, strings of beautifully polished brown *kukui* nuts, bowls of monkeypod, sprays of pink and black coral, and shell necklaces of tiny white shells, some with tiny images of gods carved in pendant form.

Her father loved the library the best, and she could not blame him. He worked there daily, enjoying the fine volumes, the magazines, and up to date newspapers. He was intensely absorbed in the work. The books were in glass cases, protected against the damp, and the library tables were glossy mahogany, with oil lamps of beautiful rose porcelain. The chairs were deeply comfortable, some in fabric, and some simply bamboo, which was more comfortable in hot weather.

"Here you are, what a lovely sight!" Terry's drawl broke into Rosalind's reverie. She felt a twinge of displeasure and some alarm. He had taken to seeking her out, a smile on his handsome face, always with some flattering remark. She distrusted him, and she disliked how little attention he paid to Victor. He glanced at the child now, patted its head condescendingly. Victor stared up at him, his face sober, not recognizing him as among his favorite people.

Terry flopped down into a chair near to Rosalind and gazed at her.

"Prettier every day," he smiled.

"Thank you." She gathered up Victor, ready to take him inside.

"Don't run away, I won't bite," Terry laughed. "Every time I come near you, you leave. What's the trouble? Don't you like me?"

She was tempted to tell the truth and walk away. But he was Peter's cousin, and a Darien. She held Victor against her bosom, and patted his back, and he gazed contentedly into the distance and gurgled.

"Not at all," she said coolly. "I mean, of course I . . . like you. What do you want?"

"Do I have to want something?" he sighed. "You work like the devil. Can't you just relax? Peter should be more considerate of you. You shouldn't have to work like a native in this climate."

She stared at him, he smiled blandly back at her. His blue eyes flickered, he gave her a wink.

"I don't know what you mean," she said coldly. He infuriated her without half-trying. Calling the Hawaiians natives in that condescending way.

"Oh, come on now, you aren't stupid. Peter married you to get you to work like an animal for him," he said, leaning back in the chair. "He knew you would work like everything. But you should relax and take things easy. He won't know."

"Is that your philosophy?"

He laughed. "Of course." He flipped his hand nonchalantly. It was bronzed like Peter's, but somehow looked softer. There were no callouses on the fingers and palms from rough work with ropes and cattle. She preferred Peter's hands, they looked tough and masculine, somehow reassuring. And when he touched her at night, stroking her sensitive flesh, they were sensuous and exciting. Their very hardness told of what he was, how he lived.

"Someday you might grow up," she said, and his eyes flashed. She realized she had touched a sore spot, and was a little sorry. She did not mean to promote trouble. But he was so immature, taking his pleasure where he wished, and not caring who was hurt.

"Someday," he said, leaning toward her, "I'd like to show you . . . just what kind of man I am!" His voice was softly dangerous, sensuous and tough at the same time.

Rosalind's mouth curled a little. She could not resist. Fondling Victor, she noted "Oh, you have shown us . . . this. But that isn't the making of a man, to be able to create a baby. It is caring for the child and mother, taking responsibility, being the kind of a man on whom one can lean and trust."

He drew in his breath sharply, his eyes glittering. Terry would have said something nasty, but just then Peter came from the stables, striding in his boots onto the patio. He saw them together, talking with their heads close together. His heavy brows drew together in a frown. Terry instantly changed mood, and laughed up at him.

"Working hard, cousin?" he drawled insolently. "I've been enjoying a little chat with . . . lovely Rosalind."

Peter looked from one to the other in anger. Rosalind stood up with the baby clenched tightly to her. "I'll take Victor inside. It's time for his supper," she said, and fled. She heard Peter's deep growl, and Terry's lighter mocking tone. Damn him anyway, he loved to cause trouble. Terry loved mischief, just as his sister did.

She took Victor to the nursery and fed him herself, loving the feel of the child, his dependence on her. If only Terry could understand that. It was good to be responsible for a child, Terry ought to have learned that.

Peter knew it, even though the child was not his— unless Eileen's taunting words were true.

Rosalind drew in her breath in a sigh, and Kinau looked at her understandingly. "Men get difficult, yes? There is much trouble in this house, and day not yet come when trouble go away." She shook her greying head ominously.

"I feel it also. From where do you think it comes? From Terry?"

"Him, pooh. Him a child. No, it comes, more serious," but Kinau would not say more, looking off in the distance, then gathering up Victor. "I take care of baby now, you go change and make yourself pretty for your man."

Rosalind slowly descended to her rooms where Peter was already washing up. His mouth was set tight when he looked at her.

"Hello," said Rosalind in trepidation.

"I wish you would stay away from Terry," he said tautly. "I know he is charming and makes suave remarks. But you are my wife, and don't forget it!"

Astounded, Rosalind started to refute his words angrily, but was stopped by the slamming of the dressing room door between them.

"Well!" Refusing to give in to Peter's ill behavior, Rosalind took off her dress and defiantly put on a loose muumuu. Damned if she would go out of her way for him! He could just glare at her! She had not invited Terry's attentions, and she did not want them.

The dress she chose was light blue with short ruffled sleeves and low neckline. She left the room before Peter re-entered, going down alone to the drawing room before dinner. Aunt Honora was bringing in some flowers and Rosalind went to help her arrange them in the silver epergne in the center of the table.

Aunt Honora wore a green muumuu, and looked comfortable with her greying hair twisted into a brisk knot at the back of her neck. Aunt Norma entered the dining room shortly thereafter to glance over the table. She wore her white widow's cap with streamers down the back, and a tight black satin dress with a bustle and long sleeves.

"My, it is so very hot today," she murmured. Aunt Honora looked at Rosalind, and briefly raised her greying eyebrows. Rosalind wanted to giggle, but restrained herself.

When Peter finally came downstairs, his jaw was set and grim. Eileen trailed behind, catching up, she put her hand on his arm, and hugged herself against him. She was perfumed and lacy, in her favorite pale silk, her blonde hair in a lovely coronet.

"Darling Peter," said Eileen clearly, "You're working too hard. I wish you would rest and relax more. Why don't we ride out together tomorrow?"

Peter looked at her and his face softened. "You want to herd cattle?" he teased, and she pouted her luscious red mouth in answer, which made Rosalind's stomach turn.

Terry arrived promptly for dinner for a change, looking leanly elegant in a grey suit with an open-necked white shirt. He was gay and teasing, and he and Eileen and Mr. Corey kept the conversation going. Peter was silent most of the meal, staring down at his plate, or frowning at Rosalind. She felt miserable. Didn't he see what Terry was doing? Terry loved to cause trouble. He didn't care a bit for Rosalind, but if it would provoke Peter, he would pretend anything.

Mr. Murray, blissfully ignorant of the tension, talked to Aunt Honora. They shared a mutual interest in Hawaiian stories, and she had a rich fund of them. Mr. Corey tried to get Peter to talk about the island, but Peter was rather sullen tonight and Corey was defeated in his efforts.

They retired to the drawing room and Rosalind served coffee to those who wished it. Terry, like Eileen, was drinking some rum and fruit concoction which made them act silly. Mr. Corey drank one glass of it, and pronounced it very potent.

Peter was restless, striding up and down the room. Finally at nine o'clock, he said abruptly, "Come along, Rosalind, we're going to bed."

It was so obvious and rude that they all stared at him. Eileen flushed and dangerous, Terry amused. Rosalind rose at once, feeling apprehensive.

"Yes, of course, Peter."

"Yes, Peter, of course, Peter," mocked Eileen, pouting. "Don't you have a mind of your own, Rosie? It's too early to go to bed! Why don't you play so we can dance, Peter?"

"You can make your own music," he answered rudely, and left the room. Aunt Honora looked wise, Aunt Norma worried. Rosalind gave them a smile of apology, and hurried after her husband. She thought he was going to lecture her, and she preferred for it to be done in private.

She felt angry and defiant. She had done nothing wrong. If Terry chose to make mischief, all she could do was try to avoid him. And scowling at her in front of them all, Peter was acting like a child himself!

Peter waited for her at the stairs and they went up together. His fingers gripped under her bare arm. He practically pushed her along the hallway and into their rooms. She turned to face him as he slammed the door shut, still holding her.

"You are hurting my arm. Did you need to make such a scene tonight? I have done nothing wrong."

"Only inviting Terry's attentions," he said furiously. There were white lines alongside his large, generous mouth. "Are you so starved for attention . . . have I neglected you so much . . . that you have to listen to his flattering nothings?"

"No, I don't. But he is your cousin, and I have to be polite. . . ."

"Do you? Or do you enjoy his sweet talking? Oh, he has all the gifts, he has," mocked Peter, angrily. "He knows just what to say to a lonely girl, to make her feel good. . . ."

Rosalind flung back her head. "You are insulting me," she said vehemently. "I have not invited his attentions. You know as well as I that Terry likes to make mischief. He would like nothing better than to hurt you . . . and me . . . and cause trouble between us. Can't you see that. . . ."

"I saw you this evening . . ." he said under his breath. "Staring admiringly at him. . . ." He came up to her, and drew her into his arms. He felt hot and fierce, his arms hard around her. She was afraid of him suddenly, and pulled back. He held her the more tightly. "Don't pull from me! I have every right. . . ."

"Don't talk about rights, Peter! You . . . you make me . . . afraid . . . don't hold me so hard. . . ."

"You are my wife!"

His mouth covered hers, hot, furious. Rosalind felt his heat as she pressed her fingers against his chest. But he was strong and as aggressive as a young bull.

"Peter . . . don't . . . you are hurting me!"

Paying no attention, he dragged her to the sofa and threw her into the soft cushions. She lay against them, and felt the passion of his body against hers. He sought her throat, shoulders, arms, then returned to her lips. Seemingly unsatisfied, he pulled down the delicate bodice in order to release the full breasts in which he buried his face.

"You're coming with me," he said thickly, then picked her up to carry her into the bedroom. In panic, she began to strike at him. He ignored her blows as though they were so many taps from Victor's small fists.

He flung her down on the bed where without bothering to fully undress, he hurt her, and tears welled in Rosalind's large eyes. After awhile she realized it was fruitless to struggle anymore against his superior strength. His body pressed on hers, he had her, and came quickly to his own satisfaction. She turned her face away, resting a cheek against the pillow. In all her life she had never felt so humiliated, so used—just an object in Peter's iron grip.

Breathing hard, he rose and went into the dressing room. The thudding sounds that followed made Rosalind realize Peter had not even bothered to take off his boots! She still felt the hard pressure of the buttons of his shirt on her bared flesh, the dress had been half torn from her body. She could not move. Tears cascaded down her cheeks unchecked, and soaked the pillow.

The room was dusk-dark, lit only by the glow of the moon that flowed through the open windows. He came back and bent over her.

"Rosalind?" His voice was calmer, husky. "Shall I help you?" Touching her face, he discovered the wetness. "Oh, Rosalind!"

She did not want his comfort or his pity.

"Leave me alone!"

He stiffened. "I'll help you," he insisted.

"I don't want your help!"

"Come along now," he said, more gently. Finding the nightgown laid out by Akela, he propped Rosalind against the head board. He took off her slippers, the remains of the dress, and her thin petticoat. She felt rigid in his hold.

"I want to wash," she said sullenly. She slid from him, taking the nightdress from him, and went to the basin.

"I'll light a lamp."

"No, don't!" She didn't want him to see her. "I can see . . . in the dark."

She bathed, using only the dim light of the windows to see. Tears still poured down her cheeks; she could not seem to stop crying. She scrubbed her face fiercely. She was so hurt—so disappointed in him. He had been so gentle before. She had come to trust him—

Finally, unable to delay any longer, Rosalind stepped hesitantly toward the bed. Peter seemed to lie breathing quietly, perhaps he was asleep. She slid under the mosquito netting, and lay down.

He turned to her, put his arm across her.

*"Don't!"* she cried adamantly. It was the final insult. He did not remove his arm.

"I am sorry I hurt you," he said quietly, against her arm. "Forgive me. My temper ran away with me. I would not have harmed you. I will try not to do it again."

Her throat was tight from the effort to not let him hear her. She lay stiffly under his arm. His voice coaxed her. He had charm—like Terry, she thought bitterly.

"Rosalind?"

She could not speak for the tears. He drew her closer and held her. Eventually, Peter seemed to fall asleep, but she lay awake for a long time. Her life seemed to have shattered. No one had ever hurt her so much. She had never expected so much from anyone, she had become vulnerable to him, and he had hurt her. Let that be a lesson to herself, she thought as the hours wore on. Don't trust anyone, don't trust—don't give your heart—but that advice was too late. She had already given it to Peter.

Eileen had been absolutely furious when Peter walked out early with his meek wife in tow. His bed should be her place, not that of the milky stupid girl! She wanted to scream and kick as she had when a child and something she wanted was denied her. But Peter could not be given to her by her devoted mother or by Terry or anyone else. Eileen glared at the purple dusk with furious eyes.

Mr. Corey grew bored with her silence, and went back to talk to Terry.

"I'll go up also. I'm tired, Mother."

"Tired, Eileen?" Norma was startled. Eileen was never tired. Bored yes, tired never.

"I'll go to bed, don't bother me when you come up, will you?" Eileen yawned, and walked out. But she was not about to do as she'd said. Her blue eyes rebellious, she walked out to the patio and flung herself into a chair. She glared up at the stars. So early in the evening, and Peter had dared to abandon her!

She would show him. She would have fun. She would get him back, he would be madly jealous of her, she would have him under her thumb. And she would demand a trip to Europe, a long long honeymoon, once she had gotten rid of Rosalind! Peter would pay for the way he had treated her. She had always meant to have him, and she always got what she wanted. Eventually.

Presently she was aware of quiet footsteps around the edge of the patio. Someone walking back and forth, back and forth. Curiosity made Eileen call, "Who's there?"

The footsteps paused, someone came into the dim light of the lamps. "Joe Smith, ma'am."

"Oh . . . what are you doing here? Is there trouble with one of the horses?" She came closer to him, he intrigued her. There was a mystery about that tall drawling cowboy from Texas, and she was bored tonight.

"No, ma'am."

"Well, then, what?"

He hesitated, and shrugged. "Just walking, ma'am."

"Then I'll walk with you," Eileen said, on impulse. She slipped her arm into his, smelled the dust on his clothes, and the masculine odor of him. He had ridden hard today. She enjoyed the smell, like that of a real man. Not like Glendon Corey, with his pomade and perfume, like a parlor dandy.

Smith had stiffened at her touch, and gently removed the confidently placed gesture. "No, ma'am, that won't do. You best go back indoors."

"It's a lovely night. Why can't I walk with you?" she pouted. "Peter trusts you, doesn't he?"

"I hope so, ma'am."

She put her hand back into his arm, feeling the rippling muscles. She smiled into the darkness as they walked along past the border of the patio, back into the area near the stables. She smelled the drying hay and groomed horses. It was all so primitive and exciting And Smith was exciting, this tall enigmatic man. She began to feel a surge of interest.

"Didn't you like our rides this week?" she murmured.

"I don't think you should come out with the cowboys," Joe answered, with reserve.

"I enjoyed watching you handle the steers. You're very skillful, aren't you, Joe?"

His sombrero was low over his face, but she could not have seen his eyes anyway. She knew they were a deep grey, hiding secrets. She enjoyed secrets.

Eileen increased the pressure on his arm. "My, you are strong. Your muscles are hard as iron."

He said nothing. He strode on slowly, and seemed to be listening to the darkness She continued to cling to him and hopped along, mentally cursing her high-heeled slippers and tight dress. She should wear muumuus, but she knew the tight gowns set off the curves of her figure.

"Joe?" she whimpered plaintively. "Don't walk so fast, I can't keep up."

"You should go back to the house," he drawled

"Don't want to go back to the house," she said childishly, in a high voice, and giggled. The rum she had had was running pleasantly in her veins, making her hot and carefree.

"Do you know what you want, ma'am?"

"Stop calling me 'ma'am.' My name is Eileen."

"What do you want from me?"

He paused in the darkness and turned to look down at her. Maybe his keen grey eyes could penetrate the darkness. She peered up at him, but could not even see his face. They had gone far from the house, and now stood in the thick beyond the flower beds.

"Just a little talk. I get so bored, Joe."

"You should try working," he noted, and began to walk on.

"Joe!"

"What?"

"Don't leave me. I'm . . . I'm afraid."

"Of what?"

His voice was even, low, and drawling. She had heard him bawling out a man one day for mistreating a horse. She had never heard a soft voice so deadly, even Peter's. She began to feel a thrill of anticipation.

"Of the night. And the strangeness. Don't you feel it sometimes when there is a storm coming on? Or trouble?"

"Yep, reckon I do. I'll take you back to the house." As he turned, she caught at his arm. "What do you want?"

She stroked her hand slowly over his hard arm. "Don't you know what I want?" she asked softly.

"Tell me."

Eileen smiled in the darkness, her tongue licking her lips like a cat after cream. "Aren't you man enough . . . to know?"

He put his arm about her, hesitated. She snuggled closer, raised her face. His other arm went about her, he pulled her tight against him. His mouth came down on hers, crushing, not slow and easy. She trembled with pleasure. He wasn't like Glendon Corey, just kissing as though he was afraid of her. And he smelled all man, masculine and sweaty and dusty.

The arms went tighter. Joe's lips burned on hers, and moved, to press on her cheeks and her throat. One hand went up and down her spine, and then grabbed her hips, pulling her tightly to him. She felt his member against her, and felt a pleasurable thrill of fear. He was so big, so tough.

She would let him shake with desire—then leave

him, and walk back to the house. It was fun, to upset a man like this, to bring him to the brink of want.

She let Joe kiss her, and her hands roamed over his shoulders, stroking over the big arms, down to his wrists behind her. "Let me go now, Joe," she said finally, turning her head away, as he sought her lips again.

He did not answer. Instead he abruptly pulled her into the grass. Annoyed, Eileen resisted because she did not want to get stains on her clothes. As she attempted to extricate herself, Smith pinned her under his body.

"Joe . . . let me go!" she panted, getting really angry.

"Like hell!"

The silk dress rode up and his calloused hand groped at the dainty undergarments. She was furious; he was ripping her clothes.

"Joe . . I'll scream!"

Eileen should not have warned him. Instantly, his mouth closed over hers. His big body had her down where he wanted her. In moments, Smith found the tender portion between Eileen's legs and thrust violently into her. She moaned, arching involuntarily to meet his penetrating maleness.

Their mating was animalistic, without tenderness. He took his satisfaction from her, and she acquiesced. His panting breath was in her mouth, and his large tongue—big, hard, and sure, like himself—flicked in and out. When Eileen fought beneath him, he temporarily allowed her to regain her breath, only to resume his actions, holding her closer than ever. Somehow he used her struggles to make her receive him even more. The storm broke in her, and then he lay exhausted on top of her, panting for air.

At last he got up. She rose, flaming with fury, mussed, clothing torn. "You just wait, Joe Smith! Just wait till I tell Peter Darien what you did!"

He stood, dark and shadowy above her. "Are you sure you want him to know about you?" Joe drawled.

"Damn you for a devil!" Eileen raged.

"You asked for it. Just as you always ask for trouble. You and that brother of yours, you love trouble. Don't cry when you get it," he said, with a deadly note in his voice.

"I suppose you enjoyed tonight," she flared, her vanity wanting him to admit he had adored her, maybe even that he loved her.

"Not specially," he countered, in his slow calm way. "You're a beautiful woman, on the surface. But inside, you're ice, you got no heart at all. I won't want you again."

She gasped in shock. Never had she been so insulted! She raised her hand to strike, but he caught her wrist easily, and said, "I wouldn't. I'll see you back to the house."

"I'll find my way!" Eileen shot out, and tried to blunder off. But she was still caught in his vise.

"It ain't that way, ma'am," he said politely. "This way, ma'am," and he pulled her with him, back to the patio. He bowed at the edge of the flagstones, and left her, his sombrero pulled low over his eyes.

As luck would have it, Terry was in the lower hallway when she entered. He looked his sister over with amusement.

"Well, well, you've been having fun, huh, Eileen? Who's the lucky man?"

"Go to hell!" she spat, and ran up the stairs to her room in a wild fury.

# 10

❦ ❦ ❦ ❦

ROSALIND CANTERED across the quiet dusty plains toward her favorite lagoon. She had tied a sarong on the saddle before her, along with a towel.

She felt tired, troubled, uneasy. Kinau said a storm would break, and she did not mean rain and wind.

Peter had been kinder to her, anxious. But Rosalind had turned cold and frigid to his attentions. She could not forget his cruelty that night a week ago. They would lay in bed now, and she would be unreceptive when he tried to kiss her. He would sigh, turn over, and go to sleep quickly while Rosalind lay awake for hours night after night.

The marriage could not work this way. She must forgive him and start again. But she could not forgive and forget. The memory of his rough cruelty ran even through her dreams, making them nightmares.

Peter grew cross and said little. He would rise early and ride off before she was up in the mornings. Everyone in the house must know they had quarreled. Eileen was mocking, Terry teased and tormented. It must suit them very well, to have Peter upset. Rosalind believed they resented him deeply, even hated him.

Yet, where would they be without him? He ran the ranch, he made the plans, he earned the money for them all. Without him, they would have to sell out. They could not run Darien without Peter.

She sighed deeply, and slid from the saddle. Rosalind tied up the gentle mare so that the horse had a long rope with which to circle the tree and crop at the sparse grass. She went to sit for a while at the edge of the waves, to gaze out over the Pacific.

The ocean was quiet today, the waves rolled evenly, beautifully, in white combers up to the sand, and melted away in foam. There was something eternal and peaceful in the movement of the water. The blue-green near the sand, the deeper blue out further. Not a soul was around. She would relax and rest, and think, before she went for her morning swim.

"Hello, there, darling Rosalind!"

The taunting light voice just behind her made her start violently. She sprang up, to turn around and stare at Terry. He was just tying his horse beside hers.

"What are you doing here?" she demanded harshly.

"Following you, my dear!" He left the animal, and walked across the beach toward her, his mouth laughing, his brilliant blue eyes glittering. She wanted to run away in terror. Rosalind had never been so alone with Terry. . . .

"Go away, I want to be by myself here," she said, as he approached. She lifted her chin defiantly. If she showed fear, he would be pleased.

"Come on now, be friendly . . . cousin!" He came closer and glanced across at the ocean waves. "Going swimming?"

"No."

"Then why the sarong?" he smirked, pointing to the garment and the towel.

"I thought I might. But not today." She picked them up, and started toward the horse.

"Oh, come on, Rosalind, don't be coy. You can swim with me. Let's have some fun. You don't think your dear husband goes without his pleasures, do you?"

"What he does is his business," she retorted curtly, and started to walk around him. His arm caught at her, and she went stiff with fear.

"Come on now," he said purringly. He had a practiced manner that she distrusted. "What's wrong with going swimming together? I'm sure you look beautiful in the water."

"Let me go."

"I'm not holding you, my dear!" he chuckled, his

hand gripping her arm. "If I really held you . . . there wouldn't be any doubt." His handsome bold face was very close to hers. "You know, Peter is lucky . . . to have such a charming devoted wife ; . . as well as all the little *wahines* he wants!"

Nausea coursed through Rosalind. Terry was confirming her worst fears. Peter wanted a wife for himself. But at the same time, he would have his fun. He was a very virile man, she knew. And she had seen him with that Hawaiian girl.

As though reading her thoughts, Terry said, "You don't think he works all the time, do you? When he comes home so tired, he hasn't been herding cattle all day, honey! All the *wahines* adore him, and he has the child to prove it."

Rosalind didn't try to answer that. He watched her sharply, he could read her face if she wasn't careful. She kept her head averted, her lashes lowered over her eyes. "Let me go," she said. "I have to get home."

"You just got here," he said, smiling. His arm slipped around her. "Come on, let's go for a swim. I bet you swim like a fish. Being alone at the lagoon of yours all those years, I bet you really learned to swim. Come on, show me how good you are."

She had worn only slippers and a loose muumuu. She wished she had worn boots, to kick at him and get away. Her lips tightened as he went on coaxing and drew her against him.

How to get away from him? The mare was tied securely. It would take a minute to get her loose. By that time Terry would be after her. She felt panicky, and drew deep breaths to calm herself.

He was so much stronger. If she fought him, she was certain he would assault her. She could not risk arousing him.

"All right," she said, relaxing in his grip. "Why don't we go swimming? I'm so hot. . . ."

Terry stared down at her. Finally he let go her arm. "All right, honey. I'll undress . . . you go on, there's a bush over there if you want to be private." His grin taunted her. The bush was thin and sparse, he could see right through the branches. And it was far from her horse.

Rosalind kicked off her slippers, set them with her sarong and towel, and tied them together. "I don't need to change, I'll swim like this." She laughed at his startled face, and ran down the sand to the water.

She had swum before in a muumuu, when she was hot and tired.

"Hey, wait for me!" he called, pulling at his boots. She glanced back over her wet shoulders. Her hair had come loose and her muumuu was wet through, revealing her sensual figure.

Terry's shirt came off next, then his pants. He was naked when he flung himself into the water.

She swam further out, confident of herself in the water. A wave came, she rode it in. Terry stood up. She averted her gaze then swam out again, as Terry passed on an incoming wave.

Rosalind picked another huge wave, enjoying it, her nerves quivering as she judged the distance between herself and Terry. He was laughing and calling to her.

"You swim beautifully, darling! Wait for me! Come on, let's go in together!"

She flipped her hand carelessly at him, and swam out once more, deliberately far, to repeat the dangerous game of avoidance.

Taking Terry off guard, she reached shore and ran to catch the clothing, and made for the mare. She unfastened the rope with wet desperate fingers, and hurled herself into the saddle. Thank God she had learned to ride astride. She got up, and was off, as Terry screamed after her.

"Hey . . . wait for me . . . damn you!"

The wind caught at her hair, tearing it, streaming it across her face. She was cold with fear. She gripped the bundle before her, and galloped away into the trees. She kept looking back, but the cattle and cowhands were on the plains.

Terry did not follow. She finally reined in among some palms, wrung out her soaked hair, and plaited it with shaking hands. The wind and sun would dry her muumuu on the way home. She put on her slippers, and rode on more slowly. She must be completely dry before she got home.

It had been such a close call, she felt shaken for days. She would not dare go out to the lagoon again alone. She must never be alone. Terry was a devil. He would have raped her, she felt deadly sure of that. He had no respect for any woman. It would have titillated him to have Peter's wife. He would have told Peter also, Rosalind knew. She shuddered when she thought of it.

She stayed close to home. Peter looked at her, puzzled, and asked her what was wrong. She shook her head. "I'm fine," she said. "It's been hot. Kinau says a storm is coming."

"She's crazy," he said shortly. "The storms are over for now. We won't have more until autumn."

Kinau worried about her, she knew her Lokelina. "What wrong, what happen to you, my baby?" she coaxed Rosalind as she sat with Victor on the *lanai* overlooking the gardens.

Rosalind clutched Victor close to her. She still shuddered whenever the incident of Terry crept into her mind.

"Oh, Kinau, I must tell you. I am . . . so afraid," she said, in a low tone.

"What happen to you? Who dare hurt my baby?" asked Kinau fiercely.

In a whisper, Rosalind told her what had happened. "And ever since," she added, "Terry looks at me, and laughs, and whispers to me to come to the beach. Oh, God, if Peter hears him, he will be furious. . . ."

Kinau was shaking her iron grey head. Her round brown face was unusually stern. "That is a bad man, that is," she murmured. "No, you must never go out alone. Sometime I come with you, we swim again. I miss our lagoon, and my sons. Ah, it was fate that you marry with Peter, but sometimes my heart is sad, longing for the old days."

"Mine too, Kinau," Rosalind whispered. She dashed the tears from her eyes, hugging Victor until he squeaked in protest, then flung his chubby arms about her neck. "I am homesick at times, thinking of the peace of our little house, and our happiness and the quiet, and how alone we were."

"It was not good for you, you met no young men. Now, you are troubled and hurt," sighed Kinau. She patted Rosalind's hand. "It will be well one day, but we must go through trouble first, my Lokelina. Hold fast to the promise of Pele, it will be well for us."

"I will remember, thank you, Kinau."

It was comforting, and she felt soothed.

Rosalind stayed at home, helped in the gardens with Aunt Honora. The roses burned up in the heat. They still had hibiscus, though, white and pink and rose and cream. The jacaranda trees bloomed, and their flowers showered to earth, creating blue pools around them.

The yellow allamanda flowered again, and Rosalind cut some for the table arrangements. The plumeria was fragrant, and she and Kinau made leis to wear. Eileen might scorn her, but Rosalind sat at the table in her blue-green muumuu with a gold plumeria wreath about her neck and felt at home. She would not care what the other woman said.

The white and the torch ginger bloomed, and they were even more fragrant. She worked with Aunt Honora, and hummed as they worked in the early morning or the late afternoon.

"I hope you grow happy here, my dear," said Aunt Honora, straightening her wiry back, and putting her hand to her hip. Her near-sighted eyes blinked at Rosalind. "You are a very nice girl. Don't let them torment you."

Rosalind had not thought Honora noticed, but she was learning that Aunt Honora noticed everything, even though she could not see so sharply as Aunt Norma.

"Thank you. I shall . . . manage," she said with

reserve. "Father is happy. I think we shall send two more stories in the next ship. Did you see the magazine with his story of Pele?"

"Yes, yes, splendid. The world should know of these myths before they are forgotten," said Aunt Honora, fingering a bird of paradise flower thoughtfully. "I wonder if I should trim these back?"

"What do you mean, forgotten?" asked Rosalind sharply. "Why would they be forgotten? The Hawaiians will always remember and recite them."

"Oh, my dear," said Aunt Honora. "You don't understand. The more white people come, the fewer Hawaiians will remember their heritage. The old songs are not sung by the young, they sing the songs of the mainland. They go to mission schools and the youths learn Latin and Greek and religion, instead of the legends of Pele and the other gods. Who will lead the Hawaiian people, and keep them in the ways of their gods?"

Rosalind stared at her. She had thought such things privately. But she had not thought other white people considered this. The Dariens owned this island, the Hawaiians worked for them, no longer owning the land. Peter said he had brought in Hawaiians to work, but the islands had been all Hawaiians before the white men came.

"They will . . . forget," she said slowly.

"If they do not have pride in the stories, and their heritage . . . If the white men jeer at them, and teach them new ways," said the older woman wearily. "If the gun is mightier than the spear . . . and it is . . . If trumpets are louder than the sound of the conch shells."

Rosalind had not thought that Honora had so much poetry in her. She studied the leathery face of the spinster, the old fashioned frizz of hair, the bend of her back as she leaned again to her beloved flowers.

"What can be done about it?" asked Rosalind slowly.

"Done? Little. Your father helps, though he does not realize it. When the words are put on paper, they will be in magazines and books, and the Hawaiians will read them and remember. And when you ask Hilohilo's wife to recite the songs, and all listen, there is more remembering. When you sing and speak Hawaiian, it will be remembered. When you teach Victor, he will remember. A long slow process, but it must be done."

She bent again to the flowers.

Rosalind was thoughtful that night. She was thinking of the taking away of the Hawaiian heritage and land. She was thinking of the fury of Lydia Pauahi's father, when his daughter betrayed him and her tribe by mating with an unworthy white man, Terry Darien. His son was half-*haole,* and Chief Pauahi had wanted to kill him.

Eileen was talking and laughing, vivid red dotting her cheeks as she strove for Peter's attention. Peter was responding, smiling back at her. Terry egged them on, casting little glances at Rosalind. Rosalind did not return them nor answer him.

In their bedroom later, Peter said, "What ails you, Rosalind?" He had a puzzled look on his face. "You have been acting strangely lately. Is the sun affecting you? You are out in the garden too long, I think."

Not bothering to speak, she shook her head and continued to slowly braid her hair, having already brushed out the glossy brown locks. "No, I'm used to the sun," Rosalind broke the silence. "I enjoy the garden and working with Aunt Honora."

"Then what is it?" Peter came behind her and placed his hands on her shoulders. She could not keep from stiffening, and he frowned into the mirror. "Aren't you happy?" he asked quietly.

Happy? She stared down at the brush in her hand. Happy? No, she certainly wasn't now.

"Sometimes you stare into space. What do you see?" he persisted. "What are you thinking?"

"Must you know my thoughts as well as . . ." she stopped abruptly. Her face flushed, which was a change from its recent pallor.

Peter's mouth tightened, but his thumb rubbed caressingly near Rosalind's slender throat. "I want to learn to know you better," he said, without anger. "How can I, if you will not open up your heart to me? We have been married almost three months, but we are still strangers to each other. What are you thinking when you stare at the sea, and do not hear us speak?"

"I am thinking of home," she said bluntly, bitterly, wishing to wound him as she had been wounded.

He flinched. "Home? This is home," he said quickly.

"I mean . . . my home, at the lagoon, where it was peaceful and quiet, and no one fought and said nasty things. We were so calm, father and Kinau and I."

He was silent for a minute, thinking. His thumb continued to stroke her shoulder. "Rosalind, all must change. You could not have remained there, removed from the world," he said, gently. "I had to take you away. You were not a native Hawaiian, to be satisfied with fish and *poi* and palm trees and a beach. There are depths in you, intelligence, a maturing woman. I could not leave you there."

She shook her head wearily. "But here, Eileen hates me, and Terry does also. And they hate you. I am not used to hate," she said, her eyes filling with tears. She tried to blink them back, but he saw them. "They will be happy only when they have driven me away."

His hands tightened on her. "No, that is not true," he said sharply. "They are my cousins, they want my happiness. . . ."

"Oh, Peter, don't be blind! They detest you also. They are destroyers! They want to destroy our marriage. They are trying every way they can to ruin it and will not stop at lies, at anything," she faltered, thinking with a shudder of Terry and the way he had held her.

He stared into the mirror at her face, his own dark and troubled. "That cannot be true. They welcomed you . . . Terry is always trying to follow you about, he flatters you. . . ."

"He despises me," Rosalind cut in flatly. "He thinks I am a goose to be such a fool as to believe anything he says. No, he hates me, so does Eileen."

"No, no, they like you. They will learn to love you. . . ."

She interrupted him passionately, turning on the vanity bench to face him. "Love does not destroy, love does not wish to hurt badly! It is hate that does that. Hate is wicked, it stings and punishes, and commits violence. That is what they do. It's obvious by their actions! Love is gentle, kind, wishing the best for the one loved. They do not wish me any good!"

He was silent for a time. Peter's hand caressed her cheek absently, as he thought over what she said. "You are upset," he said at last. "Come to bed, rest, you work too hard. I wish you would not work so long in the sun."

"You think the sun has addled my brain?"

"I don't know what to think," he responded in a barely audible voice. "I know cattle, ranching, a few other things. I am beginning to believe I am ignorant of women, especially my wife." He smiled a little, bending to kiss her gently. "But I shall delight in learning to know her better."

Rosalind followed him to bed only to lie there stiffly. Peter, however, put his arm about her, and coaxed her to his side. "Come, my dear, I shall not distress you tonight. But I want to hold you, and feel you sleeping against me," he whispered, against her neck.

She did feel better for sleeping, and slept hard that night. In the morning, Peter was still there when she wakened, and bent to kiss her mouth before he rose.

"You look more rested, my sweet. Stay in bed if you want. There is no need to rise so early."

"I'm fine," she said, and got up after he had washed and was dressed. She did feel better, for having spilled out her feelings. Perhaps he would take more seriously her warnings about Eileen and Terry.

Before he left the room, he said, "When the work lets up, I'll take you back to your home for a visit," and he smiled at her. "You will want to go with Kinau, and she will enjoy seeing her family again. I think you are both homesick, she goes about with a gloomy look to her. We could stay for a couple weeks. How about it?"

"Oh, I should like that, Peter." But after he had left, she sighed. She did not think a couple weeks would restore her to peace, not while they had to return to Darien and its problems.

Peter went out on the range, but returned early. He had been thinking all day about what Rosalind had said. Her words stuck like burrs in his brain. Hate. Terry and Eileen. But no, Eileen was always hanging on his arm, listening to him, laughing and pouting and paying him attention. He thought she was too fond of him, and he had had to be firm with her. And Rosalind thought Eileen hated him? Now Terry, he could believe. Terry was a troublemaker, and Peter had been cracking the whip over his head.

Rosalind's words kept ringing in his head. "They want to ruin our marriage, they want to destroy our marriage. They hate you, they are destroyers."

He stopped at the cottage of one of his *paniolos* on the way home, to confirm his suspicion. His cowboy was upset, and he told his boss plenty. Peter came home in anger, and looked for Terry.

He was not hard to find. He lounged on the patio, a drink in his hand, his clothes dusty from the range. His blue eyes mocked as he held up the glass in salute.

Coming from the stables, Peter halted before him. The others were not outside yet, so he could say what he wanted freely.

"You've been hanging around Dorisa again," he said, without preliminary.

"Dorisa?" mused Terry. "Which one is she?" There was a devil in the glint of the blue eyes.

"You know damn well! Her father is furious. He has arranged her marriage when she is a year or two older. I won't have you wrecking her life as you did Lydia's!"

"Mind your own business. Those native girls are

159

hot for it. They beg for it." Terry resumed drinking the rum and orange in a dismissive fashion.

"You *will* leave Dorisa alone! By God, I'll send you away to the mainland if you won't. You can try earning your own living, and see how you like it!"

"If I leave here, I'll take half the money from the ranch with me!" Terry sat up and set down the glass on the table with a bang. "Half the ranch is mine, and I'll take the money along, and see how you can manage then!"

"You don't own half, not even a fourth, not a tenth," responded Peter. "The money is your mother's, and it goes to her. And if you leave, you won't get one red cent! The shares will be divided eventually, but if you leave, you won't get any. Grandfather saw to that."

"Damn you to hell!" rasped Terry. "You can't do me out of my inheritance! A good hunk of this island and the cattle, the house, the jewels, belong to me, and you won't do me out of them! Think you're the big boss? You'll see!"

"If you don't settle down to work, and let the Hawaiian girls alone, you'll get sent away, and don't forget it!"

Terry settled back in his chair, and began to grin. "Oh, well, you have yours, why begrudge me what I can get? I don't blame you for enjoying your Rosalind, she's a sweet piece."

"Keep your tongue off my wife!" Peter did not raise his voice, but it rang ominously. He had never been so furious in his life.

Terry teetered on the back legs of the chair, smirking up at Peter: "You haven't seen her in the lagoon, have you, with her hair wet down her back, and riding the waves? By God, she has a terrific shape under that muumuu, all wet and plastered down. Curves in just the right places and those pretty brown legs. . . ."

Something seemed to explode in Peter's brain. He pushed at his cousin's chair, and it went over with a bang, dumping Terry onto the cement floor. The other man was up like a panther, the grin wiped away. He charged at Peter like a bull.

Peter was ready for him. He struck him on the cheek, and opened it with a slash of the ring on his finger. Terry struck back, they used to be evenly matched, but he was softer now. They fought, knocking over the tables, the drinks, the chairs, until women came to the doors. Kinau hung out the upstairs window, watching, her mouth agape.

Aunt Norma cried, "Boys, boys, stop it!" just as she used to. Peter did not even hear her. He was filled with blind rage and jealousy—that he should speak of Rosalind like that! Where had Terry seen her, in such a revealing manner? Peter struck out again, and connected with Terry's chest. The man went down, but came up once more, his fists ready.

Eileen screamed, "Someone stop them! Stop them! He's hurting Terry! Stop them, you fools!"

Peter vaguely heard Rosalind's voice, "Stop them yourself. Terry probably asked for it." She sounded cool and uncaring.

Peter's fist shot out and connected with Terry's jaw. The head snapped back, Terry went down in a heap. Eileen flew to him.

"You've killed him. You beast!" she screamed, and cradled her brother's limp head in her arms.

Corey, who was coming in from the stables, said, "My word, what a fight. What's going on? A little bet?" His bright curious eyes went from the limp unconscious man to Peter standing over him, nursing his bleeding knuckles.

Peter did not attempt to answer. He watched as Norma brought water, and bathed Terry's face, until the younger man sat up. He glared up at Peter as he came back to consciousness, and there was a sullen dangerous look on his face. At least he had stopped grinning, thought Peter.

Rosalind turned and went back inside. Kinau's head disappeared from the window upstairs. The maids clucked and giggled, and went indoors when Rosalind called to them.

Aunt Honora was watching them all thoughtfully. Glendon Corcy seemed oddly pleased, as the bruise on Terry's cheek turned red and purple.

"I say, you have taken a beating," said Mr. Corey, sympathetically.

"Go to hell," retorted Terry. He got up with his sister and mother helping, and limped heavily indoors.

One of the Hawaiian boys came out with a broom and dustpan and started cleaning up the broken glass, as Aunt Honora directed him calmly. She was setting up the chairs and tables again. Peter went inside, and up to his room to clean up.

It had been curiously satisfying. He had wanted to hit Terry like that for a long time. He had controlled himself, until now he'd only used words. But for pure satisfaction, there was nothing like a fistfight. He took off his filthy shirt, and examined his ribs curiously. Several bruises, but nothing broken. His face was unmarked, Terry had not connected there.

He was humming as he prepared for dinner. He felt good, as though a storm had come up and blazed over him, and gone again.

Then, staring in the mirror as he brushed his hair, he remembered Rosalind's broken words. "Terry hates you. Eileen hates you. They are trying to destroy our marriage."

Had Terry lied about seeing Rosalind at the lagoon? Peter, in his fury, had meant to question Rosalind about that. He decided it was just what Terry wanted, to cause a rift between them. No, Rosalind was loyal to him, and she detested and distrusted Terry. If his cousin had seen her, it was by no wish of Rosalind. Peter would keep his mouth shut, though he wanted very much to learn the truth.

To his surprise, Terry came down to dinner, prominent bruises on his cheekbones and flashing eyes. Peter kissed Rosalind's cheek as he came in. She was wearing his favorite rose dress, with soft lace at her throat and wrists.

"You look lovely tonight, my dear," he said placidly. Terry glared at them both.

"Thank you. Do you want a drink, Peter?"

"No, thanks. Later on."

They went in to dinner. Terry was sullenly quiet, brooding and wincing obviously. Aunt Norma showed him little sympathy. Eileen kept petting him and putting food on his plate, as though he were an invalid.

It was Corey's reaction which interested Peter tonight. The man seemed excited, stirred out of his torpor, strangely pleased by the fighting.

Peter thought about him. He often rode out alone, no longer with Hilohilo and Joe Smith. He asked few questions about the cattle. He should have left long ago. But he wanted something. What was it?

Well, patience would bring out the answers, Peter decided. He smiled down the long table at Rosalind, and she finally smiled back. It lit up the golden brown of her beautiful eyes and made her whole face radiant.

That evening, Peter played the piano again. His hands stung, but he didn't mind. He felt peaceful, happy. Rosalind brought her flute, and they played more Bach and Chopin. Terry left early, growling something uncomplimentary about the dull entertainment. Eileen followed him.

"I'll bring the salve, Terry darling," they heard her say.

Aunt Norma sat still in her chair, her fingers busily working at her tatting. She was making a lace tablecloth that would probably take years to complete. But she did not mind. Darien was her life, the house had been her domain, and she loved it. Peter glanced at her thoughtful face, and noted that she had not hastened upstairs after her son. Perhaps she also was tired of his tantrums.

Aunt Honora was crocheting and Alfred Murray was reading over a manuscript. Barton Darien was wheeled in, and sat listening to the music, his fingers beating time on the arm of the chair. Peter wondered if he knew about the fight. Probably, his Hawaiian boy told him most things. But he did not seem upset, rather satisfied.

Funny. Was Rosalind right? Had Terry been making trouble deliberately? He would not fall for that game again if he could help it. Peter flinched whenever he thought of that night he had taken her so cruelly.

As they played, Peter vowed not to make that mistake again. Rosalind was faithful, she was the loyal kind. She would not betray him, and he would not be fair game to Terry's lies again.

She reached forward to turn the page, and the light fragrance of plumeria drifted toward him from the lei she wore. How lovely she was, how gentle, how sweet. He would be more careful from now on. She belonked to him, and he would be as careful of her as of the most precious glass ornament in the Darien collection. She was worth more than anything in the world to him.

# 11

🌱 🌱 🌱 🌱

IT WAS A HOT SUNNY JUNE DAY when the conch shell echoed over the island of Darien. The Hawaiians stopped, turned grave with fear, then ran for their spears.

Peter rode back from the cattle, and Hilohilo and Joe Smith galloped to join him. Terry was nowhere to be seen. Peter stood on the dock in front of the massive white Darien home, and waited.

A long canoe was approaching, with half a hundred Hawaiian warriors paddling it. In the bow stood a chief, immense, tall, in a yellow feather cloak, with a tall headdress of leaves and small glistening golden feathers.

Peter knew him by sight and reputation, and a chill of fear and anticipation ran down his spine. He sent Smith for his rifle, and waited.

The women were at the windows of the house, they had orders to stay inside. Peter watched curiously as the boat came up. He thought they had not come to fight, they came openly. If they had wished a battle, they would have come with stealth, and brought a dozen such canoes. But the man was Chief Kaahumanu Pauahi.

As the craft drew up, two Hawaiians jumped into the water and dragged it onto the sand near the dock. Then the chief stepped out with dignity.

Behind him walked four other men, with their spears on their arms in ceremonial gesture. The Chief strode forward, alone, his hand upraised in the peace gesture.

Peter stepped forward. Behind him walked Hilohilo

and Joe Smith, one on either side, with weapons. Joe could draw and fire a revolver five times in less than thirty seconds. And he was no less deadly with a rifle. Peter had seen him in Texas, and he kept in practice even on Darien.

"I am Peter Darien. The Chief named Kaahumanu Pauahi is welcome to my island," said Peter deliberately, in slow and clear Hawaiian.

The chief's eyes flickered in acknowledgment, that the white man spoke his tongue. Although Hawaiian was his first language he knew some English.

"I am the Chief Pauahi. I do not come as an enemy, this time."

Peter bent his head in acknowledgment. He was over six feet tall, but the man towered over him. He must be at least seven feet tall, Peter thought, a bronzed giant, huge and powerful, in his prime, probably about forty years old. Bronzed arms rippled with muscle, his chest under the yellow feather cloak was scarred with spear marks, his broad face was calm and commanding.

"My daughter is dead and buried in the rocks and caves of the big island."

Peter bent his head again. He searched for what to say. "She died bravely, supporting her baby. She showed the courage, the honor, the nobility of her birth."

The chief was silent, his black gaze intent. Peter thought he saw a flicker of regret, of feeling on that hard face, then it was gone again, all emotion wiped out.

"Her son was not with her when my people found her and the three warriors who were dead with her."

"I have the son. He is a Darien, he will live here."

"He is my grandson."

Peter nodded. "He is also related to me. You have rejected him, as you rejected your daughter. So I shall keep him."

He folded his arms as he said this, and waited. If all hell broke out, he would just have to do his damndest. He was not going to give up Victor.

"If my daughter had lived, I would have received her again. My anger has cooled, as the volcanoes cool their fire when all is spent."

"Your warriors would have killed her and also the son, had I not reached her first. She died of hunger and thirst."

Hilohilo stirred uneasily. This man was a great chief, he should be treated with respect. If they gave up the boy, the Chief might forgive the Dariens.

Peter knew his mind, but would not listen to him. He had not listened when Hilohilo told him what he thought, in the past, about this matter.

"The son is well?" inquired the chief. "Or does he languish with the white blood in him?"

Peter recognized the insult, and his tone was dry as he replied, "He flourishes, and laughs, he grows rapidly. He is already attempting to walk upon his sturdy legs. His arms are strong. His tongue is ready, his cries are loud. He shall be a fine tall man one day."

The chief stood there, imposingly, in the hot sun, as though he did not feel anything. The sweat was running down Peter's back and his forehead. But he stood with his arms folded and waited.

"I would see this . . . sturdy son."

Peter gazed past the chief thoughtfully, toward the open blue sea. Did the chief mean to trick him, and take Victor away? Peter would fight for him, for the principle as well as the boy. He had vowed to Lydia to protect him, cherish him, and save him from all harm.

"I made my vow on my solemn oath that I would protect him," said Peter finally, his voice grave and thoughtful. He spoke slowly and clearly, so that all the Hawaiians would hear him.

Behind Peter came the Hawaiian cowboys. They had gathered, and now they walked forward slowly, with dignity, from where they had come on the open range. They carried their spears, they were ready to fight and to die if necessary.

"I wish to see the son of my daughter."

"The Princess Hoakanui Pauahi entrusted the son

to me. She put her hand on my head, and I bent my head, and vowed it. I held the child as she was dying, and upon him she put her gaze. She said to me, 'Keep safe my son, with your dying breath.' 'I will do it,' I said to her. 'I vow to protect the child Victor Darien, the son of the Princess Hoakanui Pauahi, to my death. So help me God.' And this I will do."

The chief had listened intently to all the words. Now there was a long silence of thoughtfulness and gravity on that beach. The Hawaiians seemed to hold their breaths. Inside the house, Rosalind held Victor to her, hugging him tightly. Would the chief fight to get his grandson? And if he did, if he got Victor, would he murder him as he had vowed, for the white blood in him? The chief's honor had been stained, would only more blood wipe it out?

The chief spoke again as Peter did not answer.

"I say on my sacred honor, and on the goddess Pele, that I shall not harm the child this day, nor attempt to take him from you. I shall not touch the child with my hands. I wish merely to see the child of my daughter."

Peter thought he caught a note of wistfulness in the voice. The impassive face of the chief did not change. He would not plead or beg. He was too proud for that.

Peter finally nodded his head. "I will bring out the child Victor that you might see the boy."

He turned and started back to the house. But Rosalind came out just then, through the opened great wooden door, carrying Victor. She wore a blue-green muumuu with a lei of plumeria about her neck. Her long dark hair was loose about her shoulders. The boy clung to her neck, and gurgled as Peter came to them.

Peter reached for the child, she shook her head. "I will carry him," she said in a low tone. "Then your hands . . . will be free."

She had courage, he thought, his heart swelling with pride in this woman who was his wife. She walked beside him with steady graceful step, in her grass slippers, only her fine carved features showing her white blood. She was tanned, her brown hair loose and straight. She might have been a Hawaiian woman, with the bouncing child in her arms.

She knew the danger. The chief might figure that his word to a white man was not worth keeping, he might seize Victor or kill him with his knife. Yet her head was high, her face proud and as free of worry as that of the chief. She had dignity, she moved with grace.

They came to stand before the chief, who had been watching them approach with his keen black eyes staring.

"This is my wife, Rosalind Murray Darien," said Peter. "She is the daughter of the man who writes out Hawaiian stories and songs so they will not be lost. She speaks Hawaiian, she sings Hawaiian songs to the boy. And this is the son of Princess Hoakanui Pauahi, Victor Darien."

The chief had been studying Rosalind with a straight keen look. Now his gaze went slowly, reluctantly, almost fearfully to the boy who clung to her. She turned him around so that he could see the immense giant of a man who stood about three feet from them. The baby's eyes widened, he stared upward. For a long moment, they gazed at each other, the black gaze and the baby brown gaze. The chief looked at the boy, his firm arms, the round face, the muscular legs and long feet. The baby seemed surprised at the vision before him, of the huge man, with the tall headdress of yellow feathers.

There was an intense silence on the sands before the Darien home. The Hawaiians peered curiously at the boy, not a murmur came from them. The chief stared at the child intently, looking him over from head to foot and back again. Peter watched the chief for any sign of treachery.

"Say Aloha, Victor," said Rosalind.

A babble of words came from the baby, in his unusually deep voice. Then he lunged forward, and touched the feathers of his grandfather's cloak. The bright colors had attracted him. The chief's arm moved, as though he would take the boy, or touch him.

Rosalind caught him back, not defensively, but holding him erect. Peter let out his breath. The chief did not grab at Victor, though Peter could practically see the longing in him to do so.

"He is . . . strong," said the chief, reluctantly.

Rosalind said clearly in Hawaiian, "Victor Darien will one day be a great chief of his Hawaiian people, but for now he is in our charge. He will learn the history of his people, the stories and the ways. And one day he will be great. Pele has promised this."

Peter glanced at her, taken off guard. He, like the others, was shocked. The gasps and whispers were quite audible.

The chief said, "I will take the boy and raise him. He shall be a prince."

Peter shook his head firmly. "I have promised the Princess Hoakanui Pauahi. The child will be in my charge."

"I want the boy!"

Pauahi's men murmured, the spears raised. Behind Peter the Hawaiians moved.

"Take Victor back to the house and stay indoors," Peter said to Rosalind in English.

"Wait!" ordered the chief, his hand upraised. "I will give you much for the boy. He is my only grandchild. I will give you the precious gems that you value. I will give you much sugar, cattle, what you ask. Only give me the boy."

"No, he is a Darien."

"He is Pauahi," said the chief firmly. "I take him!"

Rosalind moved backwards, and began to carry the child back to the house. Two Hawaiian young men behind the child moved forward and stopped her, one reached for the child, one moved to grab her arm.

Peter said, distinctly, "If anyone touches my wife or the boy, I shall kill him!"

The two men fell back. Smith had drawn his pistol, and held it lightly trained on the chief. The faces had clouded.

Peter said, "You gave your word you would not try to take the boy. Now, you may stay and have *luau* with us. We will feast and talk and be friendly."

"No," grunted the chief, staring at Victor as Rosalind carried him back to the house. "I do not eat with you."

"You will take water then, for the long journey. Fresh water," said Peter. The laws of hospitality were strong.

The chief shook his head. "No food, no water. We do not eat and drink with you. The boy is mine!"

"He remains here."

"You will regret this action," said the chief, and a fury began to blaze in his black eyes. "I will have the boy, very soon. But before I take him, much blood will be shed on the island of Darien! And you, Mr. Darien, you be first!"

"Those are words, not deeds," said Peter, his arms folded, his gaze steadily meeting that of the huge angry chief before him. "They mean nothing. I will keep only my word. There is no more to be said on the matter."

"I will have the boy! Today I go, for I gave my word!" and the chief turned abruptly, motioned to his men, and they parted to let him walk among them out to the canoe. He took his place in the long boat, and his men followed. Two of the number shoved the vessel into the water, and all picked up their paddles in unison.

As they began to move, the chief gazed toward where Rosalind stood at the entrance to the house, Victor in her arms.

"I shall return," he said in his powerful deep voice. "And then thunder shall rage, and rains pour, and fire strike! I shall call on the gods to avenge me and give me my grandson! My daughter shall be avenged! And you shall all feel my wrath!"

As the boat moved out, Peter suddenly felt the ground giving way beneath him. He lurched, caught himself, but several *paniolos* fell to the ground, crying out in fear.

171

An earthquake, a slight tremor, Peter's mind told him. But the superstition that ran through the islands and touched them all said differently. The chief had cursed them, and the ground had confirmed his words.

The chief watched their reaction, and a slight triumphant smile touched his large graven lips. "I come back soon!" he called threateningly, and shook his big fist. The canoe moved further out, it caught the waves and lifted above them, and the group paddled out beyond the coral reefs.

Hilohilo said, "The earth moved, Pele is angry!"

Peter's mouth tightened. "It was just chance," he said, as he watched the rapidly disappearing canoe.

He turned back then, to find the Hawaiians staring at him in fear. They seemed turned to stone as they crowded behind him. Only Joe Smith moved, to put away his pistol, his face in shadow under his huge sombrero.

Peter told Hilohilo curtly, "Take the men back to work. And post guards at all points on the islands, night and day."

"He will return," whispered Hilohilo, his eyes wide with fright and shock. "The earth moved when he spoke. Pele is with him! You should have given him the boy."

"Nonsense. I will keep Victor, he is a Darien. Go on back to work, everyone," said Peter, and gestured firmly. The men finally scattered, and he saw the women in the background, where they had watched and listened.

He went inside to the house's cool hallway. Kinau and Rosalind were standing together, as though protecting the child. Victor was sleepy, it was past his nap-time, and his head rested on Rosalind's shoulder. Peter caressed the curly hair, and the child opened his eyes and grinned sleepily, murmuring, "Da da."

"Did he say that to me, or is it my imagination?" asked Peter, surprised and pleased.

"He did," smiled Rosalind. "He has been saying 'mama' to me for several weeks now. What a smart boy," she crooned, pressing her lips to his forehead. "Smart boy, good boy."

"Take him up to bed. I'm going on out on the range," and he bent and kissed Rosalind's cheek, so near the brown one of Victor.

Her eyes shadowed. "The threat, and the tremor . . . oh, Peter, could Pele be on his side? She promised us. . . ."

"Now, don't be superstitious," he said, in a low tone. He saw the others peering from the drawing room, and Eileen's mocking expression.

"He threatened us, and the earth shook. Do you think that is superstition?" she asked gravely.

He sighed. "I can't answer that. It is probably coincidence, and it worked well for him. The earth shakes ever so often, you know that."

"Yes, and sometimes Pele makes the volcanoes erupt afterwards. Oh, Peter. . . ."

"There are no live volcanoes on Darien," he countered firmly. "The only ones are on the big Island, Hawaii. Don't worry, forget it, take the baby up to bed. And for goodness sake, don't let Kinau tell you all sorts of stories and scare you to death!" He grinned, caressed her cheek, kissed her mouth, and went out humming.

The chief had come and gone, with no danger. Perhaps if he came again, Peter could persuade him that Victor was safe in their charge. They might even become friends.

He thought of the events that had happened. Lydia Pauahi had been a spirited and demanding young girl. She had begged her father to let her come to Darien to learn white ways, to be the guest of the Dariens. He had reluctantly consented. Then Terry had chased—and caught her, enchanting her briefly, long enough to make a child. They had fled together when Peter bawled them out. Terry had returned alone, sullen, from a long drunk in Honolulu. It had been a time before Peter had discovered that Lydia had had the child, and had fled to the hills and caves to escape the wrath of her father.

Now Lydia was dead. Peter wondered a little, grimly, where Terry had hidden himself today. He was not a very courageous person, when it came to facing wrathful parents.

Just as well, the chief might have gone after Terry, and Peter would have been obliged to protect him. Well, that was over, the contact was made. The old chief had seen his grandson, and admired him, that was evident. One day, they might even be friends, and he would let the boy stay with his grandfather for periods of time.

That was the future. Now was the cattle range and the long hours of work to do. Peter swung into his saddle and started out once more. Four more hours of work, then he would come home to a cool drink, change of clothes, dinner, and the evening with Rosalind.

# 12

🌷 🌷 🌷 🌷

"I AM WORRIED, Kinau. Should we have given the child to his grandfather?" Rosalind asked, watching the sleeping little curled up body.

Kinau shook her head. "I think not," but she did not sound as sure of herself as usual.

"Chief Pauahi seemed to want him. And if Victor is to be brought up as Hawaiian. . . ."

"He might yet kill the baby. He still has the volcano of fury in his heart."

Rosalind sighed, and gently touched the small arm where it was twisted under his head. She straightened it, and he sighed and tried to turn over on his side. She turned him. Victor smiled a little vaguely, half-opened his eyes, and went to sleep again. He was such a good child, so strong and happy, so sweet and lovable. She would feel as if a piece of her heart had gone if he left.

But she must not consider herself, she must think of his future. "I wish I knew what to do."

"We could consult Pele again."

"How could we do that?"

They moved away from the baby's crib to talk freely.

"You could ask your husband to take us back to our home, that I may see my sons again, and my grandchildren. He would do it for you," smiled Kinau wisely, her eyes half-shut. She studied the pink peachbloom of her baby's cheeks. How lovely was Rosalind, now that she was opening up to the love of her man.

"He said when the round-up was over, he might

take us back to the cove for a couple weeks," admitted Rosalind.

"That will be in another few days."

"But how could we go out to the volcano?"

"It can be managed."

Rosalind went away thoughtfully. The more she considered it, the more difficulties there seemed. Peter might take her to the cove, yet she thought he was jealous of her longing to be alone there. And if they did go, how could she and Kinau go out to the volcano and consult Pele? Peter would not allow it, or he would take them and scoff at their superstition.

He did not believe in the Hawaiian gods. She was not sure how she felt herself. Yet she had seen their power, the strength of Pele as in wrath the goddess spewed forth the lava and fire from her home in Kilauea. She had witnessed the awesome power of the rain and wind storms blasting their way across the groves of palms and uprooting strong trees. She had felt the power of the ocean gods, pulling at hardy Hawaiian youths, and carrying them out to sea. How could one not believe?

The Christian god was all-powerful, she had been taught in the church. Yet the God Almighty they spoke of, the Jehovah, seemed so distant and aloof. She vaguely pictured him like one of the mission pastors, with white hair and a kind saintly face, good and absent-minded.

The Hawaiian gods were part of Nature, they were part of life itself on the islands. The rain gods were destructive, yet they were also kindly, bringing water for drinking and for the crops. The volcano goddess was cruel and merciless, yet good to those who were humble. Pele added to the land, with her flows of lava, and Hawaii grew yearly with her generous gifts. Rosalind had been so filled with stories from her babyhood that she scarcely knew what to believe. Her mind told her one thing, her heart told her another.

Yes, thought Rosalind, it would be a good idea to consult Pele, yet she must do it without letting Peter know. How could she manage that? She did not want to deceive him. The first step was to get back to the big island.

Peter seemed in a good mood that evening. They played music in the drawing room, then retired early. As she was brushing her long straight hair, Peter lay in bed on his side, watching her lazily in the reflection of the *koa*-wood rimmed mirror.

"What are you thinking about?" asked Peter.

Sometimes she resented it when he asked that. But tonight it was an opening. She clasped her brush to her.

"About . . . the cove," she said, hesitantly. "Kinau has been speaking of her sons and her grandchildren."

"She wants to go back home?" He was frowning slightly.

"For a short visit," said Rosalind. "Just to make sure they are well and happy. And I should like to go also."

He turned over and rested on his back, his hands behind his head. He did not speak for awhile.

"You said after the round-up," she reminded him, hastily.

"Yes. Yes. I was thinking about the chief. But I don't think he would come back so soon."

She turned around on the bench. "Do you think he will come back . . . with warriors?"

"Perhaps he might. But I shan't worry about it. He'll cool down. I think we could be friends," said Peter thoughtfully. "He is a man of honor, he keeps his word. I can understand how he feels, Lydia was his favorite child. And Victor is a worthy grandson."

She felt relieved. "Oh, I hope we can be friends. He could come and visit the child at times, and know that we take every care of Victor," she said earnestly.

"And you . . . you want to go back to the cove?"

"Yes. I should like to . . . to see the house again, and Kinau's people, and the mission people. All my friends," she said, avoiding his steady look.

"Well, perhaps we might. I'll think about it, and

see about managing things. I don't think I'll put Terry in charge. I might put Nick Darien in charge," he said, with a frown. "Terry is irresponsible. Yet Nick is so damn shy, he hasn't come up to the house for a month."

"Doesn't he . . . like to come here? Is it me?" She stood, took off her robe, and came to the bed.

"You? No, all women," he said wryly. "Terry can't leave women alone, Nick can't come near them. What a family!" He watched her lean over and blow out the lamp beside the bed, then held the mosquito net so she could get in. As she lay down, he put his arm hungrily about her.

She relaxed with relief against him. He had not said he would refuse to go. Perhaps they would leave, and soon.

Peter set his affairs in order, and gave Nick the responsibility of the cattle, and set Joe to guard the house. He had a quarrel with Terry when he told his cousin he must obey Smith. But Peter shrugged it off, and went off with a quiet conscience on the steamboat with Rosalind, Kinau, and Akela the following week.

Akela was enraptured at the idea of seeing her family again. Her lovely face glowed as she helped Rosalind unpack in the cabin. "Ah, how they have missed me," she said dramatically. "They will weep and laugh all at once!"

"I know they will. You must remain with them for the time we are there," said Rosalind. "You must have a good long feast, and tell them you do well with us."

"Yes, yes, I will tell them of your kindness. And Mr. Darien, who gives me much money to give to my family. He is of a great heart!" said Akela joyfully.

Victor, after much thought and planning, was left on Darien. Aunt Honora had solemnly assured Rosalind she would look after him, and so would Aunt Norma. One of the older Hawaiian girls, from a large family, would see to his meals and sleep. She had already started helping Kinau in his care. Joe Smith had his orders, if the chief should return. But Peter did not think the big Hawaiian would cause problems in the near future. Even if he meant to attack, he would need time to prepare his warriors, gather the long canoes, and prepare for the expedition. It was one thing to sail to Darien for a day. It was another to plan a siege.

They reached Kailua the next day about noon. A crowd came to greet the boat, and among them was a relative of Akela, who greeted her jubilantly and took her in charge. It seemed they met every boat in hopes of hearing from her. Rosalind saw her off, promised to call for her when they were ready to leave again.

It was mid-afternoon before their gear had been taken from the steamer, and they were at the hotel. Rosalind and Kinau wanted to hire a carriage immediately, but Peter teased them for their impatience.

"You women! I want to send word to Hoke that we are coming. It takes time to hire two carriages. And you want to be off right now on the nearest donkey, I suppose!"

He settled them firmly at the hotel, and would not hear of leaving until the next morning.

But the next morning did come, although the two women had felt it never would, and they set out. Rosalind's eyes shone as they came closer to her old home. She would see it all soon, her dear cove, the dear house where she had been born, Kinau's family. She watched and watched, then cried out, "There is the black cliff! I can see it!"

Peter watched her indulgently, and clicked at the horse to encourage it to go a little faster. Presently, the lovely curve of beach that circled some of the blue-green waters lovingly came into view. And then the house, recently painted, with the green shutters, the green roof, the open veranda. And Kinau's whole family running out to greet them, the grandchildren jumping up and down and screaming!

Rosalind almost fell out of the carriage before it stopped. She grabbed the nearest boy and hugged him. He was beaming from ear to ear. Hoke came forward ceremoniously, a broad smile on his big kind face, and shook both her hands. Then he was helping his mother down and hugging her fiercely.

Everyone talked at once. Above the din, Peter arranged for the luggage to be carried into the house. Hoke's family had moved out for them, generously, and set up a couple of shacks to live in for two weeks. Rosalind went back to the bedroom she had lived in so many years, and tears filled her eyes. It was so dear, so familiar, with the view out over the bay, and back to the dark protective cliffs behind the little house.

"Not here," said Peter gently, in the doorway. "Hoke has set up a big double bed in your father's room."

Reluctantly, she left the small chamber, and went to see what the arrangements were. It seemed odd to think that Peter had the right to make these plans for her. And to sleep with him every evening still seemed a little strange to her. Sometimes she wakened in the middle of the night, having dreamed she was back home in her narrow bed, only to find herself in the wide bed at Darien with Peter, his dark head on the pillow beside hers, his arm possessively across her body.

Hoke had set up a *luau,* and the smell of the food was enticing. They sat down to a feast at noon, which lasted from afternoon till dusk. They laughed and sang, and related what they had done all these months. They talked and wondered at each other, and how the smallest children had grown.

They had roast pig which had been cooking in a firepit, covered with leaves, since early morning. There was also *poi,* and tiny fish from the sea, sweet potatoes, corn, plantains. When they were stuffed full, they lay back and talked. Presently the women brought around more food, sweets, and fruits. They ate the fresh mango, papaya, and chunks of dripping sweet pineapple. With the fruits they ate some coconut pancakes with coconut syrup.

They talked more, ate more, drank coconut milk, sweet and chilled. It was like the old days, only Peter lounged beside Rosalind, and his sundarkened face gleamed in the firelight. Everyone looked at him with great respect and listened to his words.

She felt happy for the first time in months, truly deeply happy. There was no fear here in the cove, it was blessed with the lovely memories of the past, the sunshine of her growing up, the friendship of Kinau's people. A small girl fell asleep with her head on Rosalind's lap, and she stroked the thin shoulders, thinking of Victor.

Finally the day ended, and night fell in purple splendor, with bright stars pricking the velvet of the sky. The children were led off to bed, the adults also grew sleepy, and drifted away. The men doused the fires before they, too, left.

Rosalind was reluctant to go inside, it would feel stuffy after the fresh cool air, the sand of the beach, the breeze, and scent of palms and plumeria.

But she did go in, and went to bed, sleeping so deeply that when she wakened the sun was already high. She got up hastily and found Peter sitting on the veranda, lazing in the sunlight, his eyes half-closed to the brightness.

He turned his head and smiled. He looked more peaceful than usual, as though he did not have a hundred worrisome things on his mind.

"Hello, darling. Want to swim before breakfast?"

"Oh, yes, I should like that."

"Kinau has shooed away the children, they won't come back for a time," he said, and they went down to the water. Unselfconsciously he shed his trousers and shirt, and walked into the waves with only a short pair of underpants on. She went back for her sarong, and wrapped it about herself, then ran down the beach to join him, diving into the water with delight. He laughed as he saw her.

"My petite wife is half-fish," he teased, and splashed water on her back. They swam together far out to the breakers, and he was amazed when she stood up and rode a wave in.

She laughed back at him, happily. "Oh, I have

swum in these waters since I was a baby. Hoke taught me to ride the waves."

They rode another wave in, and another, and then rested in the sparkling warm waters. She gazed up at the black rocks behind them, and thought of the night that Peter had slid down that cliff, the baby Victor in his arms, seen the light in the house and come there for shelter.

He must have been thinking about it also. As they lay on their backs, he said, "I was almost done for that night, with the storm, and the exhaustion. I was beginning to think I could not make it. Then a light flared below. I thought I was seeing things. But I soon realized it was a lamp in a house. I made it down the cliff. . . ." He shook his sleek wet head. "I don't remember much about it, except falling in that door, and seeing you, sitting there reading, and the calm sweetness of your face. I thought you looked like an angel, and I was having feverish dreams."

"I remember," she said softly. "I could not sleep for the storm, and got up to read for a time. If I had not . . . If I had not lit the lamp. . . ."

"I would have found you anyway," he said positively. "It was fate that brought us together."

Fate? She wondered if it was fate, or if that might be another word for the storm god. Someone had brought Peter to her, and small Victor.

And her whole life had changed completely.

They went in, and hungrily ate the magnificent breakfast Kinau had prepared. She was laughing and chuckling over something Hoke had told her.

"You are happier, eh?" asked Peter, looking up from his scrambled eggs and pork. "You see your family again? I should have brought you before."

Kinau patted his shoulder. "You have much work to do. Now I am with my children again, and we are happy. Time works out all matters. I am gone long, they miss me more," she said wisely.

They would be here two weeks. But already Rosalind began to worry about how they would get out to the volcano without Peter finding out and stopping them. He might think it too dangerous to approach the volcano.

They lazed the day through, sleeping on the sand in the afternoon. They wakened toward evening, to find Hoke and the others preparing another feast. They would all eat together on the beach, and talk and sing and make music.

A couple of days passed. Rosalind felt more relaxed. Peter also seemed to have benefited from the holiday. He grew even more bronzed, playing in the water half the day, or lying on the beach except in the hottest times. They sat on the veranda and talked, or were silent, in companionship they had not felt so closely before.

After the heat of the afternoon, one day, Peter and Rosalind went into the azure ocean. Hoke considerately left the beach to them, he and his family went further down the coast to another inlet. Kinau had gone with them that day, to talk and inspect the houses of her daughters-in-law, and make suggestions. They listened to her with respect. Did she not have a high position in the house of the Dariens, with charge for the grandson of a great chief?

The sun had been burning hot, and Rosalind felt ready to soak in the cooling waters of the lagoon. She had wrapped her sarong about her, loosened her hair, and enjoyed the water, splashing vigorously, until she felt refreshed. Finally she returned to the beach, and lay back in the cool shade of a coconut palm.

Peter followed her after a time, and flung himself down beside her. "This has been good," he said contentedly.

"I am glad you have enjoyed it. Kinau's children are good to us."

Peter lay on his side, facing her, his damp head on his arm. "I have been subtly trying to find out what to give Hoke in return for his hospitality," he said, with a rueful smile. "He told me finally that he wished for nothing, he was very happy!"

"Yes, he is. He wants nothing."

"I still want to thank him. What do you suggest?"

She thought, frowning. "Perhaps more chickens for his run," she suggested. "He likes to raise them. If he had more, he could sell some. Or another pig."

"I'll see about it. I have to go into Kailua one of these days on business. I'll talk around at that time, and see what I can find."

He put his arm across her, and began to unfasten the sarong.

"Peter!" she said, her hand over his, to protect the garment. "Not here. . . ."

"No one is around. And you look so lovely with your wet hair all down about you."

His hand unfastened the sarong, he bent over her as he drew it back, to reveal her softly rounded body. She flushed at the look in his dark eyes, the demanding possessive look she dreaded, yet half-welcomed. He had not been cruel after that one night, yet sometimes she felt stiff with him, a bit afraid.

He leaned to kiss her brown shoulder, then moved his lips gently to her plump breasts. He took a nipple in his lips and pulled at it. She felt the response beginning inside her, as his large hand moved down her body to her thigh.

The long fingers caressed her deliberately, slowly. She squirmed a little as he went on, and her breath came more quickly. His lips returned to her mouth, and he opened her lips with his, and thrust his tongue inside, to play around with her tongue. The heat of his body burned against hers. He reached down and ripped off his underpants, and he was hard against her softness.

Both hands played with her, stroking over her shoulders and arms, over her breasts, as he kissed her. He murmured love words in English and Hawaiian, the music of them playing over her as he did.

"You never say words to me," he murmured, nibbling at the lobe of her ear.

"Speak to you?"

"Love words," he amplified, and gave her another sharp little nip. It sent shivers down her spine.

"I . . . I don't know . . . what to say. . . ."

"Say the words, darling, love, honey," he coaxed.

"D-darling . . ." she stammered.

"Good. And another. . . ."

"L-love. . . ."

"And more. . . ."

*"Hiwahiwa,"* she murmured shyly. He kissed her, and she repeated the words with a sigh. "Oh, *ipo,"* she whispered. *"Ipo."*

He kissed her more passionately, and there were no more words. His body moved over hers, he held himself over her with his elbows in the sand, and his muscular movements sent thrills of delight singing through her body. His thighs were so hard and taut, moving on her rounded softness. His arms moved under her, and he held her to him closely, his head buried in her shoulder, and he moved his face against her thick hair.

The sand beneath them moved as they moved, and they dug deeply into it as their passion increased. He pressed hard and she held him closely to her, her fingers digging into the muscles of his back, playing over his spine, and the arch of his body. Then she cried out, softly, as delight spun her into quivering response. She was shaking as he finished, and finally reluctantly drew off.

"Oh, you are beautiful, my lovely," he whispered. "Your cheeks are pink as the hibiscus flower, you are fragrant as the plumeria, you are carved to delight the eye and the body. How I adore you, from your head to your delicate toes," and he stroked his hands over her in what she would have considered a brazen manner only a few months ago.

They were both covered with sand when they were finally done. He laughed, and drew her with him, naked as they were, down to the waters, where he enjoyed bathing her teasingly, while she protested and tried to push him away, and laughed at his attentions with the blushes burning her face.

When they were tired, they lay again on the beach,

and she wrapped the sarong about her, in spite of his protests, and they slept until dusk.

Kinau returned when the lamps were lit in the drawing room. She had had a good day with her family, and she sang as she prepared the evening meal. Rosalind came out to help her.

"You look happy and womanly," said Kinau slyly. "You have a good day also alone with your man?"

"Oh, Kinau!" Rosalind began to blush all over again, and Kinau laughed at her lovingly.

"You both need this time. You need time alone together, with no bad words darting at you like spears," said Kinau wisely, briskly chopping up the taro root. "You go sit with your man, and talk or read, and be happy. I fix the meal. You go on, Lokelina. Your man wants you beside him."

She pushed Rosalind out of the kitchen firmly. Peter looked up from the newspaper as Rosalind shyly joined him.

"She doesn't want help," said Rosalind, avoiding his eyes. She sank down on the sofa, and he promptly came over to sit beside her, casting the newspaper away as he came.

"Fine, I can kiss you until dinner, then," he said, and proceeded to begin. She pushed him away, her hands on his broad shoulders, and he laughed down at her and kept his arm about her.

The serenity of the evening could only have been enhanced by the inclusion of Victor. If they could stay here, away from Darien, away from Eileen's malice and Terry's deviousness, then they could be content.

But Peter would not be happy long. He was a man who must work hard and achieve high goals. He had been brought up to manage Darien and would never be happy for very long away from it.

Peter began to talk about other holidays they would take. "I want you to see Europe," he said. "There are so many places you would enjoy—concerts, operas, recitals. You would like that so much. You respond to beauty. I long to show you Italy, and Greece."

Rosalind's eyes widened as he talked on, enthusiastically. It did not seem possible she would ever see these places he described.

"And America," he said. "San Francisco is a fascinating city. The buildings are tall and brilliantly lit, and the women very fashionable. We shall buy you dresses, with lace and silk and jewels, and you shall outshine them all!"

"Oh, Peter," she said soberly. "I am not even pretty."

He looked at her, and slowly smiled, and shook his head. "Not pretty—beautiful. And properly outfitted, you will make all heads turn. I can see you with diamonds in your hair and ears, or emeralds on a green silk gown. . . ."

When he talked like that, it frightened her. She would enjoy seeing those places, but she would rather observe from a dark corner, and watch everything that was going on. Like a little shy lizard on the wall of a house, with its bright eyes looking everywhere, she thought. Not like the belle of the ball, as he described. That sounded more like Eileen Darien.

A couple of days later Peter decided to go into town. He would start early in the morning, and come back by evening. He wanted to order some goods and have them ready by the time they departed for Darien. The days were slipping away, a week had already gone by.

Kinau spoke quietly to Rosalind as they were in the kitchen that night. "Tomorrow, when your man goes off to Kailua, we go out to take gifts to Pele."

"Oh . . . can we?" gasped Rosalind, the fruits dropping from her hands. She grasped the table edge, as though feeling the world rocking under her feet. "What if he finds out?"

"The carriage is good and light, the horse is fast. Hoke will drive us. As soon as it is light, Mr. Darien goes. Then we go, with offerings. And come straight back. If we have to stay overnight," she shrugged, "then we stay over, and tell Mr. Darien we go for a drive to see friends. But we must go, I feel it in my bones."

Rosalind finally nodded, but she felt scared. So far she had not done anything against Peter's will or knowledge, though she had defied him at times.

The next day, Peter left as he'd planned. He was cheerful, and full of ideas. He wanted Rosalind to come with him, but she refused.

"Very well, I'll smother you with surprises," he threatened. He teased her chin and kissed her lips.

"Please, Peter, no more! I don't need anything."

"But I enjoy seeing you enveloped in beauty. I like that pink dress you're wearing today. Did you put it on for me?" he murmured in her ear.

She smiled, and looked away shyly. Soon he was ready, and went out to the carriage.

As soon as the sound of Peter's carriage had died away, Hoke brought another carriage around, with a powerful gelding fastened to the traces. Kinau hurried about, and put her large baskets, blankets, and bottles of fresh water and coconut wine into the carriage. Rosalind climbed in, a scarf about her against the cool morning breeze. It was scarcely daylight, and she was frightened. Something told her that there was going to be difficulty. But she must consult Pele, Kinau was sure of it.

The journey was long. As before, Kinau whiled away the time with chanting, and telling the old stories, especially those of Pele. Even though she had heard them numerous times before, Rosalind was still interested in them.

They did not pause for long at lunch, eating hastily, so that by early afternoon, they had reached the canyon road around the rim of Mount Kilauea. Rosalind noted uneasily the steam that rose from the Crater Road, the noxious smell of sulfur.

There was a rumbling in the earth beneath their feet when they got down from the carriage. Hoke led the horse and carriage back a distance, looking uneasily over his shoulder at them.

Kinau had grown silent as they approach. Her broad smile had been replaced by a troubled expression.

She took the wreaths of plumeria and red ginger they had made on the way, the coconut wine. Then they cautiously made their way up to the rim, until they could see into the red-hot heart of the burning crater.

There was a deep rumbling beneath which had not been there before. Rosalind licked her dry and parched lips, nervously.

Kinau began to chant and sway on the edge. She was calling on the goddess Pele. "We need advice," she was saying. "We need your approval and wisdom, oh, Pele," she was singing. "Give us counsel, and bless us in our adventures. Bless the child Victor, who is of your own people and kin."

The rumble increased. Rosalind threw in the leis, and they were consumed into burning ashes before they had gone a dozen feet. Kinau tossed in the wine, and the bottles exploded as they touched the hot lava. Kinau kept on singing, even as the sulfur odor increased.

Hoke shouted, and they turned to listen. He was pointing frantically to the cindery road they had taken.

In the path had sprung up little tongues of flame!

The volcano was going to erupt!

Kinau grabbed her arm, and they began to run toward the carriage. Hoke had untied the horse, and was soothing it. The horse reared, trying to get away, but Hoke was able to hold it through sheer force.

Several times they had to jump over the leaping fires. Suddenly the earth cracked open before their steps.

"The goddess is angry! Pele is angry with us!" Kinau gasped, and pulled at Rosalind to hurry.

They skirted the flaming patches and yet more appeared on either side of them. At the carriage, the small group jumped in, and the frantic gelding needed no urging to quicken its pace, causing the carriage to jerk and bump over the rough earth.

Then the volcano gave a mighty roar, and flames shot a hundred feet into the air. Rosalind glanced back, felt the heat on her face, and saw the molten lava begin to fall over the lip of the crater toward them!

The horse raced faster and faster. But while they might escape the relatively slow moving lava, there seemed slight chance at avoiding the dry earth that was cracking all about them.

Kinau held to the arm of the carriage, prayers for safety whispered under her breath. Her face had turned almost green. Rosalind felt terrified to death. They had done wrong to come—but they had had to. Yet Pele had been angry!

Hoke shouted and pointed straight before them. About two hundred yards ahead the road narrowed and the earth had split apart with tremendous flames rising from the crevice.

They were cut off. There was no way around. And the lava would pour down slowly, relentlessly, cutting them to burning pieces, as it did the trees and shrubs in its path. A horrible, slow death.

# 13

❧ ❧ ❧ ❧

PETER HAD FINISHED his errands in Kailua, commissioning a dozen more dresses for Rosalind to be finished by the time they left within a week. He ordered a half a dozen chickens and two pigs to be sent to Hoke after they had left. Also he stopped in to see Mr. Chan, the jeweler.

He ate a quick lunch, then began the long drive back to the cove. For some reason he felt uneasy. He was away from Rosalind, and he tried to laugh at himself for feeling odd about it. She would be there, playing with Kinau's grandchildren, waiting for him when he returned.

Yet something urged him on. He arrived in early afternoon to discover the house strangely still. Perhaps Kinau and Rosalind had gone down the beach to the homes of the others.

He tied up the carriage, leaving the horse in the traces. He strode over to the house and called, "Rosalind!"

A small boy popped around the side of the house, gave him a wide grin. "Hello, Mr. Darien! *Aloha,* hello, *aloha,*" he repeated, proud of his English.

"Hello, there. Where is Kinau? Where is Rosalind Darien?"

"They go to Pele."

Peter felt the blood drain from his head. He caught the boy by the shoulder. "Where is your father?" he asked, chokingly.

The lad pointed. A young man, a younger brother of Hoke, strolled along the beach. Peter ran to him.

They met on the sands. The young man looked unusually serious.

"Where is Rosalind? Where is Kinau?"

"They go to consult with Pele. I stay here until their return."

"Where did they go?" asked Peter again, cold with impatient fear. He had had this horrible feeling—was he in a nightmare? Would he wake to find Rosalind beside him, sleeping peacefully? No, the sun shone down with brazen warmth, the wind rippled the waves of the sea.

"To the mountain of Pele, to Kilauea," replied the man, pointing. "They go early this morning, with offerings of flowers and wine. Kinau, she say they must consult Pele today. I think it is bad, for the white rises above Pele's head, and she is not at peace."

Peter looked off in that direction. His eyes were not so keen as those of the Hawaiian, but he could see something like soft, smoky clouds in that direction.

"I must go to them," he muttered.

"Yes, they may need help," Hoke's brother agreed. "I tell Hoke that the ground tremble, but he shake his head. Kinau must go, and he will take her, he says."

Frantically, Peter unfastened the horse and jumped into the carriage.

"Follow the path, and if you doubt you will look ahead to Mount Kilauea!" The man shouted after him.

"Thank you," Peter managed, and waved his hand. The man gazed anxiously after him, while holding the small hand of his son.

The drive was long and hot. Even before he could see Mount Kilauea clearly he saw the deep fissures and smelled the heavy stench of sulfur. Oh, the fools, to go like this! He was furious and wild with rage. To go off, as soon as his back was turned! The knowledge that Rosalind had not confided in him, had mentioned nothing of her plans, injured him greatly.

It stung deeply that she did not trust him. She did not speak willingly to him of her thoughts. He had to pry and poke, and often she resented it. Rosalind was a private person, unused to confiding, he reflected. He must be gentle with her—but damn it, this was the end of his gentleness! If she would not tell him of something so momentous—dashing into danger —she must be protected from her impulses!

He had been riding for several hours, and dusk was coming. Ahead of him, red flames showed against the blue dusk. His heart beat heavily, he felt choked by the fumes and the craziest fear he had ever known. If she were dead—she might die in this—and if she were gone—

His own life would be over, he thought. Yes, he would go on working, driving himself and others, but nothing would remain alive inside. He knew that now. His wife meant too much to him, she was part of him, like a vine that wound tightly around the trunk of a tree, a part of it, with orchids delicate and pale against his sturdiness, making beauty where all had been barren before.

Then, unexpectedly, ahead of him he saw something blazing. Putting the lash to the horse, the weary animal responded to the command, running faster. Peter's mouth was grim and hard, his eyes strained to see in the quickly descending darkness.

Abruptly, he had to rein in, because fire blocked the entire path, along with boiling lava on both sides of the road.

Just a few feet further on the carriage was burning!

Hoke was holding the freed horse, trying to calm it. Kinau clutched the baskets, Rosalind looked across the gap and saw him.

"Peter! Oh, Peter!"

He leaped across the inferno, as though he did not even feel the heat. He stepped directly on one flame, and his boot cracked, but he did not notice. He ran to her, grabbed her arm. "Come on," he tersely commanded the others. They followed him, Kinau running in her light sandals, Hoke dragging the reins and bit of the frightened horse. They raced across the fires that flared in their path. Rosalind's breathing was ragged. Kinau cried out as fire bit at her. She lifted up her skirts and seemed to fly. Hoke brought the animal he would not abandon.

At last they made it safely to the second carriage. Peter tossed Rosalind into the seat, quickly lifted Kinau also, then grabbed the reins, in order to steer the vehicle back to the path that he had just come up. Already the flames were almost beneath the wheels. Behind them Mount Kilauea rumbled, spewing sparks into the air, the ominous steaming, reddish lava pouring down the lip of the crater, toward the mountain's incline.

Peter raced alongside the carriage, the reins biting into his palms. Hoke ran ahead of him with the other horse. Once they were clear of the flames, Peter paused long enough to leap into the carriage.

He yelled at Hoke, "Now ride him!"

Hoke nodded, and mounted the saddleless horse, gripping its flanks with his knees. He got out of there like a frightened streak of lightning. Peter urged his horse on after him. Still ahead of them, they could see some cracks in the earth, but they were not so bad.

The air grew purer, the sulfur odor lessened. Peter took a deep breath, and slowed down the tiring horse to a walk. He finally looked over at Rosalind, his eyes steely.

"When we get home, you'll explain to me what the hell you are doing out here!" he growled.

Briefly, she leaned her head against his bare arm that had burn slashes on it. "Oh, Peter, I thought we would die!" she whispered.

They were all three crushed together on the seat, Peter between the two women. Kinau said, "Pele would not let us die, but she is angry with us. And I brought offerings to her, and praised her!"

Peter bit off the words he wanted badly to yell at them both. That would wait. He drove on, into the star-lit night.

The earth trembled for several seconds. Earthquake, he thought, but Kinau cried out, and began to chant. They drove on, more slowly, the horses being close to exhaustion. But he would not stop for a rest, the situation was too dangerous.

Rosalind offered him a bottle of cool water, which they both drank from. Kinau was too absorbed in her chanting, swaying back and forth.

Finally Kinau said, broodingly, "Much trouble comes yet to us. Pele is not happy with us. Much danger comes, and we must be ready for it. Life is not easy, life must be fought bravely. We must have the hearts of sharks, and be ready to fight our enemies, from wherever they come."

"From where does it come?" asked Rosalind.

"From all around us, it comes near and does not leave. It is as close as our hands and feet, so says Pele. Danger and trouble, and we cannot see it until it attacks with the teeth of the shark."

Peter wanted to shiver, but he braced himself. He felt Rosalind trembling beside him. He wanted to bark out that it was all superstitious nonsense.

Yet only this afternoon, Peter himself had felt uneasy and worried. He had returned early to the cove, because something told him there was danger! What was that, if not superstition? Could it be that there were gods that warned of trouble? Did Almighty God watch over them so closely that He could warn them of danger?

And if God could do that, why not the gods of the Hawaiians, who were in a manner even closer to nature? Peter pondered the question, but found no answer. If he had not returned early, if he had lingered until evening. . . . He wanted to shudder. He did not think that Hoke would have been able to save his mother, or Rosalind.

And Rosalind would have been lost to Peter forever! Burned to death, choked on the sulfur fumes and lack of air. Her lovely body turned to ash. Her beautiful mind and heart gone back to its maker. Lost forever to Peter.

It was long past midnight when they returned to the cove. Hoke slid down stiffly from his horse. Cooking fires had been lit on the beach, his brothers and other

relatives hovered around them. Even the children remained, the youngest sleeping uneasily on the sand,
the older ones waiting up gravely with their parents.

All came to help. One man took Hoke's horse, another two took the carriage and horse, petted the other
animal, unfastened it from the traces, soothed it, took
it away for food and water and rest. Others helped
Kinau and Rosalind down, and even Peter, who was so
tired he felt he would fall.

"You are safe, we have been praying for you," said
the man simply, who had spoken with him earlier.

Kinau had no words, she was limp and her head
hung down. Rosalind stumbled as she walked to the
house. A woman waited with fresh water, food they
had prepared which Rosalind tried to refuse.

Peter said sharply, "You will eat and drink. Have
some tea, you need something."

She brushed her dirty hand over her face. She
looked so dazed he could not scold her more tonight.
But tomorrow, damn it! He would tell her what he
thought, and how she must act in future!

They washed, ate a little, and fell into bed. He felt
Rosalind tossing and turning, moaning in her sleep.
His arms and legs stung from the burns, he had put on
some salve quietly, not to draw attention to himself.
But he slept little.

He wakened early, unable to lie still any longer. He
went out to swim in the lagoon and the salt water
stung him even as it refreshed. He sat on the sand and
smoothed more salve onto his legs and arms, the burns
ran in ugly red streaks over his flesh. But he was alive,
and so were they. He sat there, gazing out over the
peaceful lagoon. In the air were ashes from Pele,
from Mount Kilauea. They were spilling over the
island.

Later, he went back into the house. Rosalind was
just rising. Kinau had taken fresh water to her, and he
heard them talking in low serious tones. He sat down
in the dining room, his head on his hands at the table.

Kinau came out, gave him a fearful look. "I fix good

food for you, and hot tea," she said briskly, and bustled out to the kitchen.

Feed the brute, he thought wryly. They knew he was furious.

But that would not let them off.

Rosalind came out, looking fresh in a pink dress. She was barefoot, and he looked at her feet.

"Yes, they are burned a little," she said defensively. Then she saw his arms. "Oh, Peter," she cried out. "You are burned, and so badly!"

"And my legs," he said grimly. "But that is nothing. I'll talk to you later, and to Kinau."

She put her hand gently on his shoulder above the angry red streaks. "I would not have you hurt," she whispered.

"Then how do you think I feel about you getting yourself killed?" he barked.

She looked puzzled, her golden brown eyes wounded. "But I was not killed," she said softly.

"You could have been! Didn't you realize your danger? You could have been nothing more than a pile of cinders!" He felt a little dizzy when he thought of it. "My God, Rosalind, why the hell did you go out there? Hoke's brother had warned you, the earth had been trembling, he had seen smoke over Mount Kilauea. The volcano was rumbling for days, it was ready to erupt!"

"We had to consult Pele," said Rosalind, her lower lip trembling slightly.

"Consult Pele!" said Peter grimly. "I'll give you consult Pele . . . hell! Don't you ever do that again! I won't have you listening to that damn nonsense and getting yourself killed! Kinau!" he bawled, knowing well that the woman was listening in the kitchen.

She put her frightened face in the doorway.

"Kinau, if you ever again take Rosalind with you, or think of such a trip, I'll . . . I'll skin you alive! By God, I won't have her in danger for such damn foolishness!"

She looked stubborn. "I not want my baby in danger," she said with dignity. "But it is not foolish. Pele warned me of trouble. Even though she is upset, she was good enough to warn me and thank us for our offerings! It was a good journey. I know the danger comes, and we must be ready for it."

Peter put his head in his hands in utter exasperation. He knew when he came up against the rock of their beliefs he could not win. But to draw Rosalind in too . . . he could not endure that! He had to stop them.

Kinau said, "You feel better when you eat something hot, Mr. Peter," and she withdrew with dignity.

"Let me put something on your burns, Peter?" asked Rosalind, her hand stroking over his tender skin.

"I did," he said abruptly, his head still in his hands. "Rosalind, do you understand the seriousness of what you did? Do you realize you would have died?"

"Yes, Peter," she said, quietly, and sat down opposite him, looking at him with her smoky amber eyes. "But I had to do it, and if I had to go again, I would risk the danger. It was important. Kinau learned we are in danger. We must be careful, and take every care of Victor and ourselves while on Darien."

"Don't you think I know that without running through fire and sulfur?" he snarled.

She looked at him, then down at the plate that Kinau brought in at that moment. He had hurt her, but damn it, he had been hurt also. They ate in silence, the sausages and eggs, the pineapple dripping with juice, and drank the hot tea with cream.

They said little more that day. He had had his say, and she had told him her belief. After that, silence for a time, until they both cooled down, and became rested from the journey.

Rosalind put salve on her feet as well as Kinau's, and on Peter's burned arms and legs. They had gotten off lightly, and she wanted to thank the Hawaiian gods and the Christian God as well.

The next day, she asked Peter, "I should like to visit the mission today. May we go in the carriage, if the horse is well?"

"If the horse, not the people, are well?" he half-mocked.

She smiled nervously. "You feel better, don't you, Peter?"

He put his arm about her. "I think that whenever I will remember the sight of you across that fire and seeing the carriage burning, and that damn trip . . . I'll go up in smoke! But yes, I feel better. Only I'm not letting you out of my sight for a time!"

She rested her head on his shoulder, and timidly kissed his chin. He melted at the shy caress. He knew it, but damn if he would let her know how he turned to putty in her little hands!

They went over to the mission and had a good visit with the people there. The pastor was good-hearted, intent on his work, absent-minded about eating meals and coming home at dusk. His wife was brisk and practical. The pianist was a lean spinster, timid as a bird, but pink-cheeked and bright-eyed when music was talked about. They remained for dinner that evening and rode home by starlight.

Peter had noticed Rosalind had sat in a pew for a long time that afternoon, her hands folded, gazing at the altar. He thought she had prayed, he hoped she prayed to the Christian God. He did not want her to get so involved with Hawaiian gods that she forgot her Christian upbringing. As it was, her mind must be a curious mixture of thoughts and beliefs. So was his, he had to admit, ruefully. From living on Darien most of his life, he had absorbed much of the beliefs of the Hawaiians, and he caught himself thinking of the rain god when it rained, and leaving an offering for the corn god when the harvest was good. Was it so bad, he began to ponder. Perhaps it was necessary to believe in the power beyond earthly powers, no matter what it was. All the peoples on earth seemed to feel the need to believe in something beyond themselves.

The days passed rapidly. They paid a few visits to some friends in Kailua, had Rosalind fitted for more clothes, over which she protested vehemently. Peter enjoyed being dictatorial about this, she could not very well deny that she must dress well as his hostess.

They also stopped in to see Mr. Chan. He had some jewels ready and set for her. The small Chinese-Hawaiian man bowed and smiled again and again to see them. He set a chair for her ceremoniously.

"You have worked very rapidly, Mr. Chan," said Peter, as he sat down beside Rosalind.

"When I saw the pearls, how my mind spun around and around! Ideas flowed like water from my miserable brain. I worked night and day, I awakened from sleep to feel the inspiration coming, and I must get up to draw."

Peter smiled a little in amusement at his enthusiasm. He turned to Rosalind to explain. "I brought him some black pearls to design into jewelry for you. Mr. Chan was most flattering about them."

"They were perfect, most perfect! It would have been a crime to pierce them into strings," said Mr. Chan, his talented hands fluttering. "Allow me to show you what I have done, and let me see if you approve my poor efforts."

With a flourish, he set three boxes on the table before Rosalind. With yet a grander gesture, he laid out a piece of white satin. Then reverently he opened the first box, took out a necklace, and laid it on the satin.

Rosalind gasped in amazement. Before her lay a most exquisite necklace of palest silver, wrought so delicately that each fragment looked as though it were created from magic. In each cup of silver lay an immense black pearl, so graduated that the smallest was near the clasp, the largest near the huge pendant. And the pendant was set in silver, a black baroque pearl of irregular shape, like a bulbous teardrop, almost an inch in length.

Peter leaned to survey it critically. "Beautiful," he pronounced.

"I never . . . never . . . saw anything so . . . lovely . . ." gasped Rosalind.

Mr. Chan smiled deprecatingly at their wonder. He coughed behind his thin hand. He flicked open the second box. There lay two brooches of silver and black pearls, one in a circle of pearls, the other shaped like a flower and stem. The black pearl was the center, like a black orchid, and around it enameled green vines.

Peter nodded. Rosalind was speechless. She scarcely dared to touch the objects, as though they would fall to pieces in her fingers.

Mr. Chan opened the smallest box, and disclosed two pairs of earrings. One was simple, with a single black pearl stud in the sterling setting. The other was more elaborate, with small black pearls at the ear, and a drop of a large black pearl.

He rubbed his hands as Peter picked them up to look critically. "You like them? You like them?"

"Very much. You have said nothing to anyone?"

"As you wished, sir. All the work was done by my hands alone, and I worked at night with no one around," he beamed. "The other pearls you left with me. . . ." He opened a box, and showed the black pearls. "I used the very best, these are left." He handed the box to Peter. Peter stirred the pearls carelessly with his finger tip, then handed the box back.

"Please keep them, Mr. Chan, and make up what jewelry you wish, to sell. Only, do not reveal their source."

Mr. Chan did not attempt to conceal his delight. "But I must return them to you! You insist? With reluctance, I keep them, but I will pay you high for them. . . ."

"No, no, it is little enough for your time and effort to make these items," said Peter. They argued politely, but Mr. Chan kept the gems, and bowed the Dariens out more deeply than ever.

Peter knew that Rosalind was wondering about the pearls, but he said nothing. She had little idea of the commercial value of things, that was why it amused him so much. Eileen would froth at the mouth if she could catch sight of them. She was a wise little mischief, and she would spill it, she couldn't help showing off any jewelry she had.

Rosalind preferred to wear flowers! And who could blame her? The Hawaiian flowers were exquisite and unique in themselves. Perhaps she was wiser than Eileen, after all.

They returned to Darien, after collecting Akela. She had heard something of their adventures on the journey to Mount Kilauea, and was full of awe. That they had dared to approach the goddess Pele, in her own home! That they had escaped the fierceness of the fire and sulfur! Peter had little hope that she would keep her mouth shut.

Aunt Norma was quick to notice the burns on Peter's arms when they returned. "Good heavens, Peter. I thought you went on holiday! Whatever happened to you?" She caught one of his arms in her hands, her face was deeply concerned. "These are bad burns."

"They are healing, Aunt Norma," he said, rather impatiently. "How is Victor, how are you all?"

Eileen was inquisitive. "But you haven't answered, Peter. How did you get them? Over a *luau?*"

Rosalind spoke up quietly, but definitely. "It was my fault. Kinau and I went out to Mount Kilauea, and we were caught by the fires springing up in the paths. Peter rescued us."

"Oh-ho, I sense a story," drawled Terry, from his sprawled position in a bamboo chair on the *lanai.* "Tell us all. Why did you and Kinau go out to Mount Kilauea, dear fair Rosalind?"

She gave him a look of pure dislike. It was terrible to return to his hateful malice and Eileen's darting keen looks. She felt tired again, weary before she had been back more than a few hours.

Before Peter could stop her, Rosalind said, "To consult Pele."

"To consult Pele!" mocked Terry. "To consult . . . Pele! My word, you are a little Hawaiian *wahine,* aren't you, dear cousin? And what did the dear goddess reveal to your shell-pink ears, my dear?"

Eileen laughed, her blue eyes sparkling with mirth. Mr. Corey looked uneasily from Eileen to Rosalind.

"That we are in danger," she said shortly. "That

there is much trouble here on Darien, and there will be more. Death will come before long."

Their mockery was silenced, but for a moment. Mr. Murray stirred and frowned as they laughed. "You must not ridicule these sayings," he admonished, for once aware of undercurrents. "There is often truth in the sayings of the native peoples. I have known the Hawaiians to sense disaster long before it is visible to us white people. There is a story. . . . " And he began to tell it eagerly, his greying hair ruffled.

Barton Darien was leaning forward to catch what was said. He nodded again and again, his fist pounded the chair as Alfred Murray finished his story. "True, true," he said, with a great effort. "I know . . . such tales. Once . . . on range. . . ." He looked appealingly to Peter.

"Yes, the tidal wave," said Peter, nodding. His father pounded his chair again.

"Tell him, tell . . . for his book," said Barton imperiously, his hands trembling.

"You are talking better, Father. Tell him yourself," said Peter, with a smile, and a keen glance at his parent.

"We talk every day," said Alfred Murray. "He has told me many new stories."

"Tell you . . . tidal wave," said Barton, with his head pushed forward, as though he would force the words out. "On plains . . . cattle uneasy. Hawaiians said . . . must drive to south . . . we drove them . . . wave came . . . immense . . . forty feet high, across . . . from sea . . . across . . . just in time." He leaned back, his forehead covered with sweat, but he had said the words, and he managed a twitching smile from his half-paralyzed face.

Rosalind went over to hug him impulsively. "Oh, that was splendid, Father!" she said, her tanned face glowing, amber eyes shining. "Papa must put that in his book. Papa, do talk to Hilohilo and get more details from him. That should make a splendid chapter!"

"So it would, so it would," said Alfred Murray.

"You know, I have done more writing since we came to Darien than in the five years past? Hilohilo's wife is a mine of information. And Miss Honora knows so many things. I am very happy here."

She embraced him also. Eileen was watching with a mixture of disdain and jealousy. But Rosalind did not care just then. Peter's father and her own were finding something in common, in spite of being so different. It made her heart lift to think that her father was finding friendship here, and Barton Darien seemed to be more easy in his mind also, improving every day.

Peter talked to Hilohilo and told him all that had happened while they'd been gone. Joe was present, but silent as usual.

Hilohilo listened, his black eyes intent on his boss's face. He nodded when Peter had finished.

"I have known such things to happen," he said finally. "Yes, we do not worship the same gods. But the gods know us. They send us warnings and we must heed them."

"What do you think about what Kinau said?"

"She talk to my wife much last night. She tell her about the warnings of Pele. I think Kinau very wise woman. She think much, she know people. She is close to Pele. We must be careful, post guards more. Danger will come, and death, yes. Since Kinau says it, it will happen."

Peter lounged in the saddle, idly watching the cattle being driven across the sunlit area to the shadow of trees for a reprieve from the late afternoon heat.

"From what direction will it come?" he finally asked. He was skeptical, but perhaps they did have something. He must cover all angles.

"Two dangers come, say Kinau. One of the ocean, one of the men. We must post more guards, as you say. But I think maybe we have tidal wave soon."

Peter frowned, brought his gaze back to the Hawaiian's shrewd broad face. "Why do you think so?"

"Often it happens. When there is volcano erupting

on big island, then we get tidal wave pretty soon. It comes from the north. The east shore protected by those cliffs," he waved his big bronzed hand in that direction. "House okay. But tidal wave come from the north, from big island to us. Then water come across the land. We must move cattle south, maybe today and tomorrow."

"The grass ain't so good in the south," said Joe Smith, abruptly.

"Water drown cattle," countered Hilohilo simply. Peter finally nodded. "Okay. We move the cattle, starting tonight. It is hot, so we'll wait until dusk. Tell the men, have them get some rest this afternoon."

The big Hawaiian nodded, and rode off. After Hilohilo was out of earshot Smith demanded, "You believe such talk, Mr. Darien?"

"I don't know, Joe. But I do know that things happen, and we don't know why. And there are stranger things in life than what we can see and hear and touch. So . . ." Peter's broad shoulders rose in a shrug. "It won't hurt to relocate the cattle and it won't hurt to move them back when the danger is over."

"Um," said Joe, and nodded. Nick approached them, and finally came up.

"What's this about moving the cattle tonight?" he asked.

Peter told him simply. Nick finally nodded.

"All right, we'll do it. Sometimes the natives know more than we do. Reckon we better do what they say. Simpler like that."

The men rode off, and Peter went back to the house to rest until evening. He went up to the nursery, and found Victor waking up from his nap. Rosalind had just picked him up, and the boy caught sight of Peter over her shoulder.

"Da dada . . . dada . . ." he cried out happily, and bounced so hard that Rosalind could scarcely hold the young imp.

Peter came to take him in his arms. "My, he's getting bigger all the time, and stronger," he added with a laugh as Victor pulled his hair in his little fist. "Ouch, stop that, Victor!"

"Dadadada," said Victor, grinning amiably at Peter. Peter spent the next hour with him, watched him being fed and crawling around the mat floor. He was trying to stand up; he would grab a chair leg and attempt to pull himself to his feet. He did get up once, and looked triumphantly about him. Then he sagged, and sat down hard on his padded bottom. His expression was one of complete surprise.

Peter and Rosalind burst out laughing at him, and his lip curled up. Rosalind hastened to sit down beside him and pet him.

"No, darling, it's all right. You're great, you're the best baby in the world," she murmured to him, and he dug his head against her breasts and cooed contentedly. Peter watched them both, and forgot all his problems for the time being. She was so unselfconscious with the child, forgetting to be shy in her absorption.

Her cheeks bloomed pink, her eyes sparkled, and she laughed without restraint, sitting on the floor and watching Victor play. He loved to see her like this.

They were worth the world to him, he thought. He had worked hard all his life, putting everything into Darien, all his plans, his hopes, his efforts. And now had come along two unexpected responsibilities, and he adored them both. They made his life seem richer, brighter.

He watched Rosalind with the child and thought, One day we will have a son of our own, and a daughter, and more children. They would grow closer, and become as one, loving each other, knowing each other's minds and hearts. A new life, a wider horizon for them both. Life seemed very sweet.

# 14

❦ ❦ ❦ ❦

TERRY DARIEN played lazily in the full rolling waves. His lip curled as he thought how the cowboys had raced around pushing the cattle to the south. A tidal wave! Pooh. Nothing had happened, and nothing was about to!

Those damn foolish superstitious Hawaiians. And Peter was stupid enough to fall for their stories! It was amazing. Peter was supposed to be so smart.

Nothing had occurred, except that all the fool cowboys who had done the job for the past three nights, were dead tired, sleeping all day. Damn it. Terry had gotten roped into some of the work, with Peter riding herd on him as though he was some damn calf. He was tired of Peter, mighty tired.

He had escaped today, though. He had raced out before dawn and come to the lagoon. Dorisa would probably be along by mid-morning to see if he was here. He half-smiled, and stood to ride a large wave into the sand.

He was getting a bit bored with Dorisa. She was very possessive. And she was obvious. He had his eye on another girl, a slim younger girl, shy and rather elusive. He liked to do the chasing. Maybe he would give Dorisa the push.

He came in again, and lay down on a shaded portion of the beach, enjoying the feel of the sand on his naked body. His eyes closed, he stretched luxuriously squirming until he had made shallow hollows for his hips and shoulders.

A trickle of fine grains fell on his face. He moved irritably, opened his eyes, brushed at it, and heard the giggle above him. He turned his head, caught sight of the slender legs, and caught hold of one.

He hauled Dorisa down and across him. "Damn you, girl, you got sand in my eyes!"

She giggled again, and wiggled across his body. He spanked her rounded buttocks, she squealed and tried to get away from him. He turned and caught her wrist, cutting off her escape. He threw his leg across her legs, and glared threateningly at her.

She wore a brief bright red and green sarong on her brown body, which made him blink. A crimson flower was stuck over her left ear, signifying, "I have a lover." He scowled. She was getting awfully brazen.

But she was satisfying. She knew how to make love.

He flicked his finger at the hibiscus. "Damn you, girl, are you going to advertise this to everybody, including your father?"

"He knows about us, Terry. He knows you are my lover and my man," she said confidently. "He will consent to our marriage."

"Our marriage!" he exclaimed, horrified. He fell back from her. "You are crazy! I marry nobody!"

And when he did marry, he thought, he would pick out a wealthy beautiful woman, preferably someone in San Francisco or New York City, and live it up! No Hawaiian *wahine* and a pack of half-*Haole* kids for him! He would get away from this damn island if it killed him!

"You tease me much, Terry," she cooed, caressing his cheek with her hand. "You like me very much, huh? I be good wife for you. I good cook. Father make us a nice house."

"You are crazy," he repeated. A nice little hut for him? Hell, he would have a mansion on a hill overlooking San Francisco bay, and party all night every night! He would forget he had ever ridden a horse or chase cattle or stood night watch. He would forget being dry and dusty and weary in every bone. And he would forget the Hawaiian girls and their ways. They were cute for a time, but then—He remembered

Lydia, and winced from the memory. She had been so beautiful, so innocent—until—

Dorisa's dark eyes half-closed, she looked sly and knowing. "You no like me? I think better! You like me because I know how to please a man!" And she put her hand on his hard thighs, and teased him.

"Damn it . . . quit that. . . ." But he could not resist, she did know how to please a man. He rolled over on her, and she laughed, pleased and taunting.

He held her under him, and satisfied himself on her writhing twisting young body. He smothered her laughter with his lips, and trailed his mouth over her firm brown breasts and the taut nipples, down over her flat stomach and thighs. She put her hand down between their bodies and fingered him cleverly, until he wanted her again.

The sun was high in the sky when he lay back and yawned. Damn, she took everything out of him, and all he wanted to do was sleep. If Hilohilo came chasing him today, he would send him away with a bug in his ear.

Dorisa murmured, close to him, "Do you tell my father today?"

"Tell him what?" asked Terry crossly, his eyes shut tight.

"That he makes us a house soon? That we marry soon?"

"Hell, no," said Terry. She leaped up.

"When do you tell him?" She asked it bluntly, her black eyes blazing. "He asks me when we marry, he asks me if I am with child."

Terry sat bolt upright. "You aren't, are you?" he yelled, in alarm. "I was damn careful with you, and you know it! Don't you go telling lies, Dorisa!"

Her face was sullen, she drew the sarong about her sand-encrusted body with dignity. "I do not yet have child. But I could give you fine sons," she said. "What I tell my father?"

"Tell him I do not marry Hawaiian *wahine!*" said Terry. He got up and flung himself into the ocean, swimming out beyond the breakers. He played around in the waves for a time. When he returned to shore, he was pleased to see that Dorisa had disappeared. He was tired of her.

He hated nagging women.

Lydia had nagged at him about marriage, and her father the big chief, and about the baby. He had gone with her to Honolulu, but she would not remain with him. Tearless, her chin high, she had told him, "You do not love me, for all your fine words. I leave you, and your son will never know who you are. You do not deserve him!"

He squirmed uneasily, he hated to remember her words. Fortunately, that didn't happen often, he had a convenient memory for forgetting what disturbed him. But sometimes he could not prevent visions of Lydia.

Peter was tired but satisfied when they had moved all the cattle to the south. They had scattered the animals over a wide range, for the grass was not so thick and luxuriant, and water not so plentiful in the little pools of limestone. At least they would be safe from tidal waves. The waves came from the North, Hilohilo said, the Northwest usually.

He was riding home that dusk, slowly looking across the land to the extinct volcano which was the center of the island. On the green slopes, a girl waited. A brown girl, with a red flower in her hair.

He turned, and rode toward her as she lifted a bare arm in greeting. Maybe she was lost, or had hurt her foot. He would give her a ride home.

When he came closer, he saw who it was. Dorisa, the daughter of one of his cowboys, and a voluptuous fifteen years of age. His mouth tightened. Had Terry kept on playing with her in spite of the warning that had been given to him?

He came up to her. She stood there, her feet planted apart, her hands on her hips. He had a flashing picture of the way she would be in ten years: fat, with half a dozen brown babies, plump and chuckling—a fine cook, lazy but loving, and careless about her garb.

"Hello, Dorisa. Do you need a ride home?"

"No, I walk," she answered definitely. He lounged in the saddle, looking down at her curiously. She looked furious, pouting, sulky. Then he noticed the hibiscus behind her left ear.

"You want to talk to me?"

She nodded. "I see you coming."

He swung down, held the horse's reins in his hand, and stood about three feet from her. "Okay. What's wrong?"

"Your cousin Terry. He makes me many promises. He says he is my man, and I am his woman. My father finally agrees that we marry. He will build a house for us, my father." She paused, gave an ominous sniff, and her eyes filled with tears.

His mouth tightened. "Yes, and does Terry wish to marry?" he asked, already knowing the answer.

She shook her dark wavy hair vigorously, and it flew about her brown shoulders. "He laughs at me. He says he does not marry with a Hawaiian *wahine!* I will tell my father, and he will kill that man! He makes promises and does not keep them."

"I warned you, Dorisa. Terry only plays, he does not mean marriage with a girl. Why didn't you stay away from him?"

Her dark eyes flashed, burning up the tears. "He is my man! I am his woman! We make vows!"

And that wasn't all they had made, thought Peter wearily. He sighed, and looked off the plain to the dim white house with the palm trees all about. A haven, and he was tired. But he must straighten this out.

"Did you make a baby with him, Dorisa?"

She flushed, her bare foot dug in the grass. "No," she said low. "But we will! I give him strong sons!"

"Stay away from him, he makes promises he will not keep. Do you know the story of Lydia and her son, who lives now with us?"

She glanced away from him, and he knew that she had heard. "That is not me. I am a woman for him, I understand him."

"If you do, you are the first person in the world who does," noted Peter drily.

She became furious, and stamped her foot. "You make him marry with me! You tell him, Dariens keep their word, everybody says so! He must marry with me! I make him good wife!"

"You cannot make a man marry you," said Peter definitely. "And Terry is not to be tied down. He would go away. He has done it before. You know that the father of Lydia Pauahi is very angry with him. But he can do nothing. Terry would not marry her, and she was the daughter of a great chief. No, he will marry no girl until he wishes."

"But you are the great chief of the Dariens," Dorisa coaxed, giving him a sideways look of great sultriness, which made him catch his breath. "You make him marry with me, eh? He will not be sorry. He listen to you, and we have big wedding feast, eh?"

She was a persuasive little *wahine,* and he had to sigh. She was no dignified aristocrat like Lydia. She understood only one thing. She had pleased Terry sexually, he must be ready to marry her. Among the Hawaiians, that was simple and uncomplicated.

"I will talk with Terry," promised Peter. "But he will not marry you, I think. Dorisa, listen to me. Stay away from him, he only plays, he is not serious about girls. He wishes only to steal their virtue, then he loses his interest."

"He loves me!" she flashed. "You talk to him. I want marriage, and I give him a big baby!"

She stalked away, her head high. He swung on his horse, and cantered back to the ranch, getting more and more furious as he went. Terry used every method of his charming repertoire to win the girls, and he would go on doing it. They wanted it as much as he did.

Peter rode into the stableyard and left his horse with a hand. He stalked into the house, grim-faced, and sent for Terry.

Terry lounged into the study, a drink in his hand, a grin on his face. "What is it, big boss?" he mocked, leaning against the open door.

"Come in and shut the door." Peter sat down at his

desk, staring at his cousin. Why was the man so irresponsible? He had work to do, he slacked off and sloped off all the time. He made promises he had no intention of keeping. And he had to put his hands on every girl in sight. What was wrong with him?

Peter and Terry had the same upbringing, the same inherited traits, supposedly. Norma had been strict with them both. But somehow Terry had grown up believing that the world owed him everything he could grab, with nothing given in return.

"Why? So no one can hear you yell at me? What have I done now? Neglected your precious cattle?"

"I said, come in and shut the door." Peter did not raise his tone, but his grim face must have warned Terry. The other man shrugged, kicked the door closed, and lounged over to flop down in an easy chair, lifting the drink to his lips.

He took a long cool swallow and said, "So what is it?"

"Dorisa stopped me out on the range. She says you promised to marry her. She wants me to arrange the wedding and have a big *luau*. You want it on the patio?"

He took some pleasure in giving Terry a jolt. The man sat bolt upright, the color drained from his tanned cheeks for a moment. Then he laughed. "You got to be kidding! I wouldn't marry a Hawaiian slut!"

"She would be better off without you," agreed Peter evenly, his large hand moving a pen meticulously on the desk. "However, she seems to want you, and her father is willing. Shall I arrange to get the preacher from Kailua over here?"

"Hell, no! I won't marry her!"

"She wasn't a slut until you had her. When is this going to stop, Terry? You have one girl after another, get tired of them, choose another. If you don't quit, you'll have your throat cut by some *paniolo*."

"They wouldn't dare," scoffed Terry. "You'd kill them."

"Why should I?" asked Peter calmly. "Save me the trouble of driving you around, and chasing after you to get you to do an hour or two of work. I get damn fed up with milk-nursing you."

"Then let me go! I'll leave this damn island and all those damn girls! Let me go to San Francisco, give me my share of the money! I won't bother you again!"

"No, not until the money ran out, then you'd come whining back for more. Do you think I'm a fool? You can't earn a living, you never learned to work. You'd gamble and throw it away on women. And you would be lost in a big city. Those slickers would take you for everything you have, a country bumpkin like you."

That hit Terry in his vulnerable pride. He thought of himself as a wealthy smart young man, able to handle anything. Peter watched him, hard-eyed, as Terry struggled for words.

Terry flung aside the empty glass, then got up, knocking over the chair in his fury. "You . . . you . . . you got your nerve! Calling me a bumpkin, when you're the one who hates to leave this ranch! Why, a trip to Kailua is a big deal," he sneered. "And Honolulu . . . you got lost when you went there."

"And so did you, Terry. So did you, time and again. Especially when you had too much rum to drink. No, you stay here and put some effort into working. Or by God, I'll kick you back to the mainland and let you learn the tough way how to make a living for yourself. You touch one more girl here, and off you go. That's my final word. I won't have you messing up the lives of the *paniolos* of Darien. They are good men with fine families. You're the spoiler. . . ."

"Spoiler! Me, I give those girls the first and only thrill of their lives!" cried Terry wildly. "Then they settle down with some dumb stupid cowboy and raise a dozen kids. I bet they'll remember me all their lives, the only good guy who gave them a great thrill!"

"What in the world are you arguing about now?" asked Eileen from the doorway. She looked cool and calculating, her dress icy blue and lacy at the sleeves. She came in, looked from one to the other. "I could hear you all the way up to my bedroom."

"Your brother is in deep trouble," said Peter, sarcastically. "I told him, one more Hawaiian girl, and off he goes on his own."

"Give me my money, and I'll go now!" yelled Terry.

"Are you serious?" cried Eileen. "I want to leave! Take me away, Terry, when you go! I have to get off this damn island. We are prisoners here, just prisoners! There's a whole big world, and we can't live here forever! Give us our money, Peter, and let us go!"

Peter sighed deeply, in exasperation. He stood up. "You know there is no money, just the island and the cattle. I won't sell off everything to give you some money to throw away. If you want to go to the mainland, go, but you'll earn your way."

"You can't keep my money from me!" said Terry obstinately. "I'll speak to mother. . . ."

Aunt Norma had come in, quietly, behind her daughter. Her lined face under the white widow's cap was deeply troubled. "Children, children, what is this? Why are you screaming at each other? Terry, what have you done now?"

"Nothing . . ."

"He has had Dorisa, the daughter of one of the men," said Peter bluntly. "He promised her marriage, as he did all the other girls. I told him, one more incident, and he is off this island like a shot. I won't have him ruining the families here. They are my responsibility now. My cowboys are grumbling. He stays away from the girls."

"I promised her nothing!" yelled Terry. "The girl is just a slut! She wanted it, and I gave it to her good!"

"Lydia Pauahi was not," said Norma, and put her hand to her face. "Oh, Terry, Terry, what have you done? You ruin all you touch. You have the touch of death in your hands."

There was a brief shocked silence in the room. Norma had never spoken so to her children.

Eileen rushed to Terry's defense, as he stared at his mother as though he had been struck. "You wrong him, he is bored, Mother! He wants to get away from this deadly dull island, and so do I! You make Peter give us our inheritance! We want to leave! We can go to San Francisco . . . anywhere . . . away from here! Really live, really live!" she cried, her cheeks a hectic flush.

Norma was already shaking her head. "No, we belong here. We are Dariens. Terry must learn to settle down and do his share of the work. Heaven knows he has done little to make one proud of him. He has earned nothing, not even his daily bread. As for you, Eileen, you might take lessons from Rosalind. She works from morning to night, and still sings cheerfully to the baby. You would not be so bored, if you worked until you were tired and thought more of others than yourself."

"Oh, spare me the sermons!" screamed Eileen, pounding the desk in a frenzy. "I want to get away, I have to get away, or I'll go crazy! I hate it here, I hate it! Nothing but the smell of cattle and volcano ash! We'll die here, and never have been alive!"

Peter left them there to argue and went upstairs. He felt sick at heart. Terry and Eileen hated the island, was he right to keep them here? And Rosalind, sometimes she was so tired she fell asleep within minutes of climbing into bed. Was he right to keep them all here, for the dream of their grandfather?

They could sell all, leave, and go somewhere. But he knew what would happen. Eileen would play with men, and get jilted. And he—he would be so homesick, longing for his Hawaiian island, that he would be no damn good. He had worked in Texas, in Arizona, in Colorado. He had gone to college in San Francisco for a brief time. Each place, he had left gladly, looking forward with wild enthusiasm to returning home, to Darien.

But what about Rosalind?

Supper was gloomy that night. Terry was sullen. Eileen had been crying, obvious by the red swelling around her eyes. Norma was troubled. Honora looked from one to the other, and her mouth was tight. Probably the whole household had heard the argument. You could not keep things quiet here, everyone knew what went on.

Rosalind noticed the ripples of tension that seemed to rise like heat from one and the other. She had been with Victor until supper, he was fussy with cutting teeth.

Her own contentment grew troubled. What was going on now? Peter was frowning, not eating enough, she knew he was disturbed. If only they would let him alone! He worked so diligently, he deserved to relax in the evenings.

Rosalind's violin had arrived on the boat recently from Honolulu. It had come all the way from San Francisco, and she had opened it reverently, fearfully.

What a beautiful instrument it was! Shiny and golden brown, a smaller instrument than the large awkward one she had played. The tone was sweet and pure. She had been practicing a couple of hours a day ever since she had received it.

She longed to play it tonight, but everyone looked so cross and distressed, she dared not mention it. She served coffee in the drawing room. Peter excused himself early, his face like a thundercloud, and retired to his study. Rosalind soon excused herself, and went up to see to Victor.

She rocked him for a time, gave him a cool strip of pineapple to suck, and he soon went off to sleep. She tenderly laid him down, and patted his little cheeks. He was getting so plump and sturdy, not like the thin little baby he had been last March, when Peter had burst in the Murray house with him during the rain storm. It was July, and already Victor was trying to walk and talk, and he was pounds heavier.

In her pretty sitting room, she walked about slowly, playing the violin. The touch was coming back to her, and she closed her eyes as she played the old familiar melodies. What a pleasure music was. It soothed and stimulated, it roused memories and calmed distress. No wonder each people of the earth had their own music and songs, their own instruments and traditions. It was part of the human spirit, to find harmony.

Peter came in quietly. She lowered the violin, and looked at him questioningly.

217

"Go on playing. You picked it up quickly, darling," he said, and flung himself on the sofa. He looked tired, and deep lines were engraved on either side of his mouth.

"It is a beautiful violin, thank you for it, Peter," she said sincerely. "They must have sent me the best one they had."

She lifted the instrument to her chin, and began again, almost forgetting his presence as she sought the melodies. Rosalind played for a time, then replaced the violin carefully into its case.

"There, I must stop. It is time for bed, if you must be up early tomorrow. Are the cattle all moved?"

"Yes, all of them, finally. Rosalind?"

"Yes?"

"Do you feel a prisoner on this island?" he snapped.

She stared at him, her amber eyes wide open. "A prisoner? Oh, Peter, of course not!"

"Don't you? You longed to return to Kailua, to the cove."

"But Peter . . . it was to consult Pele. You know that. And to see Kinau's relatives. I love it here, I love Darien." She gazed at him in distress.

He shrugged, and put his head wearily in his hands. He ruffled his black curly hair with his fingers until it stood up in ringlets.

"What is it, Peter?"

"Oh, another fight with Terry. He won't leave the island girls alone. He says he is bored, bored!" he mocked savagely. "If he did his work, he would be too tired to fool around with them all day!"

"Oh, Peter. Not another one!"

"Yes, and another, and another. I wonder if it would be best to send him away. And Eileen wants to go. She screamed about being bored to death, and she wanted to take off for San Francisco on the next boat."

Rosalind sat down carefully on the sofa. "Why not let them go?" she asked quietly.

"Let them go?" He raised his head, stared at her. "Let them go? They would get into trouble so fast, it wouldn't be funny! They would be prey for every slick-talking gambler and fancy man in San Francisco! They would be babes in the woods."

Rosalind was silent. Peter loved them too much. Perhaps they would get into trouble, but wasn't that better than getting everyone else on Darien into trouble? Should they not learn some lessons? But no, Peter, feeling responsible for them, would shelter and cosset them, no matter what the cost to everyone else.

"Do you want to go?" he asked abruptly.

"I? No, Hawaii is home to me," she said. Was he sorry he had married her?

He put his arm about her. "I'm about crazy with it," he muttered. "I love Darien, it always drew me back. It is home, my home, and I love it so. But they do not. It made me sick to hear them tonight, sick to my stomach. Sick to my soul. They hate it. The land their grandfather died to defend, their father died working it, and their mother raised them here. Yet they say they detest it, and would give anything to leave."

"I don't think they would give anything," she said drily, leaning against his broad chest. "They would not give up money and jewels and their position. And they would not want to have to work, would they?"

"You think poorly of them also? Odd, Norma said about the same thing," he sighed. "I never heard her speak against them with such . . . such despair."

"There is something wrong inside them, inside Terry and Eileen," said Rosalind, in a low tone. "They are malicious, and they hate anyone who stands in their way. I think . . . Peter . . . I think they hate anyone who is strong and determined. That is why they hate you."

"You keep saying they hate me. I don't understand why. I have given Eileen everything she wants . . . clothes, jewels . . . And Terry had the best of educations, any horse he wants. . . ."

"And they are spoiled with it. They should have been worked hard . . . yet perhaps that would not have done it. Sometimes I think that a person's nature is set by something inside himself," she added thoughtfully. "From the beginning, from small childhood, there is something inside that determines whether they're good or evil, firm healthy plants or a horrible rot. It is so with plants. One cannot tell until the fruit or flower grows, just how the stalk and roots are. But some are rotten from the first."

He held her close, his cheek on her soft straight dark hair, thinking about the words. And for the first time he began to consider seriously the wisdom of sending Terry and Eileen away. But where would they go, and who would watch over them?

It did not strike him as odd that he thought of having them watched over. Terry was twenty-four, Eileen was twenty-two. Yet they were like spoiled children, who would dash into trouble without a nurse.

"I must seriously consider what to do about them," he said. "But I'm too damn tired tonight to think straight." He rose, and drew her up with him. "And almost too tired to make love to you," he added, smiling at the ready blush that came into her tanned cheeks.

He came to her in bed. She wore the thin white muslin nightdress with blue ribbons, and he played with the ribbons idly as his lips nibbled at her cheek and ear. She was so sweet and straight, how had he been so lucky to find her?

He wondered if fate set the pattern for one's life. He could look back and see the events that had changed him drastically. Early in his life, the death of his mother, making him sturdy and self-reliant beyond his years. The meeting with Joe Smith in Texas, and their shootout with the outlaws, and how Joe had saved his life.

Other events went through his mind, until he wearied of it, and turned over, to move his hand gently over Rosalind's throat, her soft breasts, her arms. He moved, to lie above her, and kiss her lips, and her cheeks, and closed eyelids. His hand ruffled the long straight hair, perfumed with the flowers she had worn that evening.

With the gentle familiarity of their months of marriage, he played with her, and caressed her until he sensed her readiness. Then he came to her, and they drew together, and he enjoyed the soft flesh of her body, the quick catch of her breath, her soft words in his ears. He whispered love words to her, in both the languages they enjoyed. And she answered him, with shyness, sweetness, honeyed words he found entrancing.

They came together, their breathing short and rapid, and she cried out softly in his embrace. Ever since the time at the cove, when he had made love after their swim, she had been more open and receptive to him, and he adored it, and her.

But did she truly love Darien, his beloved island? Before he slept, he thought again of the hate in Eileen's large blue eyes, the way she had screamed out against Darien. He must think what to do about that —he must figure it out.

He could not give up Rosalind. If she hated the island, and wished to leave, there was nothing for it —they would have to go. He could not give her up, he would give up Darien first. But, oh, God, his heart would weep blood on leaving. And she had said she loved the island—he hoped that she meant it.

# 15

❦ ❦ ❦ ❦

EILEEN HAD BEEN sullenly quiet for days. Her mother pleaded with her to break out of her old ways, to help with the household, to do her part.

"Peter is right," Norma had said earnestly. "You are bored because you do nothing all day. It is right and good for people to work for their living, it gives them a glow to be useful in the world. Work could be your salvation, darling."

Eileen could scarcely refrain from spitting her rage. She was wealthy, she was an heiress, she was beautiful! What need did she have to work? Other rich people went out and had marvelous times, dancing and flirting and drinking all night. She had read about them in the illustrated magazines, greedily drinking in the words and the pictures.

Why should she work? She was no fanatic. She was no Puritan. She saw the way men looked at her, and not just the island men. Glendon Corey was from the mainland, he had lived in San Francisco and Denver. And he was no *paniolo*. Yet he gazed at her with desire, he flattered her, he wanted her. If only she could get to America—with plenty of money!

Eileen loved her brother Terry, they shared secrets, and they thought alike. But sometimes she believed he was stupid. Instead of planning to get away, he just lounged around and played with girls and got them into trouble. That just roused Peter's fury, for his beloved *paniolos* came first with him.

If Terry was smart, he would get them away, and get the money to go with it. She would not endure being poor. If she could just get away and meet some rich men, she would be set for life. She would choose the richest old man she could find, and wait for him to die. And she would have plenty of fun!

If only Peter would let them go! But he would not, not unless he had to. And to manage that—she thought some more, her fingers plucking restlessly at the embroidery of her full sleeves.

She strolled out late one night. Peter had gone to bed early with Rosalind. They would be having a baby before long, she thought in disgust. Such bucolic pleasures were not for her. If Rosalind had any spirit, she would have left him. But this island was the most luxury the girl had ever known. She must be very stupid. Peter loaded her with emeralds and diamonds. She could go off to Honolulu and have a ball, but he would never let her go alone.

Eileen had other plans. When she married her rich man, she would not have a child. It would be painful, and would spoil her figure. That was settled in her mind. Yet she enjoyed sex. That was exciting, the only excitement on Darien for her.

She wandered beyond the patio. Joe Smith was there, silent, with his rifle on his arm. She greeted him coldly. She could not forgive his insulting behavior to her. And from the taunting in his grey eyes, he had not forgotten her.

He was just a cowboy, contented with a horse and gun.

"Evening, miss. Better not go far."

"I'll go as far as I like!"

He shrugged, and melted back into the shadows. She strode on, cursing him mentally. She stumbled into the grass and cursed the tall spikes of cactus that grew among them. Why didn't Peter have the ground cleared and decent grass put in?

Another figure rose up before her, another big man with a rifle. She stifled a gasp, and peered at him in the semi-darkness. "Who is there?" she snapped.

"I am Maleko." The deep voice reassured her. She half-smiled to herself. He was a big tall stalwart Hawaiian, new to Darien. She had talked to him before.

He was handsome, with black curly hair and black eyes.

"Oh, yes, Maleko," her voice softened on the words. "Do you have to guard tonight also? How silly it all is!"

"Silly?" he asked, as though he did not know the word. Yet she knew he was smart, and knew much English.

She stood near to him in the darkness, and noticed how his voice came from far above her head. He was tall, yes, much taller than Peter, and bigger than him. She still resented bitterly the way that Peter had beaten up Terry and humiliated him before the family. If only someone would beat up Peter, really hurt him!

Her ideas began to come together and make a plan. She reached out and touched his shoulder in the dimness. She felt him jerk, as though startled.

"Maleko. I have noticed you," she said in her most alluring tone.

"You do me honor."

She was not sure if he was being ironic. No, he probably meant it. He was an Hawaiian native, and she was white, the granddaughter of the first man on Darien. A complacent smile curled her lips.

"You are so big and strong." Men liked that kind of talk. The fact that their brains were small did not occur to them. She let her fingers trail down his cotton sleeve to the bare tautness of his muscular arm. "My, how hard your arm is, so tough! I bet you are the strongest man on Darien."

"That may be," he said, retreating slightly. She moved with him, and left her hand on his arm.

"I bet you are tougher than my cousin Peter Darien," she said, softly, for his ear alone, leaning confidingly against his arm.

He caught his breath, she could feel the beating of his heart as her fingers wandered teasingly across to his chest.

"Maybe," he said gruffly, uneasily.

She licked her tongue around her dry lips. He was

big and she thought he had probably had many women. Maleko was so handsome, any Hawaiian girl would have gone to him willingly. But he had probably never had a white woman before.

"I admire the Hawaiians," she said. "I think it is wrong that Darien belongs to the whites. Even though I am a Darien, I believe that it should go back to the Hawaiian people."

He was silent, she felt the tension in him as her fingers moved slowly over the cotton of his shirt.

"If . . . we left . . . Darien would go back to the Hawaiians," she said slowly. "We do not belong here. We belong in America, in Europe."

"Maybe," he repeated.

Was he stupid? Didn't he have anything else to say? She sighed with impatience. She would have to spell it all out for him.

"If something happened to Peter Darien," she said, in her most sultry confiding tone, "we would have to leave. Joe Smith could not stay here. Terry is willing to leave. If something . . . bad . . . happened to Peter Darien . . . we would all leave. The island would be returned to you . . . to your people."

"What could happen to Peter Darien?" asked Maleko slowly. "He is smart, he shoots fast."

"An accident. He might fall from his horse or a cliff, leaving him with a broken leg or hip." In the darkness, her blue eyes had narrowed with shining intensity. "He might not die . . . but if he was crippled. . . ."

"He does not often ride alone."

"It could be arranged, could it not?" she whispered. Tentatively, she let her lips brush, as though by accident, against his ear lobe, and she felt the strong body tremble. Ah, he was a man, then! She had begun to wonder!

"You wish your cousin to die?"

She stiffened. She had not thought about Peter dying! She wanted him alive, maimed and humiliated—Wishing he had married her and taken her to San Francisco!

"No, no, just to be injured enough to give up Darien," she said hastily. "I adore my cousin . . . really!"

The man made no sound in the darkness. She wished uneasily that she could see his face. But when the Hawaiians wanted, they could look like their expressionless stone statues.

"You would . . . help arrange that, would you not? To get Darien back?" she whispered, and her fingers moved over his corded neck.

"Darien is not mine," he said abruptly.

Oh, the damn fool! To take everything literally!

"But it belongs to your people, the natives!" she said sweetly. "It belongs to Hawaiians, like yourself. Do you have a girl friend?"

"A what?"

"A girl friend . . . a *wahine* of your own?"

He hesitated, then he said, "I am promised to a *wahine*. A girl of another island. When I have proved my manhood, I will marry with her, and have land and power."

"Well, there you are," said Eileen triumphantly. "I think it should be easy to prove your manhood! You're a big strong man, and Peter is smaller than you are!"

He was silent.

"Or do you have to prove your manhood . . . another way? Have you never had a woman in your arms, under your body?"

He shifted uneasily in the darkness. Her hand wandered down to the thin waist, the narrow hips. He almost flinched from her searching fingers.

"What do you do?" he asked sternly.

She wanted to giggle with excitement. He was the biggest man she had ever met, bigger than Joe Smith, or any Hawaiian *paniolo* she had met on the plains and lain with in the rank grass.

"What do you think? Are you man enough to understand?" she taunted him.

She was not prepared for the suddenness of his response. One moment he was motionless, uneasy. The next he had grabbed her and flung her down among the grass and cactus. She tried to protest, to scream out that a cactus was under her shoulder.

But the man had thrown himself on top of her, his hand over her mouth. The other hand groped for her long silk skirts, and yanked them up to her waist. His long legs held her down firmly. This wasn't what she wanted. She liked to tease, and arouse, and make him wait and want. Then she would allow him to have a few liberties—

Maleko did not wait for any permission. He searched for her intimate parts, found her, and thrust inside, with a quick painfully direct push of his body. She tried to scream then, he hurt her soft flesh, but his mouth closed over hers, and his teeth bit into her lips, and his tongue searched for hers. A big tongue, as big as the man's size would warrant, and a big hand on her breasts, tearing at the lace, and his thighs lean and iron-hard and hurting her—

It was strangely satisfying, this coupling in the darkness. This primitive hard sweaty man, gasping over her, and holding her so hard he would leave bruises on her tender flesh. She fought him, for satisfaction and pride. She scratched at his face and he only laughed, low in his throat.

She squirmed in the grass and cactus and sand, hurting herself. He held her firmly under him, and took what he wanted, proving his "manhood" to her. She was sobbing for breath when he finally finished and drew off.

He held his hard arm across her body and kept her down there. "I am not done," he said harshly.

"Well, I am . . . let me up!"

"No."

He came over her again, and she was amazed at his virility and strength. He used her as though he had not had a woman for months. And this time she felt the passion rising in her, and she tried to arch back to take in more of him, and she gripped his lean thighs with her fingers painfully.

"Oh . . . more of it . . . more . . . more," she

groaned. "Do it . . . oh . . . my God, you are such a man. . . ."

Ripples of desire were sweeping through her, climaxing into a series of waves of such intensity that she could only rock and moan with them. He held himself still, and let her thrust herself against him, to satisfy herself. She was amazed again at his ability—yes, he had known women before! When the waves finally died down to slight little shudders of satisfaction, he moved again, and again, and she weakly shivered with him, unable to fight or respond, she was so drained.

She wanted to sleep then, but she could not out here. She was too uncomfortable. Besides, she might sleep until morning, and that hateful Joe Smith might stumble over her in the dark! She made an intense effort and sat up, brushing her skirts down. Maleko lay beside her, away from her, his arm over his face. She could just make out his form in the moon-shadowed darkness.

She gulped in breath, and smoothed her hands over her belly. That was a man! Indeed.

"You come again tomorrow night."

No man ordered her about! She stiffened. "If I want to," she said casually.

"I will be here. You will come."

She got up, and brushed off her skirts. They were covered with grit. She would have to sneak up the back stairs. "Maybe," she said, his own word.

"If you want me to do what you wish, you will come." He got up, and took her wrist, lightly, but she felt the steel strength of his fingers. "You hate the Dariens, and you are a Darien. It is strange."

"You will do what I said?"

"Maybe. You come tomorrow night."

"I have given you enough!" she teased him.

"You did not give," he said slowly. "I took. That is Maleko's way. And you liked it."

Eileen could have slapped him. But he was coming around to what she wanted, she could afford to be nice to him. She reached up to kiss his chin, he reared back.

She patted his cheek instead. "I'll see you sometime," she said lightly. "Meantime, you think about what I said."

She walked away in the darkness, well pleased with the encounter. She had another man in her toils. Eileen hummed to herself as she walked toward the lights of the patio.

Joe watched her from his stance under the palms, and curled his mouth. Like an alley cat, he thought. Swinging her hips and purring!

She went into the house and he watched, motionless, as Maleko padded up to the house, looked at it, then turned and went away. Joe followed him about a mile, until he was satisfied the man was returning to his small camp.

Then he returned to his post to wait for the dawn.

Peter was out with the cattle the next days. They were restless; he thought they had not fed enough, the grass was so sparse.

He talked to Hilohilo, the man shook his head. "They feel the ground move under their feet, that is what makes them lift up their heads and shake their tails."

"Earthquakes?" asked Peter. "I have felt nothing."

"You do not wait and listen in silence for them. Soon they grow stronger. The earth on the big island is shaking. It will shake also on Darien."

"How bad?"

Hilohilo shrugged massively, his hands out. "Who knows? Only Pele, maybe other gods."

Peter was thinking about that one noon, as he rode beside a small herd of cattle, moving them from one sparce pasture to another. Terry had taunted him about it, asking why he didn't move them back to the good grass in the North of Darien.

"They want good grass and water, Peter," he had said lazily, his leg over the saddlehorn. "No tidal wave is coming, that is all nonsense. Why do you listen to those damn stupid fools?"

"Because they know a lot more than you do," answered Peter. Terry had ridden off in a temper, and taken the rest of the day off.

Peter was grinning at memory of that. Sometimes Terry was so predictable it was funny. They had been rather good friends when young, sneaking off to go fishing or swimming. But later, the friendship had gone sour. Terry hadn't wanted to grow up, Peter had had to grow up. It had made all the difference in the world between them.

Peter saw Smith across the way, on the other side of the small herd. It was amazing, the way the man could stay awake all night, snatch a small amount of sleep, then herd cattle all day.

Peter had tried to get him to take the days off. Joe Smith had shaken his head, his grey eyes shadowed under the deep brim of his Texas sombrero. "Nope. Trouble coming, I'll stay awake," he said in his slow deliberate fashion.

Peter turned in the saddle, searched out Hilohilo. He was out of sight, then Peter finally spotted him at the front of the herd, guiding the lead bull the way he wanted him to go. The herd was very restless, shifting away from the cowboys, trotting off into the trees. They had to be watched constantly, and patiently herded back.

Peter swung off to the side, swinging his rope to encourage a cow with lowered head to come back to the herd and away from the trees. She shook her head stubbornly, lowered her tail and lowed mournfully.

"Come on now. Don't be stupid and louse up this day for me," said Peter, coaxingly, in a low tone. The cow mooed again. Peter was working her slowly back to the herd, when he felt it.

A blow at his back, which knocked him from the saddle. As he fell, he heard the sound of the shot, echoing across the sloping plains. The cattle, jittery already, stampeded.

At the same time as he hit the ground, he felt something else shuddering across the plain. The shot seemed the echo of something else.

Then it came again, the quaking of the earth. The cows bawled in alarm, and the thunder of hooves shook the ground as they scattered in all directions.

Peter could not move. He could not move his legs. He felt them with his hand, but they would not work. His hand went higher, and came away. He stared at his hand. It was covered with red liquid.

Blood.

He had been shot.

And he was immobile. His back did not hurt, it simply did not function, nor his legs. Peter had to lie there—and the cattle were stampeding toward him. Even as he looked up, he saw a great bull with horns coming toward him, head lowered, blindly.

He would be crushed!

He managed to curl his upper trunk down toward his legs, instinctively. The bull rushed over him, one hoof landed smack on Peter's shoulder, and he groaned. Then the animal was gone, and another was coming. God, he would be torn to pieces!

Joe was riding toward him, scattering the herd recklessly. From the front of the herd, Hilohilo was riding back to him. But they would never get there in time —the bull was charging—

Joe literally leaped through the air from the saddle of his horse to the back of the enraged and frightened bull. His large powerful hands caught at the horns. As though he steered a boat, he turned the bull's head with sheer muscular power, and made him go left of Peter.

Then Hilohilo was down beside Peter, protecting him with the crouch of his huge body. "You hurt, boss? You hurt?" His hands found the wound on the back. His face registered his shock. "Oh, gods and merciful gods, you are hurt!"

The earth shook with the pounding of hooves. More cattle were following the bull which Joe Smith rode. Hilohilo simply picked Peter up in his arms, hoisted him into the saddle, mounted behind him on the rump of his large black horse, and kicked the animal on its way. The horse leaped, startled, and took off.

Other cowboys were on the way. Hats waving, ropes curling in the air, they were among the cattle, scattering them, pushing them away from the laden black horse. Peter was sagging, Hilohilo had all he could do to hold him there.

Joe Smith had left the bewildered bull caught in the trees, running back to catch the reins of his own patient mount. He swung up, and pushed aside the cattle to get to Hilohilo.

"What is it? What happened?"

"Don't know . . . bleeding bad. . . ." Hilohilo showed the blood on his hands.

"Peter?" asked Joe anxiously. "What happened?"

Peter's head buzzed, he could not answer. Darkness was falling fast, he had thought it was noon, but everything was getting dark, and his tongue was thick. He tried to tell them, but his head drooped down, and he was beginning to ache.

"Get boss back to house," said Hilohilo.

Joe wanted to carry the boss, Hilohilo would not give him up. The two made their way at a gallop across the plains, Joe ready to catch the sagging body of Peter Darien should he fall. But Hilohilo held him on the horse with maniacal strength, his brown face set and determined.

He thought the wound was not from the hoof of a bull. That did not make a wound of that nature. And he had heard something like a rifle shot.

At the house, Rosalind ran out to the patio as soon as they rode to the stables. She saw Peter sagging in the saddle, Joe Smith slipping to the ground to catch his boss, the stablehands running up.

"What happened? Oh, God, is he. . . ."

She saw the blood, and she wanted to faint. She had dreaded this, every day she dreaded it until he came home. Kinau had prophesied that something evil would happen, there would be death. But not Peter's death, oh, not Peter—

The men carried Peter into the house, and laid him

down on the couch in the smaller drawing room. Norma had run to see him, Honora came with quick light steps, taking in the situation at a look.

Joe's quick sure hands had the shirt ripped open. They had laid Peter on his stomach. He lay unconscious, his arms limply falling. Rosalind knelt at his head, and supported him.

"What . . . happened," she managed to say again.

"Don't know yet. The earth shook," said Joe.

"The ground quivered. The cattle, they run," said Hilohilo.

The two men examined the wound, their faces grave. Norma brought cloths, they sponged away the blood, which welled again.

"It is a bullet wound," said Joe Smith, straightening. "In the back. Thank God, it is in the flesh, not near the spine. Some salve, Mrs. Darien," he said to Norma. "More bandages, we must tie him tight."

"He needs doctor," said Hilohilo. "We cannot remove bullet."

Rosalind was caressing Peter's limp black head and shoulders. She found the heavy bruise on his shoulder. "What is this?"

"Bull step on him," said Hilohilo.

"Oh, mercy on us," muttered Aunt Honora, stifling a sob. Crying did no good, that would have to wait. She knelt by Peter and helped Norma in trying to staunch the blood which kept seeping from the wound. Such a tiny puncture, to make so much blood.

Rosalind could scarcely bear to look at it. She had bandaged others, had teased the children who scraped their arms and legs on the coral and rocks. But she could not bear to see Peter hurt and unconscious. It made her sick with fear. He could not be dying, he must not. He was so vital.

"What's going on?" Terry lounged in, munching some nuts. His eyes opened wide at the sight. "Peter got it? How bad is it?"

They made way for him, gravely. Rosalind lifted her head, her eyes glazed with tears.

"Wow, that looks bad! How did it happen? He needs a doctor!" Terry said sharply.

Joe Smith briefly related what had happened, Terry issued orders importantly.

"Hiloholo, send someone to Kailua for a doctor, get Doctor Gordon, he knows bullet wounds. Joe, you better get back to the cattle and round them up, move them to better grass so they won't be so restless." Terry had taken over and was enjoying it.

The two men looked at each other, then nodded. The women had succeeded in making the blood flow stop.

"I come back pretty soon," said Hilohilo, and departed. Joe went out with him, Rosalind heard their grave low tones as they went to the horses.

Norma was smoothing salve carefully around the wound. Honora was tearing cloth for bandages, each rip seemed to make Rosalind jolt. She felt as though her heart was breaking, slowly, painfully, as Peter's slow breathing sounded heavily in the small room.

"He'll be all right," Honora said reassuringly to Rosalind. "He's tough, and the wound is not in a vital spot. The nursing will be the worst, he'll be cross as a bear. I remember once when he was knocked unconscious in a fall. He was absolutely horrible, and he was only fourteen then!"

Rosalind could not even smile. She slowly smoothed the lustrous black hair, then touched his bronzed face. Oh, if she could only take the hurt herself! It would be more easy to bear than this.

She did not have the courage to examine her feelings. She felt weak and helpless, and half-sick. Hilohilo returned to say the man was leaving immediately on one of the sailing vessels for Kailua. It would be too long until a steamship called the next time.

"Did you tell him to hurry?" asked Terry sharply.

Hilohilo nodded, his grave face grieved as a child's. "I tell him *wikiwiki*."

"Well, he should be back in three days or less," said Terry. "Get Peter upstairs to bed, Hilohilo. I'll

go out and see that the men are working." And he
bustled out, full of self-importance.

Norma gazed after him thoughtfully. Honora
shrugged, her mouth twisted. Rosalind paid little
attention to him. Hilohilo had brought in one of the
house servants, a great man as big as himself, and
carefully they carried the prone body upstairs.

Rosalind trailed after them, Norma hastened to
open the bedcovers and place sheets beneath, in case
the bleeding started again. She took away the pillows.

Kinau padded in silently, as they were settling
Peter as carefully as possible. Her round face was
mournful.

Rosalind waited until the others had left the room.
She lowered the blinds and darkened the room so
that the light would not hurt Peter's eyes when he
wakened. Then she said softly to Kinau,

"This is . . . not the death . . . that you saw? Oh,
tell me."

Kinau shook her head. "No, not him, not Mr.
Peter," she said with conviction.

Rosalind let out a long painful breath. "Oh, thank
God!"

"But he be sick. We take care of him long, long.
Poor one," she crooned over him. "Bad trouble come
to Darien, and we must fight strong. I make good medicine. If only Pele closer to us!"

"We cannot go again now." Rosalind was firm
about that. "I cannot leave Peter."

"No, you not leave your man," said Kinau contentedly. She drew up the blanket over Peter's
shoulders. He lay so still, so unnaturally still, his face
so blank.

Rosalind pulled up a chair. It would be a long
wait until the doctor arrived. He might well be feverish before that time. She would be patient, and
watchful.

A sound at the door drew her attention. She
glanced around, and saw Eileen. The blue eyes were
as chill and cool as her pale blue dress.

Eileen moved into the room, her gown rustling with her graceful languid steps. "How bad is he?" she asked baldly, looking curiously at Peter's face. She showed no sorrow, no excitement. Only something glowed in her face, some secret satisfaction. Rosalind felt strangely repelled.

"He has a bullet in him," she said shortly. "Terry has sent for a doctor."

"Too bad," said Eileen, in her drawling, idly contemptuous way. "He'll be sick for a time, I suppose."

"Yes," said Rosalind. The perfume that Eileen wore was so strong that she felt sick with it. Or was it something else she brought in with her, some sense of evil?

Kinau was glaring at Eileen. Eileen ignored her, and moved to stand at the bedside, and leaned to stare into Peter's face. "Is he asleep?"

"He is unconscious. Please don't get so close!"

"Why not? He is my cousin. I'll help you nurse him," said Eileen, with a little cat smile curling her lips. "You always complain about me to him, that I don't do any work. I'll nurse him. I'm sure he would enjoy that!"

"I don't complain about you," said Rosalind, with restraint. "And I prefer to care for him myself."

"Jealous?" murmured Eileen. "Anyone can sit at a bedside and pat the patient's hand. Go away and get some rest, you look haggard. I'll tend to him."

"No," said Rosalind, firmly.

Eileen dragged forward a chair, as though prepared to sit down and wait.

"Get out!"

"Are you talking to me in that rude way?" Eileen drawled, the smile leaving her. Her blue eyes blazed. "Terry is in charge now, and you'll see . . . he won't cater to your every whim!"

"This is my bedroom, and you will get out!" said Rosalind, not caring how rude she was. She only knew she would be sick to her stomach if that woman remained.

"I'm going to stay and nurse him," said Eileen.

Rosalind looked desperately at Kinau. The woman nodded, and moved over to Eileen. Easily she picked up the startled girl by the waist and moved her to the door. Eileen screamed.

"What the hell are you doing—let me down, you damn native!"

"Get her out of here, Kinau!" Rosalind bent to Peter, but the noise had not disturbed him. He did not move.

Kinau put Eileen down with a jolt in the hallway. When Eileen raised her hand to strike Kinau, Kinau lifted her hands also. And the Hawaiian woman was so much bigger that Eileen hesitated.

"You go away, not disturb my Rosalind," said Kinau, definitely.

Norma came along the hallway with fresh bandages. "What in the world is going on!" she asked amazed and frowning. Her face was white under her widow's cap, accented by the stiff black of her gown.

"That woman . . . she put her hands on me, and threw me out of Peter's room!" cried Eileen. "I want to nurse Peter!"

"Nonsense," said Norma briskly. "You couldn't nurse a dying cat. Go find something useful to do. What about that embroidery I gave you?"

Eileen gave a little inarticulate cry, and rushed away. Norma shook her head. "What a fuss," she said wearily. "She must not go into Peter's bedroom. It is not proper."

"No, Mrs. Darien," agreed Kinau, all amiability. "I take bandages, yes? Mr. Peter, he sleeps."

"That will be good for him. I am afraid he will be feeling a great deal of pain when he wakens." Norma went into the bedroom, bent to touch Rosalind's head gently. "Dear child, send Kinau for me whenever you want any help. I'll keep Eileen away. I think she means well, but she is so spoiled."

Rosalind shook her head, but said little. The smell

of Eileen's strong perfume lingered in the room, but gradually dissipated. The sunshine peeped through the cracks of the blinds, and she rocked slowly in the chair, waiting, waiting, until Peter should wake up.

# 16

❦ ❦ ❦ ❦

WITHIN THREE DAYS, Dr. Gordon arrived on Darien. It had been a fast trip for a sailboat, but it had seemed weeks to Rosalind and the others.

The tall, grave Scotsman bent over the patient, and examined him thoroughly. "Well, the wound has not festered, that is good."

Peter had been unconscious most of the time, wakening only briefly to take broth or hot tea with a little brandy in it. Rosalind was sent from the room, and Kinau took her place. Two of the strong husky Hawaiian house servants held Peter carefully, with their brawny hands keeping him from moving, while the bullet was removed from Peter's back.

Then he was bandaged again, and the doctor came out. He smiled reassuringly at Rosalind.

"A good clean wound. Too near the spine for comfort, but it missed it, thank God. Want a souvenir?" and he dropped the round pellet into her hand. She gazed down at it, shuddering. This little grey-black piece of lead had laid Peter low. It might have killed him.

The doctor had called Hilohilo and Joe Smith, as they lingered anxiously near the house. They came in, sombreros in hand, tiptoeing over the carpets.

"I'll have to make a statement to the authorities in Kailua," said the doctor as he sat down at the desk in the small drawing room. He laid out paper and pen carefully, meticulously, his skillful hands moving over the desk as they had examined Peter's body. "Will you tell me exactly what you saw and heard?"

Rosalind, Norma and Honora listened also as the

two men, in their terse way, explained the little they knew of the circumstances. For the first time, Rosalind realized what those two men had done, daringly rescuing Peter.

The doctor listened, bent his head over the papers, and began to write. The sunlight shone on his greying red hair. He scribbled for a time. The men watched him, turning and turning their hats in their hands.

"You saw no one fire the shot?" he finally asked, looking up.

Hilohilo and Joe Smith both shook their heads firmly.

Hilohilo said, "If I see, I kill."

The doctor smiled faintly. "If you see or know, you will tell the authorities, and they will take care of the matter. You stay out of trouble."

Hilohilo's generous mouth became thin and set. Joe said nothing, but his grey eyes glowed with fire.

The doctor finished his writing, read out the statement. The men came over, Hilohilo scrawled his name, and Smith wrote his slowly and carefully. Norma signed as a witness, then the doctor let the pages dry before he folded them.

"You will stay for a day or two, Doctor Gordon?" Norma asked, and Rosalind listened anxiously for the answer.

He nodded briefly. "I'll stay for three. He should be conscious and beginning to heal by that time. Any complications would show up. Meantime, I'll set up a clinic, and have a look at the people here. Might spread the word."

Norma gratefully did as he requested, and the doctor saw a stream of patients, mothers and babies, small children with scratches or fever blisters, a few cowboys with injuries they had not bothered to take time to go to Kailua to have treated.

The doctor was a fine guest, as well. He had amusing ancedotes to tell at dinner time and later in the drawing room. Norma, Rosalind and Honora were taking turns remaining with the patient. The doctor lightened the gloom of the household, with his fund of tales from all parts of the world.

Peter began to recover. He was irritable, yet too ill to make much trouble. Rosalind slept on a nearby cot so she would not disturb him, and he slept better at nights. During the day, he was often wakeful, though feverish, wanting to know what was going on, demanding reports.

Terry would bustle up in the late afternoon, with complaints about how Hilohilo had disobeyed him, and Joe Smith refused to have the cattle moved north again.

He upset Peter, and finally Rosalind told Terry bluntly, "You handle the ranch as best you can, Terry, and let Peter alone. He is too ill to manage right now. You'll have to make the decisions, or let them go until Peter is better."

"Well, damn it, the men won't listen to me," he grumbled, and went off to complain to his mother.

Glendon Corey returned from a boat trip around the islands. He came in, one evening, tanned and rested, and glanced about in surprise. "Well, Doctor Gordon, what are you doing here? A blessed event?" he smiled knowingly at Rosalind.

She did not even blush at his grey flinty eyes, as he looked her up and down significantly.

"No, Peter has been injured," she said shortly.

"Peter? That man is indestructible," said Corey, shaking his head. "What happened?"

Rosalind left the room as Norma began to explain. She disliked the man, and could not bear to hear again what had happened to Peter. It made her ill whenever she thought of what might have happened, his death under the hooves of the cattle, stampeded by the shot and the earth tremors.

Rosalind had tried to thank Hilohilo and Joe Smith, but her voice had faltered and broken. Tears filled her eyes, as she pressed their calloused hands. "I can never thank . . . thank . . ." she began.

"You do not need to say words," said Hilohilo for them both. "He is our friend," said the Hawaiian,

243

"and one day I get the man who shoot the bullet. I tell you this, I get him. Peter my friend always. Good to me ever. I get that damn man who shoot!" and his black eyes blazed.

Glendon Corey was full of amazement, and wanted to ask all kinds of questions. Everyone got thoroughly tired of him, and Rosalind thought of asking him to leave when Dr. Gordon departed on the weekly steamer. But she could not, he was a guest. Just because he was irritating was no reason to be discourteous. No Hawaiian would act like that.

Dr. Gordon expressed himself satisfied with Peter's slow recovery, and Peter thanked him for coming.

"Call me. I'll come by sailboat again, I enjoyed the journey," the doctor smiled. "Any time. The fishing here is excellent!"

Terry had taken him out twice in a boat, with Hawaiian men to manage the sails, and the doctor had caught a huge *ulua*. They had all enjoyed the eating of it, the most delicious of the game fish. This one must have weighed more than fifty pounds, the doctor had boasted proudly.

Terry had shown himself at his best in entertaining the doctor. Rosalind wished he would always be so genial. But after the doctor left, Terry again attempted to dictate to the cowboys, and the men would not accept his orders peacefully. Always they would look to Hilohilo or Smith in order to doublecheck whether they should do what Terry Darien said, and it made the man furious.

Peter was sitting up every day now, in a wing chair near a window of their bedroom. It was hard to make him rest, he insisted on seeing the ranch papers and getting reports from the men. But he was too weak, his hands would shake as he tried to hold the papers. He had lost much blood, the doctor had said, and it would take some time to rebuild strength.

Rosalind came in about mid-afternoon with his cup of chicken broth and thick bread with butter. She found him bent over the desk, his head on his hand.

"Oh, Peter, you are doing too much!" she said, reproachfully. He lifted his head, his face was white with weariness. "You must lie down again."

He managed a smile. "Yes, I guess so. I'm as weak as a baby." He let her help him back to the bed, and slid into the sheets. "Speaking of babies, how is Victor? I haven't had sight or sound of him for two weeks."

"Oh, he is fine. He asks every day where is dada? And he pouts when I say he cannot see you."

"Bring him down to me. I long to see him," said Peter, with his old imperiousness.

Rosalind hesitated dubiously. "He is a very lively fellow, he will bounce all over the bed, Peter."

"No matter, I want to see him."

So she went up for the child, and got him up from his nap. He was still sleepy, and blinked and yawned as she got him dressed in a soft yellow suit. She carried him downstairs to the second floor, and into the bedroom. Victor woke up completely then.

"Dadadada!" he cried, and held out his arms to the man in bed. Peter grinned at him, well pleased, and extended his good arm. His other shoulder was still tied up and bandaged, with thick grease on the deep bruise where the bull had stepped on him.

Rosalind let Victor down carefully on the large bed and he crawled into Peter's arm, leaning his head against Peter's neck.

To their surprise, Victor just curled up and cuddled down contentedly. "Did you miss me, my little fella?" asked Peter tenderly.

"Dadada," said Victor, crooning it to Peter's neck.

Rosalind sat down cautiously on the edge of the bed, ready to grab Victor if he made a lunge to one side or another. "He really has missed you, Peter. He keeps looking around, and when we go outside, he must go over to the stables and see if you are there."

Peter patted the little sturdy back. "I think he has grown some more," he said, studying the legs and arms.

"He is eleven months old. And he is walking by himself," she said proudly. "We have to watch him every minute, out on the patio. He can get up by himself and grab something before you can say boo."

"Boooo," mimicked Victor, and gave a happy little chuckle. Peter laughed aloud, the first time he had done so in weeks. He ruffled the black curly hair. Victor rubbed his cheek against Peter's neck, and cooed to himself, garbling words with nonsense sounds.

"Peter, you have got to tell those men to mind me!" Terry burst in on the peaceful scene. His hair was a mess, his face red. He did not seem to see anyone but Peter, until he approached the bed. Then he saw Victor and his face underwent a sharp change. There was fury, shame, a strange look in his eyes. He looked at his son a long moment, then away, as though he could not endure to see him.

"I'll take Victor back to his room," said Rosalind hastily. She reached for the child, but he defied her with a chuckle, and curled more deeply against Peter.

"No, leave him. Now what's the trouble, Terry? I told you to leave the cattle where they were," said Peter sharply.

"It's damn silly!" stormed Terry. "They aren't getting enough to eat. When we market them, they won't fetch half the money. They have to get to good grass, and that's on the north slopes. A tidal wave! Hell, we'll never have one. They don't happen but once in ten years."

"You'll leave the cattle where they are. If they don't gain weight, we'll keep them off the market for awhile. It won't hurt anything," said Peter.

"Won't hurt anything! We have to have the money! How do you think Eileen and I can travel to the mainland if we don't have funds?" asked Terry furiously. "You promised we could go this year. . . ."

"I said *if* we had the money."

"Oh, hell! You promised Eileen she could go, you know she wants to get away! She wants more clothes. . . ."

"She can't wear half of what she already has."

The sharp voices had made Victor sit up and look with troubled eyes from one man to the other. As Terry came closer to the bed, the baby shrank from him, back against the hard frame of the man who held him closely.

Rosalind had slid to the chair near the bed. Terry continued to argue, his head down like a bull about to charge. He was weak—but stubborn. He could quarrel on and on for hours. She looked, troubled, at Peter's drained face. He was lighter in complexion, the tan having faded in his weeks of confinement. His dark head moved wearily on the pillow. She longed to throw out Terry as she had Eileen.

"That damn Hilohilo was insolent to me!" went on Terry, listing his many grievances. "He as much as told me he would not obey my orders! Well, I'm the Darien, not him! And I told him if he didn't do what I said, he was fired!"

"Nonsense," said Peter, his voice dragging. "I wouldn't fire Hilohilo for anything. He is worth his weight in gold. Tell him to come and see me."

"You tell him! Or send your devoted wife!" sneered Terry. "He won't listen to anything I say! And that damn Joe Smith, he listens, then without saying a word, rides where he damn well pleases! Well, let me tell you. . . ."

"I could hear your voices clear downstairs," Norma said reprovingly as she entered. "Terry, you know you must not upset Peter, he isn't strong enough yet. Do go and wash up for dinner."

"I'm not a baby!" he yelled at her.

"Then don't act like one," smiled Norma, and took his arm gently and led him away. Rosalind sighed with relief.

Peter was gazing at Rosalind thoughtfully. He didn't like the new gauntness in her face nor the dark shadows under the amber eyes. She had been with him constantly. When he wakened in the night, thirsty and feverish, her gentle voice had soothed him, she had held cool water to his lips, her hand had stroked over her shoulder. She was worn out with nursing him.

Victor's small body relaxed against his. He realized then that the baby had been tense with alarm during the argument. The small black head burrowed against his shoulder. He patted the head soothingly, and Victor began to croon again, some little song he knew.

"You are tired, my darling," said Peter.

Rosalind jumped, he saw the slight movement of her shoulders and arms. "Oh . . . no . . . I'm getting plenty of sleep."

"Are you? Up half the night, and your sleep interrupted when I turn over. I'm glad I'm much better, you shall finally have some rest."

She came and smoothed the counterpane around him. "No . . . Peter, it isn't that. I'm . . . worried."

"About what?" he asked cautiously. "Terry blusters around, but he isn't dangerous."

"Isn't he?" She hesitated, then sat down beside Victor, and patted his sturdy legs. "Terry was . . . out on the range, that day you were shot, Peter."

His eyes narrowed. "So, all the cowboys were."

"Could he . . . would he? . . ."

"Shoot me? I don't believe so, *makamae*," he said quietly. "I know. I've lain here, now that I am in my right mind again. I've gone over and over who it could be, the man who shot me. But I can't figure it out. Terry isn't like that. He blusters, and he lazes away his days and nights. But he doesn't hate, not like that."

She was silent, tracing an invisible pattern on the counterpane. He reached out past Victor, and touched a long glossy brown braid.

"Been worrying about that?" he asked softly.

She nodded. "And if . . . if anyone . . . might do it . . . again," she managed to get out. She was pale under her golden tan, and the amber eyes were frightened.

"Well, I don't know," he said, practically. "If it was done to frighten me . . . or cripple me for a time, that succeeded. If it was to . . . to kill me, the person might try again. But I'll be on the lookout from now on."

"How can you be?" she burst out passionately. "A coward who would shoot from behind the bushes or trees, someone who shot you in the back when you were herding cattle, who knew the danger of a stampede . . . Oh, Peter, I am scared!"

"So am I," he said, with a smile. "Come on, Rosalind, there's nothing that can be done here, not in the house. A stranger would get halfway in the door, and one of the men would half kill him."

"What if it . . . was not a stranger? We know almost everyone except for . . . only a few stray fishermen, who come and go, and they don't come up to the house usually."

Victor had been sucking loudly on his finger. Now, ignored and feeling the pangs of hunger, he began to fuss.

"Here, now, young fellow," said Peter, struggling a little to control him. His face contracted as a stab of pain shot through his shoulder.

"Oh, let me take him. Come on, you rascal," said Rosalind, and leaned to pick the baby up. "He's hungry, I'll take him up to Kinau."

"Right. And don't worry. This isn't your worry, darling," Peter told her. "I'll work it out."

She shook her head, and carried Victor away. Peter lay back, thinking. He did not believe that Terry would shoot him. He would rage and threaten, bluster and storm. But shooting in the back—no, that was not Terry's manner. If he fought Peter, it would be openly.

Eileen? No, she didn't know one end of a gun from another.

Norma and Honora were devoted and loyal.

He thought over the house servants, went over one after another. Most had been here longer than Peter himself, or they were children of some who had served the Dariens for decades. No, he could not believe them capable of such action. Besides, what reason could there be to kill him?

He counted over the *paniolos*. Dorisa's father was enraged at Terry, but he confided frankly in Peter. Joe Smith was his devoted friend, they had saved each other's lives several times. Hilohilo—no, he could kill, but not Peter. Peter he loved, and Peter loved him, with the inarticulate devotion of men who had faced grave dangers together.

He thought then of the strange Hawaiian men who had come fishing, and lingered. The big one, named Maleko, he was a question mark. He was silent and prowled around often. Joe was uneasy about him. But what reason could he have?

The days drifted by. He was healing more quickly now, and getting restless. The day came when he was able to go downstairs to the drawing room, to sink into his own big chair and grin at his father in the wheel-chair. Barton rolled closer, and touched Peter's hand, and smiled.

"Better . . . now . . ." Barton managed to say.

"Sure am, Father. Coming along fine. I'll be up on horseback in a week or so," he said cheerfully.

Alfred Murray wandered in, book in hand, and peered at Peter. "I say, you've been ill for days," he exclaimed. "You look pale, my boy. Shouldn't you see the doctor?"

Peter laughed, and the sound brought Aunt Honora bustling in, her thin face lively. "Peter, dear, you're up! Does Rosalind know? How do you feel? Shall I get you a pillow for your back? Any pain?"

Peter managed to remain with them for luncheon. Terry came in, grumbling because it was hot and the men were insolent as usual. Glendon Corey accompanied him, looking a little more dusty and less immaculate than usual. He had been riding the range, he said. A pistol hung through his belt. Peter looked at him speculatively.

Rosalind was happy, her tanned face radiating joy, her eyes glowing as she sat at the foot of the table and directed the servants. Peter ate with hearty appetite, he was making up for weeks of slops, he said.

"Slops," said Norma, wrinkling her nose. "How inelegant, Peter. They were good for you."

"Not like fish steak and baked potatoes and *papaya*," he grinned back at her.

After dinner, Rosalind insisted on having Peter lie

down on the chaise longue in the drawing room. "I feel like a damned invalid," he grumbled.

She said sweetly, "That's exactly what you are, my dear!"

He had to laugh. His eyelids felt heavy, he felt pleasantly drowsy, and he soon fell off to sleep during the hot hours of the afternoon. It had been an effort to come downstairs, after dressing and shaving. But it was worth it, he felt more himself, and the tug of pain in his back was only a faint reminder of what he had gone through. The skin itched a bit where it was healing.

He had dinner on a tray in the drawing room. Rosalind refused to let him sit up during another long meal. But the others soon came in to join him, with Rosalind keeping a watchful eye.

"Well, splendid to see you with us, again, Peter," beamed Corey, his grey flinty eyes shining in the firelight.

"Good of you," said Peter drily. The man made him feel like a guest in his own home.

They talked a bit around the fire. Peter lay back and listened, as Eileen rambled on in a discontented way about the postponed shopping trip to California. Terry complained about the cowboys. Rosalind was sewing a new suit for Victor, it seemed he was outgrowing his others. Norma had offered to help, she was making the jacket. Honora was reading over one of Alfred Murray's manuscripts intently, paying little attention to the conversation of the others. Barton Darien was listening eagerly, his hand tapping the arm of his wheelchair. Mr. Murray had gone to the study to read again.

"I say, Peter, I have a proposition to put to you. No hurry, of course," offered Glendon Corey. Somehow Peter did not like his smile, it looked sharp, like a man about to pull something. He realized that, cordial as the man was, he did not like him. Something about him grated.

"What is that?" asked Peter.

"I've been thinking, riding about your ranch. It is

really too big for one man to manage . . . two men even," he added hastily, as Terry lifted his blond head. "I represent a cattle syndicate, as you know."

"So?"

Terry had caught his breath, and was leaning forward. Eileen stopped picking at the lace of her sleeves, and reached for the tall cool glass of rum at her side.

"Accidents can happen," said Corey smoothly, glancing about at the intent faces, Terry, Eileen, finally to Rosalind. Then he gazed again at Peter. "If anything else happened to you, Terry would have a rough time of it. It's a big place here, admirably run with devoted men, but still difficult."

"So?" asked Peter again, drawling it out. With an effort, he remained relaxed against the back of the chaise longue.

"So I'd like to make an offer to buy you out, in the name of my syndicate. I've written to them, they are offering you half a million dollars for the island, the ranch, everything."

There was a short tense silence in the drawing room. The log in the fireplace popped, and Rosalind jumped. She had her hand at her throat. Peter glanced at her, then again at Corey.

"No dice," he said quietly, definitely.

"No?" smiled Mr. Corey. "Oh, come on, now, don't be so sure about it! I meant for you to consider it carefully, talk about it with your family. With half a million dollars, you would all be secure for life. You could go anywhere and live, San Francisco, New York City, London, Paris, Rome. If you like, half could be paid down, and the rest would be paid in yearly installments to each in terms of the shares you own in the ranch. Then you could be sure of having a lifetime income. My syndicate is very reputable. I'll be glad to present papers, give you information. . . ."

"No, never. I'll never sell Darien," said Peter. "That is final."

"If you think the amount is not sufficient, I'll go back to my syndicate," persisted Corey. His hands were clenched on his knees. "Say, half a million dollars down, and a set amount to each person for life. What do you say? I'll have to ask, but my people are anxious to have a base on an island, and I must say this is the most suitable spot. You have to have fresh water, and all that. . . ."

"No," repeated Peter, flatly.

Terry rushed into speech. He had been sitting forward, breathing heavily. "Peter, you can't refuse. It's the best offer we ever had! My God, think of it! San Francisco . . . Paris! We'd never have to work a day again in our lives!" he cried, his face radiant.

Eileen said, "You must consider it, Peter. You must accept! Think of us! We won't remain isolated on this island forever! It would save having to buy us out, our shares. . . ."

Peter was silent, gazing into the flames. Oddly, he was not thinking about Terry's and Eileen's impassioned arguments. He was wondering if Corey had really been on a boat trip around the islands on the day Peter had been shot. If he might have been hiding instead on some part of the island, with a rifle in hand, ready to shoot—How good a shot was he? He wore a pistol with ease, the holster was quite used.

"Mrs. Darien, you urge him to sell out. I have seen your concern for him," said Glendon Corey. Peter's attention returned to them, and he looked at Corey. "You are concerned about him, you don't want to see him have another accident. . . ."

"It was no accident, Mr. Corey, for Peter to be shot in the back," said Rosalind, bluntly. "No, I don't want Peter to sell out. He loves Darien, and he belongs here. His father and grandfather made Darien what it is. No, I don't want us to leave."

Eileen cried out against her. "You're selfish, selfish! Just because you're happy with messing around with babies and cooking and gardening . . . you're so dull! You haven't seen the big cities, the really big ones! If you ever did. . . ."

"It would make no difference," said Rosalind. "This is Peter's life, I don't want him to lose it. I don't care if I never see any city in the world."

Eileen sneered at her. "Just because you don't, that is no sign we don't. And we are the ones who own shares. . . . Peter, you must sell out. . . ."

"Peter, don't listen," said Rosalind angrily, spots of color in her cheeks. Her amber eyes shone with fury. "Eileen is the selfish one. I bet she could spend the half a million in one year! And the island would be gone, spoiled!"

"Spoiled! My dear Mrs. Darien," said Corey, smiling at her, but with a nasty gleam in his grey eyes, "what do you think we are? The syndicate will run the island as before, with the Hawaiians as content as children. They will work for us just as willingly. They don't care what happens, so long as they have their fish and their *poi!*"

"And that, Mr. Corey, shows you how little you know of the Hawaiian people!" Rosalind snapped sharply. "They have emotions and feelings, loyalties and beliefs. They have come to love the Dariens and will work for them. Why do you think they will stay on and work for you? Why should they?"

For a moment, he looked disconcerted. Then he shrugged. "If they don't like it, they can leave and get jobs elsewhere. We shan't try to hold them."

"Nor help them, nor see that they get medical care and proper food," she raged, jumping up. "Don't listen to him, Peter! He only wants the ranch for the money he can make. He doesn't care about the people here at all!"

Eileen turned to the silent Barton Darien, leaning forward in his wheelchair, listening intently, his good ear turned forward to the conversation. "Uncle Barton, tell him!" she cried. "Tell him he can't keep going! Why, he might get shot again! And the work is horribly strenuous! You don't want him to collapse and live in a wheelchair . . . do you?"

Peter turned to his parent. "Well, Father?" he asked ironically. "What do you say?"

Barton shook his shaggy iron-grey head. He managed to speak in the suddenly quiet room. "You . . .

decide, Peter. You . . . work. I . . . can't. Must decide. Leave it to you."

Corey intervened hastily. "Now, there is no reason to decide tonight! I didn't mean to bring on such feeling," he smiled at them all. Like some benign banker about to foreclose, thought Peter bitterly. "I want you to think it over calmly, Peter, and all of you. Talk it over, discuss it, the advantages, the disadvantages. Meantime, I'll write to my syndicate, and see whether we can raise the offer to something more pleasing to Peter. Yes, we must think it over," and he lifted his drink and drained the glass, with satisfaction.

Peter leaned back, his face felt tired, his eye muscles twitched. He put his hand to his face. Rosalind came to him, bent over him.

"I'll help you upstairs, Peter," she said, the fury spent.

"Get one of the men, I'm too heavy for you, my dear," he said wryly.

She called to a burly Hawaiian servant and between them they got Peter upstairs. He was glad to undress and sink into bed. That had been quite a scene. But he was more interested in Corey, and why he had chosen this particular moment to make the offer.

Peter was getting stronger. But he was still a semi-invalid, weak and prone to anxiety. Did Corey understand that, putting the pressure on at the time when Peter was most likely to give in?

"I could have hit him tonight," said Rosalind savagely, as she smoothed fresh salve on the back wound before setting a bandage carefully in place. "Bringing that up tonight, your first day downstairs!"

"You defended me like a little tiger cub," he grinned into the pillow. "And Darien, you sounded like you love the island."

"The island . . . and the people. He is a cold-blooded man, he cares nothing for the Hawaiian people. Oh, Peter, don't listen to him."

Her fingers felt gentle and soothing. "You know," he said, testing her, "you might like California and some traveling. I do mean to take you away someday."

"Oh . . . Peter!" Her fingers stopped. "Not forever!"

"Of course not, silly girl. We both love it here. No, just for a vacation."

"That's all right, then," she said, her hand rubbing the salve soothingly on his back. "There, does that feel better?"

He smiled to himself. The trip meant nothing to her. Perhaps she would like to go one day, but he would have to talk her into it. How her amber eyes would shine, though, to hear the opera in San Francisco. Rosalind would enjoy seeing the grand sights all over America and Europe. Yes, he must take her on a journey one day, before long. They had never had a real honeymoon. He would like to have a honeymoon with her, a trip around the world. When he could get someone to take charge of the ranch, and run it well, though. Not before.

He rolled over after she had finished bandaging him. He watched her dainty movements as she undressed for bed, turning her back to him as she removed the last garments. Even as long as they had been married, she was shy as a girl. But he delighted in looking at the slim smoothness of her shoulders emerge from the dress, the soft whiteness of the flesh on her back, the small waist, curving hips, and tapered thighs. The nightdress slid on over her head, and she wriggled unconsciously until the gown fell to below her knees.

She blew out the lamp, and lay down on the cot.

"How long am I going to have to go to bed alone?" he asked.

For a moment there was complete silence.

"The doctor said to wait until you were completely well." Her voice sounded meek. He grinned in the darkness. She was about as timid as a spitting tiger when she got going!

"Well, I'll soon be well," he said casually. "So don't count on sleeping by yourself much longer."

Rosalind said nothing. He stretched in the bed, and thumped the pillow before settling down. No, he would not wait much more. He was used to reaching out and holding her softness next to himself. It was lonely without her.

However, his last thought before sleep was not of his wife. He thought about Corey and his offer, flung into the chaos of emotional relationships of the Dariens, into the aftermath of the shooting, the problems of the ranch intensified by the fear of earthquakes and tidal waves.

He wondered again if Corey had been on a boat. How to find out? Hilohilo might be able to discover the answer. He would put him to work on that tomorrow, Peter vowed. He wanted very much to find just where Glendon Corey had been on the day of the shooting.

# 17

❦ ❦ ❦ ❦

PETER HAD BECOME much more restless, since getting up for a time every day. He was still weak, however, and Norma Darien warned Rosalind.

"We must keep him busy and quiet at the same time, my dear. Or he will be out with the cattle, and working from dawn to dusk before he is strong again. Can't you think of something?"

"I wonder if he could go swimming?" asked Rosalind thoughtfully. "The exercise might do him good and he could lie on the beach in the sunshine."

"A splendid idea! Take Peter out for the day, have the cook pack a lunch for you," Norma beamed, and patted her shoulder in an unusually affectionate gesture. "You can use a rest yourself, Rosalind. If Peter says anything, I'll tell him he should go out for your sake."

"Oh, no, don't, he would only worry about me," said Rosalind quickly. "I'll tell him I long to go for a swim. That should do it. I think he wants to get out."

She approached Peter cautiously that evening. "I have been wishing we were near the lagoon on Kailua," she said, watching him as he sat up in bed.

He smiled. "You long to swim again? I think you have missed your freedom there, my dear," he said, so gently that she came to sit beside him and lean her head on his shoulder. His arm curved about her, feeling almost as strong as before.

"One day, when you feel stronger, perhaps we could go out together," she said, waiting for his reaction. "Kinau could come with me, but if we are gone all day, Victor will miss us."

"No, I'll come with you," he said quickly, stretching against the pillows. "Ah, to get out into the sunshine! Let's take the carriage and make a day of it tomorrow."

"Tomorrow?" she asked, a little dubiously. He had gone downstairs only four times this week. "Isn't it a little soon?"

"If I don't get out, I'll climb out the window," he sighed. "I dislike being laid up like this."

"We can try it," she said, her cheek against his shoulder.

As they prepared to set out the next morning Peter was having difficulty getting into the carriage.

"You be careful, boss," said the stablehand. "Want me to drive for you today?"

"No, I'll manage," and Peter picked up the reins.

The man knew it was useless to argue with Darien's manager so he satisfied himself by putting a basket of food into the carriage at their feet, added a rug and bundle of towels, and waved them on their way.

It was early morning. Peter had been awake before dawn, talking eagerly of the outing. They had departed before the rest of the family had risen. Rosalind felt lighthearted and eager to be starting out at dawn with Peter.

The eastern sky was tinted pink, and a softer pink reflected off the clouds in the west. Before them loomed the jagged peak of the extinct volcano that was the center of Darien. Many long years ago, the lava had risen from it, flowing down its sides in reddish-black molten rivers, forming the island out of the sea. Now Darien was covered with grass, shrubs, even palm trees brought in from outside. A green and pleasant land, thought Rosalind.

The horse was fresh and anxious to run. Peter let him out on the road to the north. Rosalind had never gone that way, always to the south to swim. She glanced at him curiously.

"Where are we going, Peter?"

He grinned, looking younger and even more handsome this morning, she decided. "A surprise. Nobody goes there but me, but I want you to see it. I think you'll like it."

He was mysterious, teasing her about her curiosity, and their laughter rang softly on the cool morning air. She was wearing her favorite muumuu, pink with rose hibiscus flowers on it and short ruffled sleeves. In the bundle of towels were Peter's shorts and her sarong for swimming. She relaxed as she saw that Peter could competently handle the reins, in full control. He was much stronger now. Yes, he would be chafing to get back to work.

In the distance they saw some cowboys lounging over their saddles, silently waiting for the full sun. Only a few steers were with them, yet Peter's frown told of his displeasure.

"They should be south," he muttered. "Damn Terry. He's moved some of them. I'll have to get after Hilohilo to relocate them back again."

"Maybe the danger from tidal waves is over," Rosalind suggested.

He glanced over his shoulder, back toward the sky, where steam mingled with the clouds hanging over the big island of Hawaii. "No, the doctor told me before he left that Kilauea is still active. They expect a big explosion one of these days. And if that happens, we'll need to buckle up to endure a tidal wave here, maybe more than one, depending on the force of the explosion. We've been feeling earth tremors on Darien, so have they on Hawaii."

He was silent for a time, concentrating on guiding the horse, looking with keenness over the plains, and Rosalind was content. He was looking over his domain with pride and confidence, and she was beside him, and for once they were alone. No one to burst in the door and interrupt them, no one to complain and bring problems, no one to watch and sneer as Eileen did. They were completely alone in the morning dawn.

It was a longer drive than she had anticipated, some ten miles, she estimated. She looked up at the cliffs as they approached the northwest. They loomed much higher and more abruptly than she had believed. Before this point there were low level plains, where she could see the blue-green sea as it rolled in breakers to the sand.

"I thought we were going to swim along here," she said once, questioningly.

He shook his head. "No, not here. It's nice, but not as nice as the secret place I know," he grinned across at her. He sounded like an excited boy.

"Doesn't anybody else know about it? Not Terry, or Hilohilo?"

"Oh, they know of it, but they don't go there," he said. "You'll see why when we go. Years ago, it was dangerous. The cliffs were falling into the sea, there was a landslide. No one went there, especially after the second ship went on the reefs."

She sensed a story. "Oh, tell me, Peter! What ship? And what was the first one?"

He settled himself on the seat, slowing the horse to a walk. "Well, many years ago, my father had sent in for some supplies, and a ship foundered on the reef in the northwest. He was annoyed, and blew up at the captain when he finally appeared, wringing wet and the cargo lost. The seamen were saved, but the reefs got a bad name. There's no way in over the coral, for it rips the ship's bottom to pieces. The captain thought he would be smart and save a journey around the island." Peter smiled. "He got another lecture when he told Father that! I thought Father would explode!"

"What is the place like? How can we swim there?" she asked apprehensively.

"Well, you'll see. There is a lagoon with rather deep waters, maybe ten to twenty feet in places, and it ends sharply at the reefs. The waters boil in over the coral, making it look like the ships could come in. But everyone knows now how dangerous it is. No ship can come, not even the long canoes. But about ten years ago, another ship came in that way. A captain strange to these waters had missed his way in a storm, making for Kailua, and put in there. I'll tell you, his vessel went to pieces on the coral. Fortunately his passengers could swim, and they made it to shore. But their feet were badly cut by the coral and the tales they told were enough to keep everyone away from the lagoon."

"Except you," she said wryly.

A mischievous sparkle shone in Peter's dark eyes. "Yes. I discovered the lagoon for myself some time ago, and kept going back. You'll see why."

And then he was provokingly silent, looking out over the range and whistling a tune.

To her surprise, they left the plains and drove up a precipitous road to the top of the cliffs. There he got down rather painfully, and unfastened the horse to turn him loose at the end of a long rope, to graze the sweet grass at the top of the cliffs, a safe distance from the edge. He lifted Rosalind out, then the basket and bundles. She insisted on carrying her share, and he gave in.

"Okay, we go down a steep path, so watch your step. Hold on to me, I'll go first, because I know the way. You have your sandals on? Good."

Puzzled, she followed him into some bushes that seemed to hang over the cliff edge. Only someone who knew it was there would have found the path, hidden by overgrown vines and lantana. They started cautiously downward, Peter seeming to find his way by sheer instinct, as the path wound casually among bushes and ferns. Bright fuchsia bloomed in the ferns, rosy blooms over which Rosalind wanted to linger.

Peter called over his shoulder, "Don't stop, there's more below."

"Coming," she said, gasping, and wanted to grab his shoulder as the path steepened. She heard rumbling, a funny odd sound, and they came to a waterfall. The path wound almost to its edge, and Peter paused to smile at her in triumph, as though he had produced it himself for her admiration.

The waterfall ran in a thin crystal-clear stream from the ferny deeps of the cliffs. "Fresh water," said Peter, held his hand under it, and extended his cupped palm for her to drink from.

"How strange, how could it be fresh?" The water was ice cold, delicious and tasteless at the same time.

"I figure it rises through the limestone by some sort of sea action, which purifies the water and leaves the salt and minerals behind. Then it comes out through the rocks and falls down into the lagoon. The ferns and flowers along here bloom only where fresh water is near. You won't find them in any other part of the island."

They went on down the path slowly, for it was slippery in places with mud from the spray of the waterfall. She wanted to pause and exclaim over the flowers, small lavender orchids, miniature pansies, or heartsease, more fuchsia, a riot of color and bloom among the dark green of the leafy ferns.

They made it to the bottom, Peter held out his hand to her, and she scrambled down the last part of the path. How would they ever get up again, Rosalind wondered, for Peter was not well yet. She scolded herself for letting him come. Yet—how enchanting a place!

The lagoon lay circled with reefs, and the blue-green sea blustered beyond, breaking over the coral in white bubbles. Within the lagoon the sea was deep, but placid. The waterfall ran right into the lagoon, making a gentle splash as it fell. On either side of the waterfall lay ivory beaches, untouched, clean and pure. Shells lay on the sand; many shapes and sizes, small clam shells, fascinating curlicues, larger black shells she had never seen before. Rosalind longed to drop down and examine them all. But Peter just brushed the shells aside, swept the sand clear of them, and spread out the blankets and towels and basket.

"I'm longing for a swim," he said eagerly, his face shining. "Just one thing, Rosalind. Never come here without me. I know these waters like the back of my hand. You can swim out almost to the reefs, but don't go near them, your feet can't endure it. And over to the east, don't go there," his hand indicated it. "The tides are very rough there, and you may get swept beyond the lagoon. Just stay within this area, and you'll be fine. You don't swim very far under water, do you?"

"Well, I can go down ten feet or more," she said, gazing about with shining eyes. "What a perfect place!"

"Like all perfection, it has its hazards," he said, rather grimly. "Don't go deeply over there," and he indicated the left of their area. "The coral is fairly close to the surface. Watch carefully, go where I go at first. I'll point out the places that are dangerous." And he watched her anxiously to make sure she knew he was not fooling.

"All right, Peter. I'll be careful. Oh, it's so beautiful here!" and she gazed about at the slim crystal fall of the water, the deep green of the ferns that came almost to the water's edge, the glint of pink and rose and yellow of flowers among the ferns. It was so thick and quiet and peaceful—like a paradise. "What about eels or dangerous fish?"

"Once in a while I used to see a Moray eel, but not in recent years," said Peter. "We'll watch for them, though. I'll chase them out to sea!"

He was unfastening his trousers, preparing to put on his trunks for a swim. Modestly she turned aside, and slipped off her muumuu and undergarments. She wrapped a bright orange and green sarong about herself, and turned back to see him gazing at her. Promptly she blushed, and he laughed gently down at her.

"We're married, remember?" he asked, then caught her hand, and they went into the waves.

She swam and paddled and swam again in the cool waters. They were somewhat sheltered from the sun, though it shone brightly enough near the reefs. Occasionally a rough wave made its way beyond the reefs, and churned up the waters, and they rode the wave to the beach, laughing together at the exhilaration of it.

She noticed he was tiring, and said, "I believe I need to rest, Peter, I'm going in." As she had hoped, he followed and they flopped down without bothering with towels, letting the sun and wind dry their tanning bodies. When he rolled over, she saw the deep red scar of his wound, and a fresh tenderness came over her. He had been so close to death, so close! She touched the injury.

"Does it hurt?" she asked, a catch in her voice.

"It only stings a bit in the salt water," said Peter, and rolled back to face her. Gently he lifted the wet hair from her neck. "Rosalind, you are so lovely . . . so lovely. . . ."

She knew that tone in his voice. He had been looking at her, touching her, wanting her. When he unfastened the wet sarong, and bent to press his lips to her breasts, she sighed a little, with desire, and curled her hands about his neck. It had been a long time since they had met in desire, and passion.

She loved him profoundly, she knew that. She had liked him, feared him a little, been infuriated at his assumption of possession over her, yet—yet been drawn to him as to a magnet. He was so masculine, so virile, so sure and competent, and so sweet a lover.

"Oh . . . Peter . . ." she murmured against his throat as he kissed her hair.

"So long . . . so very long . . ." he muttered, and smoothed his hand over her waist and her thighs. He kissed her over her entire body, her breasts again, following his hand, rousing her passions as only he could. He knew her now, and knew how he could build up her emotions, make her yield and respond and thrill to him.

The small lagoon was silent then, as they moved and caressed and finally embraced deeply on the churning sand. The waterfall splashed softly, a bird began to chirp over their heads. But for the singing in her ears, as the blood pounded, Rosalind could not hear any bird. She heard only Peter's voice as he muttered to her, urging her, and her breathless response, her gasps of pleasure. . . .

He lay above her, and she lay motionless, holding him in her, glory in her bones, joy in her throat, so that she wanted to sing and chant to him of her love.

Her hands shaped his bronzed shoulders, and ran across his aching back. He buried his face in her throat, and his lips pressed to her pulse-beat as he moved on her slowly—then more rapidly, urgently. Her hips lifted to meet his, ardently, wanting more and more, forgetting her shyness, forgetting any thought of retreat. The passion wiped out all coyness, she wanted only to reply and reply—answer each kiss and touch.

Her hands moved over his back, remembering the wound, avoiding it gently, the fingers playing over his spine, encouraging him, teasing him, down to his hard thighs. He groaned and came to her in love and desire. When the movements were finished, they lay silently holding each other for awhile.

He rolled over and released her. He flung out his arms. "Oh, my God, that was good. Oh, Rosalind, you are the sweetest woman in the world!"

She turned to her side. Her eyes were wet with tears of joy, her limbs lax on the sand. He put his hand to her waist, and they lay quietly, drowsily in the sunshine, letting the wind dry the sweat of their bodies. She knew when he dozed, and she was happy, and half-asleep herself.

She felt a little chilled, and sat up to wrap the sarong about herself. A large ebony colored shell lay near her, and she reached out for it idly. Peter slept deeply, on his back, his long lashes as pretty as Victor's, she thought, with an adoring smile. His black hair was crisp with the salt water, and one curl lay over his forehead. She did not press it back, fearing he might waken.

Instead, Rosalind played with the shell. It opened to her curious fingers, and she gazed inside at the wonder of the mother-of-pearl inside, the intricate formation of the oyster. She noted that, embedded in the flesh of the oyster, there was a large dark object. She pressed it, it was hard to the touch.

More curious now, she reached in the picnic basket for a sharp knife. She cut into the oyster, and removed the object. Then she stared at it, blankly, as it lay in her hand.

A black pearl!

Large, perfectly round, glistening a little with the oyster flesh. She washed it off in the fresh water of the waterfall, and it lay drying in her palm, a steel-grey color, black in the sunlight, showing glints of lighter color as the sun played on it.

She turned it over and over in her fingers. Was this where the pearls had come from? Had Peter found the pearls? The jeweler, Mr. Chan, had been so excited over them. They were supposed to be very valuable. But why here? In this lagoon?

She waited for a time, wanting to ask Peter about the pearl. But he slept deeply, worn out by the climb to the lagoon, the lusty swimming, and his love-making. His face was peaceful, she would not waken him for the world.

Cautiously, she got up and went searching for more of the same black shells. Rosalind discovered a few on the sand and more in the shallows. She knelt in the water, and found even more of the shells.

She brought them back in a basket, from which she had emptied some sandwiches and fruit. Busily, she opened them, found a few tiny black pearls, several small round ones, and another huge black one, this one irregular in shape. She remembered that they were called Baroque. This one looked like a little bee. She laid them all in a napkin and contemplated them gravely.

She was beginning to get hungry when Peter finally woke up. He lay gazing up at her blankly, then smiled at her. "Hi. Did I sleep long?"

"The sun is overhead," she pointed out.

"Noon? I'm wasting time," he joked, and stroked over her shoulder with his warm palm as he sat up. She blushed, and he laughed gently at her. "How long will you blush for me, Rosalind? All your life and mine? How pretty you are in that sarong. It's wet . . . you didn't go in swimming again, without me, did you?" His teasing turned to anxiety.

"Yes, but only on the edge of the lagoon. Peter . . . I found a black shell . . . and a pearl in it. And so I went out, and I found more . . . look." She opened the napkin and displayed the gems to him.

He did not look surprised. He took the cloth in his hand and poked the precious objects with his big finger.

"That is a very good one," he said of the first she had found. The baroque one he took up in the other hand and studied closely. "That would fetch a pretty penny," he finally said, and set it back with the others.

"Is this . . . where you found the others, Peter?"

He nodded. "Yes, but I don't want folks to know. We'll put them in the locked box in the bedroom. Mr. Chan can make a fine pendant of this baroque fellow," he finally added, and folded up the napkin. He set it back into the basket.

"How do they form here, and why aren't they anywhere else?" she finally asked.

"From what I can figure," said Peter, "they take the fresh water in the lagoon, combined with the rougher action of the waves rolling in from the ocean. I have heard that oyster pearls are formed more quickly and beautifully under conditions like these. They lie dormant in warm waters. That's about all I know on the subject," and his broad bare shoulders shrugged.

"Why are they black, Peter? Isn't that unusual?"

"Very, that is why they fetch a higher price," he said. "There are some white shells here . . ." He got up, roamed the beach, his gaze on the sand, and finally brought back three creamy white oyster shells. He pried them open with the sharp knife. She gasped with pleasure at the interior. The shells inside were of shining rainbow hues, and each oyster held in its little body a tiny white blob.

Peter cut them open deftly, and rolled the pearls into her hand. One held three small pearls, and they looked beautiful to her. "Too small for price, but pretty on a string," he said.

One held a huge white gem.

"Now, that's a good one," he said.

The third was larger than the others, and held some blister pearls on its shell. He cut them off. "Might do for ornaments," he said. He washed them in the fresh water of the crystal-clear waterfall, then dropped them into the napkin with the others.

"All I know about them," he said, "is that the white

shells bring out white pearls, sometimes rather pink in color. And the black-lipped pearl oyster brings out black pearls. And they seem to flourish here. Last year I came out several times and harvested a whole basket of black pearls. Those are the ones I took to Mr. Chan to make your jewelry from."

She studied the jewels seriously, curled up with her legs under her on the sand. He watched her as she stirred the pearls with her finger.

"But Peter . . . these must be worth quite a bit of money."

He nodded. "For several years, I took them to New York City. I had brokers sell them anonymously, so no one would know that Darien was the source. I don't want people to flock here. The source is limited. I found that if I took too many, there were fewer pearls the following year. So I take some every year, but not too many. About a dishful each time."

"And no one knows about them?"

He shook his head. "Father's doctor bills were high. I had to get more money, for him and to buy more cattle when Terry had sold off some for one of his trips. They don't know where the money comes from. The cattle and hides produce some. But the rest comes from the black pearls."

"You should have sold some, not made them into jewelry for me," she said, in a low tone.

He smiled, and ran his fingers through her loose wet hair. "We aren't hard up now, darling. Things are going fine. Mr. Chan will keep the secret. He had better, or he won't get more black pearls. I trust him completely. Whenever we get short of money, we can harvest more pearls. Until then, we can keep what we want. Did you know that pearls last for thousands of years?"

"Thousands of years?" she gasped. "In their shells?"

"No, that is only a few years, maybe three to six, I don't know. But once harvested, they last for centuries. I have seen a museum where the jewelry of early Indian rulers is kept. And among the faded silk garments are sewn bright pink and white pearls. The headdresses and crowns are full of pearls, still bright and shining. There are ropes of pearls, thousands of years old. A king's ransom and more," he added lightly.

"And black pearls?" she asked, holding the little baroque black pearl she had discovered, with a little possessive feeling. She had discovered it, lying on the ocean floor! It was her own personal treasure, and she wondered what would become of her little black bee.

"They are much rarer. One crown was set with hundreds of pink pearls, with a single black one in the center, as the focus of attention."

She shook her head, and folded the cloth, her face serious. "It scares me, Peter," she said.

"Nothing to be scared about," he said lightly, but gave her a sharp look. He teased her chin with his finger. "Something else should terrify you."

"What?"

"I'm a hungry starving man," he said solemnly. "If I'm not fed, I might go mad . . ."

"Oh . . . you!" she laughed. Rosalind placed the precious gems in the basket, and set out their lunch. They ate by the side of the waterfall, not needing the bottled water, which was warm by this time.

They ate beef sandwiches with fresh slices of lettuce and cucumbers. She was pleased at how hungrily Peter ate, and how he munched the slices of pineapple and *papaya* that followed. They drank fresh water, and ate nuts and berries, idly lying on their sides.

After they had rested again, they went swimming once more. The sun had warmed the waters, so they were milder than in the morning. Rosalind sighted more black-lipped oyster shells, but she left them for now. She had enough to worry about.

They swam cautiously over to the remains of the two shipwrecks, and climbed over them, where they had draped over the coral reefs. Only fragments remained, but they clogged the harbor, and kept the larger fish out. Waves swept over them as the ocean rose, and the surfaces were salty with brine. The masts lay across the entrance to the lagoon, and the ships lay on their sides, slowly rotting to mere shapeless hulks compared to the once magnificent beauty of their proud craft.

"They are useful. They keep people from sailing in and being wrecked," Peter said, thoughtfully. "With the ships lying there, others won't be tempted to make harbor here. And the secret of the black pearls will be safe for a long time."

"I hope so," she said, somberly. "When I think . . . Peter, people would kill for pearls like that, and the money they bring. Wouldn't they?"

"I'm afraid so," he said.

She was sorry she had said that, for the smile left his bronzed face, and the lines were carved more deeply beside his generous mouth.

They left soon after that for when dusk came they would not be able to see the path. The route was slippery, and they had to move cautiously. Once Rosalind slipped, but caught at a vine to hold on. Peter was just behind her, but she didn't want to strain him. He was weak yet, for all his slow recovery from the wound.

"Are you all right?" his voice came sharply from behind her.

"Yes, just careless, Peter. I'm fine," she said cheerily. She watched her steps more closely. The wet leaves made the path treacherous, she found, as much as the mud.

They climbed slowly up to the carriage, and found the horse sleeping peacefully at the end of his rope, having cropped fresh sweet grass most of the day.

They drove home slowly as the sun began to sink and make glorious scarlet banners across the western sky. They drove into the stableyard at full dusk to find Hilohilo waiting for them anxiously. His broad face lit up at their arrival.

"Say, boss, you gone all day!" he accused.

"Can't I even have a vacation day?" Peter laughed back at him.

Hilohilo relaxed. "You look good, have good time, eh, with your woman?"

"Had a great time with my woman," said Peter, and laughed down at Rosalind.

Hilohilo chuckled and put the horse and carriage away, a jaunty relief in his steps. Rosalind and Peter went up to their suite, to change for dinner.

"Let's eat in our room," suggested Rosalind impulsively. It had been such a peaceful day, with no jealous-eyed Eileen staring at her, no gripes from Terry.

"Fine," agreed Peter, and Rosalind had one of the maids bring up trays for them. After all, Peter was still a semi-invalid, they had a good excuse.

And he was tired. She locked up the pearls and put the box away, they ate supper and talked a little. But he had undressed after supper, and soon went to bed. He was asleep before nine o'clock, and she was pleased.

The day had wearied him, but in a pleasant way. He was more tan for the day in the sun and water, and he looked rested. She looked down at him, and then blew out the lamp to go to bed herself. She was happy with the day. And she would worry some other time about the pearls.

# 18

🌷 🌷 🌷 🌷

ROSALIND HAD DISCOVERED that the one sure way of keeping Peter somewhat quiet as he convalesced was to remain near him. They went out swimming more frequently, to closer places on the south shore. Or they lounged on chairs in the front veranda, she with her sewing, he with a book.

On one particularly nice morning, Barton Darien wheeled himself outside and came to a stop near them. Rosalind smiled at him, and made to get up.

"I'm fine, girl!" he growled, with a scowl. "You don't have . . . to wait . . . on m-me."

"Of course, you're coming along fine," she said placidly. "Are you quite comfortable?"

He nodded, and his fingers drummed on the armchair. Alfred Murray wandered out from the study, a pile of papers in his hands.

"Ah, good morning, good morning." Rosalind smiled up at her father's greeting. He too was looking so much better. The good food, the rest, the peaceful existence with no worries at all—they had all helped him to recover from the disease which had ravaged his lungs.

"Good morning, Father. What are you working on today?" She was busily mending clothes for Victor.

"The story of Kelea, the surf-rider princess," he replied. "A charming story, and so significant of the place of high-born women in Hawaiian society. Barton here put me on to it. I declare, he knows more tales than Hilohilo's wife!"

Barton eased his drumming motion and managed a crooked smile, well-pleased. Murray seated himself on a comfortable bamboo chair beside the wheelchair and looked over the pages.

Peter had laid down his book. "Is that the story of the girl who enjoyed surf riding so much she declared she would marry a surf board?"

Rosalind looked her amazement. The other three laughed. Alfred Murray nodded.

"That's the one. She told her brother the king, when he wanted to find a handsome husband for her, that the surf board was her husband and she wanted no other! Amazing woman. And the story is not unusual. Many Hawaiian women rode the surf on boards or on their bare feet, even in the old days. They seemed to have had much freedom also, in spite of the tabus."

"I know another girl who liked her freedom to ride the surf," said Peter jokingly, and reached out to take Rosalind's hand. The fathers looked over at them indulgently. Barton's face was softer than usual.

"Yes, I thought of my daughter often as I wrote," said Alfred, gently, giving her a sweet smile. "How many times I looked out from my study to see her riding the waves before the house. She seemed to have taken to the water from the time she was a baby."

"Like Victor," said Rosalind thoughtfully, lifting the small pants to study the size. "He enjoys the water so much. I must take him down to the beach again before long."

"Are those for little Victor?" asked Peter, fingering the material. "I thought babies all wore dresses."

She grinned mischievously at him. "It's your fault, Peter. I found him one day with a pair of your shorts from the laundry basket. He had managed to climb into them, and how he wailed when I took them off him! Like dadadada, he kept saying. So I decided to make him some trousers of his own."

They all laughed. "He's a lively young fellow," said Peter, with satisfaction. "And how he grows!"

"We can't keep up with him, his clothes seemed to shrink right on his little body," and Rosalind shook her head, and picked up her needle again.

"Read . . . story," said Barton imperiously to Alfred

Murray, indicating the manuscript pages. Alfred, pleased, began to read.

Peter laid down his book and leaned back with his eyes shut to listen. Rosalind listened also, but between the paragraphs the men were discussing, she marveled again at the two parents. So different, yet they had become such friends.

Barton Darien was impulsive, dynamic, rough-spoken, a burly businesslike individual before his stroke. Even now, he could scarcely contain his impatience, and was ready to roar.

"Don't forget the part . . . about Kalamakua saying to his cousin the king . . . how he would m-marry the girl if Lo-Lale turned her down. Find a beautiful and young girl, one he would . . . m-marry if his cousin did not."

"Yes, I have that a little later," said Murray patiently. His greying hair was blown by the morning breeze, he looked happier and healthier, for all his thin frame, than Rosalind could remember. So gentle a scholar, so dear and absent-minded and sweet, and yet he managed to get along easily with Peter's father!

Two more different men would have been hard to find. But their mutual interests had transcended the difficulties. And Alfred Murray had the endless patience to sit and listen to Barton as he stammered over his words. He hated it that he could not express himself so fluently as he had before his stroke. Murray would listen, and untangle the words with his quick perceptions, sometimes finishing the sentences for Barton.

Peter fell asleep during the reading, but Rosalind continued to sew. This was so good for Peter, this quiet atmosphere, without the quarrelsome Eileen and the impatient nagging Terry. She finished the trousers and sat with the material on her lap, gazing out absently toward the docks, where several sailboats rocked gently on the waves at the ends of their lines. How lovely was the sunshine today, how vividly blue the sky with only a few whipped cream clouds over the island. She could smell the yellow plumeria from the bushes near the veranda, and the golden shower tree was in bloom nearby.

Her father's gentle voice went on with the story. It was a charming one about how the cousin Kalamakua had gone out adventuring, to find a young and beautiful wife for his sad cousin, the King, whose love had died many years before. Kalamakua had spotted the beautiful princess Kelea swimming in the waves near her own land, where her brother was king. Cleverly the large handsome man from Oahu had persuaded her to ride in his canoe, then a storm had come up. They had drifted from shore, and he took her back to the land of his cousin.

Lo-Lale saw her, loved her, and with gentle poetic words persuaded her to marry him. Yet, in spite of three children, beautiful Kelea was not happy. She missed the waves of her surf, she missed the riding of the wild white breakers. She would make visits to the shore near where Kalamakua lived, and she was the finest swimmer and surf rider of them all. Finally she left Lo-Lale with his reluctant consent, and went to the handsome cousin who shared her joy in the sport. There was a chant, fragments of which remained, which showed Lo-Lale's grief at their separation, "Farewell, my partner on the lowland plains . . . O Lihue, she is gone!"

It was sad, romantic, inevitable, thought Rosalind. They had loved and mated, but that had not been enough. They had not shared enough of the same interests, and the marriage had foundered. Sometimes she had worried about that very thing. Would Peter tire of her? Did he long for a bright social life, sophisticated women, a wife like Eileen who would chatter like a brilliant bird and draw every man's attention?

When the story ended, Barton stammered out several places where he thought the action should be elaborated. Alfred listened carefully to his friend's comments, then they went off into a discussion of the meaning behind the story. Rosalind lost track of the conversation, hearing only the murmur of the masculine voices.

Presently Norma came out. "Here you are," she said brightly. "Time for lunch, all of you!"

Peter wakened and stretched. "It can't be noon, I just dropped off for a moment," he proclaimed. Barton managed to laugh around his twisted mouth, his eyes bright with pleasure in his son.

"You slept almost two hours. I s-saw you snoring away!"

"Snoring!" yelled Peter, outraged. "Did I snore, Rosalind?"

Laughing, she shook her head. "Come on in, all of you. I'm hungry," she said, changing the subject quickly. "I think Hilohilo brought in some fresh fish this morning, he must have been out all night catching them."

The meal was excellent. But Terry grumbled about the cattle all during lunch and Eileen seemed to encourage him. She had gotten up late, her eyes glittered with a strange light.

Recently, she had started to go to bed early, leaving the company before ten. Yet she always seemed tired in the mornings, thought Rosalind, and never got up until noon. Did she go to bed—or was she out somewhere? What was she up to?

Glendon Corey had returned with Terry from working the steers. Unlike his host, he had washed and looked immaculate in a grey suit and fresh white shirt.

"Corey has renewed his offer," Terry abruptly told the group. He leaned forward earnestly to speak to Peter at the head of the table. "You've got to listen to him, Peter. We won't get such a good offer from anyone else! Sell out and give us our share of the money! Eileen and I are crazy to be off and see something else beside cattle and dust!"

Peter's mouth compressed, but he answered calmly enough. "You have my answer. No. I'll never sell out. This island belongs to Dariens. And I'll keep it for my sons."

"Your sons? You mean that brat you dragged home?" sneered Eileen. Rosalind glanced up to glare at her, but was distracted by Terry's facial expression. Did he wince, had his face sobered? He was staring down at his plate.

"Victor shall have his share. However, I mean to have other children as well," Peter said, smiling at Rosalind.

"Is this an announcement? Or are you just counting your sheep . . . pardon me, your brats . . . before they arrive?" cried Eileen.

"Eileen, that will be enough! You are both rude and vulgar," said her mother ominously. Eileen tossed her blond head, her eyes filling with tears.

"Peter keeps us all here for his convenience!" Eileen stormed. "He doesn't care if we are happy or not! All he thinks about is *his* family, *his* wife, *his* children! What happens to us? Why, I'll never find a husband here on Darien! Who is there to see me dressed in my gowns, or jewels? Nobody! Nobody but natives! My God, I'll go mad!"

Rosalind noticed that though tears streamed down Eileen's cheeks, she did not leave the table. She carefully wiped her eyes so that her makeup was not disturbed, and sniffed alarmingly.

"Eileen is right," chimed in Terry. "She should get away. And I have no wish to be a damn cowboy all my life! Sometimes I think I'll never get the stink of beef out of my nose!"

Barton Darien was stiff and furious, unable to speak for rage. Rosalind put her hand on his, and he relaxed a little, looking at her. "Leave it to Peter," she said, very softly.

He nodded, his throat moved as he gulped.

"We never have any fun, we never go anywhere for visits, no one comes to see us," wept Eileen, in spite of her mother's frowns. "It's so deadly dull here! So very deadly dull! I'll go mad!"

"We ought to have visitors," said Peter slowly. He forked some fresh fish into his mouth, chewed thoughtfully. "I have been thinking about that. We used to have a big party at least once a year. The injury I had has knocked that for a loop. Maybe we could still throw it."

Eileen looked ready to scream. Corey said hurriedly, "Why don't you consider selling out to us, Peter? I have made you a very fair offer. If my syndicate knew the truth of it, about the volcanic eruptions, they could lower their offer. I feel I must warn you that they might withdraw it completely. Think about it carefully."

Peter's mouth was grim. "I have. As far as the volcanic eruptions are concerned, you need not worry. Only the volcanoes on the big island of Hawaii have erupted in recent centuries. The only danger to us is tidal waves, and we can cope easily with that."

Corey shrugged. "My syndicate might not understand that. One big eruption on an island in the chain, and they might panic."

Peter's eyes gleamed with sardonic humor. "If they are that timid, I would advise them to get right out of the cattle business. It isn't for the fearful, volcanoes or no volcanoes."

"Oh, come now, that isn't what I mean," said Corey impatiently. His cheeks had flushed slightly, but his grey flinty eyes never seemed to change expression, remaining watchfully icy. "They are far away, in Texas and New York City. They have never been to Hawaii. One island is like another to them. If it hits the newspapers that the volcanoes are erupting on Hawaii, they will immediately begin to reconsider. They might not withdraw completely, but they will surely lower their offer, it would be too much money to risk."

"We should take it up now," said Terry eagerly, almost falling across the table in his excitement. "Come on, Peter, listen to him. It's for the good of all of us! Think of Rosalind! Why, she has never even been to the States! You could take her around the world! Why shouldn't she have a good time? She has worked hard all her life. . . ."

Peter's gaze went to Rosalind. She said, bitingly, at once, "Don't make me your excuse, Terry. You know I love the islands, and everything about them; the flowers, food, people, legends, music. I have made my home here, there is no other place I would ever want to live. . . ."

"How do you know?" smiled Terry. "You have never been any other place!"

She could have struck him, sowing seeds of doubt in Peter's mind. "You don't know me," she said coldly. "I love the life here. This is my home. If you want to leave, then leave. But stop making everyone miserable around you. Just because you don't like cattle and dust and hard work, don't think everyone else feels the same way! Thank God, we aren't all alike!"

"Cheers," said Aunt Honora, briefly.

"You say, leave!" cried Eileen, flying to her own and her brother's defense. "But Peter won't give us *our* money to leave! How can we go when we are kept in poverty? We have to have money to live on."

"Have you ever considered working?" asked Aunt Honora, peeling a small bit of core from her pineapple slice with great care.

Eileen glared at her aunt, then flung herself around, back to Peter. "You must do something, Peter! Sell out, give us our money. If you want to buy a ranch somewhere, that's your problem. But let us be free!"

Peter sighed and shook his head. "You would get into trouble so fast, then someone would have to go and rescue you," he said wearily, lines etched beside his mouth. "It has happened before, it would happen again. You go through money like a hot knife through butter. And you have no sense!"

Eileen pounded the table with her fist, and the crystal glasses rattled. "Stop treating me like a child! I am grown up . . . a woman! If you don't do something, I will! I'll do something desperate, then you'll be sorry!"

"Quiet!" said Barton Darien suddenly, managing to articulate the word clearly. He glared at Eileen. "You're a fo-foolish w-woman! Spoiled rotten. Spoiled."

"Nothing ever happens around here!" cried Eileen, and her face crumpled up. "We don't even . . . d-dance anymore!"

It was so ridiculous that Norma shook her head, and Rosalind could have slapped Eileen. Peter had just recovered from a grave wound inflicted by an unknown assailant, they might have a tidal wave, Victor's mother had died of starvation, and Eileen complained nothing ever happened! She was so bounded by her selfish little world, she saw nothing beyond it, except as it affected her.

"We could give a dance," said Peter, ignoring the tantrum, as Eileen slammed the furniture again. "I think it is about time I introduced Rosalind to society. We could invite some people from Honolulu and Kailua. What do you think, Aunt Norma?"

"Splendid, as soon as you are well, dear Peter," said Norma, her hand on Eileen's arm warningly. "It would be like the old days, with all the guest rooms and houses full, and great *luaus* every night. I'm sure the women will dance for us also, and we could have a small band from Honolulu."

Eileen's face smoothed a little. "Oh, do say you will, Peter, right away!" she urged. "It won't be like getting away, but it would help. . . . Just to see other people in the world! And you'll see . . . ask any of your businessmen friends. They'll tell you to sell out! There's no future here!"

Peter smiled a little to himself, and cut the pineapple before him into smaller pieces. He popped a juicy piece into his mouth. "Let's talk about it later, shall we?" he suggested.

But Eileen and Terry didn't want to put off the discussion. Eagerly, endlessly, they talked about a party; who could be invited, who would be the most fun; no, not that one, he was too stuffy and his wife was a horrible bore; that pretty girl, that handsome man, a woman because she was amusing and a great gossip. Peter met Rosalind's troubled look and gave her a wink, as though to say not to worry about it.

Peter said it in words later on, when they were alone in their suite. "Don't fret about the invitations, Rosalind. Norma and Honora and I will plan that end of it. Eileen is silly about her likes and dislikes. I want you to meet the finest men and women on the island; a banker friend of mine, an artist, the doctor and his wife and daughter, a writer your father will enjoy. Don't let Eileen prejudice you against the party. It will be great fun for you, or I won't go through with it."

She managed a smile, though her eyes were grave. "All right, Peter, I know you want to see them yourself, also. I'll be . . . glad to meet them."

"Little gallant fibber," he said, touching her chin with teasing fingers. "It terrifies you to meet strangers, and so many at once. However, I can promise you that you will like this lot, and they will adore you. I think we'll have a great *luau* every night, that will take care of the food. And our Hawaiians will sing and dance for us. It will be a great feast, and they will take pride in making all go smoothly for us."

# 19

❦ ❦ ❦ ❦

INVITATIONS WERE SENT out to Honolulu and
Kailua and some places on outer islands. Replies
came back, by way of sailboats and the island
steamer. And after several weeks of preparation, during which Peter healed completely, the party was on.

Within two days the guest rooms at the great house
were full, and the guest cottages vacated by several
single Hawaiian young men. All had been cleaned
and decorated, with flowers, coral strands, and fresh
fruit placed in each room in a beautiful calabash.

Rosalind was bewildered at first, how could she ever
match name to face, and husband to wife to child? But
soon she sorted them out, with whispered help from
Honora.

The early October days were crisp in early morning, warming to heat by noon. Perfect for swimming,
fishing, boating, sailing, or just sitting on the veranda
or the patio and talking.

The weeks of preparation had paid off. The Hawaiian *paniolos* and their families took part in the evening
*luaus,* building up pit fires and roasting huge pigs, with
ears of corn and potatoes all wrapped in *ti* leaves and
steamed to perfection. Bowls of *poi* were ready for
those who enjoyed the taste of the sticky paste that
was a staple of the Hawaiian meal. Small clams, oysters, chicken, and beef were also served in infinite
varieties.

Along with the vegetables, green beans, and tomatoes, sweet potatoes, seaweed, and so on, were bowls
of the fresh fruits of the island. Sometimes they were
served in huge dishes, just washed and ready to be

peeled. Sometimes they were chopped in great colorful heaps, covered with bits of coconut. Rosalind's
favorite was a mixture of fresh mango, papaya, and
pineapple, sprinkled with coconut and nuts.

Dr. Gordon and his wife Katherine, with their
daughter Julia, just a little older than Rosalind, were
among the first guests to arrive. The doctor briskly
gave Peter an examination, and pronounced him
healed. "But duck bullets, my boy," he said, jovially,
as Rosalind winced. "The best thing is to avoid
them." And he gave a hearty laugh.

Rosalind did not think it was funny.

With them had come Mr. and Mrs. Chan from
Kailua, the jeweler and his small exquisitely lovely
wife, in Chinese silk garb and tiny little slippers. Mr.
Chan bowed deeply as he formally presented to
Rosalind a guest's gifts; a length of rose silk embroidered with white pearls, a silver bracelet that he had
made himself, with a tiny carved dragon curling about
it. Mrs. Chan presented to Peter cuff links of silver
with black pearls in them. Glendon Corey especially
exclaimed over them, and wanted to examine them
closely. He seemed very keen over black pearls,
thought Rosalind.

Rosalind began to protest as she realized that all
the guests had brought expensive and elaborate gifts
to her. They were wedding presents, Dr. Gordon informed her brusquely, as she tried to refuse the huge silver coffee urn and matching creamer and sugar bowl.

"My dear, one only gets married once," said lovely
Mrs. Gordon, as red-haired as her husband. "Do enjoy it!"

Eileen looked on in envy, her lips tightly compressed as one present followed another until the
drawing room looked like a wedding reception room,
strewn with colorful papers and scarves in which the
gifts had been wrapped.

Mr. and Mrs. Monroe—Peter's banker-friend from
Honolulu—had brought their children. Hank at
twenty-five was brisk and already pedantic in speech.
He was becoming a banker too, and was working for

his father. Sallie, at twenty-one was a pretty, appealing girl with blond curls and a sunny smile. They brought a set of silver trays, and a pair of matching bud vases in sterling.

Mr. and Mrs. Noguchi, the Japanese silk merchants from Honolulu, arrived on the sailing vessel with Mr. and Mrs. Renwick, the professors at a college there. Mr. Renwick was also a writer, and keenly interested in the legends of Hawaii, which gave him much to discuss with Alfred Murray.

The Noguchis presented Rosalind with lengths of silk brocade, and a full kimono of green silk and matching wide *obi,* showing her how to put it on and wear it. The Renwicks brought books, saying with bright smiles that Peter always liked more books. They were some of the latest volumes from America and England, and Rosalind longed to pore over them. A whole packing case had been presented to them.

Then came Mr. and Mrs. Basilio Dalbono, their son Sebastiano and daughter Martina. They were a musical family, and they gave a small concert every evening. Mr. Dalbono was a violinist, and directed their little group. Mrs. Dalbono played the piano beautifully, Sebastiano, a handsome young man of about twenty-six played the cello, and his sister the flute. Rosalind soon joined them in their ensemble. Their gifts were music books and scores, and also a jade dragon which Rosalind adored, and took up to her bedroom to place on the mantel there.

Mr. and Mrs. Eriksen arrived on the ship with the Dalbonos, friends of long standing. He had been a ship captain, retired only recently at the age of seventy, still hearty. Norwegians, they were somewhat stiff and formal, yet good-hearted, fond of Honora and Norma, and full of advice to Rosalind when she asked. They knew everyone on all the islands, they had heard every bit of gossip, they understood human nature, and had a gift of calming troubled waters. They brought fine wall hangings of Norwegian origin, of bright reds, blues, scarlets, and purples.

Last to arrive were three handsome bachelors, and

Eileen's eyes brightened. Tom and Jimmy Winchester were a young team of farming brothers who had decided to grow exotic plants in their greenhouse. They had built it with their own hands, and now were in the second year of trying to grow orchids in hothouses. Everyone was eager to hear of their progress, and they had brought some delicate blossoms for each of the ladies. They also brought some plants for Rosalind. She appreciated them, and planned at once to set them out in a sheltered place. Not only orchids were given to her, but several other varieties of Hawaiian flowers, from scarlet anthuriums to delicate pansies, bright yellow allamanda, and several hibiscus bushes of colors she did not have.

The last arrival was Antoine Launay, who came with the Winchesters. He was French, black haired, melancholy in appearance, though later Rosalind began to suspect that as an artistic front, which he felt was expected of him. Handsome, intense, he studied each woman in turn as though about to put her onto canvas. "I must paint you, I must," he declared to Rosalind when their introductions were scarcely over.

"Me? Oh, no," she said nervously. "Do paint Eileen, she is so lovely."

"No. You have more delicate charm, and more character," he declared, and began following her around, sketching her when she least expected it.

He was the only one who had not brought a gift. He declared to Peter, "I shall paint a marvelous portrait of your wife, and give it to you for a wedding present."

"I should be delighted," said Peter. "Why don't you stay on after the others leave, and take plenty of time for it?"

Antoine Launay accepted with delight, and Peter confided to Rosalind later that the man made his living by going from one place to another, one island to another, painting the wives and daughters of the Hawaiian planters and ranchers, and the merchants in the cities.

"For all his posing of himself, and his appearance,

he is really a fine artist," said Peter. "It took me a time to see under the flowing ties and waving hair and distracted expression. But he is a sharp businessman, and manages to make a good living at his art. Anything extra he invests with Mr. Noguchi, he has a little share in that silk business. Mr. Noguchi is very fond of him, he has no son of his own. And they both admire art intensely."

Peter kept telling Rosalind little stories about his friends, which made her feel more comfortable with them, and she learned to know and appreciate them more quickly. The Chans were good friends of the Noguchis, and they often exchanged visits, having much in common. The silk merchant often sent lengths of silk to Mr. Chan to be embroidered with pearls and semi-precious stones, and Mr. Chan was always on the lookout for special gems for Mr. Noguchi's silk brocades.

On the steamer with some of the guests had come the five-piece Hawaiian band that Peter had sent for. Kenny and his Five Hawaiians were quite good musicians. Every evening they played on the veranda so the guests could dance. Some of the Hawaiian *paniolos* and their families would come after the *luau* had everyone stuffed and comfortable. The music would steal softly through the cooling air, and the sea breezes would echo with the plaintive or cheerful lilting arrangements.

Rosalind encouraged the singing and the performances of some special Hawaiian dances. She was eager that the Hawaiian culture should not be forgotten by the younger ones, and so the children were always special guests, sitting in the front rows on the grass near the veranda, where they watched and listened with delight. Rosalind even brought out Victor early in the evening, and held him to get him accustomed to the sounds of his Hawaiian heritage. He bounced up and down in time to the rhythm and when she put him down he tried to dance as the men were doing before them. It seemed built into his lithe bones, and he laughed charmingly as he bounced. How strong and lovely he was, with his black curly hair showing some light brown, his dark eyes gleaming, his golden skin glowing in the lamplight. Rosalind noted shrewdly that Terry sobered when Victor was near, and sometimes even turned and went away.

Later in the evening, she had put Victor to bed and returned to the veranda. The music had turned to the waltzes and more sophisticated American music.

She noted that Eileen was hanging on Peter's arm, coaxing him to dance. He had not seen Rosalind return, and Rosalind remained in the shadows, watching thoughtfully, with a little pang of jealousy she tried to dispel. Peter was loyal to her, she knew that now. But—but he was attracted to Eileen, she was so pretty and glamorous and exciting tonight, in a crimson silk brocade with a scarlet hibiscus in her glowing blonde hair.

Rosalind felt outshone, though her brocade dress of silver-white with pearls sewn on the bodice, the skirts crackling delightfully as she moved, had been especially ordered by Peter from Honolulu and brought by the Monroes. She wore flower leis of plumeria over the bodice. Now she wondered if she should have worn something more exotic, more expensive, such as the black pearl necklace. Perhaps tomorrow night she would ask Peter to get out the jewelry he had bought for her, the diamonds—no. If he wanted that, he would have taken them out. But Eileen wore diamonds with her crimson silk, and little diamonds flashed in her ears.

I am becoming discontented and spoiled, thought Rosalind, and turned to smile at Tom Winchester.

He asked her for a dance, and she agreed, circling about the veranda with him. "Great party," he said enthusiastically. "I came last year, first time ever. Jimmy and I had just arrived in the islands. Your husband made us feel right at home, and helped us get set up. He's a great guy!"

"I think so also," she said demurely, and smiled up at him.

"I should think so! We were surprised last year,

such a handsome fellow as Peter not married, and with all the Darien land and all," he said, with American bluntness and ingenuity. "He said he was waiting for the right girl to come along, and I guess he found her all right!"

His words warmed her heart, and Rosalind thanked him. Peter came up behind them. "Rosalind, I didn't see you come back," he said. When Tom had let her go, Peter took her in his arms for the next dance. He seemed eager to hold her, to dance with her, smiling down at her happily.

"Are you enjoying the party now?" he asked, whispering into her ear.

He smiled as she nodded vigorously. "Your friends are so very pleasant, Peter."

"They admire you also," he said gently. "And envy me a little, I think. Does Antoine follow you everywhere? He showed me some two dozen sketches of you, even of bathing Victor!"

She crinkled up her nose. "Yes, everywhere. I turn about and there he is, and I'm mussed and wrinkled and my nose is shiny . . . he even made a drawing of me as I was trying to plant the hibiscus bushes! What a mess I must have looked, but he wouldn't let me see the sketch."

"He's a good sort," said Peter. "And he promises me a fine portrait one day."

Eileen was watching them from the shadows now. Her eyes were spiteful and overly bright, her lip was sore from biting it. She had tried again and again to lure Peter to her. He used to be so much more amiable! Until Rosalind had come along. Now he couldn't see anybody but her! How stupid he was, and how dull he had become. Always lecturing her about doing what Rosalind did, and thinking of her future, and becoming a good housewife, and learning to cook and direct the maids. Anyone could order servants about, that didn't take learning! She would wait until she had married a rich man, and then she would make the servants fly about!

If only Rosalind had not come, Eileen might have

been married to Peter by this time. He had used to be kind to her, he had been fond of her. What had Rosalind done to him? She had watched sharply to see if Rosalind was pregnant, but the girl showed no signs of a thickening waist. So he hadn't made her with child at Kailua, that theory was out. So why had Peter bothered to marry her? She was somewhat prettier than when she had come, and she certainly dressed better. But putting flowers with that stunning dress! How silly! Eileen would have demanded a great array of expensive jewels, the dress deserved it.

Eileen saw her chance then, Rosalind had gone off to talk to Kenny and his musicians. Peter was standing there, looking after her, turning to talk to Mr. Monroe. Eileen came up to them, smiling, put her hand on Peter's arm, and leaned against him.

Peter broke off what he was saying, and looked down at Eileen. "Enjoying yourself?" he asked. "Tom was looking for you."

"Oh, he's dancing with Martina now," said Mr. Monroe, tactlessly. "I think he's got a thing for that girl, been hanging over her for the past several days. She is a lovely girl, and will make a fine wife and mother. What a sweet expression she has!" And the men looked at Martina, dark-haired and intense of eye, and the handsome American dancing with her.

"She'll probably have a dozen babies, and enjoy it," snapped Eileen, spitefully, then was sorry as Peter frowned at her. Mr. Monroe looked shocked, he was a conventional old soul, she thought.

"She would enjoy it, I am sure," said Mr. Monroe. "We have but two children. God was good to us, but He would not allow us to have more. I know we would have enjoyed a dozen, should He have given them to us."

Pompous old jackass, thought Eileen, and smiled up at Peter. "Do dance with me, you're the best partner around," she coaxed, softly.

He went with her, and they danced, but she felt his mind was not on her, rather it was enraged. He left her with Glendon Corey. The man was easy enough to dance with, but she didn't care much for him. He rarely bothered to flatter her anymore, and she had the feeling that he had done so only when he thought she had some influence with Peter, to get him to sell out.

Well, she did have some influence, and she would get him to sell. This was a stupid party, Peter had not invited her own special friends, and she felt bored, bored, bored. All these older people! Why hadn't he invited more eligible young men, who would have been interested in stealing a midnight stroll along the beach in the moonlight? Now she had the feeling that if she coaxed one of them with her, he would do nothing but hold her arm to keep her from stumbling, and quote poetry at her, as that artist had! And wanting to go swimming! Jimmy Winchester was silly and too boyish for her. He had said he wanted to go swimming in the moonlight. And get her hair all wet! She would do nothing of the sort.

When her dance with Corey was over, he left her with a bow in the corner near her mother. Norma was talking animatedly with Mrs. Dalbono, Eileen pricked up her ears. But they were talking about how to cook rice so it would come out dry and fine! My God, what a waste of music and moonlight!

She looked about for Peter, he was dancing with Rosalind again, his dark head bent over hers, their bodies pressed close together in the slow movements. She raised her face, and glowed up at him. Peter pressed his lips to her hair, and Eileen felt nauseated.

Eileen moved gracefully down the steps, hesitating as though wondering what to do. But she knew where she was going. Maleko had been staring at her during the early evening. He had taken part in the dancing of the Hawaiian warriors, and how fine and strong he had looked in his brief garments. His naked chest had glowed in the firelight, he was taller and stronger than any other native around.

She would find him, he was probably hanging about.

She strolled around the corner of the huge house, back toward the lighted patio. There she found Tom

Winchester and Martina Dalbono strolling slowly, arm in arm, and Mrs. Noguchi walking with them, for chaperon, thought Eileen. Silly creatures!

She avoided them before they could see her. She slipped off into the bushes, and bumped into a hard body. Hands caught at her waist.

She said nothing, she went with him, a half-smile of satisfaction curling her lips. He had cat-eyes and could see in the dark, Eileen thought. They walked through the bushes, back to the darkness of the palm trees, and there she halted, stubbornly.

"What do you want?" she asked Maleko curtly.

"I have not seen you alone for many days."

"You mean nights?" she mocked.

"Days and nights," he said. "Why do you not come out to the lagoon?"

"Too many people around," she said carelessly, her shoulder turned to him.

"You like the young white men?" he asked jealously.

She smiled in the darkness, and licked her tongue around her lips. "Of course. They are my kind, they are white," she said smoothly.

She heard Maleko grunt, and smiled. She had been feeling battered and bruised, her ego had taken a beating these days. She felt like striking out, and why not strike at him? He could do nothing to her, he was only a native.

"Which one you like best?"

"Oh, the artist," she said, lying. "He is so handsome, so beautiful a man."

Maleko made a sound of contempt. "He has no muscles," he said simply.

"He has a brain, and he draws very well," she told him sharply.

"I can draw in the sand."

"He draws with colors on paper, and makes much money with it," she told him. "He is very smart."

Maleko was silent for a time, she felt his heat and smelled the strong masculine scent of his body. "You always talk money, money, money," he said surprisingly. "You think of nothing else, huh?"

Eileen shrugged. "I think about other things, like men," she said provocatively.

"But you like the money the best. I am sorry for you. You do not think of the flowers of Hawaii, of their fragrance. You do not think of honor and glory, you do not work in the fields, you care not for children. What a poor woman you are!"

She turned and struck at him blindly, using her fingernails on his broad chest. He gasped at the sudden attack, then laughed low in his throat, caught her hands, and held her still.

"At least you can fight," he said, with a contemptuous note in his deep voice. "But not as a warrior. Just as a woman does. That you can do."

"You let me go!" He was like the others, always jeered at her.

"When I choose."

"I'll scream! If my cousin finds me with a native, he'll kill you!"

"He does not know what you do, then?" asked Maleko. "He does not know how you go to Hawaiian men for your pleasure? He does not know how you take one man and then another for nothing but the night?"

She opened her mouth to scream, in rage, but his brawny hand was over her lips. He dragged her with him into the bushes, tearing her crimson dress, she could hear it rip on the sharp thorns of the cactus plants.

She fought him, but one arm was about her waist, one hand covering her mouth. She was puny in the grip of the huge Hawaiian. He pulled her down to the sand and dirt, and yanked up the dress. She fought, enraged that he should take her when she did not wish to give. She bit and scratched and clawed, but he only held her down with his hand, and with the free one he pulled her clothes apart and freed her white body to his fondling.

Then he was over her, and thrusting himself between her thighs. She gasped, and went limp at the fierceness of his taking. She writhed in the sand, and her hips hurt from the grit and cactus strands under her. But in the hurting she took pleasure, he was a real man, sweating and panting above her, hurting her because he was so big in her.

The pleasure made her softer, and she yielded to him. Her hands went fiercely to his back, and she clawed at him in desire and passion, and pulled him down to her. He felt the difference in her, and settled on her, and they moved and played the love-game with more intensity as emotions swung high. He finished, and lay gasping while she mewed in her throat and thrust herself upward at him to finish her pleasure.

He felt her movements, and after a time he began to take her again. He had not moved off of her, and his bigness surprised her—it was so soon. Again she thrust her hips at him, fiercely, able to do what she wanted, because he was only a native and would tell nothing about her. Peter would kill him if he learned of it, he thought Eileen was chaste and pure, wanting only a little flirtation now and then. She smiled to herself in the darkness, and Maleko's mouth came down on hers, and opened it, and his tongue probed again and again into her mouth, searching out the tongue and teeth and the lips, licking at her. The sensuousness of his caresses made her come, and she cried out in fervor. Eileen arched up like a cat in heat, seeking erotic pleasure.

She lay weakened, drowsy with delight. He rolled off her, gasping for breath, his great chest heaving rapidly. She reached over lazily, and stroked her hand on his wet torso, and felt him shiver in reaction to her touch.

Finally she sat up, pulled her clothes together. The dress was ruined, and that made her cross all over again. She got up, and he stood also.

"You come again tomorrow night," he ordered, his hand on her arm. His fingers were so large, so hard, he would bruise her.

"Maybe. If I choose," she said indifferently. "You ripped my dress! I should slap you for that."

"The Dariens must be weaklings. To produce such a woman as you in their midst. Their line must be nearly finished."

She swung to strike him, but Maleko caught her hand and bent it back. "You devil!" she raged. "For a native to talk like that about me! I am a Darien, and we are a wealthy white family! You are only a gross native!"

"I have seen your brother, Terry. He is weak also. Only Peter Darien is strong. What of the child Victor? The son of Terry must be weak. They are all finished."

"Victor is a fine strong boy! He is exactly like Terry! Only that silly Lydia Pauahi was an idiot to think he would marry her! He would never marry a native girl, even one carrying his child! She should have known better. Next time, he'll choose a white girl!"

"And you?" asked Maleko softly. "If you had a child of me, what would you do?"

"Throw it into the sea from the cliffs!" Eileen blazed. "But I'll never have your child! I would fling it from my body! Besides, I bathe in cold water after meeting you."

He laughed softly, menacingly. "That does no good. You know nothing of a woman's body, for all your body is softness and perfume. You could have a child from what I have done to you tonight. Are you not woman enough to know that?"

For a moment, fear gripped her. A baby—and that of a native! Her mother would weep, Peter would rage! But she would not. She had had no child from any of her encounters. She had been careful, douching after every coupling, no matter how sleepy she was.

She tossed her head. "No danger. I won't be caught like that! I'm going to marry a rich man! And I'll leave Hawaii forever! I hate it here!"

She turned and walked away indifferently. He

called after her, "Tomorrow night, little cat that walks in the dark!"

"When *I* choose, not you!" she called back, disappearing in the darkness.

Maleko stared after her, his strong hands gripping his clothing. He did not feel the coolness of the night air. "And for her I waste my seed," he muttered to himself. "For that one who lies with any! Why do I linger? I must return home. I know enough. . . ."

Muttering, he walked off into the night, and bathed in the cool waters of a lagoon. But still he was angry at himself, and at her for enticing him. She was no good, she was not worth the smallest finger of the girl he loved in his own village.

Yet he kept lingering about the great Darien house, waiting for her, watching what went on, thinking about the Darien family. If they were all like Eileen, the line would soon be over. Yet—was it true? How many were like her? Or was she the mongrel bitch that sometimes appeared in any great dynasty? He must wait and watch for the answer.

# 20

❧  ❧  ❧  ❧

PETER DARIEN was troubled, for all his smiles and charm for the guests.

Captain Eriksen, old and wise, and knowledgeable in the ways of Hawaii, had come to him as soon as he had arrived on the ship.

"Peter, there is much talk about the islands," he told the young man. "I wanted to come to warn you, as much as to enjoy your hospitality."

"What is it?"

"About Chief Kaahumanu Pauahi. They say that the chief is very angry and brooding about what happened to his daughter Lydia. After his fury cooled, he regretted that he had refused her his home. And now he wants her son. He says you refused to give him his grandson."

Peter's eyes narrowed. "The chief would have killed Victor," he said simply. "He sent his warriors after Lydia to murder her for mating with a white. She died first, of hunger and exhaustion. Should I have turned over the child to him? He might still try to kill the boy, for the white blood in him."

The blue Norwegian eyes that had seen so many oceans gleamed in comprehension. "Yes, yes. However, the chief talks of war against the weak and delinquent Dariens! I am quoting, Peter, this is not what I think! There is talk about Terry, how he goes off and leaves his work to seduce Hawaiian girls. And there is gossip about . . . Eileen. I am sorry to say it, my boy, but there is much talk about her."

Peter bit his lips. He had closed hs eyes to what she did, he had shut his ears against rumors. But he might have known they would fly about anyway. With sailing vessels going from one island to another, the truth of her conduct must get out. He had tried to be strict with her, to keep her under his watchful gaze. And Norma had tried all her life.

But somehow the girl wandered out, and her morals were not at all firm. What he had feared would happen, had happened. Eileen did not merely flirt with men outrageously. She must go all the way with them.

"What do . . . they say?" he asked painfully.

"That she seduces the Hawaiian men from their women, just as Terry takes the young girls," said the ship captain simply. He had seen too much of the world to be shocked by it. He saw things as they were. "It's too bad, Peter. Can't you send her away?"

"Eileen needs protection from herself," said Peter, with a sigh. "I would have to go with her, and Norma. She can't live alone in San Francisco, or New York, where she longs to go. She would go wildly on her whims. And she would be murdered, I think. Here, at least I can save her life. Terry loves her, but he laughs and is amused by her antics. He would not stop her."

"It is not for me to advise you," said the old man gently, patting Peter's broad shoulder. "But if you could find her a man to marry, she might settle down and have children."

Peter was polite about it, but frankly he could not see Eileen with children. Eileen had nothing motherly about her, nor wifely. He could see her as the pet of a wealthy old man, but she would upset even him with her determination to do whatever she pleased.

Tom and Jimmy Winchester rode out with him on the range the next morning. The two brothers seemed to have something serious on their minds, and they soon had him off to themselves away from the cowboys.

"We've been hearing some talk, Peter, thought you should know," said the more serious Tom. Jimmy nodded, his face grave for once.

Peter wondered if they would warn him about Eileen.

"The talk is about some young Hawaiian warriors of the chief Pauahi," said Tom. "I understand he is in deep mourning for his daughter Lydia. And he wants the boy Victor. Can't blame him, he's a charming fellow, and looks as though he will be a big and strong man. A future chief."

"What have you heard, exactly?"

Tom thought, his face intent. "Well, it seems that some of the young men are talking war. It seems they think they can storm the island, and the Dariens are too cowardly to resist. They have some war canoes ready. I think they have been going up in the mountains, praying to their gods, and making themselves stronger by undergoing all sorts of endurance tests."

"Things like going naked and hungry for days in the hills," contributed Jimmy, more fascinated by their customs than by the significance of it. "I hear they run about naked, and go fasting for a week, and all that. Sounds wild."

"Sounds like the Indians on the plains of Texas," said Peter thoughtfully. "They will prepare themselves for weeks for a campaign. Joe Smith tells me the Apache Indians can live for months on jerked beef and water, that they are as lithe as panthers and tough as snakes. They fast and pray to their gods for nights and moons before a battle."

The Winchester men listened avidly and questioned him about that. But they soon returned to urging Peter to make defensive preparations.

"We could stay on for a week or so. We brought our rifles and pistols with us," said Tom. "They might bring as many as a hundred men, you know. That tribe is rather large, and they are devoted to their Chief."

Peter thanked them, but refused. He did talk to Joe and Hilohilo, however. They had also heard the rumors.

"They'll get a warm welcome," said Smith grimly,

patting one of his revolvers in the twin holster at his hip. "I've been practicing up."

"Do you have plenty of ammunition?" asked Peter. "I ordered more from Honolulu. But I hate to think. . . ." He did not finish the sentence.

Joe Smith said, "I ordered plenty more. Got enough for a long siege."

"We got gunpowder in the blockhouse," noted Hilohilo, referring to the cement structure where they stored gunpowder for the times when they had to blast loose tree roots or stones which lay about on the green grass of the plains. "I got plenty."

"I think we had better set out guards day and night," Peter decided. "Hilohilo, always have the guards on the cliffs at the points of the island. Joe, choose about a dozen of the young Hawaiians and teach them to shoot straight. They don't have to use up ammunition, just point at objects and get used to handling the rifles and pistols."

"Will do, boss," said Hilohilo, without his usual cheerful smile. His broad brown face was solemn with thought. "Boss, you know them fishermen, they're still here."

"I know. Do they fish?" asked Peter drily.

"Oh, sure, they catch plenty, they give it to the women, make friends with the children. But I don't know. They keep themselves apart at night, and I've seen that huge one, Maleko, roaming about. So silent, you can't hear him coming, nor see him until he's there. Gives me a jump now and then."

Peter frowned. "I wonder if we could confine them to camp. . . ."

Hilohilo stared at him. "Confine them? Take two dozen of us to confine them four men, boss," he said. "Slip away and laugh at us, they would. They young tiger sharks."

He sounded rueful. The men were young, eager, and alert. And Hilohilo was almost forty, worn with years of toil, though his muscular body showed little sign of slowing down. But he was no match for a man in his twenties, like the young fishermen.

"If they are from Chief Pauahi, they stay long," Hilohilo mused. "I wonder if they do come from him, and what they want. If any attack comes, I'll kill them first off."

"They have not shown themselves enemies," said Peter, shaking his head. "We can't kill just because of suspicion or rumor. No, wait and see, and we'll keep guard. I'll check with the guards daily to see what they have noted on the waters."

The party went on. Peter felt tense and nervous inside, and checked daily with his foremen and the guards. But nothing was noted. His guests were happy, Rosalind was delighted with their pleasure, and she seemed more relaxed and confident. That would be worth it all, he thought.

He studied her face as she watched the dancers one night. She had Victor on her lap, and he was bouncing so hard she could scarcely hold him. She finally let him down to the floor where he swayed and uttered little cries of pleasure. Her tanned face was glowing, her amber eyes flashing with light, her lithe young body swayed with the music and the effort of holding Victor.

How pretty she was in her flowered blue and green muumuu with the wide lace sleeves and the leis about her slim throat. She outshone even Eileen in her brilliant silks and jewels. Peter was proud of his wife. She was a thoughtful hostess, there were fresh flowers every day in the rooms of the guests. She thought of their comfort, provided hot milk at night for Mrs. Eriksen, saw that Professor Renwick had a chance to talk quietly every day with Murray about the history of Hawaii, saw that Barton was included in the activities, yet not tired by them.

The meals were many and varied, colorful. Some were served outdoors on the patio, buffet style, and guests would wander in and out, eating when they pleased. The evenings were devoted to *luaus,* with singing and dancing and games.

Norma and Honora were always there, helping tirelessly, but it was Rosalind who directed it all, Peter noted. He came upon them consulting about menus with the cook, arranging the buffet tables, the seating in the formal dining room for two dinners. He found Rosalind picking flowers in immense baskets with the assistance of two young Hawaiian girls, and the making of leis went on under her direction. And she still had time to play with Victor, take him for walks on the sands before the big house, and sing to him before he slept. Often, when she went out with the guests, she was carrying the sturdy child, or walking very slowly as he clung to her hand and took his uncertain steps.

"Mamamamama," was his constant cry, until he spotted Peter, and then it was "Dadada!" imperiously, to be picked up. He sat down hard on the grass, wailed, then beamed at being picked up, soothed, and petted. Then he struggled to get down again, and was off on his pursuit of a butterfly, his investigation of a hibiscus bush, his wide-eyed gazing at the fishermen as they returned from a day's catch. He was everyone's favorite, and he got used to being patted on the head and chucked under the chin by everyone in passing.

"He'll miss all that attention when they go," laughed Peter.

Rosalind shook her head ruefully. "How will I ever entertain him again? So much activity going on, and he has to be in the middle of it all!"

Peter noted that Launay continued to follow Rosalind around. He had seen some of the sketches, and begged for them. The artist frowned. "Not until I have completed my painting!" he said. "She has so many moods, so many changes of expression, I am at a loss as to how to paint her." And he went on, drawing intently whenever Rosalind stopped for a minute for any task.

In the late afternoon, Peter returned from the range, where he checked on the guards and watched to see that the cattle were still grazing peacefully on the scanty grass in the south. Terry was sullen about his refusal to return them to the north, yet Peter felt in his bones that the Hawaiians were right. They could expect a tidal wave this year, for the volcanoes on Hawaii were grumbling and spitting out flames.

Tidal waves came too quickly to give notice of their arrival. They would have no time to move the cattle once the wave appeared. And that would ruin everything, for the cattle would all die. No, better to be prepared, even though they would not be able to butcher much this year. They would get by. If worse came to worse, Peter could harvest some more black pearls.

Mr. Chan could be trusted to sell far away. That was a possibility.

So he waited and watched, and planned as far ahead as he could.

The trouble with too much advance planning, Peter had found, was that the problems that hit you were not the ones you had anticipated. Time and again, he had allowed for some eventuality, only to find that some other problem hit him on the head, out of nowhere. Such as his father's stroke. Such as Terry's fathering of an *Haole* child. Such as Lydia's death.

And other things much more delightful, he thought, as he strolled downstairs after changing. He heard the sounds of music coming from the drawing room, and went in quietly. A dozen guests were sitting about, silently, their faces rapt, scarcely noting their host coming in. The Dalbono quartet was playing, with Rosalind accompanying as second violinist.

They were performing something by Beethoven, and the sonorous melodies were soothing and beautiful. Peter dropped into the nearest chair to lean his head back and listen, his eyes half-closed, focused on his wife.

Today she was in rose color, a flowered muumuu that flowed to her ankles. The ruffles at her throat were low, showing the golden tones of her flesh. Her graceful arm was raised with the bow in her long fingers, her gaze intent on the music on the stand before her. Mr. Dalbono nodded decisively, and the next movement began. Sebastiano was at the cello, and the deep mellow tones echoed through the room and out to the flower-scented dusk. Martina on the flute was beautiful in her slim green dress, her dark eyes glowing. Tom Winchester seemed unable to keep from staring at her the whole time, thought Peter with quiet amusement.

What a delightful surprise Rosalind had been, stealing into his life and heart, thought Peter as he watched them playing. He had seen her at the church in Kailua, had been amused and touched at her shy beauty, the way she slipped away rather than meet the fashionable crowd.

Then—then sliding down the cliff with the child in his arms, seeing the light of that little house, and crashing inside. To find Rosalind with her wide eyes horrified and compassionate. The feverish days that followed, and the nights when he was vaguely aware of her cool hand on his forehead, the water she held to his lips, the food she coaxed him to eat in her quiet womanly voice.

All woman, she was. She had seemed a slip of a girl, too thin and all bones, but now she was filling out a little, and her skin glowed with good health. It made him shudder a little to think of how she had lived before he came, so carelessly, with never enough to eat, too much work to do, the anxiety of a sick father.

Now—now she looked alive and beautiful and radiant, his wife, the dearest companion a man ever had. She matched his soul as she matched his body, and he adored her. Still reserved, Rosalind seemed hesitant at times to express her thoughts, and he had to urge her and coax her. But one day she would be totally his, as close to him as he desired. He wanted a companion for life, one of those rare marriages he had seen a few times, when man and wife were so close they were like two matched halves of a peach.

Peter thought Mr. and Mrs. Dalbono had such a marriage, they even looked alike after years of living together. Dark-haired, a little plump, Italian, smiling, intent musicians, they could just glance at each other, and begin to play their instruments in perfect time and rhythm. Captain and Mrs. Eriksen were another such couple, tall raw-boned Norwegians. She had traveled much with him, and was almost as sunburned and hearty as he was. Nothing shocked her.

It was good to see good marriages that lasted, thought Peter contentedly. He wanted a marriage like that, and he thought he had found it. Rosalind seemed to enjoy the same things he did: swimming, surfing, a quiet picnic on the sand, being alone together, good music—

And children. Victor, and their own children one day. What a mother she would make of his children! The more he looked at Victor, the more he thought that one day Victor would return to his Hawaiian heritage. He was more Pauahi than Darien, thought Peter. Yet he would keep the boy, raise him, and he would be a link between the two peoples, the Dariens and Hawaiians. Hopefully, if God willed, he would help peace come between them. If he would but understand both parts of his heritage, and would be accepted one day by the Pauahi as one of them, as well as a Darien—it might work out.

The Beethoven concert ended, and the five musicians put aside their instruments, and bowed to the light applause of the dozen in the audience. Rosalind came over to Peter.

"I must see to Victor, then I'll change and come down," she whispered in his ear. He caught at her hand, raised it to his lips and kissed it.

"I will see you, my love," he whispered back to her, enjoying the quick tide of color in her cheeks. She strolled from the room, and he sat back to talk to Captain Eriksen, still thinking of his pretty wife.

When they all came out to the veranda, the deep pit fires had been lit and burning for hours, and the roast pigs were cooked. The tempting smell of the meat and the other dishes laid out on the long trestle tables was delicious to the hungry guests. Some had returned from swimming or fishing, others came out from resting.

One of the Hawaiian children came to Peter. "That

man, Maleko, he wish to talk to you, boss. He over there."

Tension rippled along Peter's nerves. He nodded, and went casually over to where the four Hawaiian fishermen, the strangers, were standing. He noted again with wonder the height and breadth of chest of the tallest one, Maleko.

He had met them, but had scarcely spoken to them. They kept themselves aloof and on the edges of the crowd. But Peter had seen that they were welcomed at feasts, fed well, and in return they had brought fish to the great house.

Now he greeted them formally, saying his name. "I am Peter Darien. You are my guests on the island of Darien. Welcome."

They all bowed to him. Maleko came upright, and said his name. "I am Maleko, fisherman who enjoys your hospitality on the island of Darien," and he introduced the other men by first name only. Peter noted he said no tribal name. Was it deliberate? Were they really of the Pauahi tribe, owing allegiance to Chief Pauahi?

He pretended not to notice this omission. Perhaps they would believe that as a white man he did not know the custom.

"I hope you are enjoying the feasts. We are grateful for the fish which you bring daily. It has been enjoyed. You are good fishermen, and must go out deeply for the excellent catch."

They acknowledged the compliment with unusual dignity. In fact, they stood like warriors, head erect, arms folded over their broad chests. Maleko spoke for them, the others only watched with glittering black eyes.

"We have enjoyed your feast, O man of Darien," said Melako, very formally. "You have made us guests here. We wish to express our thanks to you. We wish to entertain your other guests in some manner pleasing to you."

Peter hesitated. Was this some trick of Maleko? But there were armed guards about, and he had noted

Joe quietly in the corner of the veranda, with his rifle at his arm, and the guests politely pretending not to notice this.

"What did you wish to do, Maleko? We should be honored by any demonstration of your singing or dancing."

"I have heard, O chief of Darien, that nobody does the fire dance to Pele here."

Peter was surprised. He himself had seen the dance only a few times. It was tricky and dangerous. It took much dexterity, strength, and practice.

"You are correct, Maleko. It has not been done on Darien for many years, since one was here, and was injured in the doing. He was burned, and my father forbade any others to injure themselves in this way."

Maleko bent his head, his eyes flashed. "I can do it, and well, without injury," he said, his voice firm.

Peter showed his indecision. "I am reluctant to allow my guests to risk harm for the entertainment of others. It is not wise to invite the displeasure of the gods in this manner," he finally said.

Maleko flashed him a look of some surprise, quickly covered by proud indifference. "I will not be hurt. I am skilled in this dance, all know it in my tribe."

Peter longed to ask him outright what his tribe was, but manners forbade it. He beckoned to Hilohilo, anxiously nearby, obviously dying to know what was discussed. The foreman hastened to them.

"Hilohilo, this man Maleko, our guest and friend," said Peter very formally, "has suggested that he will perform the fire dance for us. As you know, it has not been done here since the man was injured many years ago. What do you think of the matter? Shall we allow it to be done?"

Hilohilo's gaze darted from one to the other. He bit his lips, frowned. "It is dangerous," he said at last.

"Maleko can do it well!" insisted the man proudly.

"If we have buckets of water at hand, and blankets to put out the fire," said Hilohilo, "perhaps it could be done with safety."

Maleko grew angry, his head high. "I need not such things!"

"It would be safer for the guests," said Peter quickly. "Well, we shall try it. You do all with two sticks, yes?"

"Four sticks," said Maleko, his mouth tight, his eyes blazing.

"My God," said Peter, simply, and the man realized his horror, and he relaxed, his face showing amusement. "You must not do it with four sticks, Maleko!"

"I do it first with two, then with four. You will see how I can do it," said Maleko proudly.

"In that case," said Hilohilo, "I myself will stand with a pail of water in my own hands, and throw it at you directly I see you on fire! I promise it!"

The man laughed in his throat, huskily, seeming greatly amused now. "No, it is not needed."

"Hilohilo is right, the water must be there, and blankets. You must not be burned. I still think it might be better not to risk it . . ." Peter was hesitating.

Maleko insisted, Peter finally agreed, and went over to tell his father. Barton frowned, but finally got out the words, "Whatever you th-think b-b-best, Peter," and left it up to him.

Maleko went away to prepare himself.

The singing and dancing went on after the grand *luau*. Presently the line of dancers performed the *hula*. Gracefully, the girls moving to the quick rhythmic beat, the slower ones with grace and joy. The guests applauded heartily.

Peter saw Maleko standing at the edge of the clearing, near the fire there. Maleko had stripped himself, and now wore only a loin cloth of *tapa*, the brown and white pattern stark against his bronzed skin. His broad chest was wide, his shoulders seemed enormous, and the muscles rippled in his arms and thighs. He was an erect, striking, commanding figure, standing without moving at the edge of the fire. In one hand he held two long sticks, each about a yard long, with pitch at either end of both sticks.

Peter stepped off the veranda and went over to introduce Maleko. First he asked, "Do you wish music with your dance?"

"Only the drum, if you will, chief of Darien."

Peter nodded to Kenny, who had been warned. The Hawaiian musician, his eyes flashing with pleasure, stepped forward with the drum, and stood to the side of the crowd.

Maleko stood with two sticks of pitch in his hands. He attracted the attention of all, as Peter raised his hands for silence.

"Tonight we have an unusual dance for you, the rare fire dance, offered by a guest of this island, Maleko. It is a dangerous and difficult one," said Peter, in English. "Please, move the children back and keep hold of them, so that in the excitement they may not dash forward."

Obediently the parents restrained their children, and the circle about the central fire was made wider.

Peter repeated the announcement in Hawaiian. "It is good of Maleko to show us his skill in this difficult fire dance. We are grateful to him for sharing with us his dance to the goddess Pele, an offering to her for her mercies."

He strode back to the veranda and sat down. He felt unusually tense as Maleko bowed to the applause. The drummer began a slow beat, watching Maleko intently.

Maleko tossed the dry sticks up in the air, as though testing their feel. He pitched them about himself, under and around his legs, over his head, high up in the air, catching them easily. Peter wondered if he would throw them so high once they were on fire!

The drumming went on, increasing in tempo so that gradually one did not note it, until the heart beat began to increase with it. Maleko leaned to the fire, first one end of a stick blazed instantly into flame, then another. He lit both sticks, and as easily as he had tossed the others, he began moving about with them in a slow and dignified dance, the blazing torches in his hands.

Peter glanced to make sure Hilohilo had the buckets of water—he did, with two of his men, and blankets on the ground beside him. Another of Maleko's men stood at one side, with two more sticks touched with pitch in his hands.

Then his attention returned to Maleko and did not leave it. The man was massive, graceful, his bronzed chest gleaming in the firelight. As he worked with the blazing torches, sweat came out, and glimmered in the light, so he looked almost on fire himself, all of his naked body shining. Rosalind reached out and clutched Peter's hand. Victor sat still on her lap, his fascinated gaze on the man handling the lighted sticks as though they were beanpoles.

Maleko tossed one straight up in the air. While it was up, he sent the other after it, caught the first one, sent it back up. Both sticks seemed in the air at once, as his huge hands tossed them up effortlessly, catching them precisely in the center of each stick, to throw them upwards again. The air made the torches glow more frighteningly, and bits of pitch came off, flaming harmlessly into the sand at his feet.

The drum was beating more rapidly, following the increasing rhythm of the large man. The fire sticks were tossed about his body now, around his legs, between them, and up over his shoulders, dangerously close to his hair. Around, down, over him and around again, his hands and arms moving so swiftly they were a blur of movement lighted only by the torchlights he flipped about.

There was no sound from the guests and the Hawaiians watching. All stared in fascination and awe at the dexterity of the big man. Then, suddenly, he paused and the drum made a soft abrupt beating, slowing, slowing.

Someone started to applaud, but was stopped abruptly, as the friend holding two other sticks held them to the fire, and then flung each in turn to Maleko. He held two sticks in one hand, and across the high bonfire he caught the light stick in the other hand, easily, as though it was child's play for him. Peter realized he had not been bragging. He knew the fire dance, and could do it.

Peter was holding his breath painfully, and his wife's hand was clasped so tight in his that he felt the pearl ring cutting into his palm. He eased his grip, but could not look at her for staring at Maleko.

Now the man held four lighted sticks, and eight flames blazed around him. He tossed them like matches about him, but they were burning pitch. Around his body, around his shoulders, in between his legs, four sticks moving into a blur of sheer speed and light. The drumming increased to a frenzy to match that blur.

Maleko seemed to respond to it. His legs apart, his bronzed body gleaming with sweat down to his thighs, he began tossing the lighted sticks one at a time high up into the air. Before the first came down, he tossed the second, then the third, catching the first stick with one hand as he threw the fourth into the air. Up, up, up they went into the purple night sky, higher and higher, until he was sending all up into the air, and standing there with his arms out to catch the first and send it back.

The children were crying out with awe and admiration. No one could hush them. "Higher . . . higher . . . there they go . . ." they squealed. Peter feared it would distract Maleko, but his concentration was such he did not even seem to notice.

Then, one by one, the sticks came back down. He held all four of them, two in each hand, so that they formed crosses. He held them up high, flung them up in the air that way, and deftly caught them all as they came down in every direction.

Then Maleko stood, bowing in a slow dignified manner as the drummer banged one last hard time on the drum.

The applause broke out then, long and hard and enthusiastic. Cries in English and Hawaiian were heard, "Great show! Splendid! Marvelous, never saw such a show! Wonderful fire dance! Tremendous! What a figure of a man. What a man he is!"

Peter rose, still clasping Rosalind's hand, and went down the steps to where Maleko stood. Maleko tossed the sticks into the huge bonfire, and bowed to him with formal dignity.

Peter bowed back, then impulsively reached out. Maleko permitted him to embrace him, Peter touched each cheek with his own, then stepped back.

"You have honored us," said Peter, clearly, so all could hear. "It was a splendid dance, an honor to Pele, goddess of fire and volcanoes. She will be pleased with you, as we are tonight."

Beside him, Rosalind reached to remove the plumeria and orchid leis from her neck. She stepped forward and Maleko bent his tall head so she might place the leis about his neck.

"It was splendid, Maleko. Thank you, from our hearts." Her voice, though soft, was clear also, and applause broke out once more at her gesture.

Peter found time to wonder at the expression on Maleko's face. It was proud, wondering, as he stared down at Rosalind smiling at him. She clasped his hand, and bowed to him, gracefully, before returning to the veranda with Peter's hand in hers.

Kenny's band began to play. Maleko and his friends slipped away in the darkness, and the party went on. But all else seemed anticlimactic. They had been so awed by the fire dance, and the splendid man who had showed what he could do, fearlessly.

Peter found time to wonder the next day about the dance. Had Maleko merely given in to an impulse to show off, in a magnificent way, to the Darien guests? Or had some darker, more sinister impulse moved him?

If he had come as a spy from Chief Pauahi, what had the dance been meant to accomplish?

"He was sure showing his muscles out there," said Hilohilo admiringly. "With his strength and the way he move, he could sneak up and kill two men without they know it."

That made Peter think all the more. Yet—yet he wondered. Maleko had shown no animosity. Rather he had seemed to be proud to show his great skill. Not

314

once, never one time, had a single stick slipped from his hands, never had he missed a catch. The fire had sizzled close to his skin, but never close enough to burn.

He was a powerful man, probably a great warrior as well. He was no simple fisherman, nor were his three friends. So they must be spies—but from Chief Pauahi? And if so, why did they linger so long, content to fish every day? What did they want, and would they strike, just four men?

It sometimes kept him awake nights, and always accompanied him on his rides out on the plains. Glendon Corey seemed content to sit back and enjoy the guests, and showed no signs of leaving. Perhaps it had not been Corey who had fired the shot. It might have been Maleko or one of his friends. Yet, it did not seem like them. Maleko was proud of his great strength, he seemed contemptuous of weakness.

And shooting in the back was a sign of cowardice.

# 21

❦  ❦  ❦  ❦

MOST OF THE GUESTS departed, swearing it
had been the most memorable time of all, offering
their own hospitality. "You must come soon to Honolulu, and we'll show you about," or "Come soon to
Kailua, we want to show our gratitude," or the Winchester brothers, "You must look us up, and we'll
show you around our land. If you want more bushes,
or any flowers at all, just let us know."

Only Antoine Launay remained to set up his
canvas and paints in a back room, intent on his
portrait of Rosalind. He was still making sketches,
following her about, but he was withdrawing into the
silent period which usually preceded his burst of
energy into an oil painting.

Peter was relieved that the guests had departed,
much as he had enjoyed them. And Rosalind seemed
more confident of herself, she had been a splendid
hostess, they had become friends with her as well as
Peter. However, the worry of a possible attack by
Chief Pauahi while guests were there had bothered him
a great deal. There were no signs of attack. He figured
there would not be much warning. The Chief and his
war canoes would simply appear one day, and must
be dealt with.

To that end, he had Hilohilo increase the guards,
watch over the four fishermen, and train along with
Joe the dozen or more young Hawaiians who needed
to learn to use their rifles as well as their spears.

Peter wanted to be alone with Rosalind. It seemed
months since they had had time exclusively to themselves. And he wanted more black pearls, he had

spoken privately to Mr. Chan before the Chinese jeweler's departure. Mr. Chan would be delighted to make up a long necklace for Rosalind, and also to send some pearls to the international markets without revealing his source.

"It will be much pleasure to me, to handle such beautiful gems of the ocean," said Mr. Chan ceremoniously, his round face crinkling up into a big smile. "You must trust my discretion. You honor me by your confidence."

"You realize how important it is that no one understand the gems are from Darien," said Peter, quietly. "We would be overrun with treasure hunters and poachers in our waters. And they might be desperate men, intent on finding such rare pearls. They would stop at nothing."

The smile disappeared. "You speak truly, my friend, Mr. Darien. I shall keep complete silence on that matter. I shall send pearls only to those in whom I myself have complete confidence. And the prices I obtain shall be of the highest value."

Peter had turned over to Mr. Chan before he departed a leather bag of some of the best pearls, including the pretty bee-shaped baroque black pearl of Rosalind's with instructions on making that into a fine pendant. Mr. Chan had been almost speechless with delight over that pearl. "Truly a treasure in itself! How I shall enjoy designing some splendid setting for this glowing jewel."

"And I shall have more jewels for you presently," said Peter, with a smile. "I want a long necklace for Rosalind, and you have my instructions on which ones to sell. The blister pearls and the other small ones I shall not wish to keep."

"I shall follow your instructions to the letter."

So the guests had departed. And Peter suggested to Rosalind that they pack a picnic lunch and go off on their own for a day. She was happy to comply, he noted with delight that she was no longer reticent about showing she wanted to be with him. She was still timid in her caresses, but she permitted him almost any liberty in bed. And she seemed pleased with his kisses, and answered them.

He must be content with that for a time, but one day he would have her confessing that she loved him as much as he loved her. That was his goal. He put his arm about her waist as they went upstairs to get ready.

"Bring your sarong, we'll swim in our favorite place," he murmured in her ear, and kissed the soft lobe.

"Which one?" she asked innocently. "I enjoy them all."

He smiled teasingly, and kissed her mouth as they reached the door of their bedroom. A shadow stood at the back of the hallway, Peter noted it in the corner of his eye. When he turned to look, the shadow was gone. He frowned slightly. Who had stood there, who had tried to listen?

He forgot it again, in the joy of starting out in the early morning freshness. The horse was sturdy, eager to be off. A large picnic basket was at their feet. He took up the reins and Rosalind settled herself beside him, her amber eyes shining in the morning sunlight.

She looked to the north. "It looks cloudy over there, Peter. It wouldn't rain today, would it?"

"It's mid-October, it could. But probably not until late afternoon," he reassured her. "And we need the rain, the water reservoirs are drying up some. We'll be home before dusk."

They set off at a good pace. He noted no cattle on the wide plains as they took the north road to the western tip of Darien. Good. Terry had not moved any cattle back. He had ordered Terry to leave the operations alone. Terry was sulking again, but it was necessary to make him understand there could only be one boss on Darien, and that was Peter Darien.

"Why are you frowning, Peter?" Rosalind's voice came to him. He realized she sounded anxious.

He reached out and took her hand in his. "Only thinking of some problems. However, I am going to forget them for today," he told her lightly, and smiled down at her peach-bloom face. "Have I told you lately how lovely you are?"

The peach-bloom turned to rose as color came deeply into her rounded cheeks. The amber eyes half-closed, the long lashes covered them. "Yes, you have," she said, in a muffled tone.

"Don't you like it?" he teased.

"Well . . . it's very nice to hear."

He laughed out loud, the problems sliding off his broad shoulders. He was out with his girl, and he would forget all troubles today.

"Why don't you tell me how you feel about me?" he asked, provocatively, watching the curve of her pink mouth.

"Oh, Peter!"

"Do you dislike me?" he urged, softly.

She shook her dark shining head, vigorously.

"Hate me?"

"Oh, no!"

"Then what?"

She flushed, and looked off in the distance.

"Just wait until later, I'll get you to tell me what you feel," he threatened, and chuckled as she turned her head further away.

They reached the sunny lagoons on the north shore, and he went on driving toward the steep cliffs. Rosalind realized at last where he meant them to go, and looked forward with shining happiness.

"To the cliffs, Peter?"

"Yes. I thought we would gather some more pearls today," he said casually. "If a winter storm comes up, we could lose some. So we'll gather them, all the bigger and older black-lipped shells, and some of the white ones, if we find some. Then during the winter they can rest and lie dormant, and next summer we'll get more."

"We could bring back some oysters for the table, also," said Rosalind, practically. "Everyone would enjoy that."

He was silent, then nodded. They could shuck the oysters after they returned, and take out all the black pearls, without anyone knowing what the shells had contained. He could put the black-lipped shells into the basket, and take them to their room. He would need some money from the sale of the blister pearls and small ones, he might realize some fifty thousand dollars from them. That would carry them over for a year or more, and let Eileen and Terry and Aunt Norma have their mainland trip also. If Rosalind wished, he and his wife would also take a journey—alone!—and go to San Francisco, New York, Europe, wherever they wished. That would be fun. He would enjoy showing her the world.

They reached the steep cliffs by mid-morning. Peter slid down, helped Rosalind down, thankful that by this time his complete strength had returned. He no longer felt like a rag doll that could frighteningly lose all power over his legs and arms and spine.

He took out the basket, then let the horse loose to roam on a long rope. Then he and Rosalind climbed down the slippery path through the bushes, enjoying the fall flowers and vines.

The allamanda bloomed brightly, yellow against the green of the leaves and ferns. Wood rose blossoms surprised them, a soft pink. Star jasmine glowed in the dimness near the waterfall, sending its delicate perfume to them. He noted several clumps and bushes of tall stately Birds of Paradise, their orange and purple like bird beaks.

And always the plumeria bloomed, pink and orange and yellow, scattered through the delicate ferns like so many fallen flowers. The hibiscus bushes were deeply rose and pink and cream. The path down was like a path in paradise, so beautiful it was, and the waterfall made merry music beside them.

They reached the beach and smiled at each other. Rosalind's face was flushed pink with exertion, she had worn her pink muumuu and looked like a flower herself, thought Peter. She moved with the light grace of a tiare flower on its stem.

They went swimming, Peter in his brief trunks and Rosalind wrapped in a sarong from her arms to her thighs. He enjoyed watching her, she was fearless in the water, it was her second home. They gathered up some of the black-lipped pearl oyster shells, setting them in the picnic basket and then on a rope in the water, with the lid closed on the basket. They would stay wet and alive for the trip home. He located several of the black shells on the beach, opened the shells and took out several pearls. Some of the black pearls were small, but two were large and splendid, perfectly round.

They ate of the fried chicken the cook had packed, bowls of greens, then ended the meal with fruit, papaya and pineapple slices, and some sweet cherries. The cook had added several sweet coconut cakes, and Rosalind ate two with enjoyment. Peter noted idly that she had become more rounded and seemed almost plump in the waist. He was glad she was rested more, and her cheeks were fuller. She had much better color than when she had come to Darien.

As they lay back on the blankets, he felt his eyelids closing. He had been up many nights in the week that his guests had been there, and Rosalind had been up early in the morning and to bed late. They both needed rest. He slept, his arm close about her, her soft thighs against his hard limbs.

He wakened as the sun blazed down on them. He lay for a time watching Rosalind's sleeping face. How pretty she was, with her dark lashes against her rosy cheeks, the sweetness of her pink mouth enticing, the small perfectly formed ears, the gentle swell of her breasts, the golden tan of her shoulders and arms. His gaze wandered lower. The drying sarong clung to her waist and legs, and he put his hand softly on her thigh.

She stirred, sighed, opened her eyes dazedly. His hand moved, and she smiled sleepily at him, cuddling closer.

"Hello, darling."

"Mummmm," she murmured, stretching against him. It stirred him, reminded him they had both been too tired to stay awake nights and make love this week. His arm closed more firmly about her, and he bent over her. His free hand stroked back her wet hair from her forehead.

He leaned to kiss her forehead, slid his lips down over her cheeks to the ear lobe, then down below then to a sensitive spot which made her shiver as he kissed. Then he nuzzled at her shoulder, under her chin, and around over the pulse beat. Gently he unfastened the fold of her sarong and opened it. How her rounded breasts enticed him, the pink nipples hardening under his eager lips.

He made love to her slowly, drawing it out, enjoying the feel of her salty silken body under his lips and hands. He moved over her and began to embrace her deeply, and enjoyed her response. She was still half-asleep, and she moved her hips, and opened her legs as he directed, her senses awakened though her mind was not yet alert.

Over her, he teased, "You haven't told me how you feel about me." He smiled down into her darkened eyes. Slumbrous with passion, they were more beautiful than ever, amber-golden-brown, shadowed by the dark lashes.

"Oh . . . Peter . . ." Her words were like a groan, and she moved beneath him, her thighs opening wider.

"Peter. . . ."

"Tell me you love me. . . ."

"Oh . . . please . . . go on . . . don't stop. . . ."

"After you tell me . . ."

"What shall I say?" Her head turned away from him. He kissed under her ear again, and she shivered deliciously.

"Say you love me."

"Ohhhhh. . . ."

"Say it."

"I love . . . love you . . ." He kissed the words from her lips joyously, and began to move more rapidly. Her hands clung to his back, the roar of the sea increased deafeningly in his ears. Only it was not just the ocean, it was the blood pounding through his body, on fire with desire.

Afterwards, he was contentedly drowsing on her

shoulder when she exclaimed, "Peter, it's getting so dark!"

"Probably rain," he said, and sat up. Then he stared at the sea. It was dark also, like the darkening sky. The waves were roiling in a strange manner. He had seen them like that a few times—

Tidal wave coming—it must be far out—

"Come on . . . fast!"

He grabbed her hand, they came up. He picked up the clothes, thrust them into her arms. "We'll have to run!"

"Oh, what is it? A storm?"

His face set, he did not answer. He started toward the path, the blankets in his arms.

"Peter, the oysters!" She had left him to go rescue the basket still hanging in the water. He cried out to her.

"Leave them. . . ."

"No . . . we must. . . ." She was struggling with the rope. Cursing under his breath, he went after her, took the rope, sawed it with his sharp knife, and pulled out the basket full of black-lipped oysters. He carried them and the rugs, and sent her up the path before him. At the top they might be safe.

He cast one look at the sea before they scrambled into the tangle of vines and flowers up the wet path. He slipped once, and caught himself. It would not do to slide back, there wasn't much time.

He was thinking ahead. The cliffs were slick and dangerous. The rocks could crumble under an on-slaught of a heavy relentless tidal wave. They must get away—but where?

The plains were flat, until they came to the central plains, where the volcano rose about two hundred feet into the air. If they could make it—

On the cliff's edge, he did not pause to look out at sea. Rosalind did, and gasped.

"Peter . . . waves . . . far out . . . they are higher than I ever saw in my life!"

"I know. Get in."

She obeyed his tight-lipped command. He unfastened the horse, put him to the shafts, and jumped in. He took up the reins, and they were off.

They started down the cliffs to the east. Rosalind clung to the side of the carriage, her face pale. At her feet the basket rattled, and she put one leg on either side of it to hold the basket in place.

"See if you can get into your clothes, it may turn cold," he ordered. She nodded, blushing but obedient.

She managed to get off the wet sarong even as the carriage careened down the cliffs to the plains. She struggled into the muumuu, and pulled it down over her legs. "Now, you, Peter. I can hold the reins. . . ."

He nodded, gave her the reins, watched keenly as he struggled into his trousers. He got them on and fastened them, then grabbed his flowered shirt. He got into it and fastened the buttons. Then he took the reins again. His boots could wait, he could manage with sandals.

She had handled the horse well, he noted. He must let her drive more often. Then he turned his attention to the sea.

Far out he saw the great wave coming. It was coming from the north, as Hilohilo had predicted. Roiling, massive, it dwarfed all the other waves. Frantically he glanced about, and turned the horse to the southeast.

Far ahead of them lay the volcano with its sheath of green which had grown over the centuries since its last eruption. Sanctuary, if they could but reach it.

"Hang on tight," he said grimly, and whipped up the horse. The animal started, the carriage jerked, and they were off.

Rosalind had glanced back, had seen the wave out at sea. It would come in, recede, then come back again in full terrible force. That was the way of it.

Her hands gripped the side of the carriage until the knuckles were white. "It's coming," she managed to say, quietly.

"Yes. We have to be up high before it comes the second time."

He had scarcely finished speaking when the tidal wave roared in. It swept across the level land, the green soil of the island, straight toward them, and the horse whinnied in fright, as foam curled about its legs. Peter was half-standing in the carriage, holding the frightened animal in check.

The water boiled about the carriage wheels, lifting it off the ground. Peter staggered, he felt himself losing balance. Then two firm hands grabbed him, and pulled him back onto the seat. Rosalind was holding onto him frantically, with a grip that bit into his sides.

The water boiled on, the carriage settled into the grass, and the horse ran off, the carriage bouncing and swaying behind it. The water died down, the volcano hill was just beyond them. The water receded, and ran back the slight slope to the sea.

They would have a few minutes before the next devastating assault, the real thing. Peter concentrated on getting to the slope of the volcano. It had never seemed so distant.

But they made it. They were rising up the steep slope, the horse scrabbled in the rocks at the height, as the tidal wave began to come again, across the land, from far out at sea. There was nothing to halt its foaming progress except the slope of the volcano.

On and on it came. Peter halted the carriage at the top of the volcano, near the very lip of the empty crater, and got out to hold the frightened horse. They were up more than one hundred fifty feet, maybe closer to two hundred. The tidal wave roared across the land. It was a frightening sight, covering trees, bushes, grass, all in one relentless motion. The huge wall of water, more than sixty feet high—but they were higher.

Rosalind was staring at the water, her hands gripping the carriage. Peter looked up at her, smiled encouragingly. She had saved him, the darling, he thought. She had all the courage and daring in the world.

The water foamed futilely below them. The trees were covered for a time, until the water slowly receded again. Peter looked out over the land, until he could see the trees clearly, then the bushes which had not been uprooted and swept out to sea.

When he could see the grass again, he breathed a great sigh of relief. The cattle were safe, the water had not gone south. The volcano slope was enough to avert the force of the sea. He came to the carriage, got in.

"The gods are angry with us," whispered Rosalind intensely. She seized his arm. "Oh, Peter, what have we done?"

"Done?" he asked furiously. "We have saved ourselves from a tidal wave! What are you talking about?"

"It was a warning from the gods! They are angry with us!" She was shaking. "I must ask Kinau what it means. We must make offerings to the gods. . . ."

He compressed his lips, but had to yell. "That is superstitious nonsense! I am surprised you believe in such matters. You know how tidal waves are formed! The volcanoes on Hawaii erupt, and later the earth must move and adjust to the eruption. That creates tidal waves."

"But Peter, you believe in the gods of the Hawaiians, the gods of earth and air and fire. I heard what you said to Maleko, you told him that Pele would be pleased with him. I heard you!"

He was anxious to get her home, and safe. He wanted to make sure all at Darien were safe, and his *paniolos* and his cattle. He did not guard his words, furious with her.

"Rosalind, I was being courteous to a guest! He believes in Pele. I was just being grateful in terms he would understand! Of course, I don't believe in gods any more than I believe in the Greek gods of ancient times! The stories are amusing and interesting, as they point out the beliefs of other people of long ago. But we are both Christians, we know their gods do not exist!"

"Peter!" He looked at her, she was pale again. "How can you say that?" she whispered. "They are real, they have power. . . ."

"Don't be absurd!"

She sank back in the seat, and turned her head away. He scowled at the road ahead. The path was wet, hard to drive on. It was only a dirt road at best, now it was a sea of mud. The horse had been frightened, now it was tired and trotted along with its head bent down. He would be glad to get home. He would straighten this out with Rosalind later. Surely she did not really believe in Hawaiian gods! They were primitive superstitious objects of worship, nature worship, and some of the stories were crude and cruel. He would point out the differences between them and the real God of the Christians.

They came into the stableyard to find everything in confusion. The hands were busy soothing the horses. Most of the wave had spent its strength beyond the house, but enough water had come in to terrify them. The grass and patio were covered with water.

A hand took the horse, and promised to rub him down good. "We was scared about you, boss," he said simply. "Miss Norma, she always asking about you, all the hours."

Norma hurried out from the house. "You're safe, thank God!" she said fervently. "The men are out with the cattle, they are so nervous and jittery. Hilohilo wanted to go search for you, but I told him you would get home as soon as you could, you knew the sky. What kept you so long?"

"We fell asleep after swimming," he said briefly. He lifted out the basket of oysters.

"What in the world do you have there?" asked Eileen curiously, trailing languidly after her mother. She looked into the basket. "Black shells, and so many of them!" Her gaze sharpened. "What do you have, oysters? Or are they pearl oysters?"

Peter ignored her. "We'll go up to our rooms," he told Rosalind curtly. "You must have a rub-down and get warm. Or you may catch a chill." And he followed her up the stairs inside. Eileen looked after them narrowly, then peered inside the carriage. She found an oyster shell that had fallen from the basket, picked it up with a gingerly touch and a grimace, and carried it to the kitchen. To the surprise of the cook, she demanded a knife.

Taking the shell away from the curious glances of the Hawaiians, she opened the shell with some effort. Then she stared at the oyster inside. With the knife, she cut away the flesh, and dug out the object within. Her eyes glazed over, she was thinking hard. A black pearl!

Upstairs, Rosalind dried herself, washed the salt water from her hair, and was drying it with a towel. She had put on a simple negligee, she would dress later. She felt bruised all over, both from the jolting of the carriage and from the words of Peter. He did not believe in the gods! Surely they would hurt him for his angry words. She shivered, and Peter frowned at her.

"You're chilled, Rosalind. Get into bed, and get really warm. I'll tell Honora to make you a hot rum drink."

"Oh, please, no, Peter. Just some hot tea or coffee, that's all I want."

He went to the door in his shorts holding the towel, and opened it. Eileen was standing there, her fist clenched before her. She came in before he could stop her.

She shut the door after her. Opening her hand, she showed Peter the pearl.

"So the pearls come from Darien," she said, harshly, her blue eyes blazing. "You got them from somewhere on Darien! And I want my share! These are worth a fortune!"

Peter scowled at the pearl in her hand. "That's just a stray pearl, Eileen, you got lucky," he said grimly.

"Don't lie to me! I've seen Rosalind's pearls! And so have other people! And I want my share. I'm a Darien, I own some of this island! These pearls could get me away from here! I want my share!"

"We won't discuss it tonight," said Peter, after a pause. "And if you're smart, you won't advertise the pearl anywhere. We'll talk tomorrow."

She gave them both a long cool look. Rosalind with her long loose brown hair, Peter barefoot in his shorts.

"You've been swimming, and you got the shells somewhere there," she said with calculated intensity.

"I'll find out where, if you don't give me enough! Be warned, I'm going to tell Terry. You owe us plenty!"

She went out and slammed the door, taking the black pearl with her.

"Oh, damn it to hell," said Peter. He rubbed the towel on his shoulders, put on a shirt, and squatted down beside the basket. He began to shuck the oysters into a dish on the table, putting the shells into a wash basin. "We might as well finish this and get the pearls out, or she'll have them all."

"How will you keep her quiet, Peter?"

"Can't," he said briefly. "She will tell Terry and Norma, Terry will have it all over the island. Well, nobody knows where we went today, and we won't say. And people have looked for years for oyster pearls." He shrugged. "With luck, nobody else will know."

He glanced up to see her frowning in worry. "Now, don't fret about it, darling. It was bound to come out sometime. We may be able to keep it among ourselves. And if not . . . well, we own the island, and have some say about who comes here. The undesirables can just stay away."

He finished shucking the oysters, briskly. He found a good dozen excellent black pearls of first quality, some half a dozen blister pearls, and a fine array of small pearls. The oysters were sent down to the kitchen by the maid, the shells were sent out by a houseman, to the trash. The pearls he washed carefully, and set to dry on a towel on the dressing stand.

As Rosalind finished brushing her hair, she looked at the gems sadly. Would they cause more trouble between Peter and his cousins? Perhaps the tidal wave had been the warning of Pele that more trouble was to come.

Where would it end? Peter came over to her, and kissed her bare shoulder. "You're still cool, love," he said, in his usual calm tones. "Lie down under a blanket for awhile, and get really warm. I'm going to have a hot bath and soak for a bit."

He lifted her face with his finger under her chin,

smiled down into her large eyes. His lips touched her lightly, then more firmly, till they were crushed breathlessly against hers.

He lifted his head. "I adore you," he said.

She held his wrist in her hand, her fingers could scarcely close about its thickness, long as her fingers were. He was so tough, so hard, like his harsh beautiful land.

"Peter . . . about what you said," she told him in a low tone. "It . . . hurt, that you don't believe in the gods . . . did you mean what you said?"

His face grew stern and he straightened. "Rosalind, a man makes his own fate," he said. "The gods of the Hawaiians are just idols whom they worship because they don't understand the forces of nature: the sun, the sea, the volcanoes, the winds. I don't intend to worship any of them, nor will I allow you to do so! I admire the Hawaiian people, and want to see them retain their happy ways. But as for believing in those superstitious fears and making offerings . . . I will not allow you to do so!"

She bent her head, and her hand rested quietly on the edge of the dresser. In the years of emptiness after her mother had died, and her father was so ill, her faith had been all that had sustained her. Her faith in the Hawaiian gods, and the good people who had been so kind to her. Was she to throw away all that, the beliefs of so many years and experiences?

"We'll talk another time, you're tired," he said firmly. "You'll come to understand what I mean, and to believe me," and he went off to the bathroom, to run the water and sing in the tub.

Drearily she thought, we will talk, and he will convince me he is right—as always! What use was that? He can never be convinced he is wrong! Yet he expects me to be changed and listen obediently and believe whatever he says!

Her mind was going around in circles. She decided to lie down and rest. She was weary and her body ached. She fell asleep between two blankets, and did not hear him come back quietly into the room. He gazed down at her sleeping face, his own hard face softening. He did adore her, he had never loved anyone in the world as he loved her.

He would adorn her with jewels, he would gown her in the most beautiful of dresses, he would show her off proudly around the world, but no one else could touch. Rosalind belonged to him, heart and mind and soul. One day, he would convince her that she belonged to him, and he would know everything about her, her thoughts, her beautiful ways, everything.

# 22

❀ ❀ ❀ ❀

TERRY AND EILEEN cornered Peter the next morning in his study before he could start out for the day. He was anxious to see how the cattle had fared, to reassure himself that the tidal wave had not hurt the grass. The salt would have been deposited on the grazing land in the northern part of the island and it would take many rains to wash it all off.

His mind on his problems, he looked up absently when the door was opened. Terry came dressed in his usual casual slacks and shirt. Eileen, though, had not bothered to dress. She had flung a blue silk negligee over her nightdress. Norma would have had a fit to see her wandering about the house in that sheer outfit, thought Peter wryly.

"Yes, what is it?"

Terry shut the door after them. His blue eyes glowed with excitement in his handsome tanned face. "That black pearl, it's worth a fortune," he breathed.

"Hardly that," said Peter, coldly. Eileen held the pearl gripped tightly in her little fist. Had she slept with it? "I advise you to forget the pearls, and get down to work. Were you with the cattle yesterday?"

"The cattle!" Terry flared. "God damn it, Peter, you're not going to shove me off on that topic!" His eyes shifted away guiltily. No, he had not been with the cattle yesterday. More likely with an Hawaiian *wahine*.

"Yes, stick to the topic," said his cooler sister. Eileen unclutched her fist long enough to show the pearl. "We want some of these! We can sell them and go away! Make a new start in California!"

"No," said Peter. "If there is any money to be made

from the pearls, I shall take it for the good of Darien. Any other questions?"

"God damn!" Terry exploded again. "You're a cold bastard! We deserve some of those gems! Why, they must be worth a fortune! Where do you get them?"

"None of your business," said Peter bluntly. "As for deserving or earning anything, neither of you have a right to talk. Two more useless people cannot be found on Darien. Why should you have anything, just because your name happens to be Darien? No, the pearls will go for the good of all, except the ones I shall keep to adorn *my wife*. And that is final." He stood, picked up his sombrero. "Coming out to work, Terry?" he asked ironically. "Or do you intend to seduce some other little Hawaiian girl today?"

Terry glared, a flush high on his cheekbones. Eileen snapped, "You won't change the subject that way, Peter! I demand my rights! If you won't give me the money, then I want some of the pearl jewelry!"

"Why should you have it? You have diamonds, white pearls, other jewels. And all you do is complain, and want to get away from here. You have all you'll get," said Peter, nodding to the gem in her hand. "And if you are both as smart as you ought to be, you'll keep your mouths shut about them."

"Why should we?" blazed Eileen. "What difference does it make? I'll talk as I please!"

"And tell the world about them?" said Peter, moving to the door. "That won't be very intelligent. We'll have fortune hunters here by the dozens, poachers in the waters, and they won't be gentle, gracious guests either. The very hint of any wealth, and we will be attacked by a swarm of pearl hunters. So keep your mouths *shut*."

He went out, slamming the door behind him. He was furious with them, yet he understood. They were crazy to get away. They were so immature and impractical, they thought a hundred thousand dollars could keep them for life. But they could not handle money, they would be fleeced at once, and come whining back for more. He would keep them under his thumb, much as they hated it, and keep them and Darien safe. Much as he hated the situation himself! He would like to jerk the thorns out of his side, as much as they wanted to depart.

He spent the entire day out on the range, looking at the cattle. Some had been frightened by the thunderstorms of last night, injuring themselves and each other. Hilohilo and the other *paniolos* were busily treating the injuries.

Then he had gone off with Joe Smith to examine the range land in the north. It was salty, from the sweep of the tidal wave over it. They discussed how long the salt would remain before it was washed away by fresh rains, or would sink deeply enough into the limestone and lava surface of the island purifying what water remained, and leaving the grass fresh.

It would probably not be safe for the cattle until next summer. That meant not much beef could be butchered and sent off to the mainland. And they would have to live on the money from the pearls.

He was brooding over that when he went upstairs by the back way. He was dusty, muddy to his hips, and his shoulder ached from the old wound. He went into the bedroom, and found his young wife dressing for dinner.

"Peter, is it very bad?" she asked at once, her gaze on his weary face.

"Nothing that can't be helped," he said, brightening. It was good to be able to talk over his troubles without reproachful looks to greet him. "The grass is salty, some of the cattle injured, but in all we got off lightly."

"The water is hot, I'll run your tub," she said. "I laid out some clothes . . . are they all right?" She indicated the bed where his grey suit and a fresh flowered shirt had been set out.

"Fine. Thanks, darling." He stripped off the dusty clothes, sat down to haul off his muddy boots and kick them away from the rug. She had gone into the bathroom, and was running the bath for him. He watched her as she bent over the white porcelain tub in her graceful pale green silk and lace gown. Never too good to do service to others, never too dressed up to help, he thought, God, how had he ever managed to find such a wife!

Eileen spent hours getting dressed, putting on makeup, choosing the right jewels, and would never think of offering to help with the flowers or the table. And her dainty hands would not be found in dirt, or picking up muddy shirts, as Rosalind's were doing now.

She set his dirty clothes into the hamper, and put his boots outside the door as he padded to the bathroom to soak gratefully in the hot water. It drew out the aches and tiredness. Rosalind brought him a cool lime and rum drink in the tub, and handed it to him with a smile.

"Medicine, Peter, for what ails you!" she teased.

"Honey, you are the best girl in the world." He took a long grateful drink, she set the glass down on the table near the tub.

"How is little Victor? Haven't seen him for two days," said Peter, soaping his legs.

From the bedroom, Rosalind said, "Oh, more ornery than ever! He is learning how to get into mischief. Kinau says it is normal, but I can't help being startled when he throws a glass over the balcony railing and laughs as it crashes! How long does this phase last, I wonder?"

Peter grinned to himself as she went on telling him about Victor. He longed to see her with a baby of their own. He had quietly decided against adopting Victor. Victor might one day be a chief of his Hawaiian people, he seemed more Hawaiian than white, though that might change. The Darien land and ranch must go to another Darien, he thought, though he would say nothing to anyone about that for a time. It depended on his children, on the boy Victor and how he turned out. He loved little Victor, but he must be sensible about his future. Terry was careless and irresponsible. If Victor turned out like that, or if he became more like his haughty grandfather, all Hawaiian, then he must go back to his people one day.

He had almost forgotten about the pearls when they

went down to dinner. He entered the drawing room to find Glendon Corey standing eagerly waiting for him, his flinty eyes blazing with excitement. Eileen sat in a cherrywood chair near him, her sullen angry look warning Peter. Terry sprawled near them with a glass in his hand, not his first or second or third, from the looks of it; Terry had not been out on the range today.

"What will you have, darling?" Peter asked Rosalind.

"Just lime, thank you," she said, and he poured out the juice and added a stick of fresh pineapple to it.

Eileen's face was a study in insolence as she looked at Rosalind. "Can't take strong drink?"

Rosalind did not bother to answer. Her face was a mask when she wanted it to be. Barton looked at them sharply, and frowned.

Peter poured a lime drink for himself, as well. He had his back to them and they did not see that he was not adding his usual rum. He had had one drink, and from the looks of it he had better keep his wits about him tonight. He did not want them to draw him into a shouting match, or reveal more than he should.

"Well, well, you have good news for us, Mr. Darien," said Corey, with a joviality that did not match his pompous politician manner. His cheekbones were red, he could not control the shaking of his hands.

"Really, what is that? About the injured cattle, or the salt where the tidal wave covered the grass?" asked Peter, coming to sit beside Rosalind on the rosewood sofa. He took her hand in his before them, noted Eileen's look and curl of lip.

Glendon Corey laughed; it had a falsely excited note to it. "Now you are teasing me! I mean the black pearls, Mr. Darien! This will increase the value of your island! Oh, no matter about the cattle, I am sure that situation will improve! I am still interested in buying Darien!"

"And I am still not interested in selling," said Peter, definitely. He squeezed Rosalind's fingers, and she sat quietly, though he could feel her quivering. She knew that Eileen and Terry must have gone straight to Corey with their news about the pearls.

"What b-black p-p-pearls?" Barton Darien managed to ask.

Eileen answered, opening her palm, and showing the black pearl. "Your son has been hiding these black pearls from us, Uncle! He has a fortune hidden away. I'll bet he means to make off with his dear wife, and leave us all stranded on this Godforsaken island!"

Norma came in with Honora, in time to hear her. "Eileen! What are you saying?"

"More foolishness, Aunt Norma," said Peter, rising. "What can I get you to drink?"

He fixed their drinks while Eileen explained, complained, and pouted about the pearls, Peter's behavior, his selfishness, and how he had hidden the discovery of the pearls from them.

"Peter must have known about the pearls for ages, Mother! He has all kinds of jewelry made for his dear wife, but not a single piece did he give to me! And he won't tell us where he found them!"

"Well, I am sure Peter knows what he is doing," said Norma, placidly. Peter guessed his aunt knew more than she was telling. "Now, do let us go in to dinner, while it is hot. Barton, may I wheel you in?"

Barton hesitated, he hated to eat with people and be helped, but the conversation had roused his curiosity. He nodded, but Peter stopped them.

"Just a couple of minutes, I have something to say," he said. He stood before the mantel, glanced quickly at Rosalind, found her looking at him encouragingly.

"Now that Terry and Eileen have discovered about the black pearls, and have rashly told Mr. Corey," he said, "I must therefore confine all three of you to the house and grounds. You will not be allowed to go further. I do not intend to sell out to Mr. Corey, nor will I allow him to hunt about and find the source of the pearls. They belong to this family, and will be used to help finance our enterprises. I do not intend to sell. Nor shall I trust any of you to do anything behind my back."

He finished, and waited for their explosions. Eileen sprang up first. "You beast!" she cried. "I want my share! And you must sell out . . . I'll get away from Darien if it kills me! I want to live in civilization, not here among . . . among natives!"

Terry had roused, somewhat blunted by drink, but angry. "Peter, you have no right to confine us. I'll find where the black pearls are, and by God I'll take them all! You must have thousands, even millions of dollars hidden away!"

"Now, now," soothed Mr. Corey, his grey eyes glittering like ice. "No sense in being hasty about this. I am sure Mr. Darien understands you are upset. Mr. Darien, you have not heard my latest offer." He added solemnly, "One . . . million . . . dollars! One million American dollars for this island, and all you have to do is turn it over to me, problems of cattle and all, and leave within a week. And of course, tell me where you find the black pearls."

"You are out of your mind," smiled Peter, inwardly furious. How could those two crazy cousins have told Corey right away? But at least the man had showed his hand. He hadn't come for any cattle and land. He had come because somewhere, somehow he had heard of the black pearls, and learned they came from Darien. This must have been his purpose all along. "No sale. Come along to dinner."

He drew Rosalind from the couch, and led her from the room. Aunt Honora, without waiting for permission, pushed Barton, tense and excited, into the dining room, and set him beside her at the table, where she could help him without being obvious. Norma stayed to urge her son and daughter and Mr. Corey to follow them. Angry voices sounded, then the others stormed into the dining room.

Peter seated Rosalind at her end of the table, strode to his end. "And no more talk of this, especially not at the dinner table," he said, sitting down. He could have laughed at their frustration.

Yet he was furious at Eileen and Terry. They just couldn't keep their mouths shut! They had had to babble all about the pearls to Glendon Corey. He was all excited now, knowing he was right about the precious gems coming from Darien. He would not rest until he found them.

Peter was quiet during dinner. He would have to set a guard on all three of them. Damn it, more men wasted in guard duty. He would set a Hawaiian on Mr. Corey, another on Terry, and Joe Smith on Eileen. The quiet Texan could keep watch over her, and she would not make a move without his knowing it, and stopping her from going too far.

But how to keep from letting everyone in the world know about the pearls? He studied the situation. Could Corey be bribed to keep his mouth shut? No, he would blackmail them. Better to send him over to Kailua, and on his way, defying him to do anything. If, in his anger, he talked, and fortune hunters haunted Darien, Peter must deal with them as they came. If he had to turn the island into a fortress, he would do it.

Joe had several outlaw friends in Texas. Maybe he could send for two or three of his buddies, men who could ride and shoot, who would be loyal and keep their mouths shut. That might help. The Hawaiians were so friendly and inclined to trust strangers, that they might not guard.

Peter left the table after dinner and, instead of going into the drawing room with the others, he set off to have a good talk with Smith.

"Sure, I know two or three, maybe more, who would come. I'll tell them about the fishing and hunting and good life," smiled Joe, under the shadow of his wide-brimmed sombrero. "Bet you they'll come. Okay if I tell them you'll pay their way?"

"Their way and good wages," said Peter. "I'll draw you drafts on my bank in Dallas. Want any help in writing the letters?" he added tactfully, knowing Joe could not read and write very much.

Joe nodded, in relief. "I'll write the envelopes, and you write the letters, boss," he said. "Come to think of it, I'll ask the Foster brothers, all three of them. They're loyal cusses, and mean as they come. And

Bill Trent, only he might be using another name by
this time. He ran with a gang for a time, but he wants
to go straight."

"Come to my study tomorrow morning, and we'll
get the letters ready for the next steamer. Should come
tomorrow or Wednesday."

Peter went back to the drawing room to find Eileen
sullen and Terry steadily drinking. Mr. Corey was
pacing up and down the veranda outside, but he came
in when Peter appeared.

"I must talk to you, Mr. Darien," he said respect-
fully.

"Not tonight, Corey," said Peter. "Rosalind, will you
play the piano for me? I could use some music."

Rosalind nodded, and went to the keyboard. Terry
groaned and held his head. Eileen stood up angrily and
went toward the window. Mr. Corey bit his lips, and
began to reproach Peter.

"Mr. Darien, I must really insist on talking business.
You are gone all day on the range, and. . . ."

Rosalind began to play softly, and Peter raised his
hand to shush him. Norma poured a cup of hot coffee
for him.

Unexpectedly, Aunt Honora said, in a singsong
manner that told she was quoting,

Where gripinge grefes the hart would wounde
And dolefulle dumps the mynde oppresse,
There musicke with her silver sound
With spede is wont to send redresse

Norma asked mildly, "What is that, Honora?"

"Thomas Percy, 1728–1811," said Honora briskly,
in her usual tone. "I think it is nice." And she settled
back with her sewing, a little smock for Victor.

Peter repressed a grin, nodded solemnly. "Very
nice." And he settled back to enjoy Rosalind's playing
of a Chopin waltz. She followed it with a mazurka,
then something by Bach. By that time Terry was snoring against his cushions, and Eileen had stormed out
the French doors. With a thoughtful look, Glendon

Corey followed Eileen. Peter watched them go from under half-closed lids.

Peter went out early the next day to the cattle, and worked hard until evening. He came home exhausted but satisfied. The cattle would do all right, the grass was not so salty in the north that it could not be put right in time.

He paused in the drawing room, at the unusual sounds of conversation. He came in, saw that Terry was falling down drunk, sagged in a chair. Mr. Corey smiled triumphantly as Peter came in. He had a long paper in his hand, and he waved it at Peter.

Eileen sat nearby, a cat-smile of satisfaction on her lips.

"Well, we've done it, Peter," she said.

"Done what?" he asked sharply, his gaze on the paper.

"They have sold out to me. Sold me their shares in Darien," said Mr. Corey, grinning. "I have it in writing."

Terry was so drunk he could not hold up his head. His handsome blond head lolled on the cushions. "S-shold out, Peter," he said, grinning vacantly. "Now we'll have . . . good timsh."

"You fool," said Peter sharply. "You can't sell out, you have no shares to sell out. It was never set up that way. Norma and Honora and father had the shares, father has given his to me. You have none until your mother gives you some."

"No matter," said Corey, with a smirk. "I have their signatures on this little paper," and he waved it at Peter. "That's good enough for me. Welcome, partner!" And he had the gall to hold out his hand to Peter.

"They can't sell something they don't own," said Peter, pointedly ignoring the hand.

"Take a look," said Corey, and held out the document. Peter stepped closer to the fire to take a look, and Corey grabbed the paper. "No, you don't! It won't do you any good to destroy it, I can just write it up again."

Peter read over the page, with Corey holding on to

the edges. It said that Terry and Eileen signed over all their rights to Darien to Glendon Corey, in return for half a million dollars outright. A check was attached.

Peter's eyes narrowed as he read. "It says nothing about a corporation in Texas which you represent, Mr. Corey," he said, blandly.

The man's grin became set. "Oh, I can sign for myself, the others can sign later," he explained hastily.

"I think you do not represent any corporation or syndicate, Corey. I think you have represented yourself all along. And you have no interest in cattle, as such. You want Darien for the black pearls. Right?"

"Well, why not? I have a right to work on what I wish," the man blustered, his gaze shifting to the paper. "If I choose to turn this island into a ranch for harvesting oysters instead of herding cattle, why not? It's my gamble."

"And you don't give a damn what happens to the Hawaiians here, how they will live, what happens to them," said Peter sharply.

Corey shrugged. "They can move on elsewhere," he responded indifferently.

"Where did you hear about the pearls?"

"Well . . . I saw some in New York. I traced them back to Hawaii. I looked around in Honolulu, saw a few, but nothing like the quality of the ones at the jeweler's in New York. Then I saw some in Mr. Chan's, and traced them to you and to Darien. When I saw your wife's engagement ring, I knew I had the clue."

Terry was listening with foggy attention. Eileen's blue eyes were sharp and eager.

"Now we can sell out, Peter," she snapped, as though she had authority. "The secret is out, and you might as well sell also. Mr. Corey will have all the time he wants to hunt for oysters, and Terry and I can go off and have our good time. I'm going to San Francisco! I intend to go to balls, and be seen at the opera, and. . . ."

Peter leaned over, Corey had relaxed his grip on the paper. Almost casually, Peter ripped the pages in two, and tossed them into the fire. Corey screamed out in rage, and came at him, fists up.

The man was lean and fit, but older and a little paunchy in the waist. His reflexes were slower also. He got in one punch at Peter's cheek which knocked Peter's head back. Before he could get in another, Peter had knocked him down. Rage was in his blow.

He knocked Corey clean to the rug. When the man got up and came again, Peter put even more force into the next blow. This time Corey sagged to the rug, and was out.

"You've killed him!" Eileen screamed. She picked up the pitcher of lime juice, and poured it on Corey's face. He sputtered, and came to, his arms flailing on the carpet.

Norma came in hastily. "Whatever is going on?" She stared, aghast at her daughter with the empty pitcher in her hands. "What are you doing, Eileen? I thought you were resting before dinner!"

"Peter tore up the contract! He is a bastard, a whore-son of a bastard!" yelled Eileen, her face contorted in rage. "He burnt it!"

"What contract?" Norma was asking, "And do stop cussing, Eileen. It isn't becoming to a lady. . . ."

Eileen had forgotten all about being a lady. She was hopping in fury. Peter explained coldly.

"Corey got Terry drunk, and he and Eileen tried to sign away their shares and interest in Darien. I burned the contract, it isn't worth the paper it was written on. They have no rights to sign away. As I have explained to them before. Nobody signs away Darien, nobody! I have worked and sweated on this land, and nobody takes it away from me! Is that clearly understood, Eileen? Nobody! It remains as a heritage for me and for my children! Darien is for the Dariens, and if you can't act like one, then you can damn well go away!"

"Peter, Peter," said Norma, in low anguish. He glared at her also.

Terry was too drunk to talk, his head was flopping, as he stared down at Corey, trying to get off the rug.

"I'll write another contract, I'll get this land . . ."

Corey was vowing. "You cannot stop me! I'll find a way...."

"You'll get off this island on the next ship!" vowed Peter in turn. "I want no troublemaker like you around!"

"I'll come back on my own ship, and hunt around until I find those pearls! I'll get them, and you won't get a cent! You wait . . . you'll pay for this. . . ." He fingered his chin, where a large black mark was developing.

"You'll go on the next ship," said Peter, grimly.

"The steamer came today, Peter, there won't be another for a week," reminded Norma.

"Then a week," said Peter. "Or I'll put you on a sailing vessel, or on a fishing boat, anything to put you off my island!"

"Your island! Your island!" Eileen was hysterical with anger and disappointment. "It is Darien island! It belongs to all of us. If we want to sell out, we can! It is not your island, Peter! Damn your arrogance!"

"It is my island," he said deliberately. "I care for it, I love it, I work the cattle here, I run it. What do you do? Answer me that! You'll never sell it away from me! I will die first!"

Corey stormed out of the room, his handkerchief wiping away some of the lime juice. He stamped up the stairs. Eileen was weeping with fury, appealing to her mother. Terry was grinning vacantly at the fire, with scarcely enough strength in him to lift his filled rum glass. A pitcher at his side was almost empty.

Peter eyed his cousins grimly, and left them to the scene.

Norma was trying to scold and reassure her daughter. Peter felt sickened. He had not thought Terry and Eileen would go so far. Now he knew that they would. Perhaps it would be better to send them away, let them get into all the trouble they could on the mainland, to teach them a lesson.

Rosalind was entering their bedroom as he came upstairs. He came in and shut the door. Her worried look took in his grimness, the mark on his bruised cheek.

"What happened, Peter?" she asked. "I saw Mr. Corey covered with lime juice. . . ."

Peter said, "He got Terry and Eileen to sign some fool contract giving him rights to Darien."

"Oh . . . no. . . ." She caught her breath, her hand went to her heart. "He cannot . . . he cannot . . ."

Peter put his hand on her waist, turned her to him, and kissed her mouth. "Don't worry, it's finished. I burned the contract. That's when he hit me, and I knocked him out. Eileen brought him to with a pitcher of lime juice." He began to grin. "First time I saw a man all green like that."

Rosalind did not think it was amusing. "Oh, Peter, can he do it again? Make them sign again?"

"It won't do any good. He won't leave this island with any contract. And he is leaving on the next steamer, in a week. I won't have him around any longer. He just wanted the pearls, as I had suspected. And he can't have the island, to ruin it. He would toss out the Hawaiians, let the cattle die, and go after the black pearls."

She listened with despair on her face. "Oh, Peter, I wish you had never found the gems. They are nothing but trouble! People will be after them . . . the greed. . . ."

"Nonsense, don't worry about it. Pearls are not trouble, it is greedy men who are trouble, and greedy women," he added, grimly. "I can handle people. You leave it to me."

"But what if Corey does leave, and tells everyone about the black pearls?"

"I'll risk it. Chances are, he'll keep the knowledge to himself, hoping he can come back one day and get them. Treasure hunters don't often go blabbing about their finds to others. No, he'll keep his mouth shut."

He stripped off his shirt, wearily, and began to prepare for dinner. He was tired, and a little disheartened. He had not thought Terry would go so far. The boy had to become a man sometime, didn't he? But he had shown no loyalty to Darien. Eileen, she was another matter. She had always been spoiled and selfish, thinking only of her own pleasure. He was sick of them both. Maybe he would send them off with Norma in another month or two, when the money came in for the black pearls. He would be glad to be rid of the pair of them for six months or a year.

# 23

❦ ❦ ❦ ❦

ROSALIND WAS deeply troubled. The tidal wave, the anger between Peter and his cousins, the way Peter had spoken of Hawaiian gods—all were beginning to add up. They were connected. When men scorned the gods, trouble came. Kinau had always said that. Rosalind believed it, for she had seen how it happened.

The gods must be angry to cause so much turmoil and anguish. They must be appeased. But how could she manage that?

There was a volcano in the center of Darien. Perhaps she might climb to the crater and beg protection. But the volcano was dead, no gods lived there. Pele had taken up her residence on Kilauea, everyone said so.

She sought out Kinau the next morning, found her with Victor, playing in the sunlight of the peaceful patio. It was very early, the sun gleamed lightly on the flowered beds of roses and bushes of hibiscus, the little beds of pansies of cream and purple and blue.

Victor was humming to himself. He beamed at Rosalind, toddled over to her, and flung his arms about her knees. She bent and picked him up, hugging his warm body to her. She went over to Kinau and sat down in a cane chair beside her.

"There is much trouble, Kinau," said Rosalind in Hawaiian. Victor beamed at the soft syllables, and tried to babble after her. She smiled at him, and kissed his soft tanned cheek. He was content for a minute, then struggled to get down and chase a butterfly which floated tantalizingly past him.

She let him down, watching carefully. He was headed for the hibiscus bushes, they were his favorite place to play. He liked to get under the shrubs and crawl about, growling like a hunter after prey, squealing if he located some fascinating turtle or bug.

"Much trouble. Evil comes," said Kinau, her broad hands flat in her lap, her face worried.

"What can we do?"

"If we were at home," said Kinau, unconsciously revealing where she thought of her home, "we could ride to visit Pele, taking offerings to her."

Both of them sat and thought about it. "We cannot here, Pele is not here," said Rosalind sadly. "I too have felt this evil. Sometimes I shiver without being cold. Sometimes my heart is touched with cold fingers, and I lie awake."

"I also feel this way," said Kinau. "Pele prophesied that evil would prevail for a time. Much trouble comes. Is she angry with us, with the Dariens? Evil lives in the hearts of two of the Dariens. And that Mr. Corey, evil is in his eyes and heart."

"I know," sighed Rosalind. Her hand rubbed over her forehead. She had lain awake last night worrying, while Peter slept uneasily beside her. She knew he jerked awake, sometimes he got up and silently sat at the window for a time, then returned to bed, moving quietly so he would not disturb her. But she was disturbed, and worried over him and his beloved island.

He loved the Hawaiian people. He was possessive, that was part of it. They were his people, they belonged to his island, the Dariens were his family, she was his wife. All his possessions were much to him, they were all. And he would fight to the death to keep them.

Yet he deeply loved the Hawaiians as well. His face lighted with friendship when he talked with Hilohilo, he bent to pick up a Hawaiian child as tenderly as he held Victor. He worried over a girl whose father spoke angrily to her because she was not being decent. He flung his words at Mr. Corey, who would have callously moved the Hawaiians away from the island.

Peter would remain here, as much for the sake of the Hawaiians he employed as for his own pride in the Darien empire. He understood them, in part. He did not believe in their gods, but he respected their right to believe in them. He respected them, that was it. He wanted them to retain their gods, their songs, their dances, their happy lives. He was protective of them, as much as with his own family. They all belonged to him, thought Rosalind.

She had not understood Peter for a long time. He had puzzled and bewildered and even angered her. Now she was beginning to realize what moved and touched him, how he felt. He loved his people. He was possessive over them, he felt he knew better than any of them what was the best future for them.

What he said went, he was the boss. But he did it for their good. Terry kicked against his arrogance, resented Peter for telling him what to do, for refusing to let him go off with his share of the Darien fortune.

Eileen hated him, so did Terry. Yet Peter still loved them, and wished their good. They were weak, he was strong, so in his simple justice he had to protect them, even when they hated him for it.

Her mouth moved in a wry smile. Peter was always protective of her also, she was his wife, his woman. He wanted all of her, her thoughts, he kept urging her to tell him the thoughts she rolled about in her mind. Sometimes it exasperated her, she had always been a private person, having her own thoughts and dreams. Yet Peter was so good to her, kind to her, giving her gifts and trying to comprehend why she did what she did.

And she loved his gentleness in bed, he had not again repeated the harshness of that one embrace. She blushed as she thought of their frankness with each other in their embraces, their love-making in the silence of the night.

Never in the wildest stretches of her imagination had she dreamed she could do with any man what she did with Peter. And it seemed natural and good, exciting and pleasing to them both.

Kinau tapped her hand. "You will come back to me, please?" she asked, with a knowing smile.

Rosalind flushed again, more deeply, and bent her shining head. "I beg your pardon, my mind wandered away."

"We speak of how to please Pele. I think we must go visit her where she lives."

Rosalind started a little. "On Hawaii?" she gasped.

Kinau nodded, her face sobering. "On Hawaii. On Kilauea. But how to go? I think we must go pretty damn quick. Better to stay on good side of Pele, she is very jealous like female."

"How to go?" Rosalind was convinced, that they should go. "The steamer was just here, and won't return for another week. Peter means to send Mr. Corey away on it. He would not allow us to go on the same one." She had noted the way Peter's arm would go about her waist when Mr. Corey stared at her, or addressed flattery to her. That possessive gesture, practically subconscious, automatic.

"Maybe we get sailing ship. I go down today to see if ship comes in with fish. Maybe a big ship. We go soon."

"Should I . . . ask Peter?" said Rosalind, in a low tone. It seemed wicked to slip away without telling him. Yet she knew him well enough to know now he might flatly refuse. He had no time to take her, he was very busy. Yet he might tell her she could not leave Darien until he had time to go. And that might be too late.

"He stop you," said Kinau simply. "No, we go, the two of us. Akela look after Victor, she keep mouth shut, she good girl, and smart. I go see about ship. You take a little bag with dress and money and sandals. We go pretty damn quick." And she got up and went away, mysterious lights shining in her dark gleaming eyes. She liked action, she hated waiting about. She had been brooding about this for weeks. Now they could go.

Rosalind gathered up Victor, who was grubbily happy from his adventures among the bushes, and they went upstairs to wash and change. Then she brought him down to her bedroom. She got out a small mesh bag, and put a dress, sandals, a change of underclothing in it.

Money? She puzzled about that. She had little. She did not want to take money from Peter. But he kept some in a drawer. She looked inside, and found only a few coins and a couple of crumpled dollars there. She bit her lips. She would have to take them, but she would apologize later, and explain.

She did not know, until much later, that Peter had deliberately locked away most of his money in a safe. He did not want to put temptation in the way of Terry and Eileen, to slip away to Honolulu. And he did not want Rosalind to have enough to leave him. Hence the very small hoard there, only enough for rewarding someone for something special. And he had dipped into it himself the other day to buy some fish from a passing sailor.

Kinau returned about noon, a look of satisfaction on her brown face. She managed to whisper to Rosalind after lunch, "We go tonight. Sailing ship waits for us. We take bottles of rum, and some bread and cheese. I fix. You ready?"

Rosalind managed to nod before Norma came out to the hallway. Her heart thumped heavily. What if Peter wakened and missed her too soon for them to get away?

They retired early, Peter was weary. He soon fell asleep, and she got up, knowing the earliest hours of the night brought the deepest sleep. She dressed quickly in the darkness, in a simple muumuu and sandals, put a shawl about her shoulders, for the ship would be cool. She picked up the bag and crept out quietly down the back stairs.

Joe saw them go, creeping down the front path to the ships. His brows drew together in a frown. But his job was to guard Eileen and keep her from sneaking away to find the pearls. He watched, and did nothing to keep them from going. He respected Mrs. Rosalind Darien, and Kinau. If they were going away, it was for a good cause, probably. Rosalind had her head on her shoulders, and Kinau was a good sharp soul.

The two Hawaiian sailors were anxious to get away. They greeted the two ladies with broad friendly grins, and soon hoisted sail and were off. Kinau had promised them a half a pig for the journey, and she had it with her in the basket.

The wind was fresh and keen. Rosalind huddled under a canvas, and waited for the dawn. She could sleep little, though Kinau snored beside her. She leaned on the broad shoulder of the Hawaiian woman who had cared for her since babyhood.

Soon after dawn, they landed in Kailua. Then did Rosalind hesitate. They walked away from the harbor.

"We need carriage and horse," said Kinau, and looked at her. Rosalind bit her lips.

"I don't have much money."

That did not bother Kinau. Money meant little in her life. "Then we borrow," she announced cheerfully. "Maybe Akela's people have carriage."

"I think not," said Rosalind dolefully. "They have not much money. They are saving for a new fishing boat."

They walked slowly through the awakening town, over the dirt streets to the shopping center. Rosalind glanced idly in the windows. She was beginning to get hungry. Perhaps they should stop and eat some bread and cheese. Oh, for a big piece of dripping sweet pineapple!

"Mrs. Darien! It is Mrs. Darien! Good morning to you!"

Rosalind turned about, to meet the beaming smile of the jeweler.

"Oh, Mr. Chan, how good to see you!" she said, impulsively holding out her hand to him.

His keen black eyes took in her disheveled appearance, her weariness, and the drooping woman beside her. "May I be of some service to you, Mrs. Darien?" he asked quickly. "You seem weary. Your husband is here?"

"No . . . no, he could not come," she said warily. "Oh, Mr. Chan, do you own a carriage?"

If he was bewildered, he hid it with polite good manners. "Yes, I do, Mrs. Darien. Do you wish to ride somewhere?"

"Might I . . . borrow it for two days, Mr. Chan? I should be so careful of it. I . . . I'll leave my ring in exchange," she offered, pulling at her engagement ring.

He held up his clever little hand that could design jewelry so beautifully. "No, no, I protest. You must accept the carriage, with my gratitude for your warm hospitality on Darien. Mrs. Darien . . . have you eaten this morning?"

"No," she said ruefully.

"Oh, please, then, to come to my low home, which is but two short blocks from here. My wife will be so happy to fix something for you, while I prepare the carriage. Come with me!"

And he took them briskly in charge, turning about from opening his shop, and trotting down the street with them. At his "low house," which turned out to be a two-story mansion on a tree-shaded side street, plump cheery Mrs. Chan hastened to order servants about, and soon Rosalind and Kinau were seated at a table.

They ate eggs poached in white sauce, a dish of white rice, all they could eat of freshly sliced melon and pineapple. Then they had hot tea to drink.

Mrs. Chan hastened to fill a bottle with more hot tea. Neither of them questioned where they were going or why Mr. Darien was not with them. If they had questions, which they surely must have, the words were hidden behind the polite mask of their courtesy.

Mr. Chan brought his carriage around, and told Rosalind the horse was very docile and well-behaved. He had put grain in a sack for the horse, and a bucket of fresh water.

She thanked him happily, and they set out with Rosalind at the reins. Kinau did not seem surprised.

"Pele wish us to come, she arrange all," said Kinau happily. "You see, all works out."

It had, and Rosalind nodded. "Shall we go to get Hoke first?" she asked, as they set out on the road to her old home.

Kinau shook her head decisively. "No. Hoke will say no, he afraid Mr. Darien get mad at him like before. We just go and say nothing till afterwards. The men don't know everything," she said with a sniff and a toss of her dark head.

So Rosalind turned off the main road and cut off across the grassy plains, avoiding the high cliff country, toward the volcano. They could see it in the distance against the bright blue sky. Streamers of smoke were rising, more clear as they came closer.

They had eaten well, they did not need to stop. Rosalind kept on, with the horse at a steady trot or walk. She did stop to water the horse, and pet his sweaty neck, and he nuzzled her affectionately.

"Yes, yes, Pele wish us to come," murmured Kinau, as she gazed ahead. She seemed to be talking to herself, murmuring as they went along. Rosalind had picked some fresh plumeria blossoms when she paused to water the horse. Kinau's quick fingers were fashioning them into large leis.

As they came closer, Rosalind began to feel uneasy. Smoke and sulfur fumes were steaming up from the black lava lands. Ahead of them at the sides of the dirt road they could see some spurts of bright red, where flames shot up from the cracks in the black ground. She remembered vividly the last time they had come, when Peter had rescued them from the flaming path. Had they been wise to come? She had been so intent on getting away from Darien, on arranging the carriage trip, that she had practically forgotten the danger here.

Kinau sensed her thoughts, as she usually did. She patted Rosalind's arm. "All will be well," she said confidently. "Pele wants us to come to her. I know this, I dream of her last night."

"That is good," said Rosalind, relaxing a little. "Oh! That flame is close!"

"It will not trouble us."

Rosalind drove on. Finally she had to stop the horse, and let the carriage remain in the shade of a tree. The horse was balking, and trembling in the traces, flinging back his head. She did not want the gentle animal to bolt.

"We climb up from here," announced Kinau. "We do not go up the cliff path."

Rosalind was relieved. They left the carriage, carrying the leis and the bottles of rum. They climbed up the volcano's steep sides, until they were panting. Above them were fissures, from which emerged steam and the fumes of sulfur.

Kinau peered about. "This good." She approached one of the wider fissures, and looked inside. Rosalind came up more cautiously, to stand beside her and shudder at the boiling hot lava that burned just below them.

Kinau began to chant prayers to Pele. "Oh, Pele, much trouble comes to us on Darien. You are all-powerful, you have much kindness in your generous heart. Aid and help us, for we have much devotion to you, O Great Pele, goddess of fire and the smoke that burns."

Rosalind joined in the chanting. She knew the words, she knew the prayers. She had come before with Kinau. They sang, chanted, prayed, sang again, and the wind blew off the mountain and fluttered their skirts and scarves on their heads.

The sky was a bright blue today, scarcely a cloud in it, but for the steam that wreathed the head of Kilauea. A great rumble came from within the volcano, and Kinau looked up. "Look, she listens and answers, our great Pele," she said, happily.

A spurt of fire came from the depths of the volcano, accompanied by another great rumble.

Kinau flung the bottle of rum into the fissure, and it was swallowed up with a crack. A lei followed it, it burned to a crisp at once. The second bottle of rum followed, as Kinau chanted praise to Pele, assured her she was the greatest of all the gods, that she was the kindest, most generous goddess in the world, that she was loved and adored.

Rosalind added her chants, singing with Kinau into the wind that now wailed about them. The last lei was flung in, to be burned instantly. The volcano rumbled and growled, steam rose steadily.

At last, Kinau stopped to wipe the sweat from her brown cheeks. "It is good," she said happily. "It is good. We go now. Trouble will come, but Pele will aid us. She has promised. Her aid is powerful."

They left the site, scrambling down the rough rocky lava to the grass where the horse grazed. Rosalind gave him another drink, then untied him from the tree, and they set out once more.

Kinau was happy, and chatted all the way back to her son's home. Dusk came, they chewed on the bread and cheese they had brought, and drank the now luke-warm tea. Dusk was darkness before they arrived at the bright beach fires where Kinau's family had gathered.

"Mama, you have come! With no word before you!" Her sons crowded about to help her and Rosalind, and to take care of the horse and carriage. "So late you come! From where do you come? You are hungry and tired? We fix food and beds for you! Tell us your story!"

Kinau reveled in their attentions. She told them of the journey, now that they had gone to Pele. "And all went well, the sailing ship carried us swiftly. Mr. Chan loaned us his carriage. We went to Pele and sang to her, and she answered us with words of peace and welcome." Kinau beamed triumphantly at them all, patting the head of her smallest grandchild who sat on her lap.

"Ah, Mama," Hoke was shaking his head, his face grave. "Did Mr. Peter Darien not forbid you to do this again? Did he not say he would be angry?"

"Is Mr. Darien a god? No? I answer to the gods," said Kinau, grandly, drawing herself up. "It was necessary to come, that is the whole of it. We have come, and done what was necessary."

They ate and drank, talked and laughed and sang together, told of what had happened while they had been apart. Rosalind said little, she was weary and so relieved.

They had accomplished their mission, and Pele was pleased. She felt a sense of deep peace inside herself, a peace that had been missing for a long time. It was good. She could face the future now, with more confidence.

Peter would be angry, but he must understand she had had to go to seek out Pele and her approval. Kinau understood, and Kinau loved her. Peter must understand, if he truly loved her. That was all.

They made their beds on the beach, it was such a warm and beautiful night. Rosalind curled up on a blanket and pulled the sides to cover herself, curling her head on her arm. How pleasant to lie beside the fire, hearing the sleepy chatter of the grandmother and her sons, the whine of a small baby, the giggle of a couple of little girls who whispered secrets. And the lapping of the waves just beyond them. How peaceful it was, how lovely with the stars shining brilliantly overhead and a slim sickle of new moon to bless them. The moon shone a path on the waters, toward Darien. Was Peter awake, missing her. Or was he furious? She thought of him lying in bed, without her, and tried to send her thoughts to him, trying to reassure him that she was safe and happy. The peace must reach out from her to him.

They wakened at dawn, and she and Kinau went swimming in their dear lagoon before dressing to return. Kinau's daughters-in-law vied in providing a fine breakfast, with bread and cheese and fried chicken to take on the trip that day.

Rosalind and Kinau then started out, with many farewells, weeping, and laughter to wave them on their way. Rosalind drove briskly, relieved and happy that the jaunt had ended successfully.

She drove to town, and they reached Kailua by

noon. Mr. Chan was waiting for them at his house, his anxious face beamed in relief as they approached.

"Ah, you have come, you have come!" he exclaimed. "All is well, now, yes? Your family is well, Madame Kinau?"

"All is well," she beamed back at him. "Now we go home to Darien, in peace."

"Good, good, good. You will have luncheon with us. I have spoken to the captain of a sailing vessel, he will take you to Darien tonight, and you will be home tomorrow morning," he said, his head bobbing pleasantly. He escorted them into his house, with exquisite courtesy.

Mrs. Chan fluttered around them, insisted on their eating a large lunch then resting against the heat of the day. Mats were set out on the second floor terrace in the shade, and they slept most of the afternoon.

In the evening, after a quick supper, Mr. Chan drove them down to the wharf. There the captain of a small ship waited for them.

He showed them on board, courteously, anxiously, apologizing for the smallness of his boat, the shortness of his sails. Evidently he had done business with Peter Darien, and was anxious about having the wife of Peter Darien aboard.

"This is splendid, you are most kind," said Rosalind, firmly, at the tenth apology. She smiled and shook Mr. Chan's hand in farewell. "I cannot thank you enough for your kindness to us. Please tell Mrs. Chan she is a most gracious hostess, and my husband will wish to thank her also the next time we come."

Mr. Chan bowed almost double. "I cannot do enough for you, the hospitality of my poor house is yours at any time. I pray for a safe voyage." Then he whispered, "I have paid the captain all that is sufficient, do not pay him more!"

"Mr. Darien will repay you," whispered Rosalind gratefully.

"It is not necessary. The gods favor your voyage." He bowed again, and left the swaying deck of the vessel.

The sails were hoisted, and they were off. It was a longer trip against the winds, and the night voyage was rougher than before. It was mid-morning before the ship docked at the Darien wharf, to the curiosity of the Hawaiians who had gathered to watch it come in.

Someone ran up to the house to tell them, and before Rosalind had scarcely set foot on the wooden dock, Peter was striding toward her. One look at his face, and she knew he was livid.

He grabbed her arm, and held her to him. He had too much pride to show his anger before the captain. He gravely thanked him for his care of Mrs. Darien, and ordered all hospitality shown to the man and his crew of three.

Kinau scuttled off to the home, a satisfied set to her head and a cocky strut to her back as she strode along. Peter hauled Rosalind along with him, back to the house, to his study.

Norma and Honora came out from the drawing room. "My dear Rosalind, where . . ." began Norma. Honora looked at her in wonder.

Peter scowled, and would not let her stop to talk. "In here," he growled, and pulled her into his study, slamming the door. When he turned around, there were white lines beside his mouth.

"Oh, Peter, I had to go to. . . ."

"Where the hell did you go, and without a word?" he asked at the same moment.

She had not slept much, but she did feel peaceful after the trip. It had been worth it. "Peter, I had to go to Pele. Kinau and I went . . . Mr. Chan was so kind . . . loaned us his carriage . . . Pele accepted our offerings!" she said radiantly.

Peter gave her a long incredulous look, then sat down on his desk chair as though his legs had given way. "You went . . . to Pele? To Kilauea? Without my permission? Did Hoke take you . . . I'll skin him alive!"

She was immensely glad they had left Hoke out of this expedition. Hoke's gallantry would not have permitted him to refuse them, but Peter's wrath would have fallen on him.

"No, he did not know. I drove the horse, Kinau and I went alone to the volcano. Pele accepted our offerings, Peter! She told us there would be trouble, but she would be on our side, she will support us in the difficulties. She was gracious and kind to us, and all will be well."

"Damn it to hell! Rosalind, I told you not to go there! And this superstitious nonsense. . . ."

She interrupted him quickly. "Don't, don't say it, Peter! Oh, please, don't say it! Pele will be angry all over again! I believe in her, and so does Kinau, and she will help us. I feel so much better! Oh, we will be all right, Peter, don't you understand? Everything will be all right!" She radiated confidence and joy, her tanned face shone, her amber eyes gleamed in spite of her weariness.

He opened his mouth, and shut it again firmly. He put his head down in his hands, and his fingers ran through his thick curly hair. "Oh, God," he groaned into his hands.

She came over to him. "Peter, believe me. It will be all right. She told us it will be all right. We had to go, and find out, and give her offerings." She took his head and leaned it back against her soft breasts, and gently stroked his cheeks. "Peter, it will be all right," she said gently, with assurance.

He leaned his head against her, and she felt the tremor that went through him. "Don't you know . . . you could have been killed?" he whispered.

"No, no, not this time, there was no danger," she said confidently. "We felt it. Oh, Peter, I feel such peace, such joy. We prayed and sang to Pele, and she listened to us, and answered with assurance of her help. Don't you realize? Whatever troubles come, and they will be difficult, she will be on our side! Oh, I feel so good, though so tired!"

At this he got up, and turned her toward the door. "To bed with you, then. We'll sort this out later. I've been up since I discovered you missing. I could use some sleep myself."

"Oh, Peter, I'm sorry. But I was with Kinau, I was all right."

"Never leave me again," he said, vehemently. "I go right out of my mind. I go crazy. I thought of you drowning on the sea, getting lost somewhere, and burning up . . . God. I never want to go through that again! Don't you ever go anywhere without me, ever again!"

She did not promise. He took her upstairs, and raved a little more in the bedroom. She soaked in a hot bath, answered his many questions cheerfully, asked about Victor, told him of Mr. and Mrs. Chan's great kindness, and then popped into bed. She slept the clock around.

It was almost noon when she came downstairs the next morning. She felt refreshed, and the mental relief was so great. She felt a different person. Nothing and nobody could bother her now. Rosalind beamed at the servants, beamed at Norma and Honora. Eileen was not around. Thank goodness, thought Rosalind. She could sour a fresh pail of milk with her look.

She heard a great murmuring outdoors. "What's going on, a feast?" she asked, curiously, as the murmuring and singing grew louder.

"I think so," said Honora drily. "I think you are going to be the guest of honor."

"What?" Rosalind went out to the patio, to find a crowd of Hawaiians there. They cried out on seeing her. Kinau sat among them, wreaths about her neck, a green wreath on her splendid dark head, beaming at them all, her body encased in a new fine muumuu of bright red.

Leis hung in their hands. Some came up to her shyly, and began to set them about her neck. Peter came out curiously, followed by Norma and Honora.

"This is the woman," they sang in a chant, evidently a chorus had been composed especially for her. "This is the woman who dared to go great distance to consult Pele. This is the woman who rides daringly on horse.

This is the woman who rides up to the volcano of our beloved Pele. This woman is our mistress, she dares greatly, she is strong as a man in her faith, she is gentle as a mother in her care of all her charges. This is the woman we honor this day, with our flowers and our songs and dances."

And they brought up more leis and more, until her head and neck and both arms were hung with flowers. She smiled at them, rather dazed.

"I thank you very much," she said haltingly, in Hawaiian. "You must thank Kinau, who has much power with Pele, having been most devoted to Pele for many years. Kinau is the one to thank."

"We thank Kinau, and we thank Lokelina Murray, who comes like a young goddess to our Darien, to work with us, and smile at her, and be one of us," they sang. One young girl, more daring, added a verse.

"We watch for the ship that comes over the water," she sang. "We watch for the steamer, and the great puffs of smoke come. They herald the arrival of our Lokelina, who is favorite of Pele! Smoke shows she comes. We hail and honor our Lokelina, one of us, though her skin is more pale, and her hair more light. We honor her, and welcome her, and she is one of us."

Blushing, the girl stepped back to cheers. And the chorus was sung again, lustily, by men and women and children. Peter watched and listened, a strange look on his face. He knew the words, what did he think of what they said? Finally he stepped forward, as the singing finally stopped. He held up his hand.

"Tonight we will have a great *luau*," said Peter solemnly. He took Rosalind's flower-bedecked arm in his hand. "This time, it is not for the guests of the Dariens. This time it is for our Lokelina and her beloved Kinau, who have come to us and are now a part of us. Will you come, and feast with us?"

"Yes, yes, we come, we feast, we sing and dance!" they cried with great enthusiasm. They ran away, giggling and laughing, planning already for the evening.

Peter brushed back Rosalind's chestnut hair, where it had become mussed from the many leis set about her neck. "Well, darling, I hardly know what to say. I guess the thing to say is . . . now you are one of us, part of us, and we cannot live without you."

"Oh . . . Peter," she managed to say, choked. She reached up, and put her arms about his neck, and he bent to kiss her hard on the lips.

It completed her sense of joy and peace. It would be well. With faith and courage, and the love of the to Pele. Pele had straightened it all out, and all would be well. All would be well. She had been right to go people here, they would all go forward together.

# 24

❦ ❦ ❦ ❦

THE EVENING AFTER the *luau,* when they were sitting down to dinner, Peter started. And at once Rosalind heard what he had heard.

"The conch shells!" murmured Honora, turning pale. "Is it attack?"

Eileen began to scream, she knew that ominous sound. "They will kill us all!" she cried. She jumped up, still screaming.

Peter shot her a look of active dislike. "No, that is not the signal. It is a tidal wave."

He went out swiftly, calling for his horse. Hilohilo's voice was there, calling out.

"The tidal wave is coming in from the northeast! My man saw it from far out, we are calling everyone to come to high ground."

"Tell them to get to the center of the island, or come to the big house," said Peter. Rosalind had followed him out to the patio, her face paling.

"It is big wave, bigger than we ever see," said Hilohilo, shaking his head in wonder. "Good thing you return from Pele, Mrs. Darien!"

Peter gave her a shake. In her ear, he said, "Do you see? Rosalind, if you had not returned yesterday, you might have been out on the open ocean when the tidal wave came! You must never, never do that again!"

"Pele will protect us," said Rosalind strongly. "I'll get some mats and blankets. Urge them all to come here, we are on high ground, and can fix food for them also." And she ran back inside to the kitchens.

The cooks and maids were quivering with fear. "We

will drown, we will drown!" one older woman moaned, shaking in her sandals.

"No, the ground is high here. We must think of preparing food for those who will have none," Rosalind urged. "Fix big kettles of soup, get milk from the cooling house."

She sent this way and that, gave them so much to do that they forgot their own troubles. Norma came out to help, and Honora. Eileen had disappeared.

Terry looked about for his sister. "She wasn't fool enough to go outside, was she?" he asked, as he helped drag mats from the storage room.

His mother gave him an odd look. "She went up to the top floor, to be safe," she said without expression. Terry's lips tightened, he frowned.

"She would do better to remain with us," he said finally, not willing to criticize his beloved sister. He shook out some mats vigorously, and began laying them about in the drawing rooms and halls.

Barton Darien called in alarm from the bedroom. Rosalind went to reassure him. "It is a tidal wave," she said, gently. "It is very high, and people are frightened. But we will be all right here."

"It has come into the first floor of the house before, I can remember . . . years ago . . ." he managed to say with some stammering. She kissed his cheek.

"Don't worry about it, Pele will protect us," she said, and went out.

She heard him grunt. She smiled and went to reassure her father. He was in his study, he often had a light supper on a tray rather than join them for a heavier meal at night. He looked up from his papers absently.

"Anything wrong, Rosalind?"

"A tidal wave, Papa," she said calmly. "You might want to go upstairs, and take some of your papers with you. But I don't believe it will come into the house."

"Oh, good idea. Good idea. Oh . . . shall I help?" he asked, belatedly, a frown of concern crinkling his elderly face.

"Not just now, Papa, thank you. Just take care of

yourself and your manuscripts, and don't go outdoors, please." She smiled as she left him. Dear Father, and how happy he was here. This move had been good for him, and for Victor.

She found time to wonder if it had been good for herself. She had enjoyed being with Hoke and his family again. yet it had been good to return home to Darien. Darien was home to her now, and she felt she belonged here, near to Peter and his family.

Families began to stream in on foot, on horseback, in carriages, laughing, or crying, or wide-eyed with wonder. Some had seen the tidal wave far out to sea, and described it. It was immense, bigger than ever seen, terrible! From the northeast, also, which was unusual and dangerous. Often the cliffs prevented the waves from washing on Darien from that direction. Now it looked as though the cliffs would not, for the wave came in at the side, more to the north, missing the sheer cliffs which protected the big house.

Some of the *paniolos* rode in with girls and women and children on their saddles, letting them down hurriedly to ride back again for more. The cattle were in the south, and they must take their chances. The families must be protected first.

Many crowded onto the patios and the veranda, setting down their most prized possessions, laying out blankets, talking, crooning to the smallest children to comfort and reassure.

Peter rode in with a young girl on the back of the horse holding on to his waist, a baby under each arm. Rosalind was at his side at once, as he controlled the restless stallion with his knees. He grinned down at her, under the broad brim of his sombrero.

He let the babies down into her arms. Kinau padded up to take one of them. He let the girl down, with a strong arm holding her until she was safely down.

"How many more, Peter?" asked Rosalind.

"Several more families farther out. They are walking in, but we had better get them. The wave rolled out and now it will be rolling back in. And I caught a glimpse of it with the lightning flash. It is a whopper."

He bent, touched her shoulder with his hand in a caress, then turned his horse to race back across the plains. Joe brought in two women, let them down, and went away again after his boss. The yard about the great house, the verandas, the patios, all about were filled with the families of the *paniolos*.

Rosalind brought milk for the babies, encouraged others to come to the huge cook pots of soup and rice, set out dishes on the hastily erected trestle tables. But the women were not hungry, they kept looking toward the east and north, watching for the wave to come, watching for their husbands to return. The older children caught their moods, the somber anxiety, though the younger ones played about, even laughing at the strangeness of the situation.

Lightning flashed again and again, lighting the plains with its ghostly white brief glares. Thunder rolled in the hills, cracking across the large cliffs behind them. Then the wave came, tall, riding high, a wall of water so high that the lightning showed it as an ocean of black waters.

They stood and stared at it. The *paniolos* came riding in recklessly, using a whip on their horses, though little was needed to get the frightened beasts to race across the last remaining grass to the sanctuary of the high ground. Peter was among the last, with Joe Smith, watching for any horse to go down, or any of the women or children to slip from the sweating backs of the horses.

The wave rolled toward them, and past, over to the west. They had just missed it, though the waters came up to the floor of the patio, splashing the bare feet of the children.

Peter slipped down from his mount, watching keenly, holding the bit of his terrified stallion firmly in his big hand. They all stood and watched as the huge tidal wave swept in over the land where the houses and cottages and huts had been standing.

Many would be destroyed, but the people were

safe, huddling together to stare out over the ground to the west, lower than the great hill where the Darien house had been built.

Rosalind went to Peter, to slip her hand through his arm as they watched in awe and horror at the immense wall of water sweeping past them in the distance.

"Did . . . did everyone get out?" she finally asked.

"Joe and Hilohilo are counting now. I think we did," and he cast an anxious look about. "We'll have to bring them indoors. The storm is getting worse."

Some wanted to linger to watch the great wall of water, but it was soon over, sweeping across the plain, ending in a futile rush against the slopes of the central volcano in the distance. Water from the sea had gurgled to the very foundations of the Darien house, then receded. They brought the children indoors, and bedded them down to sleep, several to a mat, while their mothers talked over their heads.

Glendon Corey came out, offering a disdainful look at the mass of people all over the house. "What a din! Can't they keep quiet? I was trying to get some sleep."

Peter glared his dislike, Rosalind had to bite her tongue to keep back furious words.

"Sorry the tidal wave disturbed your peaceful rest," said Peter sarcastically. "It's one of the hazards of living on a primitive island, no matter what wealth lies here."

"Don't worry, I wouldn't live here long," sneered Corey. His polite facade seemed to have melted, and his face was cold and haughty. "I'd take what I could get, and get out."

"That's what I figured," said Peter, turning from him. Peter's arm went about Rosalind's waist, she went with him as he moved from one group to another. He inquired kindly about each family, made sure all of them were present.

Smith brought him a tally, all of the families were safe. Several of the *paniolos* had been trapped at the volcano, but they must have ridden up the slope out of reach of the water. They would have to wait until morning to make sure, but it looked like no lives were lost.

"Biggest damn wave I ever did see," said Hilohilo with gusto, his eyes sparkling. "Something to tell the grandchildren about, huh?"

And indeed, as the danger was passed, that was the attitude of the Hawaiians. They were safe now to enjoy the unusual situation, talk about their own experiences, and store them up in memory and in song for the future.

Rosalind was up all night. One baby was sick—she brought medicines and soothed the child. Milk was heated for the other infants. The cooks kept soup kettles hot, for anyone restless enough to want food. Blankets were brought out of storage as the storm continued, and the air turned chilly.

In the morning, the *paniolos* and Peter went out on foot to survey the damage. In some places the water was still hip deep, and in other places too high to venture.

By noon, the waters had receded, and they could see more clearly what had been done. The families were all right, Hilohilo had gone around to make sure everyone was accounted for.

However, a number of huts had been crushed, and swept away. Two cottages had lost their roofs, the mud lay everywhere, bedding was ruined.

"But we safe. We build again," as one older woman put it, with a laugh. "People live, that okay. Always make more huts, buy more blankets."

Some went home to begin the clean up. Others remained for another day or two to let the men have time to rebuild their huts, put on another roof, or clean out the mud and grime that lay ankle deep in the tide-swept houses.

Rosalind kept thinking of Pele. Was this the danger she had warned them of? No, perhaps not. It had been serious, but they had been on guard, and no one had been hurt. There must be some other danger, coming closer and closer, and they must remain watchful.

Peter relieved the guards at the cliff sites, and sent

in replacements, watching for tidal waves, canoes, and sailing vessels. He too must believe more might yet come.

Glendon Corey was beginning to pack his suitcases. He had come down to the kitchen the day after the tidal wave, with a huge bundle of laundry, demanding that it be done at once, and ironed neatly. He was becoming quite a pest, perhaps in revenge for his frustrations and failure.

He could not leave too soon to suit Rosalind. She kept thinking that he was trouble, that anywhere he went there would be havoc. She only hoped he would keep his mouth shut about the black pearls, or they would have more unwelcome visitors like him, and perhaps some not so easily bested.

The steamer this next week might be late, Peter thought. "The tidal wave is enough to keep the ships off the ocean for a time. If another one comes, they won't venture to sea until it lets up. I wonder if Kilauea erupted? I would be curious to find out. That might have brought this on."

"It still steaming, boss," said Hilohilo. "Maybe it blow some now, some later. We keep the cattle south, I think."

Peter nodded, and even Terry had no cracks to make out of that. He seemed subdued, looking at his sister with curious eyes, as though seeing some cracks in her perfection. She had stayed up on the top floor for two days, for fear of the waters. Then, when Eileen had come down, she had complained of the mud and the dirt, and the people sitting around everywhere, even in "her" chair in the drawing room.

Only Victor and the other smaller children seemed to have thoroughly enjoyed themselves, crawling happily over the floor mats, enjoying waking adults snatching a snooze with a happy laugh in their ears, being picked up by strangers and petted and made much of. Victor seemed to enjoy immensely the other children his size, and would sit and stare for a time at a small baby lying on a mat.

Some good had come of it. Some shabby huts had

gone down, they would be rebuilt with sturdy concrete foundations, as Peter had been wanting to do. The Hawaiians now accepted Rosalind completely, she was "The Missus," and "Lokelina Murray," to them. What she said was good, what she did was perfect, what she wanted would be done quickly.

And so they began to rebuild, and to move home again.

# 25

❦ ❦ ❦ ❦

AFTER TWO DAYS, matters calmed down. More than half of the Hawaiians had returned to their own homes. The others remained, living on the verandas, or spreading out mats on the drying ground, to sleep and cook and chat amiably through the day.

Rosalind had been working hard. She slept late one morning, remembering only vaguely when Peter left her, leaving a kiss on one cheek.

"Go back to sleep, my love," he whispered. "No need to get up early."

She murmured, turned over, and went back to sleep, to awake much later in the morning. She lay, blinking sleepily at the bright sunlight, feeling contented and happy.

Finally, she yawned, sat up, stretched—then slid out of bed and made a run for the bathroom. She retched, then leaned against the cool wall of the bathroom. She didn't want to get sick, had she caught something? The water, was it impure? No, she had had only hot tea or boiling hot coffee since the tidal wave.

She was sick again, and finally crawled back into bed, feeling depleted and sorry for herself. But as she lay there, she felt much better, and tried to think of what had happened.

Perhaps she was catching a cold, it would not be surprising. But colds did not usually make her sick to her stomach. A chill, perhaps, she had been out and soaking wet, looking after the children. She put her hand to her forehead, but she had no fever.

Her hand went back to her side, she touched her waist. That was odd also, she was gaining weight, though she was eating as usual. She had been very thin when she married, she had seemed to gain steadily—

Oh! She caught her breath, and gazed blankly at the walls. Could it be—could she be having a child? She counted—she had missed her period, but thought it was from tension and nerves. Sometimes that affected her—

But it had been more than two months. A flush crept up into her cheeks, her amber eyes became starry. A baby—a baby for Peter. She knew he wanted a child of his own, much as he loved Victor. Could it be—?

She would say nothing until she was sure. She felt terribly shy, all of a sudden.

Akela came quietly into the room, saw she had her eyes opened. "Ah, you are awake now. I bring something?"

"Hot tea, please, Akela," Rosalind managed to say.

Rosalind usually wanted cool juice in the morning. Surprise showed on the girl's face, but she slipped away, her slim feet padding in the sandals. She soon returned with the strong beverage. Rosalind drank it, and felt much better.

After a while, Rosalind got up. Akela was laying out her clothes, hesitating over the row of dresses.

"The rose muumuu, please," said Rosalind, and Akela nodded, pleased.

"That is very pretty one, with such white lace," and she stroked it lovingly with her hand.

Dresses. Would she need more, when she became more obviously pregnant? Probably not, some of the muumuus were built full, and the Hawaiian women wore them from one baby to the next.

She bathed, and put on her clothes. She had looked critically at herself in the mirror in the bathroom. She was more rounded in the waist, and her breasts were fuller. Still—it might not be. She would wait before telling Peter.

But she glowed with new beauty as she moved about the house that day. Norma smiled at her, Honora looked at her speculatively, seeing more than others realized, as spinsters often did. When Rosalind tried to lift one of the children, a two-year-old, Honora stopped her brusquely.

"The boy is too heavy, Rosalind. Don't spoil him. Come on, my lad, some lunch for you," and she took him away. Rosalind gazed after her, puzzled.

"When are those people going to leave our house?" Eileen had come up so quietly behind her that Rosalind started.

"Why . . . when their own homes are rebuilt, Eileen," said Rosalind, trying to keep her temper. "You know, many were destroyed in the wave."

"They could set up housekeeping on the grass, they're used to it. Look at the mud and dirt they are tracking in all the time," and the girl pointed disdainfully at the usually immaculate parquet floor of the hallway.

"That can be cleaned later."

"I want it cleaned now," and Eileen went storming off to find a servant to tend to the task. Rosalind let her, for she knew the hallway would be just as dirty within hours.

"You're a poor housekeeper," jeered Eileen, when she saw her later. Her blue eyes flashed with jealousy and anger. "I suppose it makes no difference to you, but I'm used to having a sparkling house, and not letting all those natives trail around."

Rosalind's mouth compressed. Eileen usually saved her darts for when they were alone. She only hoped the Hawaiians did not hear what the girl said. They all understood some English.

"The mud is from the tidal wave," she said, as evenly as possible. "We can't help having dirt and mud in here. It will all get straightened out in a week or two."

"I suppose you don't care if it ever gets clean again!" exclaimed Eileen. "This is more what you are used to! I understand you lived in a shack yourself!"

"Not so large a house as this, surely," said Rosalind, a sense of humor saving her.

"I could have warned Peter, if I had known what

he was up to. I can't imagine why Terry didn't stop him from marrying you. One should always marry in one's class," snapped Eileen. She flounced away, lifting her silk skirts disdainfully from the muddy floors.

Rosalind's mouth had tightened, her eyes blazed for a time. But she said nothing. She only wished, passionately, that some miracle would happen, that Eileen would go away. Let Eileen go to the mainland, let her marry some poor misbegotten millionaire dazzled by the beauty and charm she had when she wished to turn it on. Only let the girl leave them in peace!

Eileen obviously hated it here, she lived to get away. Peter seemed to think his cousin would get into trouble if she was not watched, but why should Peter have that chore? The girl was of age, she was old enough to be sensible. As it was, she would get into trouble wherever she went. And Eileen was shrewd, she could probably choose her millionaire without any aid or assistance whatever. *Caveat emptor,* thought Rosalind, with the spite Eileen brought out in her: let the buyer beware!

One of the Hawaiian women came to her. "Please, Missus, we leave now, with gratitude for your care. The children wish to thank you," she smiled.

Rosalind went with her gladly, accepted the kisses from the children, and wished them well. Their hut had been rebuilt, another one would go up as soon as cement was mixed and a more sturdy foundation laid. Peter was determined to make sure the houses this time would be more firm.

She went out to the kitchen then, to consult with the cooks. Some were assigned to making more soup, some to setting long trestle tables in the patio for a feast tonight. They had about one hundred people to serve for three meals a day, and it was a chore.

Hilohilo brought in some sides of beef from cattle which had died in the tidal wave. And another *paniolo* brought in two pigs. They dug *luau* pits merrily, and prepared to make a feast of the evening meal.

Much laughter rang out from the gardens, where women and children were helping with the gardening, in return for their meals. Honora was out there also, looking sorrowfully over her roses. The salt water which had reached them had not done them any good.

Peter came home late, tired but contented. Only about ten of the cattle had drowned, the others were safe. Not a single Hawaiian had died, they had all been rescued in time. The signal system was working, and he was proud of his workers.

He put his arm about Rosalind's waist. "How are things going here, honey?"

"Fine," she smiled. "We have a *luau* tonight. I think there will be singing and dancing."

"And how you enjoy that," he grinned down at her, and left a quick kiss on her nose. "I got myself a little *wahine!*" he teased, into her ear.

"You sure did," she said, more soberly. She remembered Eileen's taunts, and her heart almost wanted to droop. But Peter had chosen her, he liked her Hawaiian ways.

Rosalind put her doubts away and entered into the enjoyment of the evening. Eileen refused to join them.

"I have to live with them all day," she said nastily. "I refuse to live with them all evening! I'll have dinner in the dining room, with candles and wine, and some civilized service!"

Terry joined her, and so did Corey. Rosalind saw to them briefly, then went out to join the Hawaiians outside. It was a beautiful evening, the sky was bright with stars and a lovely moon. If the others chose to remain inside, let them, she thought with a shrug.

Peter, however, looked grim as he glanced into the dining room. Terry was drinking steadily, a bottle of wine at his elbow. Glendon Corey was staring down at his plate, his glass was constantly refilled by one of the Hawaiian men who waited on them. Eileen pushed the food from one side of her plate to the other. She was grandly gowned in ivory satin, with blue sapphires at her throat and wrist.

She saw Peter at the door, and smiled at him quickly.

"Come in, Peter, and join us! We're having a party." She waved her glass of rum at him.

"No, thanks. The party I want is outside."

"With the natives, and your native wife?" she sneered.

He stared at her steadily. "Get your tongue off my wife," he said curtly. He went out, leaving them.

Terry said nothing. Corey laughed softly. "Can't take any reference to his wife, can he? Yet he must see she hasn't a touch of class about her," he bowed to Eileen. "Unlike you, my dear Miss Eileen. She picks up those babies like her own child. And feeds them and gives them milk like a Hawaiian mother, singing those outlandish songs to them."

Terry stirred, his face flushed, and he reached for the bottle so quickly that he knocked it over with his elbow. He shouted for the servant. When the man came, Terry ordered, "Bring me another bottle, make it rum this time!"

"Yes, Mr. Terry," said the Hawaiian, without expression, and brought the bottle to him.

Eileen smiled graciously at Glendon Corey. She detested the man, but at least he had the decency to dress well and appear at a civilized dinner. "You have class yourself, Mr. Corey," she said, her speech a little slurred, she drank another half glass quickly. The rum made a glow in her stomach. "You ought to stay on, teach Peter a thing or two!"

Mr. Corey shrugged. He had no illusions about teaching Peter Darien anything. His only revenge would be to spread word of the black pearls as soon as he reached Hawaii. Just wait until he got hold of a few of the rougher treasure hunters on Oahu, at Honolulu! They would welcome the news, like a hungry and thirsty man the sight of a bar. They would come swarming to Darien, and then Peter Darien would be sunk!

The treasure hunters he knew did not play fair, they didn't play at all. They would come and find the pearls, or kill Darien in the doing. They would ruin the man and the island, and it would serve him right! Corey had figured out that Darien used some of the pearls as investment, to guard against the bad years with cattle. This could well ruin him, along with the two tidal waves.

He smiled into his glass, then lifted it in a toast to Eileen. Terry's head had sunk down on the table; the Hawaiian had quickly removed his plate so that Terry would not have his face in it.

Above Terry's snores Corey said, softly, "To our future meetings. Perhaps they will be on happier occasions. I can see you, queening in San Francisco society, or even New York City! You will stun them all with your beauty, and your background. Such a lovely woman, worldly, to come from an island so primitive as Darien! Yes, I can see you as the curiosity of the season, the belle of all society."

Eileen adored hearing all this, her head rose, her chin came up proudly. She could see it also, see herself in blue silk and sapphires, on the arm of a handsome wealthy man, who would buy her anything she wanted, for the touch of her lips. She visioned herself at a grand ball with men crowding about her. Men dressed in the elaborate fashions of the day, not in dusty cowboy pants and flowered shirts! Men in silk suits, with lace on their shirts and diamond studs at their wrists!

And they would all crowd about her, admiring her, wanting her, hunger in their sophisticated eyes! And she would wait until the most wealthy man of them all came to her, and went on his knees to propose to her! Yes, a wealthy elderly man, writing a will, leaving everything to her, so she would never again in her life have to beg for anything! She would be in control! She would dominate! She would have men swarming about her, begging for her attentions! She would choose a lover quietly, or even several lovers! And her wealthy husband would be dead, and she a widow in stunning black lace and silk, with diamonds. She sighed with happiness at the picture.

Rosalind smiled at Peter as he made his way through

the crowd to her. He would pause and smile and speak to others, but he was coming to her, to her. Her heart swelled with love and pride and adoration.

He was so arrogant and proud, so thoughtful and possessive. And he came to her for comfort and love. She loved the way his chin was always held high, his stride was as one owning the land he walked on. His dark brown eyes were deep and gentle for her, not flashing angry, or contemptuous as to others.

He came to her, and looked at her plate. "Enough?" he asked. "Shall I get you more fruit? Your favorite pineapple?"

"Nothing more," she shook her head, and the soft glossy dark hair swung on her shoulders. "You must eat, Peter. You have driven yourself so hard these days."

He touched her cheek, smiled down at her, then went away to fill a plate for himself. Again he sought her out, and sat down beside her in the chairs on the patio. They watched as their guests ranged beside the tables, seeking more slices of beef or crisp pork, dishes of *poi,* the salty little marinated fish, or dipping into one of the great bowls of fruit.

When the guests were filled, the singing and dancing began. Alfred Murray had wandered out, his attention drawn by the music. He sat down near Rosalind, smiled briefly at her before returning with interest to the songs. He looked more happy and contented than he had for years, his daughter thought fondly. Barton wheeled himself out, and rolled to a stop near them.

Kinau had come out with Victor. Rosalind held out her arms for the child, but Kinau shook her head with a smile, and a casual look down at Rosalind. Had she suspected Rosalind's condition? The young wife wondered.

Kinau joined the line of hula-dancing women, with Victor in her arms. The baby swayed and laughed happily as she moved with him. His hands clapped together as they clapped, the big-eyed tanned baby. Others had babies in their arms, or small children

swaying beside them, as all did the dances they had
learned from childhood.

The drummers pounded away, the music moved
more quickly. Peter glanced about, well-satisfied. Rosalind was looking also, as she suddenly remembered
the four young fishermen. They had disappeared before the tidal wave, she thought. Her brow crinkled in
a frown of puzzlement. They had seemed quite nice.
But they must have gone away.

She pulled at Peter's sleeve, he bent to her. "The
young fishermen, Maleko who did the fire dance, and
his friends. Are they not here?"

Peter glanced about, shook his head, frowning also.
"I have not seen them for a week or more."

"Did they say farewell?"

He scowled in thought. "No, I don't recall that
they did. Odd. They seemed very polite and well-
mannered."

She thought it bizarre also. They had lingered for a
couple months, then abruptly disappeared. And not a
word to their host. Peter had treated them well. No
Hawaiian would slip away without a word of gratitude.

She forgot it again, as Kinau began to sing in her
husky voice. It was a song to Pele, and the others
listened and swayed, and joined in the chorus. They
approved of it, applauding when she had finished.
Then someone else began to sing, another song of the
islands.

The evening went on happily. The tidal wave had
come, but they had remained, they were not harmed.
All was well, and they were feasting and drinking and
singing and dancing. It was a good life there on the
islands, they sang.

Before midnight, the songs ended and the young
people drifted away to make love by themselves, and
the older ones took the children to put them to bed.

Sleepy Victor had gone up to bed before this. He
played hard, laughed and danced hard, and when he
was ready to sleep, he drooped like a young flower,
his head wilting on the nearest shoulder. Kinau had

taken him up to his room, then returned for more dancing.

Peter and Rosalind stayed until the last guests had left, then he put his hand under her arm. "Time for us to go to bed also, my darling," he said into her ear.

She still blushed when he whispered to her, and his touch closed intimately about her arm or waist. She went with him, up and up the stairs, down the hallway to their rooms.

He closed them in, then took her into his arms, as though hungry for her embrace. Her slim arms came up to close about his neck, and her fingers played with the crisp black hair of his head and at his throat. His kiss deepened on her mouth

"Ah, I love you, I love you," he whispered, against her throat.

"I love you . . . Peter . . . I love you," she managed to say, and his clasp tightened.

He helped her remove the soft muumuu, and she slid out of her other clothes, drawing a nightdress over her head. He was taking off his shirt and trousers, and grinned at her across the dimly lit room.

"You won't need that, my love!" he teased.

She had her back turned to him, she glanced over her shoulder, unconsciously provocative. "The night is cool, Peter," she murmured.

"You won't be cool long."

She began to braid her hair, he came to her and took the brush out of her hand. "Oh, Peter. . . ."

"Forget that. I want you now," he said urgently, and picked her up and carried her to bed.

They lay together, and he turned her to him, his hands roaming her body hungrily. Would he notice the thickened waist? She was not large yet, but in another month—If it was true, she must tell him soon—

"You're so silky, so soft, so sweet," he was whispering against her breasts. They were enlarging, when would he begin to notice? She must tell him soon, just as soon as she was sure—

"What are you thinking?" he demanded, raising his head.

She evaded, "Oh, about the evening, what fun it was. I do love the singing and the dancing, don't you?"

"Yes, always." He moved his head against her shoulder, turned his lips to her throat again, against the pulse-beat. "There is something about the island that fits music. The air is made for love-making and happiness. Do you like it here, my darling?"

He did not sound demanding, he sounded anxious. "Oh, I love it here, Peter," she assured him fervently.

"Better than . . . your other home?"

Then she knew what troubled him. "Much better than anywhere in the world, love," she whispered. "Oh, much better. For you are here, and wherever you are is my home."

He caught his breath, and began to caress her more urgently, as though her words had spurred him on, and increased his desire for her. Soon their naked bodies were joined, in the pale moonlight that streamed across their bed. He lifted her to ecstasy, and felt it himself, so that their bodies twined together more fiercely, becoming closer and closer.

She lay awake when they had finished. His head was on her breasts, and she stroked lightly over his damp forehead. Her fingers moved through his crisp dark hair.

"What is it?" he asked.

She started. She had thought him asleep. But as they grew closer, he seemed to know when she was troubled.

"Oh, I was thinking. What if you had married one of those girls on Kailua, or from Honolulu," she said lightly. "Would not one of those be a better hostess for you . . . more sophisticated . . . more mature?"

"Don't be silly," he said drowsily. "I adore you. I looked for you all my life. When I found you . . . I grabbed," and he chuckled against her soft skin, like a mischievous Victor.

Her hand moved over his shoulder. She persisted, bravely, "But sometimes . . . I think I am not the right

one . . . after all, this is Darien . . . and you entertain. . . ."

"You are the perfect wife for me," he said distinctly, raising his head and peering down at her
through the darkness. "The most perfect wife I could
have found. I adore you. Everyone of our guests en-
vied me, I could see it in their eyes! Now, what nonsense have you been thinking?"

"Oh, just wondering," she sighed.

"Well, stop wondering and go to sleep," he growled,
as though cross with her. His lips nibbled at her arm.
"Um, you smell of plumeria."

He settled himself against her, and holding her
drifted off to sleep. She smiled at the quickness of it.
He was happy, and satisfied with her.

She—she must remain awake for a time. Eileen's
taunts got through to her sometimes. Yet she knew
enough of Eileen and certainly of Peter now, to know
they would never have been happy together. Eileen's
affairs would have driven him to desperation, even
murder. Her nagging would have made him wild. He
worked hard, he deserved peace and quiet and rest at
the end of a working day, not the nagging of a wife
discontented with her lot.

Perhaps Rosalind was the right wife for him, as he
affirmed. She must shut away doubts and fears, of her
unfitness to be the Mrs. Darien everyone expected.
She must just do her best, and think of others, and try
hard to please him.

And the baby—he would be happy about that. As
soon as she was quite certain, she would tell him.

If only, if only she could be sure everything was
well. But somehow a voice rang in her ears at times.
"Beware, beware, do not rest and relax too easily, do
not be off guard. Trouble comes, and you must be
ready."

What trouble? If only she knew.

Yet, trouble came without warning, there was no
preparation for it. She must watch and guard, and wait
and hope, and trust in the gods to help them.

She turned into Peter's arms more deeply, and her

hand on his back encountered the deep scar of the bullet that had almost killed him. She shivered. That was reminder enough of the suddenness of danger, attacking without warning.

She breathed a little prayer before she slept, "That all may be well, Oh God, that Peter may be safe, and all those I love. That you will be with Victor and help him grow up to be a fine man. That you will watch over and protect us all. . . ."

And so praying, she fell asleep to troubled dreams, where dark bloody faces seemed to appear before her and fade away slowly, and screams sounded in her ears. She wakened once, to find herself covered with sweat, her heart pounding with alarm.

Peter still slept beside her, his face turned to her, his body relaxed, his long strong body that needed hers, and protected her. She drew great breaths, wiped her face with the sheet, and composed herself again.

Trouble would come, she could do nothing but watch and pray.

# 26

❦   ❦   ❦   ❦

EARLY THE FOLLOWING MORNING, Peter had just finished dressing when the conch shells sounded.

He lifted his head alertly. Rosalind was still in bed, half-asleep, stretching lazily.

She sat up swiftly, eyes wide with alarm. "Peter . . . what is it. . . ."

He counted, listened. "Attack!" he said. "From the south. Damn. Stay inside, Rosalind, the women and children will come inside the house, and all of you remain here!"

And he was off, pounding down the stairs. The men were running, the women looked up from the mats on the floor, the children were grave and questioning. Babies wakened and cried as the conch shells echoed.

Smith came from the stables, running, his rifle in his hand. "They are coming across the waters to the south."

"How many?" Peter barked at him.

The grey eyes flashed with steel. "About a hundred, five war canoes of them. And Chief Kaahumanu Pauahi in the lead."

"Oh, the idiot, the fool," groaned Peter. "Get everyone inside the walls, and we will lock the gates!" he called out across the front patio toward the men who spurted from every direction.

He put his hands to his eyes, shading them so he could peer across the brightening sea as the sun was rising. Now he could see the five long war canoes, crowded with warriors. And in the lead canoe stood the impressive figure of the tall chief, Chief Pauahi, splendid in his yellow feather cloak and his tall bronze helmet.

All carried spears, and some carried rifles. Peter's mouth tightened, he turned back to oversee the women and children, running from their newly rebuilt huts.

The cowboys were riding in, as ordered. They were to leave the cattle and concentrate on protecting the families and the big Darien house. The house was structured to withstand siege, it had happened several times during the years of the Dariens.

Jealous chiefs, angry Hawaiians, foreigners from ships, all had tried to conquer Darien. None had succeeded, yet.

All were brought within the walls: women, children, their husbands, the horses they prized. The stables were crowded, the house was full from first to third floor with the families.

The gates were closed and locked with iron bolts across the steel doors. The house was constructed of stone, with some wood trim, it would withstand much. It stood on a high rise of ground, both for protection from the waters and from siege. Peter stood on the veranda, his loaded rifle on his arm, pistols in his belt.

Peter glanced from one place to the other, counting mentally. His cousin, Nick Darien, had ridden in from his guard post high in the cliffs to the northeast. Hilohilo was there, rifle in hand and a spear close to his side. Joe Smith, and the dozen Hawaiians he had trained in the use of a rifle. The other men and older boys with their spears, their excitement under control.

Then he looked out to the dock, several hundred yards away. The war canoes were landing. He squinted his eyes. He thought he recognized several of the men coming with Chief Pauahi.

Yes, it was Maleko who strode just behind the chief. Maleko, splended in tapa cloth about his loins, his chest bare. He wore the headdress of a minor chief. So, Maleko was no simple fisherman.

Had he been a spy? Probably. Maleko glanced up,

and seemed to see Peter across the space between them.

He came forward, spoke to the chief. He seemed to be pleading, his hand outflung. The Chief shook his head, haughtily. He gestured toward some pigs and cattle in the distance.

Then the yelling and the screaming began. Peter flinched, then braced himself. Noise could not harm them. He watched grimly as the hundred young warriors pulled up their canoes and fastened them to the dock. Then the young men raced ashore and began running about, screaming and shaking their fists at the closed walls of the Darien fortress.

Peter glanced back over his shoulder, sent a long slow look over the house. Yes, the shutters had been closed, the grey wooden shutters over the windows, so not a glimmer of glass appeared. The women must remain inside, they had their orders. The doors were locked on all four sides of the house. Some of the cowboys remained in the stableyard with the hands, keeping the horses calm. Behind the stable were the tall cliffs, they could not be attacked from that direction without long ropes. No one had ever dared come that way.

But they were prepared for attack from any direction. He spared a regret that there had not been time to get a response from Joe's friends in Texas. A few outlaws handy with weapons would have been most welcome. If they were as cool and deadly as Joe, they would have been worth their weight in gold—or black pearls.

A figure moved beside him. Peter glanced, then started. Terry stood there, rifle in hand, his bleary eyes blinking at the bright sunlight.

"Are they coming now?" asked Terry.

Peter clamped down on hot words. Terry had come, that was all that mattered, no matter if he had a hangover and his hands shook. He had come, he was yet a Darien.

"Not right now. I reckon they will yell around for a bit to try to raise their morale and shake ours," said

Peter, a faint smile on his lips. He turned to stare out over the plains to the west.

His mouth set grimly at the plaintive moans of the cattle. Some warriors were driving in the steers which had wandered close to the house. Now they were slaughtering them with spear and knife. Pigs were butchered recklessly, contemptuously, as though they said they cared nothing for the lives of the Dariens and the Hawaiians with them. You see?, they were saying by their actions. We kill the cattle and pigs that would have fed you. You will have no use for food when we are done with you!

Peter listened to the yells of contempt, watched the gestures of redicule which the warriors sent to them. Hilohilo was fairly dancing with rage, the other *paniolos* growled and put their hands to their weapons, lifting their rifles.

"Hold your fire!" called Peter sharply. "Wait until they are close enough! No firing until I give the word! Forget their obscenities, they merely wish to make you fire without avail! Wait for my word!" He repeated it in English, for Joe Smith's sake, but the Texas outlaw merely pulled his sombrero lower over his chill grey eyes and waited. He was accustomed to waiting, especially during a fight.

The Chief waved his hand imperiously, and pointed at the Darien wall. A dozen of his tall warriors raced toward the wall, rifles pointed in hand.

Rifles cracked, the echoes blasted against the cliffs. A dozen bullets hit the Darien house, some landing in the wooden shutters.

Another dozen warriors raced behind the first, hauling some crude vine ladders to the wall.

"Ready!" shouted Peter, as they advanced. The Hawaiians and Smith raised their rifles, chose their targets. "Fire! Fire!"

The rifles cracked, some with deadly aim. Several warriors fell, one remained motionless, and the others dragged him away. The Chief glared at the fortress, his helmeted head high, the plume waving, his yellow cloak making him a prime target in the bright sunlight. But he was too far away for their rifles to reach him.

Joe Smith rechecked his weapon, blew the smoke from the rifle barrel. The other Hawaiians danced around gleefully. The first blow was theirs! Hilohilo spoke sharply, they calmed and returned to their positions.

The hundred warriors retreated. They took out their fury on more cattle and pigs. Several men rode up on horses, and Nick Darien gave a groan, his face drawn in anguish. "They'll kill them," he muttered, clenching his fists about his rifle.

As the Hawaiians rode the horses up closer to the gates, then slipped down, holding to the ropes about the necks of the splendid animals, Peter felt nausea in his throat. His beautiful animals! His horses, so carefully hand-picked and trained.

If only they could have had the time to secure more of them in the stables!

"There's Beauty," groaned Nick, and raised his rifle. Peter caught at his hand.

"No, it's too far, you'll only waste a bullet," he said sharply. He moved his hand from the rifle to Nick's shoulder. "I understand," he said, more gently.

They all flinched as the horses whinnied in anguish. They were slashed about, then their throats cut. Horse after horse went down, and the warriors screamed in joy and tormented their enemies by shaking their bloody knives in the air.

"Ten of them, ten of them," muttered Nick. "By God, I'll get ten of them warriors for that!"

"Don't let them rattle you, Nick," warned Peter.

Terry was blinking in amazement at the sight. "But why the horses, Peter?"

"To show us their power over us, Terry," explained Peter, patiently. "To get us riled up, so we shoot crooked."

"The Indians in Texas call it making bad medicine," said Joe, strolling up to them. His face was as calm as ever, he had paused to roll and smoke a cigarette, his rifle loosely in his right hand. "They screech and kill the cattle, and all, to make their enemies believe they are all powerful. Then when everybody is shook up, they move in for the real kill. You just have to ignore it, figure on staying cool and shooting straight. It's people that matter the most, you have to remember."

Terry looked at him with more respect than usual. "I expect you've seen plenty battles like that."

"Plenty," said Joe, with a brief crack of his lips that might pass for a smile. "Apache Indians are the worst. Brave as hell, proud as sin, and when they die they go straight to their heaven. So what is there to fear? They come yelling and screeching like them Hawaiians, and kill as much as they can before they die. That's their code."

"The Hawaiians also," added Peter gravely. "If they die in battle for their chief, they will go to their heaven, and the gods will all honor them." He sighed briefly. "How much better to live with honor, than to die with honor. If one has a choice."

Terry was listening, his face unusually serious. His rifle shifted in his nervous hands. He stared out at the tall magnificent chief who might have become his father-in-law.

They all watched for a time. The stench from the dead cattle and horses and pigs became almost overwhelming. Terry went away, to return with pale face from being sick to his stomach. He wiped his mouth and tried to grin as Peter looked at him.

"All right, Terry? Maybe you better go inside and lie down."

To reinforce it Eileen's shrill voice came from an upstairs window, muffled by the wooden shutter which closed it. "Terry, get in here! This isn't your fight! They can have this whole damn island if they want it!"

Terry grimaced. "I'm staying!" he called back, without looking up.

Hilohilo looked at him, for once his contempt was unconcealed. "And it is your fight, boy!" he spat out. "If you hadn't dishonored the daughter of the Chief

Pauahi, none of this would have happened! He is a proud man, and he loved his Lydia much!"

Terry stared down at the ground. Peter did not try to rebuke Hilohilo. The truth was there, all could see it and know it. And in the moment of battle, when death was close, that was the moment for truth, the best time of all. One needed to know why one fought, and for what cause. And one needed to know why the enemy fought, to gauge his determination. Chief Pauahi had cause.

Now the great loud voice of the chief rang out, startling them all.

"Come out of hiding O dog Dariens!" yelled Pauahi in his powerful voice. He stood a little apart from his warriors, his yellow cloak thrown back from his broad brown chest. He lifted his head, and his voice boomed across the plain before the walls. "Come out, and fight like men, before you die! It is the least that weaklings such as you can do! Die like men, if you do not live like men of honor!"

"Why, that dog!" cried Hilohilo quickly, and lifted his spear.

"Too far," said Peter drily. "Let him rage. He's just working himself and his warriors up for another attack. Be ready."

There was silence in the house, and on the veranda as they waited.

The chief called again. "Come out and fight me! Is there none who will fight the chief of the Pauahi? Come and kill me with your firing sticks! Or with the spear I will fight! I burn with the longing to kill! Why do I waste my time with weak dogs? Because they have dishonored my house! They do not deserve to live! They are not men, they are pigs who die in the pits!"

One of Hilohilo's men yelled in reply, "Our Darien is a man to follow, a chief to follow! He is greater than you, O Chief of the Pauahi! He is a splendid man to follow, we are honored to be of his house!"

"You follow a white man, weak and thin and of no account!" the tremendous voice roared back. His warriors gathered about him, grinning with pleasure at this exchange. They adored words, and this was a fine battle indeed.

"Our Chief is tall and good!" yelled back Hilohilo with gusto. "He could defeat you in any battle! Come and do your worst! Our chief of the Dariens is worthy of any chief of the Hawaiians! He is powerful! He is strong! He has the word of the great Pele that she will protect him and his! His woman goes to Kilauea and receives the blessing of Pele! What say you to that, O Chief of the Pauahi?"

There was silence, and muttering then among the enemy. Maleko was nodding his head emphatically, and the chief cursed, and flung his spear into the ground before him.

Hilohilo watched happily the effect of his words. He added some for good measure. "When the chief of the Pauahi spurned his lovely daughter and turned from his own grandson," he roared, "who took care of them? Who took in the grandson of the chief, who denied his own blood? It was the Dariens! Our chief of the Dariens is good and compassionate. Our Missus Darien is of a great goodness and worth! Even goddess Pele listens to her, and she will answer our prayers, and fight with us!"

The chief could not endure these taunts. He yelled, his fists shaking at them, great powerful brown hands, unseen behind the walls, and too far for his rifles to reach, "Come out and speak again to me of the one whom Pele will protect! Pele is our goddess! She sends the tidal waves twice over Darien to destroy it! She sends up smoke and fire to destroy the Dariens! I hear how they are caught in the fires, and almost burn to death on Kilauea, the home of great Pele! She will help me to destroy all Dariens!"

"You are wrong, oh, Chief!" yelled Hilohilo, enjoying himself immensely now. He hopped up and down, happily spitting out fiery words. "Pele listens to Missus Darien, she has powerful medicine, and is beloved of all Hawaiians! Missus Darien, she holds the little Victor in her arms, and keeps him alive! She comforts and does her wifely duties by the Chief of the Darien! The Chief of the Dariens grows stronger with her faith! Great Pele listens to us now! The tidal waves were our warning, and we knew they come! Conch shells warn us, and we take shelter. No one Hawaiian die of the wave on Darien! For great Pele protects us, as she protects us today!"

Silence from out on the plains. Kaahumanu Pauahi had turned to his warriors, to Maleko, and they were speaking to him, palms outturned in pleading, or fists clenched in wish for war. He listened to one and to another.

Peter watched alertly, eyes narrowed against the bright noon sunlight. They could move at any time, and the taunts would make them desperate.

The chief gestured. The men spread out, eagerly, and then the next attack began. The first ones made it to the walls, flung up their vine ladders, and tried to climb up. A steady firing began, as Peter directed his supporters to the protection of the walls.

The Pauahi warriors fell back. The next line came forward, with spears in eager hands. And a forest of weapons were flung into the compound, where the milling *paniolos* were fighting for a best vantage point to shoot.

Someone cried out, a spear had found its mark. "Fire!" roared Peter. "And again!"

The rifles cracked, but the spear throwers had already run back. Another wave of spear throwers followed. They were skilled in this, and with their powerful arms they could throw farther than the rifle bullets could reach.

Another spear fell onto the compound, quivering in the dirt. Still another found its mark in the shoulder of an Hawaiian. He dropped his rifle, grimacing with pain as he tried to hold the spear still. Someone went to his aid, supported him to the safety of the house.

Peter directed the firing, but the spear throwers were too far from their reach. They could fling the blades up and over the walls, and some found their mark. The pointed spears were sharp and inflicted deep wounds.

The firing of the rifles, the crack of pistol shots, the yelling of the warriors were all echoing in Peter's ears. He reloaded, fired again and again. He tried to make every bullet count, aiming for shoulder or chest. But the warriors were skilled, ducking down after flinging their sharpened spears.

He watched more intently. He saw one warrior with arm upraised, and fired before he could let loose the weapon. Joe Smith saw how he was doing, and began to fire that way. The bullet might be spent by the time it reached the distant warrior, but the constant fire scattered them.

Finally the spear-throwing ceased, the warriors retreated. The chief gestured to them, they pulled back with him into the shelter of some palms. It was high noon, and the sun was burning hot, directly over their heads.

Peter watched, then saw the battle would cease for awhile. He began to walk about, to see what injuries had been done. He came upon Nick, sitting on the veranda steps, his face stoic as an Hawaiian pulled out the spear caught in his shoulder. Blood gushed as the blade came out.

Peter dropped down beside him to examine the wound, smearing on strong medicines. He hoped that the warriors had not added poisonous materials to their points, that could kill within minutes. Anxiously he watched his cousin as he leaned, eyes closed, against a post, while Peter bandaged his shoulder.

"How do you feel, Nick?" If he were dazed, faint, it would mean poison. . . .

"Mad as hell," said Nick, in a strong voice. "That damn spear got me in my right shoulder. And me needing that arm."

Peter got him inside, Rosalind was waiting there, her face pale and anxious. He smiled at her briefly. "Look after him, darling."

"Do you need more bullets? We are making more."

"Yes, bring out what you have when they are

398

cooled," he replied. Presently she handed out the little pail of bullets, and he passed them around. They all paused to drink a cup of cold water and chew on a sandwich without appetite, glances alert for any more of the enemy.

The warriors were grouped under the trees, talking earnestly to their chief. Maleko stood apart, his head bent. The Chief looked over at him, then turned his back on him.

Peter was curious. What was the relationship between them? He wondered if Maleko was a Pauahi. That would account for much.

Yet the chief did not seem to be listening to him. He was listening to some fiery young warriors who fairly danced with impatience as they spoke to him, shaking their fists from time to time at the great house.

Leaving Joe Smith on guard, Peter strolled around the house to see what damage had been done. The great white house was pockmarked with bullets, and spears stuck in two window shutters. Behind, at the stables, he found the horses nervous, pawing the ground with fear, and the grooms had all they could do to keep them from breaking away in panic.

Fortunately, everything was basically in order, no one had been injured there. The warriors had not gone around the house, to try to breach the walls at the back. Still, it would pay to keep guard. Peter ordered four more men to the rear, with rifles.

Terry was padding around after him, listening and watching, his usually merry face quite somber.

As they walked back to the front, Terry said, "I can't understand why Chief Pauahi attacked us. We were always friendly, I mean, until. . . ." He paused, embarrassed at the fiery look from Peter.

"Until you seduced his daughter?" asked Peter. "It is enough to make him fighting mad."

"I know, but why now? Why has he waited so long? And what did they mean about the weak Dariens? Oh, I know he was making fighting talk, to encourage his warriors. But I caught what he was saying, and he seemed to mean it."

"I guess he figures we are weak, according to his lights," said Peter. They had returned to the veranda. "Did you notice Maleko out there, Hilohilo?"

The husky foreman nodded, and spat in disgust on the ground. "Him one damn spy, that one! And stay for months! Eating our food, coming to *luau,* and eating our salt! No good, that one."

"I wonder," said Peter, thoughtfully. He remembered how Maleko and the others had watched and listened at feasts, around campfires, padding off into the darkness. Spying, yes. But what had they found? It seemed that Maleko was trying to persuade Chief Pauahi to another course.

What had Maleko decided about them? He was contemptuous of Terry probably. But why conclude that all Dariens were weak? Maleko had had respect for Peter, he showed it, and also for Rosalind. He had bowed deeply in respect to her. No Hawaiian of his nature would bow to a white woman without meaning respect.

Eileen. Peter thought of his cousin, and wondered again. Had Eileen made advances to that young Hawaiian? Had she given herself to him? Peter had few illusions about Eileen left. She might have been attracted to his strong lithe body, and she was bored and discontented here.

He remembered times when she had gone off early to bed, only to sleep late the next morning, appearing with drowsy eyes and satisfied look. Had she gone catting off in the darkness, to meet Maleko? If so, there was no wonder that the Hawaiian had contempt for the Dariens. No Hawaiian girl would act so. She would go to her true love, and meet him unashamed. But she would not go to one man after another. That would be disgraceful.

Yet with Terry weak, and dishonoring Lydia Pauahi —and Eileen meeting a Hawaiian warrior on the sly without her brother's knowledge—it might add up to something in the minds of the Pauahi. Perhaps they had concluded that the Dariens would not fight for their own island, their possessions and people.

If that was the case, thought Peter, they would have to think again. He would fight to the death for his family and people. So would Nick, so would Joe, and Hilohilo, and all their people. Barton Darien could no longer hold a gun or fire it. But he had a son, and that son could fight for him and for all of them.

The hot hours of the afternoon wore on. The warriors lounged on the grass under the trees. They built no fires, they ate a little fruit and drank. They seemed to be waiting.

Dusk, thought Peter. They would come at dusk, rested, and fighting fit.

He strolled about. He saw to the injured. One man was seriously hurt, he ordered him removed to the house in spite of the man's urgent request to remain.

He went inside the house, spoke to Rosalind. He looked about. The great house was crowded from top to bottom, even the steps were full of children crawling up and down. But they were quiet, anxious, waiting also, in spite of their play. The guns would crash again, like thunder.

He looked around, saw that they all had food and water, and were reasonably well off. He returned to Rosalind, found her in a rocker with a sleepy Victor in her lap. Victor cooed and raised his arms to Peter.

Peter picked him up, held him close. So little, to be the innocent cause of much of what went on out there —the battles, the injuries, maybe dying. He sighed a little, kissed the plump brown cheek, and gave him back to Rosalind. He bent to her, pressed his cheek to hers.

"All right?"

She nodded. "Take care, Peter," she said, her amber eyes clear as she raised them to him. She did not seem frightened or upset, and she even smiled as she pressed her lips to his.

He ran his finger down her smooth cheek. "I figure the next attack will be at dusk," he said, quietly. "Keep them all inside, will you? And protect yourself, don't go near the windows, no matter how curious you get."

She nodded. "I will take care. Pele will aid us, Peter, I know it. She has promised. But death will come, I have seen that in my dreams. So . . . take very good care, my dear!" Her fingers clenched over his strong tanned fingers.

He opened his mouth to rebuke her speech of Pele, but closed it again. Faith was faith, and belief in the gods could not be wrong. The Hawaiians were simple people, close to nature and the gods that were the symbols of that nature. Sometimes cruel, sometimes kind, the gods of the volcano and fire and earth and the seas, the shark gods, the fire gods, all were part of their sturdy faith.

Who was he to quarrel with that? He believed in God, who had all power over heavens and earth, and he prayed to that God, and had faith that God would protect them. And then also, he thought wryly, perhaps they would need all the faith they could acquire!

"I will take care." He kissed her again, and went out.

She locked the door after him, and went back to the rocking chair. Victor cuddled against her, and she waited, as they all waited.

# 27

THE HAWAIIANS ATTACKED again at sunset, when the bright rays blinded the men inside the walls of Darien. Spears flung from strong arms found their mark on the wooden shutters and in the bodies of several men.

The shrieking and screaming increased to a pitch. The shots of the rifles echoed back and forth from the cliffs behind to the sea. Peter was deafened by the sounds, but he squinted against the setting sun and fired, again and again.

Rosalind handed out more bullets, they continued to fire. Glendon Corey peered around the door, his face greenish-white.

"They have no quarrel with me!" he cried. "Why are they attacking?"

Peter was close to amusement. How battle brought out the true natures of men! Glendon was quivering with fear.

Terry glanced at Corey, then away again. Peter finally said, "They are fighting us, Corey. Get inside and stay safe. They have no quarrel with you."

Later he realized what he had said and done. Corey did not understand the Hawaiians, he had never taken the trouble to do so. And he did not understand men, and how inflamed they could be in battle, until anyone in their way was the enemy.

The sky darkened, the Hawaiians were screaming and yelling. They had dampened down their fires. The attack was on in earnest. They watched for gleams of light, and flung their spears with deadly accuracy.

Someone yelled from the back of the house. Peter raced around there, Terry at his heels.

He found a door opened in the wall, and men struggling to shut it again, and bar it.

"What is it? What happened?"

One of the *paniolos* pointed outside. "That man, the white man who stay here, that Corey, he open the door and go outside. We tell him he crazy man, he say that they do not battle with him."

Someone screamed outside, a high shrill cry of fear. Peter raced around to the veranda again. From that height he could see over the wall.

They had Corey. They had ripped off his coat and hat and shirt. They waved the garments in the air. Someone was starting up a fire, and Peter could see the faces of the young Hawaiians.

Inflamed with battle, they lifted gourds to their lips, wiping their faces with their bronzed arms. They were drinking. He looked for the chief, the tall man stood aloof, his arms folded, watching.

"Oh, the fool, the bloody damn fool," Peter muttered, his teeth clenched. The man would go through hell before he died.

"We've got to rescue him!" Terry, his face flushed and eager, clutched at Peter's arm. "Come on, Peter, let's go out and get him! He hasn't a chance!"

Peter looked at him. "Neither do we," he said shortly. "If we open that gate and go out, half a hundred warriors will have our hides nailed to the walls before we get a dozen steps. Don't you know yet what we're up against? Our only hope is to stay inside the walls, and fight off the siege."

"But he's a white man, not a damn native!" Terry insisted, earnestly. "We have to try to rescue him . . . oh God, listen to him scream!"

He put his hands to his ears. Peter's jaw became pronounced as he clenched his teeth. This was what they could all expect, should the Hawaiians win. The men, women, and children would all be slaughtered tonight, if they could not hold off the assault. And this tormenting and torturing to death of Corey might just be the torch that lit them into a frenzied suicidal attack at the gates. Sense would not prevail, wave after wave would come on, until someone breached the barrier.

Joe Smith was raising his rifle, keenly measuring the distance between them and the fire they had lit at the feet of Corey. They had tied him to a stake, and were slashing him with knives. The fire crept to his knees.

"Too far, Joe," said Peter, quietly, sick to his soul. He had detested and distrusted Glendon Corey, but no man should have to die that way. Peter went about, instructing the men calmly which ones were to guard which gates, which ones wait in the compound, which ones to go around the back and relieve the men with the horses.

Terry followed him about like a bewildered child. "Shouldn't we have a try, Peter?" he kept saying. "My God, they are murdering him! Listen to him . . . God, he can't last. . . ."

"He was a fool," interrupted Peter, his patience brittle. "He should have known enough not to go out there. He must have thought he could bargain with them. They are not in a negotiating mood, they are keyed up to kill."

Terry shuddered. "What a horrible death," he muttered, fingering the rifle. He raised it, shot impulsively into the darkness toward the fire where Corey burned. Peter gripped his arm, stopped another shot.

"Don't waste bullets, Terry. We can't spare them. Every shot must count." His crisp words seemed to shock his cousin. Terry stared at him, his face strained in the dimness.

"But we're safe here," he protested. "Nobody can get inside the walls. They are too high . . . we are safe. . . ."

Peter turned from him. Poor Terry, always believing what he wanted to believe, always taking what he wanted to take. He never thought that fortune might turn her smiling face from him eventually.

The screams from outside died down. Corey

drooped against the stake, only thick vines held him to it.

"Reckon he's dead," said Hilohilo regretfully, fingering his spear. "He ask for it, he bad man. But me, I am sorry about it. Fool man, he should never come to Darien. Too greedy, too sly, too bad."

It was enough of an epitaph for Glendon Corey, thought Peter wearily. He rubbed his eyes. The smoke from the fires had made his eyes sting, and he was tired. He would like to rest, to eat, to sleep. But all must stay awake tonight.

There was silence for a time outside. Too much violence. The fire had been put out, and the burned body of Corey hung limply from the stake. The warriors had wandered away, the chief had disappeared. Peter narrowed his eyes, watching, waiting.

He decided to take another look around. He motioned Joe to take his place at the post on the veranda, and the man nodded. His grim face seemed tireless, his pose was alert, the rifle ready at his arm. Hilohilo prowled about, spear at the ready. He liked a spear better than a rifle, and he had his knife at his belt.

Peter started around the house. He watched, listened. Terry padded after him in his sandals. He seemed to follow Peter about like a dog after his master. Bewildered by the events, he was eager to please, on edge.

They went back to the corral, spoke to the men there. Peter patted his favorite stallion affectionately, his hand on the quivering neck of the black. "There, boy, you're all right," he murmured again and again, soothingly, thinking of the horses slaughtered maliciously outside the gates.

A slow burning anger filled him. He understood, yet he felt angry at the way the warriors had murdered cattle, pigs, even the beautiful horses, just to show how powerful they were, to make bad medicine, as Joe had said. He caught himself, he must remain calm, not letting anger blur his mind.

They left the corral and went around the other side of the house, past the flower gardens and the patio.

Only yesterday they had had the *luau* there, with laughter and dancing. Bright-eyed children dancing, slim girls dancing, women singing in their musical husky voices, the songs of the islands, the songs they lifted to the skies to cheer their spirits and remind them of their past and future. Rosalind had sat in the chair, right there, smiling, her amber eyes bright, as she held Victor on her lap and patted his legs in time to the music.

"What's that?" whispered Terry, clutching at Peter's arm.

They both paused, listened, Peter shook his head. They were on edge, tired, nervous. They walked on a few steps.

Then from over the high wall came two warriors. One jumped on Peter, knocking the rifle from his arm, hitting him with a club. He caught Peter on the side of his head, and Peter went down.

Terry dashed to his rescue. The attack was so sudden they did not yell. The warriors were silent also, ferocious, deadly.

Terry used his rifle as a blunt weapon, too close to fire. He struck one of them, then went after him with his knife. He closed in, the man gripped him with arms of steel, and raised Terry high in the air. He dashed Terry to the ground. Terry, dazed, got up to his knees, tried to grip the warrior. The man had a knife in his hand, he raised it, Peter saw it gleaming against the pale light from the night sky.

It came down, Terry groaned and crumpled, curling up against the hurt of the wound. Peter struggled up, caught his rifle, and fired in the direction of one warrior. The man groaned, went down. The other warrior was on him, knife in hand. Terry rolled over, managed to strike out at the warrior with the knife that had been in his own body, and found a vital place.

The warrior screamed, and fell over. Terry sighed, and lay back, the blood draining from his body, spilling over his brightly-flowered shirt, his arms, his face.

The rifle shot brought the Darien men running. One carried a torch, and they gasped as the light showed what had happened. Peter was bending over Terry, blood streaming from his own head wound. Terry was covered with red.

They brought a mat, and carried him inside the house, past the patio into the inner drawing room. They laid him down tenderly when he whispered, "No more . . . can't stand. . . ."

Norma came, and Rosalind, faces pale with shock. They brought water, bandages, and medicine, but they could not stem the blood that flowed from Terry. He lay, face ashen, eyes closed.

"If only we had a doctor. . . ." muttered Peter.

Rosalind turned to him with a sigh. "Let me take care of your head now, darling," she said. Her hands shook a little as he sat down, and she gently sponged away the blood, and examined the wound closely.

Peter said to Hilohilo, hovering over him, "Post more guards, all around the buildings and walls. Spread out the men, warn them. The men came over the wall. . . ."

"Yes, boss," and Hilohilo ran to do what Peter ordered, glad the boss could snap orders. Joe came in to look, and went away again.

Norma was bending over Terry, holding his hand. She could have wept, but she was still in shock.

"How bad is my head?" asked Peter calmly, of Rosalind.

"About a quarter of an inch deep, it looks like the blow slashed down the side," she said, her voice quivering a little. "I'll put some medicine on it, then bind it up. You must rest, Peter."

He thought, no. He could not rest. Not now. The warriors out there were cunning, and thorough. And the chief was a canny fighter.

They must watch and wait through the night. And the next attack might come at dawn. It was a favorite time for attack. When the men were sleepy, the enemy off-guard, and the light a dim grey. . . .

Rosalind bandaged his head, wrapping the white cloth about the side, leaving his ear free. Peter bent one last time over Terry.

"You saved my life, Terry, I won't forget it," he said, and pressed the weak hand that lay still on the mat.

A faint smile curved Terry's lips. His eyes half-opened, he winked a little, painfully at Peter. "Good. You're in my debt," he said, with some of the old mockery.

Peter went outside, and the door was locked and bolted after him. Rosalind knew it was futile to protest, but now and then she glanced through a chink in the thick shutters to make sure he was still on the veranda. He sat in a chair, but bolt upright, the rifle on his arm, his gaze on the gates.

The night had grown still, as though the whole world waited. Rosalind sat down on the mat beside Terry, and touched his hand. It was not burning hot with fever, it was chilled and cold.

She asked one of the girls to bring a blanket, and they laid it over Terry, covering him to his chin, the blood-soaked shirt and trousers, the blood-covered arms. The wound was deep in his stomach, curving upward to his chest. The bandages were thickly stained already.

Norma crouched at his other side, her face taut with grief and anxiety. The others, families who waited for their men, were still. They had taken out the little children, but others were there, women and girls and small children about six and eight.

They looked at him with great compassion, and were silent, only murmuring to each other from time to time. A few slept, the others were sitting or lying on mats, waiting for the morning.

The house was so full of people, there was no privacy for Terry. But he did not seem to mind, lying with his eyes half-shut. Now and then he squeezed his mother's hand faintly.

Eileen burst into the room, making a great clatter with her mules. She was in a slim white nightdress with a blue negligee floating over it. "Someone said . . . Terry . . . oh, Terry, my God, what has happened to you?" she cried. She wakened the people in the room, who moved over, groaned, sat up to watch with compassionate interest.

"Oh, hush, my dear, hush!" Norma warned, but it was too late. Terry wakened from the half-sleep, opened his eyes, and looked up at his sister. He managed a little grin.

"Pretty," he said, drowsily.

She dropped to her knees beside him. "He's hurt! He's got to have a doctor! Why is he lying here? Let's get him up to his room! Boy!" And she clapped her hands sharply, imperiously, for one of the house men.

Norma said gently, "They are all outside, waiting for the next attack, Eileen. Please be quiet. Terry needs to rest."

"But we must move him up to bed!" she cried out, wringing her slim hands.

Rosalind watched her curiously. Terry was the one person Eileen seemed to love. Certainly she was upset about him.

"No," said Terry, firmly. "Don't want . . . to move. Hurt. Lie here. Be quiet, Eileen."

She moaned, "Oh, my God, what happened to you?"

"Knife," he whispered.

"Knife! You shouldn't have been out there! It isn't your fight!" she cried. She shot a fierce look at Rosalind. "It's all your fault, you bitch! If you hadn't brought that damn baby back here! Give him up to his grandfather! Nobody else wants him!"

Rosalind's mouth compressed to keep back furious words.

Terry whispered, "Rosalind . . . let Eileen . . . sit there . . . must talk . . . to her."

Rosalind got up. Eileen shot another furious look at her, then sat down in gingerly fashion on the mat, bending anxiously over her brother. Her hand closed over his, as his fingers moved to seek hers. Rosalind stood near, in case she was needed, and heard what they said.

"Eileen, my dear . . . you must . . . grow up," said Terry, weakly. "Necessary. Won't last if you don't.

Know this . . . what you do will add up someday. Catch up with you. Always does."

Terry coughed, and Norma leaned over him to wipe away the bloody froth on his lips.

Eileen sobbed, once. Rosalind longed to touch her, comfort her, but knew the girl hated her so much the touch would be an insult to her. So she stood rigid.

"Never mind, Terry," said Eileen. "You'll get well, and we'll get away from this horrible place! We'll escape, you watch!"

"No . . . escape . . . for me," whispered Terry, his mouth curled slightly. "You . . . will go, my dear. Don't belong . . . here. Make a new life. But Eileen . . . remember . . . you always pay for what you get. You always . . . pay high . . . remember. . . ."

"Don't be silly," she said, bluntly. "You're feverish. . . ."

His fingers closed more strongly over hers, he moved her hand, Rosalind could see the movement. "No, listen . . . you will pay. So Eileen . . . my dearest . . . be careful . . . remember . . . I love you . . . always did . . . for my sake . . . take care. . . ."

Tears were running down Norma's cheeks, but she sat still, a frail little figure in her rustling black silk, the hot little tight garments encasing her body. Her head with the white widow's cap sat as primly as though she would dine elegantly that night, instead of sitting on the floor beside her son.

Honora came in softly, brought her tea, but Norma shook her head. Honora remained to look down at them, caught Rosalind's glance, shook her head, and finally departed.

Eileen was weeping, noisily, so overcome with her own grief that she had no thought for Terry's pain.

He urged her, "Eileen, go and get some sleep, my dear. Just . . . remember what I . . . said to you. You will, won't you? Payment time always comes . . ."

"Oh, Terry! Don't talk so . . . we have done nothing wrong. . . ."

He gave her a pitying look, and his head fell back,

as though talking had exhausted him. She gave a cry. "He's dead . . ."

"No, just tired," he managed to say.

Norma got up. "Eileen, you come up to bed, and we'll talk a bit," she managed to say firmly.

Eileen was finally persuaded to leave, still weeping noisily. Rosalind sank down on the mat again. Terry opened his eyes, managed a faint sardonic grin that reminded her of the time on the beach when he had tried to make love to her.

"All the sins . . . catching up . . . huh? The gods will be pleased," he whispered, and closed his eyes. He breathed unevenly, but seemed to be half-asleep.

Peter came in several times during the night, pausing to look down gravely at Terry.

He would sit down beside Rosalind, hold her against him, as though drawing strength from her. Then he would leave again, out into the silent darkness.

Kinau came in toward dawn. She carried Victor with her, a sleepy child, just wakening.

"He should see his father," murmured Kinau, and handed Victor to Rosalind. She bent over Terry, examining his face keenly.

"Not long now," she said, and patted Rosalind's shoulder.

Norma returned, her face grey with fatigue. "Eileen is finally sleeping, I gave her some tablets."

She sat down beside her son, looking at him. The blood had seeped through to the blankets.

"Is there nothing . . ." she whispered, touching the body lightly.

Rosalind shook her head. "The blood will not stop."

They sat in silence. Victor went to sleep again in her arms, curled against her breasts. The room was very quiet.

She did not know when she had become aware that Terry was looking at her. His eyes were opened. He struggled to speak as she bent down toward him.

"Yes, Terry? Do you wish a drink of water?"

"No. Victor."

Puzzled, she leaned closer, and the baby moved with her. Victor wakened, his dark eyes sleepy. Terry managed to reach out his weak hand and touch a sturdy leg.

"Tell . . . him. . . ."

"Yes, Terry?"

"When he . . . grows up. Tell him . . . about . . . his father. Tell him—"

"Yes, Terry, I will tell him."

"Not . . . how I lived . . ." managed Terry, coughing until the blood flecked his white lips. "Tell him . . . how I died . . . proud . . . of me?"

"Yes, he will be proud of his father," Rosalind said, over the lump of tears in her throat.

Terry smiled, his fingers touched the baby foot, and Victor stared at him in wonderment. Terry's eyes were soft on the boy.

"Looks . . . like . . . Lydia . . . good boy. . . ."

Tears streamed down Norma's cheeks. She choked them back, and took Terry's other hand in hers. The free hand fell away from Victor's foot. Terry's eyes shut, he sighed. He seemed to sleep then. They sat in silence as the dawn slowly filled the room with grey light around the thick wooden shutters.

Peter came slowly into the room, moving deftly between the sleeping bodies on the floor. He bent over Terry, whose face was taut with fatigue and pain. Fresh blood had oozed through the white bandage.

"How is he?" Peter whispered, and leaned to touch Terry's cheek. He started.

Rosalind knew then, even before he said it.

"He is . . . dead."

Norma let out one poignant cry, then covered her mouth with her hand, rocking back and forth in grief. She leaned over Terry, gazing into the face that would never smile back at her again.

"Oh . . . my son . . . my son . . ." she moaned, and people began to wake and stir around her.

Someone brought another blanket and they covered Terry's face, so handsome and young. Rosalind carried Victor away, back to Kinau, to keep safe in the third floor room. Someone had to tell Eileen, but Rosalind shrank from the task.

Honora went to tell her, and the girl screamed and cried, disturbing the whole household. The Hawaiians wakened, muttered, held to their special charms and muttered prayers over and over.

Dawn came, but there was one less Darien to see it.

# 28

❦ ❦ ❦ ❦

WITH DAWN, another attack came. Peter straightened as he saw the warriors race up in the grey light, flinging fresh spears cut from trees.

The raw white wood flashed in the dimness, the whang of the missiles sliced through the cool morning air. The spears struck in the wooden shutters, or fell harmlessly to the ground.

The spine-chilling yells of the warriors started also. Peter saw the yellow-cloaked chief urging them on, saw the spears from his great hands flung accurately to far inside the walls.

The Hawaiians inside scattered about, some around the walls, some at the stables, some near the front. Several stood on the veranda with Peter and Joe Smith, who fired their rifles steadily as the waves of warriors came closer.

"Their weapon . . . a battering ram . . ." called Joe, pointing. Several young warriors were carrying a great log up to the front gate, covered by the onslaught of their friends.

Joe fired, fired again, several of the men went down as the others took aim also. The log was dropped after one futile attempt at battering the gate.

The sun came up, bright and clear and cheerful, incongruous in the deadly morning. The eastern light shone in the eyes of the Pauahi men, and they fell back. Some were shot down, some hit by spears hurled from inside the compound, and they cried out.

A dozen men lay on the ground outside the walls, many without moving. A great shout went up, the chief waved his arms fiercely.

His men retreated out of range. They circled him, to discuss alternative strategies.

The men inside took the opportunity to reload their weapons, to sharpen more sticks into spears. They were low on spears, but more bullets came from the house as Rosalind and several other women continued to heat and mold the lead.

Peter watched keenly as the conference continued. Joe Smith muttered, "Having a pow-pow, I reckon."

"What's that?"

Hilohilo moved closer to hear.

Joe waved his hand. "Injun talk. They fight, then they talk about it, big pow-wow. Talk it all over, have a meeting, and decide what to do. I notice these fellas do the same. The chief has the word, but he listens to what the warriors say also. Interesting."

Peter's eyes burned with lack of sleep. His head ached from the wound. He turned his mind from all that. He must not think of weakness. He must think of strength. They depended on him for leadership. Hilohilo was too excitable, Joe was too detached. And Terry was dead.

He spared a thought for his cousin, he had died a man, no matter how he had lived. Terry. Should he have let Terry go away, to live the wild happy life he had wanted? No matter. The gods had decreed it, Terry had died here on Darien, where he had been born, defending the house and Peter.

Futile to look back, to wonder how it might have been. Still he must wonder, and think. How the circle moved, and was drawn, until it came back to the beginning, and all was in place, as ordained.

The conference continued. Peter watched, then ordered water brought around, and some fried fish and freshly baked *plantain*. The men ate eagerly, half at one time, then half again as the first man, refreshed, took up their weapons. Peter ate last.

He went to the door, the women there let him in. He went to seek Rosalind, and found her moving quietly about the house, supervising the cooking for the hundreds there, finding time to pick up a small baby

416

underfoot and restore him to his mother. Victor was in Kinau's arms, struggling to get to Peter when he saw him.

Peter picked up Victor, smiled into the eager chubby face, and put his rough unshaven cheek briefly against the baby one. "Hello, my little one," he said tenderly.

"Papapapa dadadada," said Victor, babbling and patting Peter's face. He looked curiously at the white bandage on Peter's head.

Rosalind said, "Do you have time to change the bandage?"

"No, I'll just have a cup of hot coffee, and some bacon." He sat down at the kitchen table, Victor on his knee, and ate and chewed, without tasting. The coffee was good, fresh-brewed and hot.

"How is Norma?"

Rosalind's face shadowed. "Numb, I think. She cannot speak, and does not seem to hear us."

He did not ask about Eileen, he had heard her wailing. Honora was helping take food to the children.

Peter got up when he had finished, set Victor on the floor, where he promptly crawled to the stairs outside to climb up the first and second ones. A small girl came over to him, to guard him as naturally as she would one of her little brothers or sisters.

Peter kissed Rosalind. "Take care."

"And you also," she said, smiling up at him. She put her hand briefly to his cheek, her rough reddened hand. He turned it over, and kissed the calloused palm. "I love you," she whispered.

"I love you, my dear."

He went out the door, and it was bolted after him. Joe Smith reported, "They're still pow-wowing, and looking over here," and he spat on the ground beyond the veranda. "Maybe they had enough!"

"I hope so," said Peter somberly.

They could stand off the Hawaiians for a week, if necessary. The steamer would come in at that time, see the situation, and rescue them with reinforcements from the mainland. He hoped it would not come to that. Too many might be killed in the meantime.

He rubbed his eyes, and straightened his tired shoulders. He looked out over the wall to the distance, where the yellow-cloaked chief in the tall helmet was approaching the wall. He walked alone, and waved back one man who would have come with him—Maleko.

"Don't fire!" called Peter.

The Hawaiians inside watched curiously as the chief approached. Those nearer the high ground of the veranda could see out over the wall as he came closer.

The powerful voice yelled out, "I would talk with Peter Darien!"

Peter hesitated, looked at Hilohilo. The man looked dubious, spread out his brown palms.

Joe drawled, "I wouldn't let him come close, boss," and his grey eyes showed a glint of worry. "He's big enough and tough enough to kill you with his bare hands."

"What do you want with me, Chief Pauahi?" Peter yelled out in Hawaiian.

The man answered in the island language. "I would speak serious words with you!"

"Speak then!"

"Inside the walls, with no gate between us!"

When the powerful voice ceased, the stillness in the compound was intense. There was silence in the house behind them, the words had been heard there also.

"Maybe a trick," warned Smith.

"He come inside, we kill him," said Hilohilo. "He kill two men, he wound many."

Peter hesitated, thinking. What was the risk? He was surrounded by men with knives, pistols, spears and rifles. What chance would Chief Pauahi have, one against many? What trick could it be?

The powerful deep voice boomed again. "I speak truth. I wish only to talk with the chief of the Dariens!"

The words were respectful. The warriors behind him lounged in the shade, or nursed their wounds, and some crouched about small campfires. None came near their chief. The closest man was Maleko, standing about a dozen yards behind him, with no weapon visible.

"Do you come alone, with hands empty of weapons?" yelled Peter.

"I come alone, with hands empty of weapons, and a heart that wishes to hear words of peace!"

Peter decided to take the chance. "We will open the gate for you! But men with rifles will stand ready for any treachery! Do you wish to come inside?"

"I will come inside!"

Joe Smith came down off the veranda. He aimed his rifle deliberately at the gate. Five others, scattered across the high ground, stood with rifles pointed. At Peter's nod, four sturdy Hawaiians, at the gates, cautiously took down the heavy bars, and laid them aside. They pulled open one gate, and the tall chief strode in without glancing to one side or another, his haughty head held high.

Beyond him Maleko watched, his hands on his chest, his arms folded impassively.

The gate was closed and bolted again. Peter strode toward the chief, as the man walked toward him. About six feet apart, they both halted. They looked at each other.

"I wish to talk peace," said the chief, in his deep firm voice.

"I had no wish for war," said Peter firmly. "You brought war to me on Darien."

The deep eyes flashed fire, then were subdued. Peter watched him sharply.

The fine head turned, the chief looked deliberately about the ground. Several men lay with bandaged limbs on mats. Their weapons were still in their hands. The two warriors that Peter and Terry had killed had been dragged into the shade of the veranda. The chief looked at them, recognized them, and his face saddened.

"There has been much killing."

"Yes. Your two men died bravely," said Peter, tersely. "You may take them out with you when you

leave our gates. Their bodies have not been dese-
crated."

The head bowed briefly. "I thank you." He finally
continued abruptly. "Where is your pale-faced
brother?"

"My cousin Terry Darien is dead, killed by your
warriors."

A flicker passed over his face. "Ah."

Peter stared straight at him. "It was a slow death,
over the night. We are full of grief for him, he died a
man."

"Ah." The chief was thinking. "I do not pretend to
be sad. He took my daughter from me, my Lydia."

"No killing will return her."

"No. But she has been avenged."

Peter's mouth tightened. "All this would not have
happened, if you had taken her back into the village.
It was you who sent her out to die in the mountains,
she and her child."

The chief's dark eyes blazed at the blunt words,
then he moved his hands slowly. "Yes, I was wrong.
I should have taken my daughter back. My honored
position was covered with dirt, I raged in my sorrow."

"It is understood," said Peter, slowly. "I feel I would
have wanted to do the same."

For the first time that day, they looked at each other
with understanding. The chief's face softened ever so
slightly, the muscle in his jaw ceased its working.

"My warriors did kill the man Terry Darien?" asked
the chief, after a pause.

Peter bent his head. "They killed him. I killed one
of them, Terry killed the other and saved my life."
He touched the wound on his head.

"Then my honor is once more satisfied, all is well,"
said the chief. "I will tell my men. The mission here
is finished. We have killed the man who dishonored
and disgraced my daughter. Lydia can rest in peace
now."

"Yes, you can tell the men. And tell them also that
he died a man, honorably, saving the life of his chief."
Pauahi frowned. He did not like the words.

420

Peter watched him shrewdly, knowing how he felt. He was a kind-hearted man, for all his tall height, his kingly appearance, his haughty ways, his arrogance. Peter felt he understood him now.

"The father of your grandchild," said Peter, "died a man. His son will carry on with honor. The son of your daughter is worthy of her and of his father, he will be a chief one day."

The dark brooding eyes lighted. "Give him to me!"

Peter shook his head. "He is a Darien. He stays with me."

"Do we fight each other once more?" cried the chief, his fist striking his chest. "You wish to hurt me once more? Have I not known enough pain?"

"I wish to give you no more pain. But the child is one of my house. He is a Darien. I am the chief of the Dariens. The boy Victor stays with me, the son of his father, to grow up here on Darien, to be trained with the cattle and the ways of my household."

"He is Hawaiian! I do not wish him to grow up white!"

Peter hesitated, his mouth set. He had no desire to carry on with the war. But he still was not sure of the chief. He would not give up Victor to the man, to be murdered if the chief felt the blood was poor. Or for revenge, or any such motive.

The warriors outside were becoming restless. They could hear their chief's voice raised in anger. They stood and looked toward the walls, they could only see their chief's head. A rumbling began among them, murmur of words, growing louder.

"I do not give up the boy Victor."

"I came for him. I do not go away without him!"

"For what purpose? If you grow angry with him, as you did with your daughter Lydia, will you kill him also? I cannot take that chance. He remains here."

The chief's face flushed dark with anger. "You do not trust my word!" he said imperiously.

"You have not given me your word. Would the boy live? And what if you mean to trick me? You do not trust white men. I am white. Do you think to give your word carelessly to me, and then betray, because a white man is not worthy of trust?"

The chief hesitated. The growling outside grew more ominous. Tension grew inside the compound also. The chief was so big and powerful, he could snatch up Peter, wounded and weak as he was, and dash him to the ground, or crush his neck in his great hands.

The chief lifted up his arms to the heavens, his head bent back so he could stare unblinkingly at the sun above.

"I call on the gods to witness what I say!" he cried in his great booming voice. Outside all were still, as they listened intently, heads, bodies, turned toward the place where their chief spoke.

Peter tensed, then folded his arms. The chief was making a speech, he would listen with respect. That was the custom.

"Many many years ago, this land was ours! We roamed about freely, we sailed the seas where we would, in our great canoes. We fished where we would, we respected the tabus, we honored each other.

"Then came the white men! They fished in our waters with no permission from us! They made no offerings to our gods! When we protested, we were told that the land and the seas were free! They could do as they wished!"

How could he stand and stare at the sun in that manner? Peter wondered vaguely as he listened to the words. The Hawaiians inside the compound were all listening seriously to the chief.

"The land was my father's, and that of his father, and of his father in turn. We are the chiefs of the Hawaiians! All honored and respected us! The women observed the tabus, and taught their children to honor the gods. Then . . . what happened?

"The white man came to our land and settled here. They built houses! They took the land, and said it was theirs, because of pieces of paper which they had. The land of our fathers . . . it was theirs because of some piece of paper! Pauuhh!" He made a long drawn-out sound of disgust, and spat on the ground.

Joe Smith tensed, Peter shook his head at him. The grey-eyed man, who did not understand all of the Hawaiian speech, watched tensely for any sign of attack.

Chief Kaahumanu Pauahi continued, in his great booming voice that could travel down a mountain side. "They took our fish without asking. Our waters were forbidden to us! Our canoes could not go into their waters, they said! How came this? How could pieces of paper take from us what had been ours from the beginnings, when our people came many generations ago from the seas to the south?"

He lowered his gaze from the sun, his blazing eyes challenged Peter. Peter remained silent, listening, beginning to comprehend what drove the chief to his desperation.

"Our women became corrupted. They go to work for the white man. When he gave them his attentions, they accepted, and had the children of those men! They did not protect their girls, and many had *Haole* children. The gods were displeased, they sent thunder and fire and volcano lava. Still the white men stayed, and our people became less than honorable."

Peter nodded, soberly. He knew what the chief meant. Encouraged, the chief continued.

"We took our children, and withdrew into the islands that others did not take from us. We fled up the mountains and lived in caves. We fished where the white man allowed us! All this . . . and still the men were not satisfied! No, one must come and take my daughter from me . . . my Lydia!" His voice broke, for the first time.

Hilohilo bent his head, as though he had done something to be ashamed of.

"The men corrupt our daughters. They take our honor from us. They take our land, our seas. When will it stop? I ask you, what must we do? Must we kill ourselves, fling ourselves from the cliffs into the sea, to satisfy the pieces of paper? Where are we to go? These islands are ours, but they take them from us. Our daughters and sons turn from us, and go into

423

disgrace. The old ways are not followed. The old tabus are scorned, and the gods are angry, they are angry!"

A low murmur came from the Hawaiians inside the compound, and outside, their faces flushed, they listened and nodded.

"The white men have crushed and cheated my people," said the chief, lowering his arms, folding them to his chest. "They have taken our lands, seduced our daughters. What is there left for us?"

He paused now, and stared at Peter, as though defying him to answer.

"What you have said is true in part, O Chief of the Pauahi. I have listened to your words, and I know what you say is the truth. I am ashamed of my people, who have done this to you. You know and I know that the land was that of the Hawaiians."

The chief's eyes gleamed, Peter raised his hand to still him, and then continued.

"But allow me to say this. When my people came to Darien, it was an empty salt-filled island. My grandfather came here, and with his own hands . . ." Peter held out his strong brown hands— "he dug and planted, cleansing the soil. He brought in cattle. He brought in men to work the land. He brought in Hawaiian men to help him, and gave them work. He helped them build houses, and encouraged them to bring their families, their wives and sons and daughters."

Hilohilo murmured, "That is the truth, that is the truth."

"We have taken land from no man!" said Peter forcefully. "I am a man of honor, men respect my word. And I say, no one has been corrupted by me! But I know what has been done, and no words can cleanse past deeds, and the blood that has been spilled. We must begin where we are, and make peace between us, as two men of honor, that no more such dealings can happen again."

"You are a man of honor, yes, I see that," said the chief. "But what of your people? You have another cousin. . . ."

"I will speak for Nick Darien," said Peter quickly. "He does not touch the daughters of the Hawaiians. He is a man of honor also."

The chief's gaze touched the silent figure of Nick Darien, noted the bloody bandage on his shoulder.

He bent his head, then said, "But you have another cousin. I speak of the woman who walks in the dark, and corrupts men. I speak of the woman who is without honor, and without respect for herself. Will she remain to mock my people with her immodest ways? All know of her, and her name is bad among us. Does she remain here, to bring up more children like herself? Such women do us no honor, O chief of the Dariens."

Peter's mouth tightened, he burned inside. So all had heard now of Eileen.

"She will leave the island, and not return," he said curtly. "I promise this."

The chief's nod was slow, but satisfied. "So. We will finish then. My daughter has been avenged. And the woman will leave, who mocks and scorns us. That is good. We can make peace now."

Peter drew a deep breath. He had feared the chief was working himself up for another assault.

"Yes, we will make peace," he said, in a firm clear carrying voice. "You will take away with you the warriors who died so bravely. We will give you water and supplies for the journey."

He nodded to the Hawaiians near the gate. They unbolted the gates, and allowed several men to come in, among them Maleko. The bodies on the mats were gathered up and borne away. Several men went to fill baskets with *plantains* and fruit.

The chief stood, his arms across his chest, his face grave as the dead men were borne ceremoniously past him. Then he turned to Maleko.

"You know this man," he said to Peter.

"I know him as Maleko, a brave man who danced the fire dance to Pele."

The chief nodded. "He is the son of my cousin. He warned us that the battle would not be easy, for the chief of the Dariens was not the foolish man that his cousin was. He was not of the softness of other whites. He is Maleko Pauahi." And he touched lightly the bronzed shoulder of the tall man.

Peter bent his head to him. "I thought he was more than a fisherman."

Maleko's mouth parted in a slight smile, his black eyes gleamed.

Maleko remained beside his chief and cousin while the bodies were taken to the long canoes, and the supplies loaded. The other dead and wounded warriors were also placed on the boats.

The chief waited. When all was done, and his men were beginning to push out the canoes into the deeper waters, he said, "I would ask one more time for my grandson. Give him to me. I wish the boy. I will raise him with pride."

The door behind them opened, and Rosalind came out, Victor in her arms. Peter stiffened. "You may see the boy, but not take him with you," he said, frowning at Rosalind.

She was looking at the chief. Her face was weary, her hands red with work, her gown mussed. But her head was high, her chin up.

"I wished you to see your grandson before you left, O Chief of the Pauahi," she said, clearly, in Hawaiian. "He is a fine lad, and you will be proud of him."

"I would take him."

"No," said Peter.

"I would hold him for a minute," said the chief, his face softening a trifle as Victor stared at him with great dark eyes.

Without hesitation, Rosalind placed the boy in his arms. Maleko beside them, his arms folded on his chest, Victor stared up into the haughty proud face, at the tall helmet, the yellow feather cloak about his shoulders.

Rosalind said, "I wish you would come and see the boy from time to time. He should hear from your lips the songs and stories of his own people, that one day he may know all his heritage. He is both Darien and

Pauahi, and one day he may unite us in love and affection."

"I will come and see him, and tell him the stories," the chief promised. He sighed. "He will be tall and great. But he is white also."

"He is also Hawaiian," said Rosalind. "Already he begins to speak his own language."

"You have spoken about him to Pele, our goddess?"

Rosalind nodded. "She says he will be a great chief of his people!"

The big hand stroked gently over the round head, down over the shoulders and sturdy back. "I will come back, small one, to see how you grow."

"Makua," said Victor, quite distinctly.

They started. He had said the word for father to his grandfather.

The chief pressed his face against the boy's head, and then slowly handed the child back to Rosalind.

"I shall come back. Without the war canoes."

"We shall welcome you," Peter told him.

The chief turned and left, Maleko following several paces behind him. The Hawaiians watched him depart, and go to the canoes. He stepped inside the first one, and they began to leave.

Across the waters came the sounds of their farewell and lament. The singing started softly, then began to echo from the cliffs as they moved out to sea. The song of farewell to their dead warriors, the song of lament for the defeat in battle, the sad wailing sounds of the lost.

Tears shone in Rosalind's eyes as she stood there, Victor clasped tightly to her. "They are losing so much, Peter," she whispered. "Their heritage, their land, their people. What will become of them?"

"I do not know," he said solemnly, wearily. He put his arm about her. Joe Smith had taken his rifle from him. It would not be needed any more—for the time being.

He thought of the bitter words of the chief, and knew they were true. Before the white men came, the Hawaiians had known these islands as their own. Then the sailors and whalers had come, introducing drink and lusting for their women. The merchants had followed, and taken away their trade. The other men had followed, to take their land, their fishing rights, and their daughters. Many of the Hawaiians were now only partly Hawaiian.

Where would it end? There was no one to protect them, and they could not fight the whole world, who wanted to move into their island paradise and snatch it from them.

For the first time, Peter began to realize fully what it all meant. The Hawaiians that were left were fighting desperately to keep what was their heritage and their land. All wanted their paradise, and in the name of progress they had stripped the native peoples of their rights to the islands they had loved for many centuries.

No wonder the chief had hated it when his daughter mated with Terry. And a man who had discarded her after taking her virginity from her! An unworthy man! It must have been the final indignity. His land, his fishing, and then his own daughter, all taken from him.

Could there be peace between them, after such blows to the pride, the honor, the dignity of the chief of Pauahi, and to all his people? Peter hoped so, but he realized it was a peace of desperation. The chief could not hope to win such a fight against all the forces against him.

Gathering his dignity about him, as his great yellow feather cloak was gathered about his bronzed body, the chief had left, his head high, but despair in his heart.

# 29

❧ ❧ ❧ ❧

THE NEXT FEW DAYS were sad ones. Terry was buried in the small churchyard near the Darien chapel. The other two Hawaiians who had died were also buried there, with much weeping and mourning.

Norma could not be consoled for the loss of her son. Her white, weary, anguished features were set in sorrow. Eileen refused to leave her own room, and wept loudly, then quietly, as her moods came and went.

Peter went to Honolulu on the steamer. He had to present the situation to the authorities there, and explain what had happened. It took two days of explanations, signing papers and obtaining lawyers to handle any cases which might come up, should the chief become angry all over again, charging them with the deaths of his warriors.

Finally it was all cleared up, and straightened out to the best of his ability. He paused in Kailua to attend to more business, then came home.

Rosalind met him at the boat, and he put his arm about her. "You saw the doctor, darling?" she asked anxiously, with a look at his freshly bandaged head.

He nodded, and beckoned to the red-haired Scotsman who followed him down the gangplank.

"Yes, I found Dr. Gordon after he had returned from a trip around Hawaii, treating some of his patients. He came back to look after our people for awhile. How is everyone?"

"Healing," she said, with a smile, and a handshake for the doctor.

"You've been having quite a time," said the doctor, with his quick smile at her.

"Yes," she agreed, with a grimace. "I hope all has settled down now."

She turned and walked with them up the hill, back to the great house. It was cleared out, and several men were working on repairing the wooden shutters. Two others were mixing paint, and carefully applying it to hide the wounds of the battle.

Several men were in the gardens, working to re-plant shrubs, more vegetables and fruit bushes. They had used the gardens heavily during the weeks of the occupation.

"The houses about finished?" asked Peter, pressing his arm secretly closer about her. He had missed her, longed for her.

"All finished, everyone has moved back home," she said, with satisfaction. "In fact, they want ·to have a *luau* upon your return, to celebrate the victory." She gave him a doubtful look as she said that.

"Victory," groaned Peter. "I've been talking for days until my tongue sticks to the roof of my mouth, trying to explain to the authorities what happened. And some relative of Glendon Corey came and demanded to know what had happened to him."

"You told him?" she asked indignantly. "You told him what Corey had tried to do, and how he died?"

"Well . . . some of it. I must say he wasn't surprised. The man was in trouble in the States for some confidence game he was playing. Seems a syndicate gave him a bundle of money to buy some horses, and he went off with the money."

"Hum," said Rosalind. "Sounds like him. Though I should not speak ill of the dead." Her amber eyes sparkled with feeling, and he laughed, and kissed the tip of her nose. He knew just how she felt. And she was too honest to pretend any grief over the death of a man she had detested.

Peter had thought about Corey, and decided that he was capable of revenge. He might have spread word about the black pearls, and brought down upon Darien a plague of brutal fortune hunters, who would not have scrupled to murder them for such a treasure. It

had probably happened for the best, that his cowardice had led to his death.

The doctor was welcomed cordially by Honora,
Barton and Alfred. Norma was keeping to her room,
apart even from her daughter in this period of mourning for Terry.

Dinner that evening was quiet but contented. It
was the way an event was when a good friend had
arrived, and others welcomed him, and there was no
discord, no spite, no whining. Rosalind sat at her end
of the table, glowing with joy. Peter, watching her,
thought she had never looked so beautiful. She bloomed
with beauty, her very skin glowed with a golden joy.
Her amber eyes shone, her laugh was soft and musical.
Barton leaned to her, from his place at her right, and
was stammering something.

She listened carefully, answered him slowly, so he
would understand. She patted his big hand, and he
turned his fingers to press a clasp on hers. He seemed
more content than he had been since his stroke,
thought Peter.

And Alfred Murray had joined them at the table,
more bright and alert than usual. Peter wondered if
his vagueness and his disappearance from their midst,
his hiding out in the study, had been more due to his
horror of dissent and quarreling than his desire to be
alone with his writing. Alfred was a sensitive solitary
soul, and shrank from loud voices and angry tones.

Aunt Honora kept a sharp eye on the maids, and
directed them when Rosalind was preoccupied. She
turned a loving attention to Rosalind, assisted her,
spoke of their flowers which were blooming lushly.
Rosalind had made the table arrangement, Honora
had done the living room floral displays.

Peter was quiet, tired, listening more than talking.
He was happy to be home. But he observed with renewed awareness how pleasant it was to be here with
his relatives and his wife. Without the whining of
Terry, for though the man had died a hero's death, he
had been difficult to live with. Without the fury of

Eileen, her pestering, her nagging. Without the anxiety of Norma.

Peter sighed a little. One more unpleasant task to do. He must see to it that Eileen was sent away, and remained away. How could he do that? Must he take her himself to the mainland, and try to find some family to take her in? She would get into trouble, he knew it. Yet here she made more trouble for everyone. Yes, he had promised Chief Pauahi that Eileen would leave. She must go soon. She would probably go willingly.

Peter had left some black pearls with Mr. Chan to be sold. There would be enough for Eileen to live on for a time. She must be careful, though, and that was not her nature.

"Peter? Have you thought about a *luau*?" Rosalind was saying, recalling him to the present. Her eager look met his. "Hilohilo was asking this afternoon if they might plan one for tomorrow. He wishes a great celebration that all will remember for many years."

"I don't know why not," he said, smiling. He could refuse her little, he adored her. "We will celebrate the victory, and everyone will make up songs and they will be sung for years in memory of this."

"I'd better have my clinic in the morning, then," said Dr. Gordon, ruefully. "By afternoon, I won't be in shape, and neither will my patients!"

They all laughed. Honora gave him a sharp nod. "I'll set it up for you, doctor. We'll start early, and do as much as possible before noon."

They drank some white wine that Peter had brought from Honolulu, laughed and talked, and Peter kept looking at his beautiful wife. How fitting she was in her place, how gracious and lovely. She had bloomed from her shyness, she was like a fully-opened rose, instead of a shy tightly-folded bud.

After dinner, Rosalind played for them on her flute, and Peter was at the piano for the first time in weeks. The doctor leaned back, listening with his eyes shut, his finger tapping the time on the arm chair. Barton had wheeled himself in and listened raptly, the weary lines clearing from his aged face. Alfred Murray sat near him, turning over the pages of a manuscript absently, his attention half on it, and half on the music.

Honora was embroidering a golden fish on the tunic she was making for Victor. Victor had discovered fish in the pond where water gathered during a rainfall, and he wanted fish on everything.

The next morning, the doctor held his clinic with Honora's help, while Rosalind and the others prepared for the *luau*. Many hands helped willingly, the trestle tables were set up, the *luau* pits were dug, the pigs prepared and set into the burning coals. Vegetables were scrubbed, some *plantains* and *ti* leaves set into the glowing pits. Other bowls of vegetables were prepared, large salads of carrots, tomatoes, lettuce. And the huge glowing bowls of fruits were set out, avocados stuffed with crab meat, salads of mango, papaya and pineapple. Of course, the bowls of *poi* were there to be dipped into and licked from the fingers. And small pieces of pickled fish, and plates and platters of banana bread and coconut pancakes.

The patio was filled with the two hundred Hawaiians and whites. Victor staggered on his uncertain legs from one person to another, the other children ran about underfoot, but were never scolded. They were fed from the adult's plates, petted, teased, sung to, patted on the head.

The feast went on and on. Norma and Eileen had refused to attend. Eileen had screamed at the very idea. Norma had stared with unusual reproach at Peter when he invited them.

"A feast? When my Terry lies dead? How can you, Peter?"

"The Hawaiians wish it," he said gently. "They have won a great victory, they have proved themselves. It is something for the legends. However, I understand that you do not wish to attend. Later, I will talk to you about plans for Eileen."

She nodded, and withdrew to her room, her white-capped head bowed.

Their rooms were on the other side of the house

from the patio. Peter hoped they would not be too much disturbed by the sounds of laughter and singing, yet—it was natural for the Hawaiians to wish to celebrate. He felt like it himself. He was so relieved that the battle was over, the chief had been placated. Terry had been sacrificed, his young life was over. But what would have happened if he had lived? Would he not have gone on as before, drinking, wasting away his days, seducing the young Hawaiian girls, sulking to have his own way?

Terry might have matured, chances were he would not have. Peter sighed, and tried to forget for a time. Terry had saved his life, he had died gallantly, let him be remembered for that, and the rest forgiven and forgotten.

Rosalind was happy. She had her man back, safe and almost sound. She had watched the doctor change his bandage, and the deep wound was healing. But it had been close; she shuddered to think how close it had been.

She saw that the platters were kept filled, she sat beside Peter on chairs a little higher than the others, watched that Victor did not get stepped on, ate of the delicious fresh foods. She dipped the spicy pickled fish into the *poi,* and licked her fingers as the others did, laughed at the crude jokes and the pointed remarks at a newlywed man, listened to the gossip of the women, watched the shy grace of the girls as they moved about the tables. The colors were so gay and pretty, all wore their best muumuus and brightest shirts. The sun shone on them benignly, as though in blessing.

While Peter had been gone on his trip, Rosalind had asked, of Kinau, "Are the troubles over for a time? Have you any thoughts that come into your mind?"

Kinau had beamed, and patted Rosalind's shoulder. "All troubles blow away now like the dead leaves before the brisk winds. We be happy now, eh? When we get next to Kailua, we make offerings to Pele, for she has kept her promise and kept us safe. She good to us, and we be good to her, and take offerings of rum and flowers, like she wants."

Rosalind had drawn a deep breath of relief. "All the troubles over, Kinau? All?"

"Never all troubles over," said the older woman comfortably. "Troubles come to us all. All the time, little ones, big ones. But the gods give us strength, if we ask. We turn to them, and beg help, and be humble before them. Then we face troubles, and they blow away again."

"All we must do is face them . . . with faith, and trust in God, and the gods," murmured Rosalind thoughtfully.

It was not what happened to one that mattered, she thought today, in the brilliant sunshine, with Peter by her side. It was the way one faced the troubles, with courage, and hope, and trust in oneself and the gods. The attitude was what mattered, the humility and trust, the faith. Then in grief, one could overcome. In death, one could hope for the next life and paradise. One learned to take each day at a time, and enjoy the bloom and perfume of it.

She had feared that Eileen would come, dramatic in black, her face ravaged, to storm at them and spoil the feast. Even Norma might arrive, for she had grown still and withdrawn, and her grief seemed to overwhelm her. But they remained away from the celebration of victory. She felt pity for them, for they truly mourned Terry.

Rosalind mourned Terry also, but in a different manner. She mourned the wasted young life, the idleness that had frittered time away. She mourned the bitterness he had left behind him, the cynicism that had infected those he loved most. She saw Dorisa today, sitting quietly to one side, her youth spoiled, for all knew she had been Terry's lover. Would she ever marry? Perhaps years from now, when a man could forget what she had done.

She mourned the young lives cut short, the warriors who had fought and died for the blasted honor of Lydia Pauahi. She mourned that Terry had given but one act of courage in his life, when he could have lived a life of gallantry.

But he had saved Peter's life, and that meant everything to Rosalind. She slipped her arm into Peter's, and he looked down at her and smiled with that special secret look he would give her. His eyes softened, those dark commanding eyes that could blaze with fury; or become steely with command. For her there was only gentleness and adoration now.

Barton Darien rolled outside and watched with bright eyes as the celebrations started. He had eaten in the privacy of his bedroom, still ashamed that he spilled food and his hands shook when he raised his glass. But he had come for the entertainment.

Alfred Murray was already there, sitting a little aside, watching and listening, with notepad and pen beside him on the small table. The Hawaiians already had a name for him, "The one who writes us down."

Honora was supervising the clearing of the tables. However, bowls of fresh fruit and nuts were left, and cakes of chocolate, coconut, lemon, pineapple. The glasses were left, and large containers of punch made of light rum and fruit juice. They would eat and drink all the afternoon, to refresh themselves between bouts of singing and dancing.

One young warrior, his arm still in a sling, was lustily banging on a drum with his free hand, making the air throb with his rhythms, his brown face grinning as the small children scampered up to him to watch in fascination.

Other drummers came, one brought a fiddle, one a guitar, and someone a flute. The music began with a swinging, and young children began to sway and sing where they stood, eagerly waiting for the main attractions.

Spontaneously, half a dozen young graceful warriors took the center of attention. They came together into a group in the center of the wide patio, and began to sing and chant of the battle that had happened.

All watched and listened, sometimes serious, sometimes laughing. The warriors mimicked the coming of the war canoes. One mocked himself, hiding behind a bush, peering out in fright, and the children giggled and jumped up and down.

Then the battle began. They mimed the throwing of spears, the shooting of rifles, the banging and banging of the gunfire. The drums tattooed a steady rhythm, the battle was on. One went down, writhing dramatically as his wound was fatal. Another took his place as he rolled to the side of the patio. The dancing went on.

They showed how the battle had ended. One played Pauahi, with an immense headdress, coming to speak to their leader, played by another man in a suit jacket, with a rifle on his arm. They spoke some of the words of the chiefs, and all leaned forward to hear again the words that had been spoken.

The one playing Chief Pauahi was especially dramatic. He repeated what had been said, making it into a song, lifting his arms to the heavens as he spoke of their lost paradise.

Alfred Murray began to write it down, dipping his pen into ink, writing so hurriedly that Rosalind hoped he could read it later. The words were splendid. She remembered vividly how he spoke in ringing words, how his despair and grief and rage had stood out. The man who recited it spoke well. He spoke for them all.

Then the chief of the Dariens actor spoke out, and the small audience turned to Peter, smiling, and nodding. He spoke well, and they applauded when it was all finished.

"This will be s-sung for m-m-many years," stammered Barton, his eyes bright as he clung to the arms of his wheelchair. "It will be a legend."

Rosalind nodded gravely, her gaze going back to the center of the patio. Now the girls were coming out, and the music had changed to light lively music. The lovely *hula* from the South Seas, swaying to the rhythm and emphasizing the words with their beautiful graceful hands.

She smiled to see them. How lovely they were, how the madness of battle and hate had been wiped out by the singing, about the beauties of Hawaii, how they loved their islands, how the sun shone.

She herself had played and sung and danced these songs since childhood. Impulsively, as they began the song of the return of a native to his homeland, she jumped up, and ran to the line of girls, taking her place at the end.

The Hawaiians opened their dark eyes widely, in surprise and pleasure. Her rose-printed muumuu swayed with her graceful hips, her slim arms fluttered in the air.

"Across the waters of the sea . . ." and their waving hands indicated how the sea waves looked.

"I have returned to my islands of the sun . . ." and they shaped the beautiful islands and the bright sun above.

"I pluck a lei of plumeria and hold it to my heart . . ." and they pointed to the leis about their slim brown throats, and Rosalind's hands touched hers.

"And my heart is full of love. . . ." They made the gesture to their hearts and pressed their hands to it in love.

"Nevermore shall I leave my island home . . ." and they shook their glossy heads vigorously, and Rosalind's hair flowed in the sunlight as she shook her head, and the long brown locks streamed about her shoulders.

"I shall fish in its beautiful waters . . ." and they mimed the catching of the fish.

"I shall climb the beautiful mountains . . ." and their hands indicated the steps upward.

"I shall swim in the blue waters of the sea . . ." and their arms moved over and over in swimming motion.

At the end of the song, Rosalind bowed with them to the applause, and began to return to her place, heated from the dancing. But the girls tugged boldly at her arms, put other leis about her neck, and urged her to the center of their line.

They danced another song, the one about a girl whose lover had left her, but he would return one day. How her heart will leap when she sees his boat appearing on the horizon, how she will love him, how she will show him his son in her arms!

And they danced another one, about the joys of their life, how they dance, and feast, and make love under the bright moon. She continued to dance and sway with them, singing the murmurous words, and Peter's eyes were bright with surprise and appreciation as he watched his wife.

Finally she laughed, and left them, and the girls ran away, to make way for a line of older women to sing and dance, the old songs of legends of the gods and goddesses and their stories.

Rosalind dropped into her chair. Peter put his arm about her, leaned to her ear. "You have even more talents than I had dreamed, my dear!"

"You did not mind?"

His grin showed he did not, his eyes were bright with approval. And the others kept looking to her, kindly, nodding brightly when they caught her gaze. She was one of them, she danced and sang and knew their words. She was their own, one of them, forever.

One of the girls brought Rosalind a coconut filled with light rum drink mixed with coconut milk. She drank it thirstily, though it made her head spin pleasantly.

The afternoon went on and on. Hilohilo was in his element, urging the old women on to dance, to teasing words of the days of their youth. There was a merry song about a joke played on a strutting youth. There was a sad song about the death of a beautiful maiden who jumped to her death when she was forbidden to marry the man of her choice. There were more songs, old ones, new ones, more dances.

Joe Smith leaned against the house, watching impassively, his sombrero pushed back from his bronzed face. He knew some of the words, he had heard the songs. Rosalind caught him once, his feet were doing a little jig at one of the more infectious melodies. She smiled to herself. Another few years, and he might become more Hawaiian than any of them!

Nick had not come, however. He was manning one of the guard posts high on a cliff. He was silent, shy, not one to come to feasts. But Rosalind had packed a basket and sent it up to him and the other men who were there also. They could probably dimly hear the music from their high perch.

There was little pause in the festivities. One group replaced another, all wanted to demonstrate their skills. Victor fell asleep on a mat, beside two other small children, faces peaceful as the joyful noise rose about them. Honora sat happily in her rocking chair, her lean tanned face bright with pleasure.

By evening, they were all tiring. More food was brought out, and they ate again, and talked, and drank cool rum and coconut. And finally as the sun set, and darkness built up around them, they began to drift to their homes. Their rebuilt huts safe once again, until the next crisis, thought Rosalind.

They came up to express thanks for the celebration. Rosalind and Peter stood to shake their hands, to thank them for coming, to wish them well, to pat small heads, and give a special clasp of the hand to the warriors who had fought so well, and the women who had served in their ways.

Then the house was finally quiet. Barton Darien had rolled himself inside, and was being put to bed. Alfred Murray retired to the study, to scribble down his notes in more readable form. Honora supervised the taking down of the tables. From somewhere came a mellow laugh, the soft reproach of a girl to her lover, the whimpering of a sleepy child. Kinau came to take Victor away, and he put his head down on her shoulder sleepily.

"Let's go up now, darling," Peter urged in Rosalind's ear. His hand tightened about her waist.

She paused to make sure Dr. Gordon was taken care of. He was chatting to Aunt Honora about her roses.

They went up to their suite, and closed the door to shut out the world. He put his arms about her. "Oh, you are so lovely, so dear to me," he whispered.

"And you are my love," she murmured against his lips. They kissed, quietly, then more deeply, standing in the pale light of the moon streaming in the wide windows.

In bed, he turned to take her into his arms. She had put on a slim thin nightdress of white muslin, he stroked his hand down over her rounded body.

"How lovely you were today. I never realized you could do the Hawaiian dances."

"You did not mind?"

"Mind? No, it makes you all the more part of us here. You belong to us, to me of course, most of all," he added, with a chuckle against her brown throat. He drew her more closely, to kiss her. "I could not have chosen more wisely had I thought for a thousand years. The one girl in the world that would suit me most," he said, with his old arrogance. "And you please our people. They will always love you and serve you willingly."

She smiled a little sadly. Serve them. Yes, the Hawaiians were there to serve them. How poignantly the words of the Chief of the Pauahi echoed in her ears. "They take our land, and wave pieces of paper in our faces, and tell us it is their land. We do not belong where our fathers have lived for many many years. How did this happen?"

She knew how the chief felt. But what could one person do? All she could do was live as the wife of the Dariens, always anxiously careful of the welfare of the cheerful Hawaiians in their charge. They could not fight for themselves, and she and Peter must fight for them.

"Oh . . . Peter . . . I do love you," she murmured, and she meant love, respect, admire, adore. She put her arms about his neck as he leaned over her, his hand stroking her body. She stiffened a little. She had not told him about the coming child, she felt strangely shy about it. She must tell him soon.

He said nothing of that. He lay on his side, and brought her close to him, and gently kissed and caressed her until they were both ready. Then he drew her more tightly to him, and on their sides they lay together as man and wife, enjoying the feeling of being as one in the wide bed.

The moonlight shone kindly on them as they moved more strongly, and came to fulfillment. The light made small patterns through the mosquito netting, and she traced the pattern idly on his muscular arm as he laid it over her.

"You smell of plumeria," he said sleepily, and put his face against her throat, to drift off to sleep. She smiled, and held him against her breasts, and let herself think of the coming child. Boy or girl? Either would be joyously welcomed into their hearts. A small boy like Peter, trotting about after his father, as Victor tried to now. Or a little girl, her sober face intent at the piano.

She remembered one little girl tonight, standing at her mother's knee, watching intently, her finger in her mouth, as they danced. Her whole body had swayed in rhythm. Soon she also would be dancing.

And one day the daughter of Peter and Rosalind would be dancing there, on the patio in the bright sunlight, smiling at her parents, her eyes aglow. It was like a promise, that dream.

# 30

❧ ❧ ❧ ❧

LATER IN THE WEEK, Peter spoke to Norma. "Eileen must go away," he said soberly.

She nodded, not understanding him. "Yes, she has been unhappy here for a long time. I will take her to the States."

Peter hesitated, his mouth tight. "Would you like to travel for awhile, then settle somewhere, such as San Francisco?"

Norma gave him a surprised look. Her face was pale and drawn with weariness and grief. "Oh, we will come back one day, Peter. Eileen talks of staying in San Francisco or New York City, but I don't know . . ."

He gazed off into the distance, they were walking on the beach near the house. He had not wanted to be overheard.

"Aunt Norma, I am sorry, but Eileen must never return to Darien."

"What do you mean?" she gasped, turning whiter, and clutching at his arm.

"She has caused much trouble here, Aunt Norma," he said, firmly. "I promised Chief Pauahi that she would go away, and never return to Hawaii. I think she would like that anyway. She may marry. . . ."

"Peter! You would banish her, but why? What has Chief Pauahi to do with it?"

He bit his lips, but decided on the truth. He could not bear to look into her worried eyes as he told her, "Eileen has proved as promiscuous as Terry was. She has seduced the young Hawaiian men, then scorned them. I know it is true. The chief felt it was a horrible

humiliation for them, another one on top of what
Terry had done to the girls, of what all whites have
been doing to the Hawaiians on the islands. He
wishes her sent away forever, and I promised it
would be done."

Her fingers bit into his arm. "That is a lie! My Eileen is a good girl. . . ." Her voice faltered as he finally looked down at her compassionately. Her eyes
welled with tears. "Isn't she?"

He shook his head. They walked on in silence.

"I must have spoiled them," she said finally, in a
low tone. "How could they act like that? How could
they?"

'I don't know, I don't understand," Peter said
sadly. "They did not seem to feel any responsibility
for their acts, they could be as . . . immoral as they
chose. And the Hawaiians resented them bitterly."

"But Terry was so attractive to women, the girls
flocked around him . . ." Norma faltered.

"Girls of fifteen are not notorious for their good
sense," he said crisply. "And how do you explain Eileen? She is twenty-two, she should have married.
But she scorned the men in Honolulu, and she has
met no one whom she wished to marry, according to
her. Instead she . . . seduced the Hawaiian men . . .
and they despise her for it. . . ."

Norma passed her damp hand over her face. "Can
it be true?" she asked herself drearily, in a low tone.
"Oh, my poor Eileen."

Peter was silent for a time. "I think she will be better off in some sophisticated society. I will give you
enough to live on for six months at a time. Don't let
Eileen get her hands on it, or run up large bills. She
wants to marry a millionaire, if she succeeds that
might be the answer!"

"Oh, Peter, don't scorn her so! She is your
cousin. . . ."

"And you have been very good to me," he said,
softening a little. "But God help the man who mar-
ries Eileen!"

"Once away from this . . . this atmosphere, and her

boredom, she will do well," said Norma, as though trying to persuade herself. "Very well, we shall go. Eileen wants to leave anyway. How can I tell her she cannot return?"

"I will tell her myself. But Aunt Norma, you will always be welcome here," he added. "When Eileen is settled, return to us if you will."

"Thank you, dear Peter," she said quietly, and her hand pressed his sadly. "So much has happened, my dear Terry . . . gone . . . I don't know what I will do. . . ."

Peter took them to Honolulu, along with Joe and Nick. Eileen was coldly angry at him, but eager to get away, trunks packed with splendid dresses, jewels in her case. They would travel wherever Eileen wished, then settle down. Peter could only hope she would find a husband to suit her. One who would control her somehow, he hoped.

He saw them off. Joe and Nick would take them as far as San Francisco, then proceed to New Mexico to contact Joe's outlaw friends, and to buy horses. They needed more range-bred horses to replace those the Hawaiians had slaughtered.

Once the ocean liner had departed, Peter returned to Kailua, and then to Darien, with great relief. He was glad he did not have the task of taking care of Eileen and traveling with her. He had other obligations and went home willingly to them. He returned two weeks before Christmas to find the big house cheerful with poinsettias, coral vines, large calabashes filled with fresh flowers, the drawing rooms and hallways glowing with scarlet hibiscus.

He went to find Rosalind, and hug her. He had returned on a small sailing vessel, and only a handful of Hawaiians had spotted him coming in. She was in their bedroom, just pulling on a pale silvery green muumuu.

"Oh, Peter, you have come home!" she cried. He strode across to her, pulled her into his arms, and hungrily kissed her face and throat. She glowed with delight, her hands on his face, which was stubbly with beard.

"My darling . . ." He kissed her again fervently.

"Oh . . . Peter . . . is all well?" she asked anxiously, drawing back slightly to study his face.

He nodded. "They are all on their way. Should be in San Francisco in a few more days. Joe and Nick will see them settled in a respectable boarding house before they go on to New Mexico."

"That is a wild part of the west," she said slowly.

"Those are wild boys," he grinned. "And they'll find Joe's friends, and pick us some good horses, I hope. Should get back to Los Angeles and get on a ship in a few months."

He reached in his cloth bag, and drew out some boxes. "Mr. Chan has been thinking of you and sends the respectful regards of himself and Mrs. Chan," he announced, and set down one long box on her dressing table. "Open it."

"More jewelry?" She murmured, shaking her head in reproof.

When she hesitated, he reached across her and snapped the box open impatiently. She gasped, and he looked with pleasure at the double long strands of black pearls. Mr. Chan had chosen the best gems, and graded them by size, so that two immense pearls were at the base of the strands, then smaller ones, to the silver clasp at the back.

Peter lifted the necklace and set it about her throat. He smiled to see how it looked on her graceful neck, against the silvery green of the muumuu. "Lovely," he murmured approvingly, and pressed a kiss where the clasp lay at the back of her neck.

"Oh, Peter, so much . . . you give me so much. . . ."

"Wait till you see your Christmas presents," he laughed mischievously.

He snapped open another box before she could protest. There lay the black pearl bee, set in a silver maze with the tiny flower at the nose of the bee, so he seemed to be sniffing at it. The broach was about two inches across, a silvery delight. He pinned it to her dress.

"Oh, my little black bee, how wonderful," she gasped, touching it lovingly. "What beautiful work Mr. Chan does! I must write to thank him with the next steamer."

"He said he was most happy to work with the pearls," said Peter. He had given Mr. Chan a number more to sell for him, and Mr. Chan had decided to make some into jewelry to sell in New York, through a friend of his. It would make a good fortune for them both, and Peter's bank account was now very healthy again.

Peter shaved, bathed, dressed, and went down to dinner with her. He was pleased to find everyone in a very amiable mood. Aunt Honora was thinking about Christmas parties and decorations, Barton was unusually happy, Alfred Murray had good news from a publisher who wanted to print a book of his Hawaiian stories.

They discussed plans for Christmas. There would be a great *luau,* of course, and Peter had some silver coins for all his *paniolos,* and lengths of cloth were coming on the next steamer for all the women and girls. Some dresses were also coming for his wife, but that was his surprise and still a secret.

Rosalind was radiantly happy. Peter was back home. She felt well and strong again after some bouts of morning sickness. She had confided in Kinau, who expressed no surprise at all. They had decided the baby would come in mid-June.

Soon she would tell Peter.

She presided over the table, saw to the serving of the fresh fish, fried in batter, the crisp sweet sticks of pineapple, the cold roast beef sliced with hot hash brown potatoes and onions. For dessert there was coconut pudding. The kind of meal Eileen scorned, and the others enjoyed. No, Eileen had not fit in here, she would be happier perhaps on the mainland. Rosalind hoped so, and hoped she would settle down, and be content there. Her restlessness had infected them all.

Two days later, the conch shells blew. Rosalind was out on the patio with Victor, and she started, jumping up, turning pale with apprehension.

The *paniolos* came galloping from the plains, Peter in the lead. They all ran out from the house to look out to sea, and saw the long canoe approaching.

"One canoe," sighed Rosalind, with some relief, shading her eyes to peer out to sea. Victor was balanced on her hip. Honora came to take the boy from her.

"Should we bar the shutters?" Honora asked anxiously.

"I don't know . . . one canoe, I don't see another. There is the chief, raising his hand to Peter. . . ." She could see him, splendid in his great yellow feather cloak and tall headdress, standing in the canoe, as a dozen warriors pulled the oars to bring the vessel in to land.

They watched as Peter and the cowboys swung down from their saddles. One man led the horses away, holding all the reins. The other *paniolos* and Peter went to the dock as the war canoe drew in.

"They are greeting him, they are talking," said Honora, in relief. "Do they have guns?"

"Not in sight," said Alfred Murray, who had come out to stand beside them, his eyelids crinkled against the bright rays. "No, they carry only the paddles. Now they are bringing the boat onto the sand. There is Maleko, holding up his hand."

The Chief and Peter started from the dock toward the house, and several of the warriors fell into step behind them, surrounded by the curious *paniolos*. Rosalind and Honora and Alfred went from the house to meet them halfway, as was courteous. Victor babbled and waved his hands at the excitement.

The two parties met, the chief bowed slowly toward Rosalind. His eyes lit up when he saw the child, his gaze lingered on him.

"The Chief of the Pauahi has come to spend Christmas holidays with us, Rosalind," said Peter, a half-humorous look on his face.

"The Chief of the Pauahi and his warriors are most welcome," said Rosalind, holding out her hand to him. He shook it hard, in the white fashion. "We will have great *luaus* and make celebrations," she said, in the Hawaiian language.

His stern face relaxed a trifle, they continued together toward the veranda. Faces peered from the windows, then withdrew hastily as the chief raised his glance to them.

Barton Darien wheeled himself out to greet the chief, who greeted him ceremoniously. Rosalind went inside to begin preparations for the feast, Hilohilo would take care of overseeing the digging of the great pits and the preparation of the pigs. Honora went to see about the tables and decorations. Kinau came to take Victor.

Rosalind went out later to see how matters were going along. To her surprise, the great chief was seated on the grass. Peter sat on a mat nearby. Victor sat between his grandfather's legs, listening intently as the chief recounted some long story to Barton and Alfred. The other man sat in a white wicker chair, with table and pen at hand, and a bottle of ink precariously poised at his left.

Rosalind sat down beside Peter, not to interrupt the story. The chief continued, his face absorbed, his great hand in the air to emphasize some point. Victor would squirm around to watch him, then cuddle close to his grandfather once more. Kinau sat at a distance, a watchful eye on her charge, sewing in her hands.

At the end of the story, Alfred Murray finished scribbling, and raked his inky hand through his greying hair. "That is splendid, Chief Kaahumanu, splendid! I had not heard that story. That explains many things about the dolphins."

The chief inclined his head graciously. "You are welcome, one who writes our stories. I know much more, I will tell the legends to you. I have heard that you write them, so our young people will not forget the tales."

"Yes, yes, they must be preserved forever," said Alfred fervently. "Sometimes the young people go to the cities, and cast aside all they have learned, and do not repeat the stories to their children. The stories must be kept, so one day they will speak the tales again, and sing the songs."

"You are good to do this," said the chief, holding his arm about Victor, with gentle purpose, so he would not crawl away. The iron arm curved about the boy, so carefully that Victor returned willingly to his grandfather's embrace. "Yes, it is sad that so many of our youths have left our camps, they forget our ways, they are ashamed of our customs. This one . . ." and he looked down at Victor, "he must not forget. He will be chief one day."

He said it proudly, and the pride was in his face. He was reconciled evidently to the fact of the boy's *Haole* heritage.

Rosalind noted several beautifully woven baskets near the chief. Peter rose, and brought two of them to her.

"The Chief of the Pauahi has brought Christmas gifts to you and to us, Rosalind. It will please him if you will accept them, with his wishes for a happy season of peace."

"The Chief of the Pauahi is most gracious," said Rosalind, formally, taking the first large basket. She peered inside curiously, to find several exquisite branches of pink coral set on beds of fern, surrounded by grasses so they would not break in the long sea voyage. "Oh, how beautiful!"

"They can be made into jewelry which the women like about their necks," said the chief, nodding to her. His stern face scarcely relaxed, but a gleam of pleasure shone for a moment in his dark eyes at her pleasure.

"I enjoy them the way they are," said Rosalind. "I think I shall set them in the glass cases in the hallway, among the carved calabashes. They will set them off beautifully."

Peter approved, she noticed. He handed her another basket, this one with small branches of the more rare deep red coral. She exclaimed over them.

Other baskets of fine weaving held plants, some she had never seen before.

"For your gardens, which are famous through the islands," said the chief. "I bring from the mountains."

There were baskets of rare orchids, several bushes with berries of scarlet and yellow, vines with roots deep in soil. All had been carefully packed and kept moist with moss. She thanked him, and Honora added her pleased words.

"They will be magnificent in our gardens," said Honora, tinges of color in her tanned cheeks. "You are most kind and thoughtful."

Two calabashes held some fruits, another held nuts. They were accepted, he was thanked, the bowls carried inside. Honora excused herself to go to plan places in the gardens for the new flowers and bushes. Rosalind stroked her fingers gently over the red coral, and the chief watched her inscrutably.

"You do not make jewelry with this?" he asked finally.

"Not with these, O Chief of the Pauahi," she said, shaking her head. "These should be kept as they are, in the beautiful form of Nature's jewels, so they will remind us of your kindness and generosity."

He seemed pleased, and nodded once, deeply. His sharp gaze had noted the black bumblebee on her dress, but he was too polite to mention it.

The *luau* that night was magnificent. The chief sat on a tall chair, and with his height he still towered over the others. Food was brought to him by the loveliest girls, they brought bowls of rum and fruit juice for him to drink, and other bowls for him to dip his fingers in perfumed waters, fragrant with orchid petals.

Women sang and danced, but Rosalind did not join them. Her place was behind the men, demurely in the background, as the two chiefs watched the singing and dancing and the playing of flutes and the banging of the drums. Maleko did the fire dance to Pele as the climax of the evening, and it was even more spectacular than before. He offered it to his chief, humbly, and the chief accepted, his stern face gracious.

During the following days, the celebrations were more informal. The chief enjoyed swimming and fishing. He asked to take Victor with him. Rosalind agreed, after consulting Kinau. Kinau would accompany them to the sandy lagoon, and sit in the shade with her sewing, keeping a sharp eye on her young charge.

Rosalind went down there sometimes, not to swim, but to sit beside Kinau and talk. She too watched curiously, as the chief enjoyed the companionship of his young grandson.

The huge man would put the child on his broad back, and Victor would clasp his arms about the thick neck. Then the chief would walk out into the waves, careful not to dunk Victor, and swim about like some large porpoise, riding the waves with Victor clinging to him and laughing with glee. He was so gentle with the child, the women no longer worried.

And he took Victor fishing, showed him how he baited the hook. Or they would watch his men fishing with nets, scooping in a run of fish. All grew accustomed to seeing the huge chief, his bronzed chest and bare back, a *tapa* loin cloth about his hips, his long legs striding along, with Victor clasped at his neck, riding "grandpapa," eagerly. They talked in Hawaiian, the chief patiently teaching him more words.

And every day the chief would sit in the shade of the hot afternoon, near the veranda. Alfred would bring out his writing supplies. The chief would begin on one of his long stories of the Hawaiian people, with Barton Darien a fascinated listener. Often Victor would sit between the great bronzed legs of his grandfather, listening also, until sleep overcame him, and he lay against his big relative and went off to slumberland, the voices echoing about him.

Peter went for a walk each evening with Rosalind,

down by the shore near a lagoon, and they strode along the sand arm in arm, talking idly of the day, or being silent together, contentedly.

She had been nerving herself to tell him about the child. She had also been thinking that she had little for his Christmas, only some shirts she had been making for him, and a couple of bright scarves, which she had hemmed.

"Why so quiet, my dear? Are you tired?" he asked one evening. They paused to gaze out to sea, where the aquamarine waves near to shore swept out to meet the deeper sapphire of the greater depths. Slow swelling waves rolled to shore, broke in white foam, and the setting sun cast a glimmer of orange across the greens and blues.

She rested her head against his arm. "I . . . I have been thinking, Peter. I have so little for you this Christmas, and you have given me so much."

He turned her to face him. "Given me so little? My dear, you have given me peace, love, a wife to adore, my happiness. I am a different man than I was this time last year."

By the look of his face, he was serious. She rested her cheek against his broad chest, thankfully. "You mean that?" she whispered. She could feel the steady beating of his heart under her cheek.

"Yes. You are a very modest little wife," he teased tenderly. "You make me comfortable, make the household run smoothly, keep Victor happy, give me love and adoration. I love you more every day. Yet when I married you I loved you so much I thought I could not love you more."

The words were very sweet to her. "You did not marry me . . . because you . . . pitied me?"

"I pitied myself, because my life was so empty . . . I had everything material in the world, but also strife, grief, problems. You brought me love," he murmured in her ear, and raised her face to kiss her lips. Their shadows were cast long on the sand, as their futures together would be long.

"I . . . I am so happy, Peter. I want to tell you something . . . I am going to give you a child," she said in a rush, turning pink with embarrassment. She looked up at him anxiously. "Are . . . you . . . pleased . . . surprised?"

He was grinning down at her. "I wondered when you were going to tell me, darling," he said. "Were you going to wait until the baby came?" He laughed at her wrinkled nose.

"No . . . no, I meant to tell you before . . . but I kept putting it off . . . you are happy?"

"Very happy, the happiest man in the world. When?"

"Mid-June, I think, and so does Kinau."

"June. Lovely. You must take great care, and not lift Victor so much, he is getting very heavy," said Peter, thoughtfully, his arm about her waist, his hand stroking slowly over her slim hips.

"I do hope Victor will not be jealous of the new baby. I shall not have less love for him, only more for everyone, because I am so happy," said Rosalind, simply. "Oh, I feel overflowing with love. How could all this be happening to me?"

"I feel the same way. How could things turn out so well, so joyfully? It must have been meant to be."

They turned, to walk slowly back along the sands. The skies purpled as the setting sun dropped below the horizon, and the sky mirrored the darkening with a deeper blue. The waves crested white against the creamy sands, roiling almost to their feet, smoothing out the shore.

Clearing away the footprints even as they walked. Smoothing out the trials of the day, of the year, leaving the sands of the island of Darien as untouched as though no one had ever stepped there.

A coconut palm swayed in the evening breeze. Torches flared near the great house, as the *luau* pits were burning for the evening meal. Voices, mellow with laughter and singing, drifted to them.

Darien, at peace once more, sheltering them all,

white and Hawaiian, living together in harmony. May it always be that way, prayed Rosalind, as she held her husband's firm hand in hers, and walked back with him to where their families waited.

# NEW FROM BALLANTINE!

**FALCONER, John Cheever**          27300   $2.25

The unforgettable story of a substantial, middle-class man
and the passions that propel him into murder, prison, and an
undreamed-of liberation. "CHEEVER'S TRIUMPH . . . A GREAT
AMERICAN NOVEL."—*Newsweek*

**GOODBYE, W. H. Manville**          27118   $2.25

What happens when a woman turns a sexual fantasy into a
fatal reality? The erotic thriller of the year! "Powerful."—
*Village Voice.* "Hypnotic."—*Cosmopolitan.*

**THE CAMERA NEVER BLINKS, Dan Rather
with Mickey Herskowitz**          27423   $2.25

In this candid book, the co-editor of "60 Minutes" sketches
vivid portraits of numerous personalities including JFK, LBJ
and Nixon, and discusses his famous colleagues.

**THE DRAGONS OF EDEN, Carl Sagan** 26031   $2.25

An exciting and witty exploration of mankind's intelligence
from pre-recorded time to the fantasy of a future race, by
America's most appealing scientific spokesman.

**VALENTINA, Fern Michaels**          26011   $1.95

Sold into slavery in the Third Crusade, Valentina becomes a
queen, only to find herself a slave to love.

**THE BLACK DEATH, Gwyneth Cravens
and John S. Marr**          27155   $2.50

A totally plausible novel of the panic that strikes when the
bubonic plague devastates New York.

**THE FLOWER OF THE STORM,
Beatrice Coogan**          27368   $2.50

Love, pride and high drama set against the turbulent background of 19th century Ireland as a beautiful young woman
fights for her inheritance and the man she loves.

**THE JUDGMENT OF DEKE HUNTER,
George V. Higgins**          25862   $1.95

Tough, dirty, shrewd, telling! "The best novel Higgins has
written. Deke Hunter should have as many friends as Eddie
Coyle."——*Kirkus Reviews*

LG-2